THE STARLIT THRONE

VIOLET WOLFE

ILLUSTRATED BY
PAULINA GOLDEN-MENSAH

Illustrations and cover art done by Paulina Golden-Mensah
pgmensahart@gmail.com

Identifiers: ISBN 979-8-9853993-0-1 (hc.) ISBN 979-8-9853993-1-8 (pbk.)
ISBN 979-8-9853993-2-5 (e-book)

Printed in the United States of America
www.violetnovels.com

Second Edition 2025

To my chosen family. Thanks for seeing something in me that I could never see in myself.

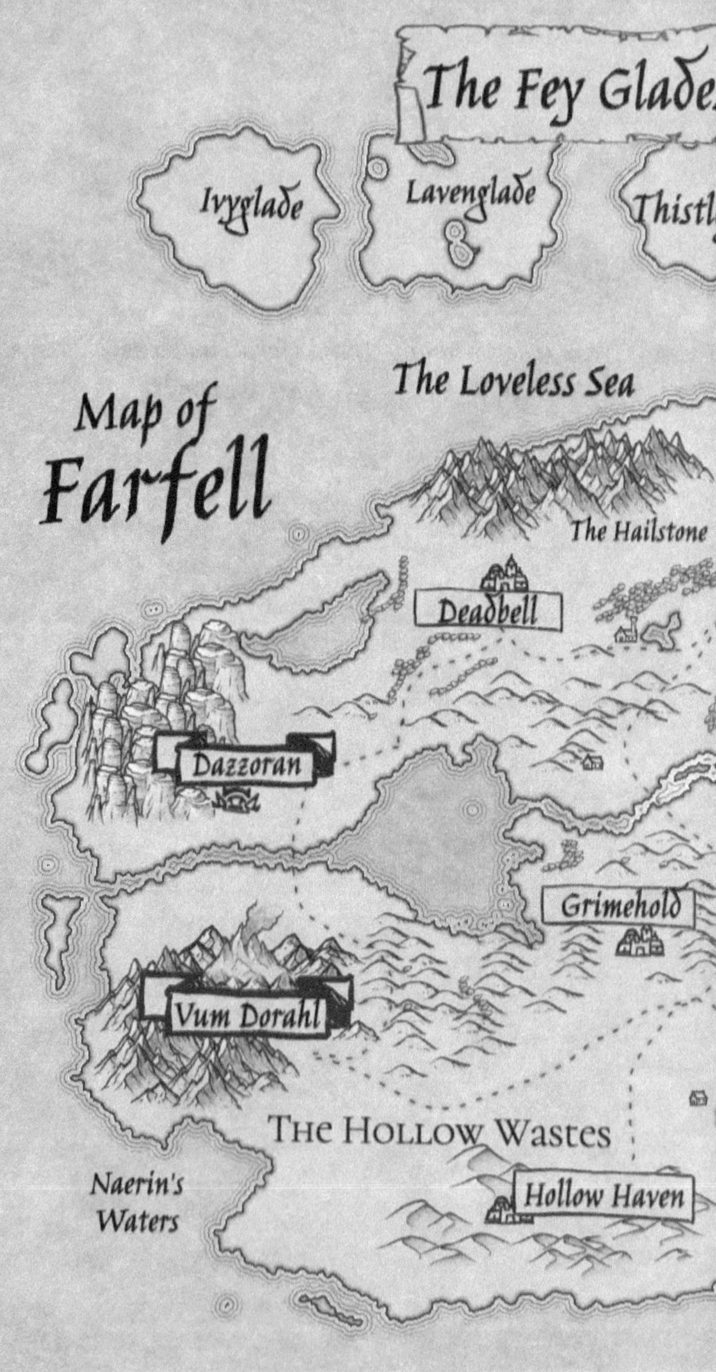

The Fey Glades
Ivyglade
Lavenglade
Thistle
Map of
Farfell
The Loveless Sea
The Hailstone
Deadbell
Dazzoran
Grimehold
Vum Dorahl
The Hollow Wastes
Naerin's
Waters
Hollow Haven

Fernglade
Starview
Candlewood
ondvale
ormire
Haelhil
Sunstill
Sugarport
of
all
To The Southern
Continent

THE DUSK PRINCESS

Centered in Starview's throne room was a dainty pool with shimmering waters, disturbed by little Faelyri's splashing. At only six years old, her pale lavender hands clapped together as if attempting to catch and flatten the liquid between her palms. The starlit strands of her hair, shimmering like a sky full of constellations, dipped into the water, their glittering ends damp as their color shifts from dark purples to pinks.

Before her stood the majestic thrones of her parents, intricately carved and adorned with the runes of their lineage. Beside her knelt Ilriel, her older brother and twelve years her senior. The water sat just below his knees as he smiled down at her antics.

"You think you can hold water in your hands?" he asked, his voice laced with a teasing laugh.

"I can!" Faelyri declared. Her brows furrowed, the faint markings on her face twisting with the motion. "I just need to practice."

"You can't use magic, Lyri," Ilriel said with an amused shake of his head.

"The other elves can," she retorted, sending a small splash of water in his direction. "They make explosive magic when they draw symbols. So why can't I?"

"Not everyone can," he replied softly. "I can't."

"Mother can," she insisted, stubborn as ever, her small hands slapping at the water. "Her magic is beautiful."

"Mother's weapon is magic, not her. That's not the same thing."

Faelyri opened her mouth to protest again, but her brother's gaze had drifted to the towering double doors of the throne room. His face hard.

"Ilriel?" her voice came out uncertain.

He snapped back to her, his expression softening. "It's nothing, Lyri. Keep playing."

But before she could respond, the doors groaned open, their echo reverberating through the vast hall. A guard strode in, armored boots striking the floor with purpose. Faelyri froze, shrinking back against her brother as she instinctively grabbed a fistful of his sleeve. Ilriel rose slowly, water cascading from his clothes.

"Stay here," he told her firmly. "I'll be back soon."

"Where are you going?" she asked, her voice trembling.

"Just keep playing the game," he said, stepping out of the pool. "I won't be long."

But as his retreating figure disappeared through the doors, Faelyri hurried after him, her bare feet slipping against the cool marble floor. The faint glow beneath her steps guided her as she padded quietly down the hallway, her heart pounding in her chest. Rounding a corner, she pressed herself against the wall and strained to hear the muffled voices beyond.

"The Queen and King are dead," the guard said, his tone heavy with finality. "Their ship was ambushed by Haelhil forces. Though they were near Starview, they didn't survive the journey home."

Ilriel's voice was calm but cold, each word measured. "And you are *certain* it was Haelhil?"

"Yes, Your Highness," the guard confirmed. "It was a high elf vessel."

"Search the wreckage," Ilriel commanded. "Ensure the Nightstrand is not lost to the sea."

"Their bodies have already been retrieved," the guard said. "The Queen still held the object."

"Bring it to me," Ilriel ordered, his voice sharp.

Faelyri's breath hitched. Bursting around the corner, her voice cracked as she cried, "What? Mother and Father are gone?"

Ilriel turned swiftly, "Lyri, you shouldn't—"

"I don't want them to be gone!" she wailed, her small frame trembling as tears spilled down her cheeks. "I want them to come back!"

Ilriel knelt and pulled her into a protective embrace, his voice low and soothing. "Lyri. We'll get through this. I promise. It'll be okay."

"No, we won't!" she sobbed, clutching his tunic as though it could anchor her. "It's not okay!"

"It will be," he insisted. "You'll see. We'll make it through this together." He turned to the guard, still holding his sister, "bring them to the burial site. Dig them a single grave and bury them together."

❧

Starview's burial grove was a place of haunting beauty, tucked beneath the canopy of an ancient, towering tree whose roots coiled protectively around the mountain's secrets. The air was heavy with the scent of wildflowers, their vivid blooms carpeting the sacred ground where the dead were laid to rest.

For the immortal elves, death was very rare.

Their parents, Starview's rulers, were lowered into a shared grave, their bodies wrapped in silken shrouds. Ilriel stood tall, like stone, his face full of calm authority. In contrast, little Faelyri's anguished cries shattered the stillness. She wiped her face as her tears and snot strings soaked her dress's sleeves.

Ilriel spoke with a voice both regal and deliberate, his words a tribute to their parents and a vow to carry on their legacy. But for Faelyri, his speech was drowned out by the roaring storm of her grief. When he finally turned to her, his gaze gentle, he urged her to speak.

She shook her head, certain that if she stayed silent, they wouldn't be gone. As if her silence could bring them back.

"Are you sure?" he asked quietly.

She nodded, silent tears streaking her face. As she stood there, the crushing weight of loss settled over her like a shroud. A bitter truth took root in her heart: love was monstrous. To love meant to hurt, and to hurt meant to break.

As the years went on, Faelyri would look back on that day with a heart full of regrets. She regretted that she couldn't do magic. She regretted following Ilriel down that hallway. She regretted never speaking at the burial site, nor visiting her parents since that day.

But most of all, she regretted that she loved her parents and now knew that if she loved nothing, she would never be hurt again. She now knew that when you feel an attachment to a person, that person will hurt you. No exceptions.

Except her brother. Because he also felt that same pain that day, and understood it, she was certain of it.

And yet, Ilriel had been able to love again. He had found a way. He had friends, a life. But Faelyri never could. She had nothing. She was nothing. Only a shadow haunted by loss and forever chained to a memory.

CHAPTER

ONE

I bet if I ran fast enough, I could make it to the bottom of the mountain. They wouldn't catch me. I could sneak out in the middle of the night. By the time morning came, I would be long gone.

I would leave a note, of course: *'See you in a few days!'* It would read in lovely Elven script. Just so everyone wouldn't worry.

Though, maybe they wouldn't worry at all.

The wind kisses my face as I lean a bit too far over my balcony. Digging into my stomach is the cold marble fence as I use it for balance. Beneath me, the eternal foggy darkness engulfs the mountain below. It always does, as I am about fifteen thousand feet up (give or take).

Maybe it would take more than a few days... I'll change the note.

'See you in a week or two!'

"Your highness, you are going to fall." The guard restlessly fidgets behind me. When I ignore her, she uses my name, "Faelyri."

My lips quickly twitch upward. I lean a little farther.

Syvis, my shadow, has the worst job in the palace: dealing with me. I feel terribly for her, as she needs to constantly ensure I'm not wandering off cliffs.

My hands grip the smooth marble fence. If I try hard enough, I can trick myself into believing I've caught a glimpse of the single ship on the mountain's base. A ship I've never seen. Not even once.

Whenever my gaze falls upon what I always assume is the location of the docks, my chest grows heavy with an overbearing longing. But shortly after, any yearning for that ship is quickly eclipsed by the hardening of my stomach.

The rapid tapping of an armored boot warns me to step away from the ledge.

I ignore her again and bend down a little farther, letting my shimmering hair drape over the fence. I shake my head, watching the color shift from hues of purples to pinks. I always gauge how long it's gotten by hanging over the edge like this. One day, it may be longer than the fence itself.

The bed of fog is denser than usual under me, swirling in thick tendrils that pulse with a life of their own. I reach out, just to run my fingers through its softness.

Just as my foot lifts off the ground, Syvis intervenes, pulling me back from the ledge. The smooth, cold surface of her moon-stone armor presses against my skin.

Taller than me by a foot, her face is as hard as her armor. Strands of black hair escape the bun on her head. I brush them aside before she releases me.

"You need to stop doing that," she commands.

I lift my hands up as I say, "I'm only messing with you. I won't fall. I promise. I would never harm myself."

No danger here, not ever.

She scowls, shaking her head, "And what if you did?"

"At least I would see the ship on my way down."

"How humorous." While very hard for her with the large armor, she manages to cross her arms. "Why do you care so much about the base of the mountain? There is nothing there."

"You know that is quite a lie," I point toward her, and then toward the floor. "People live down there. Otherwise, we wouldn't get letters."

She sighs, "We never get letters."

She scratches her head, behind her ears. They're much

longer than mine, and pointed downward. "I do not want to argue, despite how much you love to. We need to go."

Fine. But I *don't* love to argue.

She takes a step out of the way. I take my time walking to the bedroom door, leading the way for my valiant knight to follow.

My home has a stillness that I have never experienced beyond its walls. In the silence, the soft stream of waterfalls echoes through the open hallways. Each day, I follow the same, familiar, path. Over the ivy-covered bridge that connects my wing to the main palace. I make my way to the entrance, where my brother patiently waits.

Tonight, however, I'm straying from my usual path. As I walk, I pass portraits of my family (and myself), lifting my head to meet their gazes.

First is my father, wearing a large crown and a gentle smile. His pale eyes always seemed so heavy, as if he had just woken up from a nap.

"Your Highness, we should keep walking," Syvis urges.

I take a moment, waving my hand dismissively at her. As I do, my fingers brush against my hair which I tuck behind an elongated ear.

My mother's portrait is truly lovely. Moonflowers surround her. Any tension in my body melts away. Without a doubt, hers is the most striking, for sure. We have the same face, but she wears it better. Maybe the grace comes from a long life of rich experiences that I'll never have.

I can barely remember their voices now.

My brother comes next, his long hair slicked back behind his face. He is certainly not smiling, wearing a crown that outmatches both of our parents'. His is the only portrait where the subject is holding a weapon. He demanded it be repainted when he did not like the first outcome. That poor painter.

Mine is the final one in the line, and I'm slouching. I try to straighten myself now, but it causes such an unbearable discomfort. The version of myself in this portrait is gripping my hair so tightly that I almost ripped it out of my head. My brother wanted it repainted, but I pleaded not to. The artist had already dealt with him, and I could not bear the thought of sitting there for hours again.

"My hair got longer," I state, fixated on my image.

"Well, you have never cut it."

Yeah, good point. My mother would never let me cut it. I stand there for a few seconds, only tearing myself away when Syvis clears her throat.

We're almost there anyway. Our shoes echo in the hall, her's much louder. I let my head drop, watching the enchanted stone beneath my feet light up with every step. The closer we get to our destination, the louder the soft vibration in the walls becomes.

I glance up to see my brother standing outside the ballroom door. I beam at him, and he returns a warm, softer smile.

Ilriel stands tall, as always, because why would he not? He also always keeps his hand on the hilt of his sword as if something is perpetually coming for him. Next to him is his guard, Farren. Her eyes are as white as her hair.

When her gaze lands on me, I shiver.

Ilriel is a breath of fresh air compared to his awful guard. As sad as this is, He is the person I spend most of my time with. Should I make other friends? Sure. But how does one even begin to do that? How does one allow others in?

Anyway, I can't make friends here, even if I wanted. Everyone treats me like I'm delicate. Or they need to watch what they say around me.

It's incredibly lonely here.

I open my mouth, on the verge of telling him how happy I

am to see him. When he crosses his arms and says: "You're late."

Never mind.

The tapping of his foot on the ground causes me to grind my teeth. I shake my head. "I live here. I can't be late."

Farren huffs, mockery in her tone, as she mispronounces my name, "Is that what you think, Faelyri? I personally—"

Then, her brain catches up to her mouth for once, and she quickly tightens her lips. As if someone has snatched her voice from her throat. Maybe someone should.

Ilriel turns to face her. His eyebrows are pressed down, nostrils flared, and a rattle as he grips the hilt of his sword tighter.

I hold my breath, fidgeting with one of my sleeves. Behind me, Syvis is still as stone.

The only sound in the air is the muffled music coming from the door behind him. He does not speak, he never needs to, and Farren shrivels into herself.

She would never apologize, but I don't expect her to.

I only release my breath when Ilriel turns back to me and grins. When he smiles, the markings on the sides of his face scrunch. Lightly colored branches spread over his cheekbones and around his eyebrows. The same as my own.

"You are right," he says through a laugh, "you can't be late if you live here."

The tenseness in the air begins to subside a bit as I ask: "Were you waiting for me?"

Shaking his head, he says: "Someone else." He then pokes his head to the side, pointing his gaze beyond me. Or through me, either one. "But I am happy to see you, as always."

As I start to smile at him, heavy guard's boots march down the hall. I turn my head toward the sound. An armored woman is coming toward us, causing an uneasiness to rest in my stomach. I glance at Ilriel, then back to the guard.

I straighten my posture, no matter how uncomfortable it is on my shoulders.

The guard's final steps are louder than the others, but she falls into a low bow once before us. Of course, the bow is mainly directed to my brother.

"I have a report—" As she begins to speak, Ilriel cuts her off.

"Lyri," he turns to me, "go on in. Enjoy your night."

My shoulders drop, as do my eyebrows. "Is everything alright?" Why is this guard reporting to Ilriel *now*? Did something happen?

He chuckles, keeping his eyes soft. "I promise you that everything is fine. You know me, would I be this lax if not?"

I bite my lip. No, certainly not. But still... "Well, is there anything I can help with?" The words spill out before I can stop them, despite knowing how my question will be answered.

But maybe I *can* help.

"I would never want to bother you with something like this. Please, Lyri, go enjoy the party."

Right. Yeah. Run along and play.

But I *want* to stay. I should know what's going on. Ilriel is much older than I, but even at my age, he was already preparing to rule. I don't need to prepare for something like that, so I always get left behind and left to my uneventful, unexciting, unambitious life.

"Lyri, it's alright. Please don't worry."

I roll my eyes so hard that my head starts to throb. He wins. I suppose off I go. I should bow, but I don't. Instead, I turn on my heels, dramatically motioning with my hand for him to open the door, letting the laughter and music flood the hallway.

The large room, full of twilight elves, resembles the night sky. Different shades of cool colors and glimmering hair.

We tell children that each citizen of Starview is actually a fallen star dropped off on its parent's doorstep. That is, of course, not true (but I believed it for an embarrassingly long time).

Being a fallen star would be cool, though. Imagine the bragging rights.

Starview is a tiny sliver of land, home to about ten thousand citizens. Though, "tiny" is a term bound by comparison. I mean that sure, against the vast expanse of Haelhil, the realm of the high elves, and Farfell, the continent across the sea, Starview seems quaint. However, even they pale in comparison to my home in beauty. Nothing can ever rival it.

Ten thousand elves surely cannot fit in the ballroom, yet my brother hosts these events every week. They all attend at least once. They alternate. Except me. Always here.

As I step in, the silver doors close behind me.

Twin spiral staircases arc gracefully along the hall's edges, ascending to the palace's upper floor. Even without windows, the room shimmers, bathing in silver and moonstone inlaid in intricate starry mosaics. Light flows in, no flame or window needed.

I enjoy a party, really, I do. There are just *so many* of them. This endless repetition of the same music, the same feast, the same hollow pleasantries. You think they would be bored of it by now.

"Syvis, do you think they have parties at the bottom of the mountain?"

She groans. "Must you always speak of the mountain?"

A faint smile tugs at my lips, "We could go together." I offer, half-joking. "Don't you want to see it?"

"A forsaken land of shadows and caves? No. There is no large city, no Elven heritage. And, it is incredibly dangerous."

"Alright. I get it." A breath escapes me, loud but swallowed by the music.

Truthfully, I know I can never go to the bottom of the mountain. But at least it would be something to do rather than being trapped here by their endless fear. I don't want to be afraid.

"Well, what should I do then?" My arms cross, the long velvet bell sleeves cascade like a barrier.

"Dance?" she suggests with a casual shrug. Her shrug is very endearing. Her armor is so stiff that sometimes she can't be as dramatic as she probably wishes to be.

"Alone? Embarrassing." No one asks me to dance, though to be honest, I am completely fine with that.

"I've no other suggestions."

That is quite alright. This is fine for now. At least the others are having a good time, which is all that truly matters. This party is never for me, and always for them. I often wonder if they are all just as lonely as I am. Stuck here forever with no visitors. At least I live in a palace.

Syvis leans in, her voice cutting through the music, "We should move from the door."

Right. I give a sharp nod, my gaze sweeping the room. At first, nothing catches my eye: just shimmering gowns, swirling capes, and empty, practiced smiles. Then, I spot them: the circle of ladies I always spend these evenings with.

They linger beneath a stone pillar, so I weave through the crowd to take my place beside them.

Once there, they begin to dip into a bow, but I assure them there is no need for that.

I would not consider us friends, exactly, but I enjoy their company. They are much older than I am, though you would never know. Their immortal faces are still so young, with a blinding beauty. With their age come the incredible stories of the past. I love listening to them, and sometimes, I believe they love having someone who wants to listen.

I begin to ask them about their days, but I am stopped.

"Your Highness."

My head shoots to the left. A man is standing far too close to me. Why? My face betrays me as my mouth twists. My hand instinctively reaches for Syvis. Her steel-blue fingers firmly close around mine.

"Would you grant me a dance?"

I take a half-step back, away from him, squeezing my guard's hand tighter. "Why?"

He stutters. "You... smiled at me when you entered. When our eyes met. So... I thought..."

I *what?* No, I certainly did not. This is the first time I've seen his face. Sure, I scanned the hall, but I thought my face was expressionless enough. I was careful, right?

However, my teachers' voices echo in my mind: *Always be courteous, always be gracious.* So, I force a smile. "I am a terrible dancer, I'm afraid. But thank you."

The ladies make knowing glances before one of them waves him off with a flick of her hand.

He takes a stubborn step closer, parting his lips to protest, maybe. I try to hold my smile. My cheeks are sore.

Before he can utter another word, a hand clasps his shoulder.

Ilriel stands behind him, "Didn't they tell you to *move along?*"

My strained smile falls, and I attempt to rub out the stiffness from my cheeks. Ilriel delivers a final, pointed tap to the man's back, and the defeated elf vanishes into the crowd. Hopefully, never to return.

"One day," Ilriel drawls, turning back with a smirk, "I may not be around to scare off your suitors."

"What does that mean?" I call after him, but he's already gone.

Syvis's hand finally drops mine.

"Thank you." I say to the group.

I slump against the cold pillar. In my mind, there are images of waterfalls and starry nights and rustling leaves on trees. I have collected a lot of them over the years and kept them locked in my brain. That's where I would rather be.

I cast another glace over the room. There's no reason for me to be here. There's always next week.

Pushing myself off the wall, I offer a quiet farewell to the group, thanking them again. Navigating through the crowd, I shove aside those too distracted (or indifferent) to clear a path. If they won't move, I will make them move. Finally, I'm back at the entrance and slip out.

The doors seal behind me with a soft thud, muffling the music. The corridor stretches ahead, dim and seemingly deserted save for the faint whispering further ahead.

I glance at Syvis, raising my brows. She nods, understanding my fake telepathy. Her steps are far too loud, so in the silence, I mouth, "stay here."

She frowns, but concedes with a nod.

I am not stealthy. I have never needed to be. But alas, I try my best, treading as lightly as possible in my delicate slippers. As I near the branching corridor, the hushed whispers become discernible.

It's Ilriel.

"The miners claim the moonstone veins are depleted," he says, voice low and edged with frustration. "We must secure more, however we can."

I can never help myself, because I am the worst, so I step into view. "We've run out of moonstone?"

Moonstone is woven into our armor, blades, and even our walls. It is the lifeblood of Starview, and its defense. Without it, the high elves would invade, and we would all burn.

While they think I don't know much of anything, I know more than they like to pretend.

"Lyri, how long were you eavesdropping?" Ilriel spins toward me.

My mouth opens to speak, but he cuts me off.

"No," he snaps. Then, his voice softens almost instantly, "we haven't run out, and we won't."

"You just said—"

"You misheard," he insists, "this is what happens when you lurk in the dark, paranoid."

Did I mishear?

"Where do you plan to get more?" I ask, unwilling to yield. At least, right now.

His exhale is long and weary, like wind. He rubs his temples, "these mountains are vast. The miners report only one depleted vein. We've already sent teams farther into the range. There's *plenty* left." His tone sharpens, "you are being paranoid."

"Oh..." My fingers twist a strand of my hair.

Our gazes lock. His eyes are a deeper shade of purple than mine, and I can never quite read them.

"I'm sorry," I whisper.

His features soften further. "Apology accepted. I didn't mean to frighten you, but don't eavesdrop again."

"I just want to be included."

I have no desire to shoulder his burdens, but I would like to be more than a silent shadow.

Without a word, he pulls me into a rough embrace.

His leather armor digs into my skin, but the warmth of his hold feels like the quiet comfort of a vast star-lit sky.

For a fleeting moment, I believe everything is fine.

But then, he steps away from me. "It's just easier this way."

A vice tightens around my chest. It's evolving, sinking deeper into my stomach as I study my brother's face. There is some invisible crack that only emerges if I stare long enough. Only in situations like this, when he tries to shoo me away.

By the morning, it will vanish. He will laugh at my jokes, listen to my clumsy lute playing, and flash me an easy smile.

So, I always ignore the crack.

But right now, as the warmth from his embrace fades, the hollow ache remains. I can't fight it.

But I still force myself to smile. I am just going to ignore it.

CHAPTER

TWO

While it *is* dawn, you could never tell. Our island is cloaked beneath a cascading veil of stardust. If the sun shines bright, we will never see it beyond the sea of stars.

When the ancient rogue elves built this city, they used the terrain to their advantage. The city was set *in* the mountains. The craftsmanship is seamless. No discernable line marks where the palace's stone meets the mountain's face. Towering spires of varying heights pierce the sky while balconies overlook the view.

Today, Ilriel and I share lunch near the palace entrance, in a tiny garden tucked away on the side, where a table has been set for us. Over the cliffside, a small stream burbles, and the scent of the moonflowers lining it surrounds me.

I rest against the ivy-covered gate, my chin touching the cold iron. My gaze drifts, following the dancing stream until it is swallowed by the foggy abyss. I haven't bothered bringing up the conversation from the night before. There would be no use continuing it.

"I wanted to ask you something." Ilriel's voice pulls me back. He lifts a spoon, grinning as he stirs the medley in his bowl.

It takes longer than it should, but I eventually tear my gaze away, forcing my dark eyes from the water. "Hm?"

He inspects the mushroom on his spoon before eating it. After swallowing, he asks, "Would you like to join me when I travel to Farfell? Frondvale, actually. I'm to visit with the human king."

He fishes out another mushroom.

Wait, am I truly being included? He wants me to go with him?

Off the island?

"You want to leave? Why Frondvale? Why the king? How are we getting there? How long will we be gone? What do..." I hold myself back, pressing my lips together.

His eyes hold mine, shimmering with a rare light. "I'm forging a treaty. I decided it was time to stop hiding ourselves away in this mountain."

I clear my throat. I suppose he truly isn't wrong. We really have been isolated for too long. "I agree. But why a treaty for that?" My gaze lingers on the branching marks etched across his face, waiting.

His grin only deepens as he pours dark wine into his cup. Beneath the table, his leg starts its restless bounce. "It's merely formal. I'd like allies." He chuckles softly. "So, Frondvale. Will you come?"

"Is it?" I ask, sidestepping his question. My eyes flick to the trembling table before returning to him.

His gaze narrows, sharp. "Why the curiosity? Politics have never been your interest."

He's right. I never had an interest in politics. "If my life is going to change, I'd like to be prepared for it. That's all."

Am I really leaving?

His eyebrows lift, the tiny circular runes tracing their edges rising with them. "As always, dramatic."

Behind him, Farren laughs.

I flare my nostrils, resisting the urge to glare in his guard's direction. I refuse to give her the satisfaction.

"The sea is dangerous," I state. "Is allying with distant strangers, which we will never see again, worth the trip?"

I dreamed of descending the mountain and *admiring* the sea, not crossing its waves. There are far too many dark and rising dangers. I don't want to travel across the sea. I don't want *him* to go. Our parents died on the waters.

Lowering my voice, I press further. "Is this because of Hael-hil? Are the high elves planning an attack? Is that why we must leave? Is that why we need the humans?"

"Yes." He answers too swiftly for my liking.

I say nothing. If Tae'ril and the high elves are coming, they would most likely love nothing more than to get their hands on the two of us.

He is the reason we never leave. Why I spend endless hours trapped in this city, gazing down from my balcony into the starless abyss. He wants Starview (well, Starview's magic), and he is growing ever more aggressive in his pursuit. So we remained sealed away, prisoners of our own enchanted mountain.

"So, that's why you want me to come with you? Just in case?"

He sighs, "yes. So...?"

I slouch farther down into my seat, forcing my gaze onto my lunch instead of him. I wish my stomach weren't in knots. I'm getting what I want: an escape. But why is my body rejecting the idea of it?

Shifting uncomfortably, I finally take a hesitant bite, chew, and then swallow. I don't want him to go, but he will. So, he shouldn't go alone. What if something awful happens to his ship? If I go, at least he won't be alone and frightened.

"I'm sorry. I'll go," I say to him.

I do want to leave this city so badly. And I have read so many books on Frondvale. I have heard stories from many of the elder (and I mean *elder*) elves. While Starview lingered in an eternal dusk, Frondvale shone like dawn, large and alive.

I cast a glance at Syvis, who has stood silent through it all, "you'll come?"

She nods once, resolute as ever. Of course she will. What a foolish question.

"When do we leave?" I ask my brother.

"In a few days," he answers easily, sipping from his bowl.

"I guess I am just curious. Why humans?"

"Because this is my realm, and I have decided that Starview *needs* allies."

My realm. But what if one day it isn't? I have never stopped to consider, until this moment, that one day Ilriel may not rule. We do not have a monarchy. Our Goddesses choose our ruler. What if, one day, it is no longer him?

What if his rule ends, and someone else is chosen? His rule has been so long, since our mother died, I don't even know what that would look like. That's one book I never considered reading.

Though, our mother ruled for so long, *hundreds* of years. And it's odd that he was chosen after her, rather than another family.

My thoughts whirl with vivid images of the high elves, imagining them galloping into our city and slaughtering us. The mountain feels as if it's tilting beneath me, so I press my elbow against the table for stability. The rushing water causes a turning in my stomach.

He speaks again, voice steady but coaxing. "With *me*, you are safe," he promises, his tone fierce yet earnest. "I will never let anything, or anyone, harm you. You know that."

I have no idea how long it has been since I've spoken a word. My thoughts have piled up so densely that they've left my mind feeling utterly empty.

"Are you finishing that?" Ilriel stretches his spoon toward my half-empty bowl. I shake my head, nudging it toward him.

I bite my lip, hesitant but unable to suppress the next question. It burns at the edge of my mind, more pressing than any treaty, or alliance, or invasion. "What if I'm... weird? What if I don't know how to interact with them?"

Ilriel's expression shifts into that familiar, wary concern. The one he wears when he senses I'm on the brink of unraveling. My chest tightens. My fingers twist into the soft tablecloth as my heart pounds in anticipation.

He sets the bowl down gently, pausing as a servant arrives to clear the remnants of our meal. I crane my neck slightly, trying to keep him in sight.

"You are weird!" His voice is light, almost forced. Not what I expected. "But normal weird, the good kind. You're wonderful, and everyone will love you. Who wouldn't love a princess?"

My heart slows, uncertainty settling in its place. Is there a good kind of weird? I'm not sure.

CHAPTER
THREE

The bustling heart of Starview's market unfolds before me, vibrant and alive with sights and sounds. Syvis trails a step behind, her presence silent but steady, as always.

My purpose is clear: I need to gather things for my journey, including protection from the sun's blazing wrath if such a thing exists here. I've been told the touch of the sun burns and chars the skin, and burning would be terribly inconvenient.

Perhaps I should also collect gifts. Gifts are the way to friendship, right?

As I meander through the vendors and wares, I catch glimpses of the townsfolk who pause to bow as I pass. Heat rises in my cheeks.

Please stop.

I slouch as I walk, which is not the posture befitting royalty, but it's the only way I know to stave off the constant anxiety that creeps at the edges of my thoughts. My eyes dart between stalls, seeking a cloak sturdy enough to keep me protected but airy enough so I don't overheat.

Nearby, the animated and theatrical voice of a teacher draws my attention. She stands before a gaggle of children spilling out from the school.

"Beware the feyfolk," she warns, her tone heavy with foreboding. "The changelings who creep into your homes to steal children from their cradles, leaving their own wicked kin behind. And when the swap is complete, they feast upon the stolen young."

The children gasp in unison. One small girl clutches at her skirt, her face pale with fright. I feel a pang of recognition; her terror reminds me of the sleepless nights of my own childhood.

"I could tell if they were fey," a boy boasts, puffing his chest with the bravado of innocence.

"Oh? And how would you know?" the teacher challenges. "The fey can glamour themselves into whatever you most desire to see."

"Are they scary?" the little girl quavers.

"They are horrors," the teacher says grimly, "haggard nightmares that twist your will to their own ends."

Ah, I know that book. I read the same grim tales as a child and spent many nights staring into the dark, fearing that some malevolent sprite would spirit me away.

The girl's lip quivers and tears threaten to spill. I step forward, knowing this is one of the rare moments when my title can be used to my advantage.

"You do not need to worry about feyfolk," I say gently. "There are no faeries or pixies within Starview."

Her wide eyes search mine for the truth. "But what if they come here? What if they trick someone to let them in?"

I crouch slightly, meeting her gaze. "*You* are too clever to be fooled by such creatures."

The girl sniffs, a glimmer of courage returning to her small frame. Satisfied, the children scatter.

I turn to the teacher, and now I'm annoyed. "Please don't frighten the children."

She shakes her head, "it is not fear I sow, but caution."

I cross my arms, my annoyance causing me to toss aside my grace, "Do you *really* think they would ever encounter anything other than a twilight elf in this place? On this island? Where they'll never leave?"

She shrugs. "They will live forever."

Oh... right.

Immortality is a fact of life, and I know this. I see it in the ageless grace of elves who have survived centuries yet still look as though they could be my siblings.

Though, I never thought about my *own* immortality.

I'm going to live forever here. Alone.

FOUR

The night wraps around me, suffocating, and I toss and turn, haunted by my own nightmares. Too many of them.

Faeries, their twisted faces peering from shadows. Ships crashing against jagged rocks. Flames devouring my flesh under a cruel sun. Invasions that rip through the calm of my world. My body rolls in bed like a frightened child until I wake.

But a faint sound reaches me amidst the chaos of my dreadful thoughts. At first, it's barely there, a fragile note. A ringing. A soft, melodic hum, like the echo of a distant song? It lasts only a moment, and I hold the side of my head, fingers in my hair.

Am I finally losing my mind?

Curiosity, or the aforementioned madness, pulls me from the safety of my bed. Barefoot and silent, I slip into the silvered halls of the palace, the sound like a beckoning thread I can't ignore.

It winds through the corridors, tugging me farther and farther until I stand before the war room.

A place I'd believed to be long forgotten and unused.

Yet the hum grows louder here, singing to me, calling to me. It's not just in the air; it is actually inside me, vibrating through my bones. I press my palms against my ears, but the sound persists, rooted somewhere deeper, more intimate.

It feels... alive.

Inside, Ilriel looms over an open tome sprawled across the war table, his sharp features drawn tight with exhaustion. The faint glow of the room's lanterns catches the dark circles beneath his eyes. He notices me and, with a swift motion, slams the book shut.

A familiar object catches my gaze on the table: a small, unassuming marble box. I know this box well, as it holds the kingdom's most precious relic, the Nightstrand. The artifact that anchors our world.

Really, it is the only object that matters at all.

And the hum crescendos as I step closer.

"Lyri." His voice is calm, but his face is anything but. "Why are you awake?"

I scratch at the back of my neck, my nails grazing my skin as I struggle to speak. "Are you... playing music?"

Ilriel frowns, confusion flickering in his eyes. He straightens, his commanding posture contrasting with my hunched stance.

Next to him, I am so small.

His glance moves to the box quickly. "You hear music?"

The hum twists into a sharper, more insistent note, drilling into my mind. I wince, clutching at my head as if it could quell the pressure.

"My head hurts," I confess before daring to ask, "What are *you* doing up?"

His hand slides to the box, drawing it closer to himself. The instant he touches it, the hum transforms into an unbearable pleading chorus. It drowns out all thought, all sound, all light. I stagger forward, clutching at the table for support.

It feels like my ears have exploded.

Am I dying?

Get out of my head. I plead to whatever lodged itself in here. *This is my head. Get out.*

Whatever it is, it ignores me.

"Lyri," Ilriel says, his voice distant as I lose my footing.

I collapse against him, and he stumbles, dropping the box. It strikes the ground with a sharp crack, its lid snapping open.

"Hand that to me," he commands, his voice tight with urgency.

I turn toward the artifact, its golden surface etched with ancient runes that pulse with a soft, powder-blue light as my hand hovers over it.

The hum now sings through me with clarity. As though the artifact itself reaches for *me*.

The moment my trembling fingers graze its surface, a vibration courses through my arm.

It's alive.

Is it real? Or am I losing my grip on reality? Am I hallucinating?

Ilriel's posture crumbles, his shoulders slumping in a way I never thought possible. He moves faster than I've ever seen, snatching the artifact from my grasp.

The moment it leaves my hand, the light vanishes, and it

becomes a lifeless trinket. A sharp sound rings out as he slaps the artifact against his palm in frustration.

I'm not sure why or what comes over me, but when I don't have that in my hand, I have an odd ache in my heart. A hollowness in my body. I need it back.

"How did you do that?" he asks.

I shake my head, pulling myself up from the floor. "I don't know."

He rushes to the tome, flipping through its pages with frantic precision. The Nightstrand is tucked under his arm as though it might vanish if not held close.

The melody stirs again in my thoughts, pleading for something I cannot understand. I'm straining to listen, to grasp its meaning, but the melody dissolves into fragments before I can hold it.

"What are you looking for?"

"The answer to my question," he tells me, focus never wavering from that book.

"Can I look?"

He glances at me, his eyes sharp and searching, filled with curiosity and something darker.

"I think," I begin hesitantly, "I think it's singing to me. Search for something about... a song."

"*I know it sings*," he snaps. Of course he does. It is *his*, after all.

His head drops to the book again. When his expression darkens, he taps a finger against the page before slamming the tome shut with a resounding thud.

I can't help but stare at his arm, where the Nightstrand rests under it. At first glance, the artifact is unassuming: a small, golden cylinder adorned with intricate runes. Yet, its simplicity is a lie. The artifact shifts its form to match the wielder's needs, whether a blade, a shield, or something unimaginable. Only one twilight elf at a time may command it. Yet, it chooses its master and may revoke that privilege if it deems them unworthy. As easily as you can get it, it can be taken away. It has a mind of its own.

But, if it chooses you, you rule the kingdom, and Ilriel has ruled for a very long time.

I don't know what key, heroic traits are needed to wield it, but I lack every single one.

But I also didn't know it sings. I didn't know that you couldn't discern any of your thoughts from the sound of it.

"I'm going to figure out what happened," he finally admits. "But you need to tell me how you did that."

"I told you, I don't know."

"Faelyri, this is not a joke."

"I know!"

"I need this," his voice quickens, quiet but laced with something unsettling.

His eyes glimmer, though not with light. That crack is forming in his expression, the invisible fracture that only I can see.

"Does this make me—"

"Don't." His sharp tone cuts me off. "Having this does not make you a queen."

It's like he's trying to convince himself more than me. Though, I agree with him. A person who rules a kingdom must possess a wealth of knowledge that I simply lack. But Ilriel? He has it. He's always had it.

I raise my hands. "Fine, keep it. I don't want it." My voice wavers. "I can't even hear myself think when it's near me."

"I can't keep it if you can use it. Relinquish it to me."

The artifact doesn't feel like a weapon. It feels like a captor. I don't want it. I don't want the power or the burden it brings.

But why is it crying? Why does it feel like it's dying? It's in pain, and it's asking me for help. I don't want it. But I want to help it.

I *have* to help it.

"It sounds like it's dying," I say softly, almost to myself. "Like something's wrong with it. Severely wrong. Why can I use this? Did it stop working for you? We need to talk to someone, anyone."

Rapid fire questions, as always. But they call for answers immediately.

He says with a biting edge: "It *is* dying. And when it does, the barrier surrounding this city will fall. And yes," the last part sounds like it is excruciating for him to say, "it stopped working for me. Weeks ago."

Weeks? Everyone should have known about this. There should have been some announcement, and coronation, and ceremony, and lines of people touching and putting their hands on it.

"Tell me, Lyri," he continues, undeterred, "are you prepared to sit among a council and *govern* Starview?"

"No," I whisper.

"When our protection falls, do you think *you* can lead an army to fend off Haelhil?"

I shake my head wordlessly, unable to find my voice.

"What happens if you die?" His face twists in a way I've never seen before. The crack widens, splintering further.

What's beneath that mask? Is it the same face that that smiles at me each day?

"Why would I die?"

"If this dies, will you die with it?"

I don't know. I can't answer.

"And then when you die, what happens then? Are you its final partner? I find that unacceptable." He's rambling. "I will fix this. I just need to find *her*."

"Who?"

"Filauria."

Starview's first queen, the chosen of the Goddesses, was the first to wield the Nightstrand and was also the kingdom's first and only traitor. The one who was a hero by fracturing the ancient high elves of Haelhil, leading most of them away from Tae'ril to our crescent-shaped mountain.

A warrior of unrivaled power, or so the stories say. Her name was, at one point, spoken with reverence. Now, however, it is only spoken with fear.

I've known her story since childhood, and I remember my mother narrating the tale each night before I fell asleep. I loved it. I loved her.

When she decided to leave Haelhil, others followed, scattering across Farfell, abandoning the high elf stronghold for good.

But the longer the elves stayed in those new places, the more they changed, their forms evolving to reflect their surroundings. I glance down at my hands, pale and faintly lavender. What would I be if Filauria had never carved out this sanctuary? If she hadn't built this palace so close to the moon?

Her choice of location has always struck me as odd. A remote mountain bathed in starlight. It's beautiful, yes, but dangerous. Why here?

Anyway, eventually, her time was up. The Nightstrand passed from her hands to another, a man whose name always escapes me (because I never care to remember men's names). Her fury was *legendary*. Betrayed by the artifact she had wielded to build this kingdom, her wrath culminated in her murdering the new king, driving her blade into his heart in a fit of blinding rage.

The kingdom's outrage was swift, of course. They branded her a traitor, waged a bloody battle, and cast her out from the mountain sanctuary she forged. Her final words echoed across the halls of this palace, chilling and unforgettable:

'I will return when your palace crumbles, and I will wash away the filth with your blood. Remember that. Sing songs about it to your children. Warn them.'

It was all very dramatic.

As a child, I would beg my mother to repeat that line in her most dramatic voice. I know I shouldn't idolize a traitor, but I couldn't help but admire her. She forged her own destiny. She gave herself a purpose. She was an icon.

And now, according to my brother, the Nightstrand would not be dying if she were here. It would not be screaming at me to save its life.

Ilriel said that he wanted allies; he should have started with her.

"Are we going to need to leave Starview?" I ask. "All of us?"

"Will we get out in time before we're all slaughtered?" he demands.

"We need to find her." My voice cracks. Embarrassing.

"And I will, when I figure out how to use this first."

"How can she fix it?"

He yells, louder than I have ever heard: "I don't know yet!" His composure is getting more and more frayed.

I don't know what he's thinking, but *I* think I need to get the Nightstrand from him. Immediately.

My greatest strength has always been my helplessness. Some might call it a weakness, but I know better. When people believe you're powerless, they let their guard down. They don't see you as a threat. They just see you as you.

"Ilriel," I make my voice intentionally shaky, "I'm frightened and tired. Will you walk me back to my rooms?"

His jaw tightens, but after a pause, he sighs and places the

Nightstrand back into its box. He doesn't close it, though. Careless.

I step closer, lifting my arms as if seeking comfort. "Please," I add softly, gesturing for a hug.

His shoulders sag, his attention momentarily elsewhere. And in that instant, while his guard is down, my fingers snatch the Nightstrand and slip it under the folds of my dress.

He doesn't notice when I close the box.

With a nod, he gestures for me to follow, and he walks me back to my rooms. My heart pounds with every step, the weight of the Nightstrand heavy against my side. For now, it's safe.

❧

That glimmer in Ilriel's eye when he asked about my death, I'll never forget it. The image clings to me, shadowy and sharp, like a shard of glass lodged in my mind.

I gaze beyond the mountains as my mind drifts.

I sent for Syvis to come to my bedroom. Her presence is a steady pillar against the storm in my mind.

She clears her throat, coughing into her gloved hand. The subtle movement causes her armor to clink softly.

I grip the marble railing, leaning too far over the edge as my thoughts pull me deeper. Is it possible to fall into madness all at once? Or is it something that festers slowly, creeping up like ivy? Has my brother always been mad? Surely not. Ilriel was always perfect, polished, poised, unshakable. Where I would scream and wail over petty grievances, he was always calm. Always *civil*.

"Lyri."

That tone. Her voice carries just enough authority to remind me she's always watching. I straighten quickly before sinking to the cool marble floor. The smooth stone presses against the bare skin of my back, where my dress dips low.

The Nightstrand, faintly glowing, sits in my lap now, pressed close as though I could shield it. Or perhaps it shields me. Who knows.

Its song hasn't stopped. The awful melody winds through my head, both painful and... pleading. It cries for something, *someone,* and though I don't quite understand it, I feel its ache like it's my own.

Perhaps it's lonely, like me. Perhaps it needs a friend.

"I can't let it die," I whisper to both Syvis and the air itself. "I don't know why."

"Because you do not want your home taken from you?" She is so practical.

I shake my head. "Well, yes, but... it's more than that. I *feel* for it. I feel *bad* for it." My voice lowers as I ask the question, which I'm almost afraid to know the answer to. "Can you hear it?"

"I hear nothing," she replies simply.

Her words confirm what I fear: this burden is mine. Alone.

I tilt my head back, staring at the vast sky. The last spotting of Filauria was in the Northern part of Farfell, in the ice peaks. I overheard some guards whispering about it a year ago. Though, it could have been just idle gossip.

This belongs to her, and that is why it is dying. I bet it just wants its rightful keeper. I just have to find her. I can do that.

Is this it? Is this my purpose?

I drop my gaze, letting my chin rest against my chest. "Syvis," I ask softly, "what do you think of my brother?"

"Would you like a real answer?"

That makes me lift my head a bit. "Yes, of course."

"I do not trust him. Anything he says or does. I believe he is a danger to the kingdom and to you."

I sigh heavily, crumbling under the weight of everything. He was just having a bad day. He is so wonderful, and this was just a bad day.

She reaches down and takes my hand, her grip surprisingly gentle for someone who has spent a lifetime wielding steel. Her hands are coarse, the callouses thick, but her touch is kind. I trace the rough texture absentmindedly with my fingers.

"Everything will get fixed," she assures me, her voice steady and full of a confidence I cannot share.

Fixed.

It's such a simple word, but it rings hollow.

I'm not so sure anything can be fixed. Maybe it's easier to accept that empires fall than to stop it from happening.

Ilriel, for all his cracks, for all his rage, *cares*. He's dangerous, yes. But he's dangerous because he refuses to let our home slip away.

I clutch it tightly to my chest as though holding it might steady the chaos swirling in my head. Somewhere in the dark distance of Farfell, Filauria waits, if she's alive at all. I have to find her. I have to try.

"You do not have to understand it. You just have to do it." It's like Syvis can read my mind.

With that, the singing grows louder.

CHAPTER

FIVE

My worry and paranoia are my only companions tonight, and they keep me from slipping into dreamland. I stir constantly, eyes fluttering open to the sound of restless night creatures. They croon and scuttle in the dark, their symphony oddly soothing. At least I am not alone in my restlessness.

I keep instinctively clinging to my new, unwanted responsibility.

The fourth, or perhaps fifth, time I wake, I hear a faint rustling in my bedroom. I don't bother to open my eyes. It's nothing. Just some small creature seeking shelter, sneaking through the balcony I always leave open to Syvis's perpetual dismay. I often wake to find feathered visitors nesting in my curtains.

It's fine. This will be no different.

It has to be.

A small, adorable visitor.

But the rustling grows louder. Heavier. Booted footsteps against the marble floor. My pulse stumbles, and I curl my trembling fingers more tightly around the Nightstrand, shoving it beneath the fabric of my slip. My breath catches as I sit upright. I prepare to come face to face with my intruder.

I freeze.

No intruder awaits me. No shadowy figure looms in the dark.

But my bedroom is in complete disarray. Books lie scattered, their pages torn and crumpled like discarded leaves. My small dining table is overturned, its legs splayed grotesquely. Drawers gape open, their contents strewn across the floor, and my once-pristine rug is pulled up and bunched.

I didn't hear this. *How did I not hear this?*

"Lyri, are you alright?"

I scream at the sound of Ilriel's voice. My covers fly over my head, and I shrink beneath them, curling into myself as though I can make my body vanish entirely. I breathe in sharply, muffling the sob trying to escape.

"I heard the noise," Ilriel says gently, his voice coaxing but distant. "I came to see if you were alright."

I fling the blankets back and sit upright, my voice sharp and trembling. "You *heard* it? Did you catch who it was?"

He doesn't meet my gaze at first. "I didn't. They must have entered through your balcony." He gestures toward the open door.

I scramble off my bed, clutching the Nightstrand tightly. I cross the room to shut the door, slamming it with far more force than necessary. At least it's closed now. At least I'll have the element of surprise if something, or someone, tries again.

"How could you have heard it?" I ask, my voice shaking as I turn back to him. "Your rooms are in another wing."

Ilriel walks past me and reopens the door, the pale light of the moon spilling across his face, sharpening his features. He peers over the edge, down into the swirling fog that blankets the cliffs.

"They must have escaped the way they came," he says, his voice even, unbothered.

From where, though?

He turns back to me, extending his hand, and though I trust my brother, I hesitate before taking it. There's something tight and hollow in my chest.

When I do place my hand in his, he pulls me gently onto the balcony.

"I'm glad you're alright," he says softly, smiling with that familiar, disarming warmth.

Before I can step away, he wraps me in an embrace, pulling me close against him.

His heartbeat is rapid. So is mine. He rests his chin against the top of my head, just as our mother used to do when she comforted me, but there's a heaviness in the way he holds me. It's as if he's trying to bind me to him, to hold onto something slipping through his fingers.

"You're hurting me," I mumble against his chest.

He doesn't respond. It's as if he doesn't hear me at all.

"You were looking for the Nightstrand," I accuse.

"I love this kingdom," he says, his voice a murmur swallowed by the night. "All I want is to do what's right for it."

I pull back, startled to see tears tracking down his face. His expression remains stone, unyielding, but the tears fall freely, glimmering in the pale moonlight. Has Ilriel ever cried before?

He steps closer to the balcony's edge, gripping the marble railing so tightly his knuckles turn white. He leans forward slightly, staring into the dense, swirling fog below.

"What are you doing?" I ask, my voice light and shaky, a nervous chuckle slipping free.

"There is a question you always ask," he breathes, "'What

do you think waits at the bottom of the cliff?'" It's as though he is speaking to the night itself. "The fog is so thick, so endless. It's impossible to see what's down there. But it calls to you? It feels inviting?"

My lip trembles. My hands go cold. Is he going to jump? "Ilriel, you're scaring me."

He doesn't turn to look at me. "There's an emptiness in my chest I can't fill. I can't block out the thoughts. I try, but they're always there." His voice catches, for the first time, raw and broken. "But I love you, Lyri. More than anything. You know that, right?"

He shifts his weight, placing one foot onto the balcony's ledge. My heart drops like a stone into the abyss below.

"Ilriel—" I choke, my voice breaking.

He is. He's going to jump. I need to reach for him, to pull him back. But before I can move, he extends his hand to me without turning around, palm open, waiting.

I clutch my chest with my free hand, my breathing sharp and fractured. The tightness coils even tighter, like thorns around my ribs.

I gasp, my voice panicked and thin. "*What are you doing!?*"

My cry echoes through the mountains, carried by the cold winds, but there's no answer in return. Only my brother, standing there on the precipice of something unthinkable.

He isn't going to jump. He can't. This isn't worth it. He has so much more: his future, his strength. Everything beyond this small, cursed object. A life that is long and grand that stretches ahead of him.

"I'm going to find her, don't worry," Ilriel says, his voice hushed, empty, as though speaking only to himself. "The humans will help me. *Take my hand.*"

Filauria? I don't care about her, about the humans, or even

about fixing the Nightstrand. I care about *him*. I care about *now*.

He finally meets my gaze, and I truly see how hard he is crying.

I don't take his hand. Instead, I grab the fabric of his sleeve, my knuckles white as I cling to him. I need to pull him back, to anchor him to the ground where he belongs.

"Ilriel…" My voice cracks, and I realize I'm crying now, too, the tears hot and relentless. "This isn't the way to—"

Before I can finish, he pulls me close. Too close. His arms crush me against him, my face buried in his chest as though he's trying to fold me into himself.

Every part of my body aches. It's not a physical pain, but something deeper, sharper, like vines of thorns have wrapped around my heart and begun to tear. My breaths come in short gasps.

He leans close, his voice low and quiet. His cheek is wet where it brushes against mine.

"I really hope you land on your feet."

He hopes I *what*?

Before I can react, his weight shifts. I'm lifted, thrown like a ragdoll over the cold marble fence. The force wrenches something in my shoulder. A sharp, sickening pop. But I don't scream. My breath vanishes in the rush of movement, and the world spins.

My free hand shoots out, desperate, grasping for anything. My fingers close around the icy edge of the railing. I dangle there, my shoulder throbbing with every heartbeat. I can't lift my other arm; it's clutching the Nightstrand, buried against my ribs. I can't let it go. I *won't*.

The song in my head is piercing now, its cries blending with the sound of my own ragged breath.

It's only been seconds, but my grip is already slipping. My

palm burns against the cold metal, and my nails scrape uselessly. I try to pull myself up, but the pain is unbearable, and Ilriel is still there. I can't fight him. I can't.

The only choice left is to let go.

So I let my fingers slip.

The world falls away beneath me. Air rushes past me, sharp and punishing, and my body tumbles into the foggy abyss. My free hand stretches desperately toward the cliffs, but there's nothing to catch. My nails scrape against stone, splintering as they rip, and I plummet further to my death.

My head hits the jagged side of the mountain with a sickening crack. My vision spins, black spots dancing before my eyes. I don't stop falling. The fog surrounds me now, a silent witness to my descent.

And then, finally, impact.

My hand closes around something. A tree. One of the gnarled giants that grow stubbornly from the mountainside.

My body jerks to a halt, the branch shuddering under my weight. My feet find a small hollow in the trunk, and I cling there, gasping, trembling, alive.

I'm alive.

But the wood is rough, and my bare feet sting as it cuts into my skin. I can feel my blood trickling downward, mingling with the bark. My fingers, slick with sweat, threaten to slip again.

I don't look down. I *won't.*

The Nightstrand hums in my hand. It knows. It *understands.* I don't even need to speak. The glowing starlight creeps from the golden ends of the weapon, light pouring like liquid as it reforms.

A rope? A whip? I don't care. It will do.

I hook it around a jutting stone, tying it tightly, the handle tucked beneath my chin. My body weight tests the line, and it holds. The Nightstrand vibrates gently as if urging me onward.

I begin my descent.

My feet slip at times on the icy stone and the deeper I go, the denser the fog grows. The narrow ledges offer occasional reprieve, allowing me to pause, to steady myself, to remind myself I can do this.

I will not die like this. I *cannot* die. I just have to be strong enough to hold on.

Time stretches endlessly. I don't know how long I've been climbing. Minutes? Hours? The fog above has swallowed my home. And the fog below... it beckons, endless and cold.

When I finally glance down, I see it: the ground. I'm close. *So close.* I can make it. I can survive this.

But confidence is a cruel thing. My hand slips, and the Nightstrand goes with it, its light extinguished like a dying star.

And I'm falling again.

The impact is sudden and graceless, but I'm alive. Somehow, I'm alive. I lay sprawled across the jagged stone, the air driven from my lungs, my body trembling. My limbs ache, my feet sting, but nothing is broken. I should move. I *have* to move.

But I don't.

I curl in on myself, clutching my head as the truth crashes into me.

This happened. It was real.

Sobs wrack my chest, loud and unrestrained. My cries grow into screams. Screams for release, for control, for something I cannot name.

No one will come. I don't expect them to. The screaming is for me alone, a way to purge the terror and pain threatening to swallow me whole.

I don't know how long I lay there, screaming and sobbing into the cold.

But it's been far too long.

When my screaming finally subsides, a new shuffling rises through the silence. The same sound that haunted me in my chambers just moments ago.

Did he have someone waiting for me down here?

It takes every ounce of strength to push myself onto my knees. Standing feels impossible, so I don't even try. My body is trembling, my breaths uneven, but the sound is getting closer, louder, until it feels as though the very trees are rustling in anticipation. My tears have long dried, but the hair on my arms stands on end.

I slip the Nightstrand under my sleeve, its hum vibrating faintly against my skin.

A figure slithers from the shadows beyond the trees. At first, I cannot make sense of what I'm seeing, but then, *a high elf?*

She's nothing like I expected. Her hair is neatly tied back, her face clean and sharp, her oiled leather armor gleaming, untouched by the wear of battle. This isn't the appearance of someone who dwells in caves or hunts in darkness.

Do high elves live down here?

"Your screaming is making my head throb," she says flatly, pressing her fingers to her temple and closing her eyes as though my anguish is nothing but an inconvenience.

Is she serious?

My jaw tightens with anger. I've just survived the most harrowing moment of my life, and she's upset about *her* discomfort?

"I'm sorry that my screaming is an *inconvenience* to you," I snap, my voice ragged.

She steps closer, her movements graceful. When she pauses, her head turns to glance behind her.

"Do you live down here?" I blurt out. It's the first question that comes to mind, and though I'm shaking, I can't stop it from spilling forth.

Her expression twists, her lip curling as though I've insulted her. "The people who live on this island are *heretics.*"

I dig my free hand into the dirt and rock beneath me, grounding myself against the trembling in my limbs. Somehow, I manage to rise.

My bare, bloodied feet ache as the ground presses back against me, but I don't flinch. "Why would you say that?"

She scoffs, the sound venomous. "You followed that *wretched* woman here. You abandoned your rich Elven history to live among dust and shadows."

She's one to speak of abandoning Haelhil, I think bitterly. We're a long way from the golden cities of the high elves. Unless she isn't truly here of her own accord. *Oh, Gods.* My stomach twists. *Is she here for Haelhil?* Is there to be an assault?

My body shivers involuntarily, betraying me.

I keep my voice as calm as I can muster. "Why come here, then?"

"Work," she answers simply, her gaze moving behind her again, as though expecting company. "I have what I need. I am returning to Farfell."

I glance back toward the mountain, letting my eyes climb its shadowed face. The stone looms dark and uninviting, draped in fog and streaked with jagged lines.

It feels alive, almost watchful. It seems to whisper its own threats into the cold air, but perhaps that's just my paranoia whispering back.

The longer I stare, the heavier the weight in my stomach grows. The Nightstrand hums louder, matching my heartbeat.

How long would it take to climb back up? Hours? Days? Would Ilriel come looking for me? Would he care enough to search for my body, to give me a proper burial?

And if I returned, *what then?* Would he simply try again? Would I ever feel safe again?

What's the point of clawing my way back up that dreadful mountain when my purpose lies below? I need to search for Filauria. Why return home, only to descend into this shadowed world again?

But... it would have been nice to have someone beside me. A friend. Syvis.

I turn to the woman, my voice steadier than I feel. "Will your ship take me to Farfell?"

She hesitates, the question lingering in the cold air. Then, a small smile tugs at the corner of her lips.

"You want to come to Farfell with me?"

No. I want to go home. I want my bed, my balcony, and the familiar sounds of Syvis's armor clinking as she stands at my door. I want a thousand things I can no longer have.

But I nod.

And with that nod, the choice is made.

CHAPTER

SIX

My worst trait is that I'm gullible.

I should have known better. A high elf who insulted my island, who sneered at the legacy of my people, could never be trusted. I *should* have known she wouldn't be alone.

The containment spellbinding me is unmistakable: starlight chains of elven magic shimmering faintly as they snake around my wrists and ankles. The delicate glow is deceptive. These chains *burn*. The moment I shift, they sear into my skin, branding me with marks I know will definitely scar.

Very annoying.

The more I struggle, the deeper the pain carves itself into me. My arms now hang limp, dead weight at my sides, my resolve tempered by the sting of my earlier attempts to fight back.

Days have passed. I'm no longer aboard the ship, and I suppose I could call it a free ride if I wanted to make light of this nightmare.

I'm not alone in this misery. My blurred vision makes it hard to see, but I know I'm not the only one here. Others shuffle in chains, their wrists glowing faintly as mine do. Elves, high elves, and a scattering of humans, all bound as I am. I'm the only twilight elf among them, though. That, at least, seems certain and not surprising.

She really scored big with me.

Ilriel taught me once how to escape this spell. *You don't need a key,* he said, *you just need to speak.* Neither I nor the others have tried it yet. Perhaps they don't know how. As for me, I've been too seasick, too disoriented, to focus. Though now I feel the fog lifting, and I know I *could.* But I wait. It's safer this way. If I'm to run, I need to do it when we're secure in one place. Somewhere I might have a chance.

Besides, the emotional storm inside me has yet to settle. Disbelief, rage, fear. All of it churns together, a poisonous brew I can't drink down. Vulnerability hangs over me like a second set of chains, more suffocating than the first.

Why is this happening?

Why is this happening?

Why is this happening?

I don't dare ask it aloud. When I try to open my mouth, my throat burns raw, parched and ragged. It takes more energy to swallow than I care to admit.

The groans of the others pierce my heart, quiet cries that hint at their shared pain. The chains must be branding their flesh, too. Do the high elves know who I am? It's unlikely. Why would they? I've been little more than a phantom princess. A shadow of nothing.

The ache of my captivity pulls my gaze outward toward the smallest sliver of golden light creeping over the distant hills. The warmth of it seeps through the iron bars of our wagon, brushing my face. I don't know how far we've traveled, only that it has been a very long time.

The shadow of a great stone archway steals the light from us. My body slams hard against the side when the wagon jolts to an abrupt stop. My lip splits as I bite down to keep from crying out.

One by one, they pull us up by our burning shackles, dragging us from the cart. I stumble, barely able to catch myself on numb feet. Nightfall looms, the light fading into a deep violet haze. My head jerks downward when I try to lift it, a rough hand forcing me to keep my gaze low.

I only wanted to see where I've been brought...

We shuffle forward in a line, the clinking of our chains loud in the silent camp. It doesn't take long before we're corralled into a standing prison cage, three elves, myself included, thrown together while the humans are kept apart.

A soft sound carries through the air. Someone is crying. I don't blame them. I can't bring myself to join, though. I'll cry later.

The realization hits me as I glance at my companions: the other elves are women. I turn my gaze toward the humans; they are all women, too.

That's a bit alarming.

I lean forward, poking my head through the bars to scan our surroundings. The camp is small, enclosed by a crumbling stone wall, if you could call it a wall. Remnants of a long-abandoned stronghold. Its decay leaves gaps wide enough to see through, though it's still enough to keep us contained.

I linger too long. A sharp *clang* rings through the air as a sword strikes the cage beside my head, the sound vibrating in my skull. I jerk back instinctively, glaring at the snickering guard who stands on the other side.

"Don't try to escape, pretty little elf," he sneers, his voice a twisted attempt at charm. "You won't get far."

The way he says *pretty* makes my stomach turn, bile rising in my throat. I want to lash back, to say something biting, something about how he clearly doesn't know how to use the sword he's waving around, but I swallow the words. They'll do me no good.

He presses his face close to the bars, his grin sharp and revolting. "You're lucky these are separating us."

No. *He's* the lucky one.

I keep my fists clenched at my sides, couldn't fight him even if I wanted to. I barely know how. And I am still trapped, surrounded by his allies. I doubt my fellow prisoners would rise to help me, and I really don't blame them.

He loses interest soon enough, strutting away with a swagger that makes my skin crawl. I breathe a shaky sigh of relief, my chest loosening just slightly.

I whisper the spell into my shackles. The Elven words are soft, nearly inaudible, but I feel the release. The magic shatters, and the chains fall away. My wrists burn where they were bound, raw and sore, but the pain is bearable.

I sit against the cold floor, pulling my legs close as I rub my aching wrists. Next to me, the girl sobs quietly into her knees. I turn to her, my voice low. "Where are we?"

"I don't know," she says between her sobs. "I just want to go home."

I understand. I would also like to go home. But I know crying won't help us. If anything, it will feed their cruelty. I lean closer, lowering my voice further. "Do you know how to remove your binds?"

Her red, tear-streaked face lifts to meet mine, wide-eyed and curious. She shakes her head.

"Can you speak Elven?" I ask.

Again, she shakes her head.

How? How can there be a generation of elves who cannot speak Elven?

The second elf's eyes are sharp. Locked onto me with quiet curiosity. I lean closer, my words a whisper, as I speak over the trembling girl's hands. Soft Elven phrases slip from my lips, and the enchanted chains unravel. The golden cuffs clatter to the ground, dull and lifeless.

The burns left behind are cruel, worse than mine, angry welts that may never truly heal.

"Keep quiet," I murmur, "we can't lose the element of surprise, right?"

She nods quickly, determination flaring in her wide, tear-streaked eyes. I turn to the other silent and watchful elf and free her as well. The starlight dissipates with a quiet hum, and her chains fall away, leaving behind her scars and raw skin.

Both of them look at me, anxious yet ready, their newfound freedom igniting a spark of hope. They want to move. *Now.* They want to tear through the bars and run.

"No," I whisper, placing a steadying hand on the younger girl's arm. "If we fight now, we die. We're weakened, starving, and unarmed. They'll cut us down before we even make it to the gate."

Disappointment flashes across their faces, but they don't argue. There's a fire in both of them. A will to survive. That's comforting. *They're determined.*

"We'll wait for nightfall," I say, leaning back against the cage. "Guards grow complacent. They'll disperse when they retire for the night, and that's when we'll go. That's when we *run.*"

And we *will* make our escape.

They nod again, silent but resolved.

I glance around the camp, scanning for any sign of my belongings. More importantly—*the Nightstrand.* The artifact hums faintly in my mind, a song tugging at me, distant but persistent. It's close. It *has* to be close.

I let my eyes drift to the large tent at the center of the camp. Inside the dimly lit canvas, shadows flicker over tables strewn with scattered belongings: pilfered scraps and stolen trinkets. And there, beneath a carelessly tossed cloth, something gleams. A faint golden edge peeks out, catching the dying light of day.

The song in my head. It's there. The Nightstrand calls to me.

I just need to run fast enough.

❧

Night falls like a heavy curtain, and I wait. Silent. Still. Watching. I was right. Because I'm *always* right. The guards have retired for the night, their boots silent now, their laughter replaced by the whispering winds and the crackle of distant torches.

The shadows deepen, swallowing the camp whole, until even the pale glow of the moon can't reach me. It's then that I hear the footsteps, soft but deliberate, approaching the cage. A man. *Great.*

He doesn't speak at first, but dread coils in my chest like a serpent the moment his key scrapes against the lock. The door groans open, a sound that cuts through the quiet. "Come with me," he orders.

The girls press themselves against the far corners of the cage, eyes wide, bodies rigid. They won't interfere. No one is coming to help me.

"Hurry up," he snaps, his tone colder this time. To punctuate the point, he adds, "I'll kill you here if you don't come with me."

He must be joking. *He has to be.* "I'm fine here, thank you," I say, my voice trying for calm but shaking at the edges.

His hand drops to the knife at his hip, and before I can react, he draws it. The blade gleams faintly in the dim light, its edge sharp enough to sever through thought itself. He points it at me, and my body stiffens, my breath catching.

My fist clenches the hem of my slip, twisting it tightly until I hear the fabric tear beneath my grip. My eyes dart to the tent across the camp, where the Nightstrand hums. A golden glow hidden beneath the cloth, and its call has a low vibration in my mind. I flick my gaze back to him. "Where?"

He gestures with the blade toward a tent further off. It's not the one I need, but it's close enough. I nod, lowering my head to conceal my face as I leave the cage. My bare feet sink into the mud, cold and slick. The door clangs shut behind me, the lock snapping into place.

"Walk," he commands, the blade hovering just behind my back.

I obey at first. My steps are slow and hesitant. Too slow. He grows impatient. "Move faster," he growls and then shoves me.

The force sends me stumbling forward.

But his knife is no longer at my back.

Now.

That's when I run.

The mud, as disgusting as it is, becomes my ally. I slide across it, my hands outstretched as I reach for the table inside the tent, knocking objects aside as I search. *Where is it? Where—*

My fingers close around cold gold, heavy and warm with its strange life.

The Nightstrand.

Its hum fills my chest, soft but resolute, reassuring me that it's still *mine*. It has been nothing but a curse, a nuisance that has dragged me into this nightmare, but in this moment, it feels like a lifeline. *A partner,* it whispers.

The man is charging toward me.

I'm sore. Exhausted. I've never fought a day in my life. But the Nightstrand thrums in my grip, vibrating with a pulse of energy. The golden hilt grows warm as pale light begins to gather.

His hand clamps onto my arm, trying to tear the weapon away. My feet scrape through the mud, my shoulder shrieking in protest. My body acts before my mind can catch up. Pure instinct. I swing the hilt into his face with all the strength I can muster.

He grunts, stumbling back, blood pouring from his nose.

I stumble too, gasping for breath, my chest rising and falling in sharp, frantic rhythm. My hands shake, the Nightstrand still alive in my grip. It *sings* to me now, a sound like distant bells, faint and calm. Starlight spills from the weapon, trailing from the hilt like silken threads.

I don't think.

I *know.*

The threads weave into a sword. Elegant, pale blue, glowing faintly in the dark. Starlight condenses into a deadly point. My hand holds the grip. I wasn't good at sword fighting as a child. I hated it. While Ilriel thrived, I fumbled. Frustrated and weak.

But this... this is different.

The Nightstrand steadies me.

The man's face locked in my vision. Blood drips from his nose as he stumbles toward me, face twisted in fury.

I can't hesitate.

I *don't.*

I let everything go.

The starlight blade cuts through the air like a whisper, finding its mark and sinking into his stomach. The glow flares, blood welling around the wound as his body freezes, standing for a moment longer than it should.

He crumples to the ground.

My breaths come in ragged bursts. My heart pounds against my ribs, my skin clammy and flushed. I stare at the body, unmoving, sprawled in the mud as blood pools around his head. I did that. I *killed* him.

The weapon fades from my hand, its starlight vanishing like mist, but the weight of what I've done remains heavy in my hands. My stomach lurches violently, the sensation like a hurricane spinning inside me. I press my hand over my mouth, bile rising until I double over. My insides expel onto the mud, the stench of blood and sickness mingling.

The girls in the cage are crying now. I hear their sobs, faint and terrified, and I know I should move.

I need to move.

I force myself upright, swiping my sleeve across my mouth as I stumble toward the cage. My limbs heavy, my body drained, but I still manage to reach for the lock.

"I'll get you out," I whisper, my voice shaking. "I'll get us *out*."

I can finish falling apart once they're free. I can vomit and scream and mourn later.

"*Flee*," I command, my voice hoarse, as I brace myself on my hands and knees, retching. "But free the humans first."

The elves shuffle around me, the quiet scrape of their movements almost lost beneath my gasps, and the ringing still echoing faintly in my head. They take the key, their steps quick and frantic, and leave me alone in the cage I'd just opened. I hear them moving toward the human prisoners, but I cannot look up. Tears spill freely down my cheeks as I clutch my aching stomach.

I don't have time for this. I'll allow myself to unravel later, when I'm safe, when I have space to panic properly. I force my shaking limbs to move. First crawling, then stumbling, I manage to drag myself back toward the table where my escape began. My breath stutters as I gather strength, and I finally push myself into a run.

I'd love nothing more than to find a clean change of clothes, something untainted by the grime and blood clinging to my skin. Unfortunately, this camp has no such luxuries. What I *do* find is far from clean but serviceable enough.

Out here, exposed beneath the moon's faint light, I peel the filthy slip from my body. The cold air bites at my bare skin, but I grit my teeth and press on. I pull an oiled leather half-sleeveless tunic over my head, the fabric stiff and unforgiving. It fits tightly, tugging against my sore shoulders, but I manage to slip into it. The matching shorts are equally snug, ending just above my knees.

My hands shake as I fashion a makeshift belt from frayed rope I find on the table. I tie it around my waist and secure the Nightstrand to my hip, testing the contraption by drawing and replacing the weapon several times. It's crude, but it works.

Next, I tug long socks over my bloodied legs, wincing as the fabric presses against my torn skin. They reach high over my knees, hiding the worst of the damage. The boots I find are worn and ill-fitting, pinching at my heels, but they're better than running barefoot. I lace them tightly and rise unsteadily, my balance returning with each deep breath.

The last piece is a forest-green cloak, its edges tattered and its fabric heavy with dust. I fasten the brass clasp at the neck and pull the hood low over my face. My hair—my most recognizable feature—disappears into the shadows of the fabric. It isn't perfect, but it will have to be enough.

No, a bag. I need a bag.

I grab the first thing I find: it's torn, and dirty, but I don't care.

I step out of the tent and scan my surroundings. My heart sinks.

The stronghold, or what's left of it, is a ruin, barely a skeleton of stone walls and crumbling barricades. Beyond its broken edges, there's nothing but open plains stretching endlessly in every direction. The wind howls across the emptiness, carrying the faint scent of ash and earth. There's no shelter here, no cover, no safety.

But then, far in the distance, I see it: a city, its silhouette rising faintly on the horizon.

If that's Frondvale...

Ilriel could be there now, wearing the mask of the grieving brother, spinning tales of how I shattered under the weight of expectation and hurled myself from the balcony. Maybe he's consoling the court, his voice shaking as he explains my "tragedy" while quietly planning how to expand Starview's reach without me.

If that's true, I'll be furious.

Though, if I'm honest, I'm furious anyway.

Was his plan truly to *kill me* for the Nightstrand? Did he think it through at all? The moment the truth comes to light, the people would turn against him, wouldn't they? He'd be exiled. Banished to wander the world alone, stripped of everything. At least, I *hope* that's how it would play out.

The thought of him searching for me fuels a knot of anger in my chest. He must know by now that the Nightstrand wasn't left behind. He must have been livid when he realized I'd taken it with me, that his plan, whatever it was, had failed.

I don't know what I'll do when I see him again. If he even has the temerity to look me in the eye. I'd like to imagine myself storming toward him, striking him across the face with all the anger he deserves. But I know the truth. I'd probably just cry.

At least I have time to figure it out.

I inhale deeply, pulling the hood farther over my face as I turn toward the distant city. Whether it holds safety or danger, it's the only place left to run.

The anger smoldering in my chest pushes me forward, and I begin to run, each step carrying me closer to the horizon. Toward whatever fate waits for me beyond the ruins.

63

CHAPTER

SEVEN

I track the passing of time by watching the slow descent of the moon, its pale light illuminating the winding dirt path. I should have followed the other girls and let them lead me somewhere safer, but I needed to get to a city. Any city.

This one calls to me. Its silhouette promises answers, even if I have to drag them from reluctant lips. Someone there *must* know something about Filauria. She is far more important than Ilriel and his stupid schemes. I can't care about anything else.

If a twilight elf has wandered into Farfell, there would be whispers and rumors. *There have to be.*

At first, I sprinted, my desperation driving me forward. But my run became a jog, the jog a brisk stride, and now I trudge forward at a slow, aching walk.

Each step sends a dull throb through my feet, bruised and blistered inside their stolen boots. The pain gnaws at me, sharp and constant, but I push it aside.

This sucks.

The Nightstrand hums softly at my hip, its tone almost teasing, an encouraging melody that rises and falls like laughter.

"I wish *I* could be carried like you," I grumble back, my voice hoarse.

The weapon offers no reply, of course, but its song doesn't falter.

As exhaustion drags at my limbs, I stumble more often, tripping over stones hidden in the dirt. With each passing mile, my body feels heavier, and the unrelenting heat presses down like a hand on my back.

The cloak, meant to hide me, feels more like a burden now, trapping sweat against my skin. As for the blood on my thighs, that has dried in thin, rust-colored streaks.

My long hair sticks to my face, damp and stinging where it brushes against scratches and cuts. I *could* cut my hair. It would lighten the weight, keep it from tangling and plastering against me. But my mother never wanted me to cut my hair.

The path stretches endlessly before me, disappearing into the haze of heat. The world is still, save for the steady crunch of my boots against the earth.

I haven't needed to hide, at least. No one walks the roads of Farfell at night, it seems. Perhaps they're afraid of the dark.

But now, as the first hints of dawn creep along the horizon, I slow my steps even further and lift my head.

The orange glow of the rising sun spills across the path like liquid gold, casting growing shadows.

I pause, my breath uneven, as the first rays kiss my face.

I make the mistake of trying to gaze head-on at the sun itself, then recoil at the sharp stinging in my eyes.

Without thinking, I immediately try again.

And again.

I almost try again before pressing my eyes tightly shut.

Do not look head-on into the sun, noted.

But the light is so brilliant that even as my eyes are closed... I still see it?

Is this what the sun is like? Warm, bright, and impossible to escape with a domineering presence? All seeing and painful?

The city is finally closer now, its distant walls rising like dark mountains against the dawn's brilliance.

"Just a little farther," I whisper, though I don't know whether I speak to the Nightstrand, to the path, or to myself. Who even cares at this point.

Eventually, my feet bring me down the barren path until I come upon a splinted arrow sign pointing left. Its faded lettering reads:

"Grimehold"

Gross.

Oh well. I have no choice, really. The sun has begun its climb toward its peak, and I know I won't survive much longer if I don't find shelter.

The dirt path gives way to cracked cobblestones as I cross a small bridge, the water beneath it shimmering faintly with the sun's light. Beyond the bridge loom the colossal gates of Grimehold, unwelcoming and gray. The walls surrounding it are old and crumbling, their shadows stretching like claws across the ground.

I limp toward the gates, my blistered feet barely able to hold my weight any longer. The guards stationed on either side don't so much as glance at me, but as I draw closer, the gates groan open.

I step inside, and Grimehold reveals itself in all its squalid glory.

The air hits me first: thick, foul, and stifling. Rotting meat fills my nose, the stench so overwhelming I nearly gag. The buildings are hunched and dilapidated, as though they've been crushed under the weight of the timeworn stone wall encircling the city. Their roofs sag, their windows fractured or boarded up, and the crooked alleyways between them are darkened by shadow, even as the sun rises higher.

The main road is narrow and uneven. Cobblestones jut out at odd angles, while others are missing entirely, leaving muddy gaps in their wake.

The deeper I walk, the worse the smell becomes. The rotting meat fades, replaced by sewage and sweat, and I have to fight to keep my disgust from showing on my face.

There's something else, though... Chirping birds and armored boots on cobblestones are all that fill the air.

There are very few people in the streets, and those who linger do so with wary, sidelong glances. Yet, the city is far from empty. Guards patrol in numbers that outmatch the civilians. I keep my head down and my pace steady.

Please don't notice me.

When I reach the open square at the city's center, I stop short.

A massive statue looms before me. A woman, her stone foot pressing down on the head of a faceless figure as if she's grinding it into the mountain of bodies beneath her. The plaque at the base reads:

Baroness Edie

Savior of Grimehold.

She seems like a real joy.

But what seizes my attention more than that lovely work of art is the line of severed heads impaled on pikes behind it. Ten in total, their lifeless eyes staring blankly at the square. Elves, humans, and dwarfs are represented, their faces in varying stages of decay. One has no eyes at all, just dark hollows that seem to watch me anyway.

Death wasn't the end of their suffering, as the elements were not kind to them either.

A pit opens in my stomach, the nausea clawing at me again. I know little of other races' death rituals, but *this*... this isn't right. It's a mockery. It's no way to respect the dead.

This city is wrong in every possible way. Its darkness lingers in the air, the stones, and the people who seem unfazed by the horrors around them. It's nothing like home. Ilriel wouldn't be here. And Filauria? No. I refuse to believe she'd waste her time in such a wretched place.

Even so, I can't linger. I need answers. A lead, a rumor, *anything*.

Pulling my gaze away from the grisly display, I turn to the market stalls lining the square. There are only three, and none have customers. The vendors sit slouched, their wares as bleak and unappealing as the city itself.

Initially, I'd wanted a meal. A bed. Something warm and soft to make me feel alive again. But after seeing those heads and breathing this stench, there's no way I can keep food down.

I scan the signs etched into nearby buildings, their lettering faded and incomprehensible, then settle on the closest stall: a fruit stand operated by a haggard old woman.

When my gaze meets hers, I exhale sharply. She *looks* elderly. I suppose she *is*... but...

"Hello," I say, offering a small bow in an attempt to cover my rude reaction. "If you do not mind, I could use some help."

She doesn't reply. She stares at me instead, squinting as if to get a better look. Then she speaks, her voice scratchy. "Moon elf?"

"Twilight," I correct her, though I suppose she's not far off.

Her gaze sharpens. "The one they want?" she asks. "With the bounty?"

Bounty?

"Uh, what?" I manage to choke out.

The old woman's hand trembles as she raises one gnarled finger to her left. She isn't pointing to a building; she's pointing to a sign. My brows furrow as I take in the poorly drawn picture: an image of a figure that is undeniably meant to be *me.* I let out a nervous chuckle as I reach for the sign.

That's when the man strikes.

Fingers like iron close around my arm, his grip so tight I wince. My instincts kick in, and I swing my free fist toward his face. My knuckles connect with his nose, but pain explodes through my hand, and my pitiful strike barely budges him. He doesn't even drop his grip.

I should have never come to this filthy city. Lesson learned.

I fumble, scrambling to form a weapon with the Nightstrand, but I'm too slow, too exhausted. The man doesn't wait for me to succeed.

His fist slams into *my* face, and I cry out as stars burst behind my vision. I stumble backward, falling hard onto the jagged cobblestones.

He lunges for my weapon, still strapped to my side. I clutch at it desperately, my fingers locked around the hilt. We tug back and forth, neither willing to let go, until his armored boot crashes into my stomach. Air rushes from my lungs in a strangled gasp, and my grip slips.

He pries the weapon from me, shaking it triumphantly as I lay crumpled on the street. Physically and emotionally. Before I can recover, he seizes me by the ankle and begins dragging me like a child drags a doll.

I claw uselessly at the ground, the rough stone scraping my palms and tearing my cloak. My head lolls back, and I see the sky. Endless and indifferent. Farfell is awful.

Where is he taking me?

Not to his home, I hope. My heart pounds as the largest structure in Grimehold looms ever closer, its dark spires jutting against the sky like broken teeth. Fitting.

I shift my gaze away, back to the heavens, clinging to the only sliver of peace I can find, even if I'm so close to death.

Is there an afterlife? Ilriel claims there isn't one. I hope he is wrong.

I shouldn't have wished to leave. I understand the elves' fear now. Haelhil isn't the only place where monsters dwell. The world beyond Starview is just as cruel, perhaps worse. I should have listened. I should have never followed the Nightstrand's song. I should have stayed in bed. I would have continued to be miserable, yes, but alive. *Safe.*

This is all my fault.

The stone gates of the structure open before us with a grinding groan, and I'm hauled to my feet. I stagger, barely able to hold myself upright, before I'm pushed down a short flight of stairs. I stumble again, catching myself against an old wooden door before it creaks open under the guard's forceful shove.

Inside, the air is colder, heavy with mildew and damp. I blink against the dimness, my breath catching as I take in the sight before me: rows of cells stretching in a long horizontal line.

A dungeon?

The cell door creaks open, the sound a shriek of rusty metal. I try to resist as the man drags me forward, but it's no use. With a final shove, he throws me inside.

My body hits the ground, rolling until I crash against the back wall. Pain splinters through me as I groan, curling in on myself. The grime-covered floor balances me as I force myself upright, my back against the cold stone.

The guard sneers through the bars, shaking the Night-strand in his hand as though it were nothing more than a trinket. "The Baroness will come for you, traitor," he spits. "So just wait quietly."

Traitor?

As if trying to kill me wasn't enough, now Ilriel is using the work of untalented artists to draw portraits of me on bounty signs to brand me with idiotic accusations.

I've failed the Nightstrand, failed the Goddesses who deemed me worthy of it. I press my lips into a tight line, fighting back tears. I can feel its hum, distant but steady. I need to get it back. I can never lose it again.

I also need to find out how long this accusation has been circling. The trip across the sea was long, so perhaps my former kidnappers had no idea. Maybe they were actually doing me a favor. When I was with them, Ilriel couldn't find me.

He must have been shocked when my body wasn't at the foot of the mountain.

"A fallen star."

The voice jolts me, low and mocking. My head snaps to the left, my breath catching.

The source of the voice sits lazily in the corner of the cell. Her face is obscured by hair, so platinum it's actually silver, cut into uneven, wolfish layers. However, her scowl is plainly visible.

I push myself further against the wall, creating as much space as possible. Why would they put us in the same cell? There are empty ones, plenty of them. Do they expect us to fight? To tear into each other like animals for their amusement? They're going to be terribly disappointed if that's the case.

She tilts her head, brushing her hair away to reveal more of her face. She's beautiful, almost unnervingly so, but that's not what keeps me staring.

Her ears. They have a point to them.

I don't answer. I swear the room has frozen. All sound collapsing into silence. The world outside these cold, rust-streaked bars ceases to exist, no guards, no city, no sunlight. Just the pounding of my head and the thundering of my own thoughts.

Is this my life now? Dusty prison cells and untrustworthy strangers?

"A traitor? What'd you do?" Her raspy voice rattles me a bit, but I force myself not to react. When I refuse to entertain her curiosity, she scoffs.

Have they been giving her water? Are they going to starve me?

I curl my arms tighter around my knees, bracing against the sickening wave of vulnerability. "How do you know who I am?"

"There are a shitload of signs, and there aren't many people that have your face."

My fingers brush against my cheeks, tracing the faint branches. Branches that are impossible to hide. I scowl but say nothing.

Like me, she looks worn down. She must have put up her own fight when they dragged her here.

"I'm not a criminal," I mutter, turning my head away.

"Apparently, you are." She shifts, the quiet sound of her movement drawing my attention back. "How did you end up in here?"

I glare at her and throw the question back. Sure, it's childish, but oh well. "How did *you* end up in here?"

She seems so unconcerned. "I'm a thief." She says it as though it's the simplest fact in the world, as though there's no shame in it.

"You don't seem upset about being stuck here."

"That's because I'm leaving soon."

She's unsettling. "What are you waiting for, then?" I demand.

"I *was* waiting for my friend. But if the Baroness wants you, I don't want to be around when she shows up," she mutters, fiddling with the edge of her glove. Then she looks at me again; her expression is unreadable.

I turn fully toward her, confusion knitting my brows. "You would leave me here?"

"I don't care about you. But let me say, *you also* don't want to be around when she shows up."

From within the folds of her glove, she pulls something long and slender. A lockpick gleaming faintly in the dim light.

For the first time in hours, hope stirs within me.

Her gaze narrows, and the edges of her mouth curl into a

smile that stirs something else strange in my chest that I really do not want to dissect right now.

"You good at fighting?" she asks.

No, I'm not. But I nod anyway. If I have to fight, I will.

She crouches low, melting into the shadows on the stone floor. Her movements are fluid, eerie, yet graceful, like a spider weaving its web or a phantom haunting a hall. The room's silence deepens as she extends one long arm through the bars, her hand steady as it works the lock. This is her art; I just realized I forgot to get her name.

Click.

She doesn't push the door open immediately. Instead, she holds the bars gently, testing them so they don't make a sound. I tense, ready to rise, but she raises a hand. A silent order to stay where I am.

If she actually leaves me here, I swear I'll find a way to kill her.

She crawls low as she slips from the cell, movements deliberate and precise. I swallow the lump in my throat as she reaches out, her fingers brushing the hilt of the guard's knife.

She pulls it free without a sound, twirling the blade once. The motion so practiced it's almost hypnotic.

I shouldn't watch this. I should look away. But I can't. I'm *fascinated.*

The moment she rises to her full height, she strikes. The knife flashes, and before the guard can react, the blade slices clean across his throat. Blood spills in a dark arc, and the body crashes to the floor, armor clattering like a drumbeat.

The other guard whirls around, his sword half-drawn, but my cellmate doesn't falter. If anything, she seems *invigorated.*

I watch, frozen, as she crouches slightly, her stolen knife glinting in the torchlight. She blows an errant strand of silver hair from her face, her lips curling into a grin.

"What a rush."

Oh, so she's insane. Good.

I should get up. I should help. I should *run*. But I don't. I can only stare as the silent storm of blood and shadow unfolds before me.

The clash of their weapons jolts me, finally breaking me free of my trance.

Unlike her silent precision, the cell door it groans loudly for me, echoing off the stone walls. I rush toward them, but by the time I arrive, the second guard collapses in a heap.

Two guards dead, their blood soaking the cracked stone floor. Three lives gone, if I count the one in the camp. Each loss tethered to me, whether or not I wielded the blade. I tell myself these two would have met the same fate regardless, that my cellmate's hands would have spilled their blood whether I was here or not. But that doesn't stop the weight from settling in my chest.

And I think I'm going to throw up right now.

"You were *incredibly* unhelpful," she remarks, breaking through my guilt-ridden haze.

"I didn't have a weapon," I snap, my voice sharp. "They took everything from me. What exactly was I supposed to do? Fling my fists and hope for the best?" I pause, jaw tight. "I don't have time to argue with you. I have to find my stuff."

The Nightstrand hums faintly, a guiding vibration in my mind. It calls to me for help, weak but persistent, its presence pulling me toward a darkened corner of the room.

I hurry over, ready to dig through the wooden crate buried in shadow, but before I can, her arm pushes me aside.

"My stuff is more important," she says far too flippantly.

"Trust me. It truly isn't," I snap, shoving her back.

Or trying to. She barely budges, and we scuffle for a

moment, both reaching into the crate like two petulant children.

At the bottom, beneath scattered daggers and loose coins, I spot the Nightstrand's gleaming golden surface. Before I can grab it, she snatches it first. My breath catches as she holds it up, her gaze lingering on the runes etched along its length.

"Give it to me," I demand, my voice low.

She tilts it slightly, examining it as though trying to decode its secrets. Her face is cold. "Did you steal this?"

"It's *mine*," I say through gritted teeth, snatching it back.

She leans back, balancing easily on one hand, her sharp eyes are grey, or are they green? I can't tell. But they're pinning me in place.

"Why is a wanted twilight elf here? In Grimehold, of all places? Alone?"

I take a steadying breath. "I escaped a camp," I admit. "It was nearby. I *killed* my captor, and I'm searching for someone."

Maybe with my emphasis, I'll sound more threatening than I feel.

Strapping her daggers to her hips and a smaller knife to her thigh, she says, "you don't look like a killer."

That's what the human guard thought. That's what Ilriel thinks. But they're wrong. I *can* be.

She stands, and I follow, pulling myself upright as my gaze travels over her. She's dressed head-to-toe in black leather, and the armor fits snugly except for a slightly loose vest that hangs awkwardly around her middle. When she notices my lingering eyes, she adjusts it with a quick tug and shuffles uncomfortably.

Maybe I should thank her for getting me out of here. That is undoubtedly the polite thing to do.

But I just cannot get the words out.

She says nothing as well and turns toward the exit.

I hesitate, my pride nearly silencing me, but I call after her. "Have you seen another twilight elf?"

She stops, tilting her head slightly without fully turning around. "No." Her voice is flat, but there's a sharpness in her words. "Your best bet is to head to the Capitol. North. Ask someone there."

I blink. "How North? Do you mean Frondvale?"

Her head turns just enough for me to catch the tightness in her expression. "*Far* North," she confirms. Her tone hardens as she forces the word out, almost like it wounds her to say it. "And yes. Frondvale."

Before I can reply, the creaking of the door cuts through the silence like a knife. My stomach clenches painfully as footsteps echo from the stairwell above. Slow, deliberate, impossibly heavy. I might vomit here, on her awful shoes, out of fear.

My pulse races as I lift the Nightstrand. It vibrates in my hands, responding to the tension in my body, its song rising to meet my fear. The golden metal shifts, and this time, a bow manifests between my palms in a soft bloom of pale starlight. I notch an arrow, my trembling arm barely holding the weapon steady.

My cellmate glances over, eyes narrowing. "Drop your weapon. He's my friend."

I don't lower the bow completely, though I do let my aim falter.

Her friend doesn't mean my friend.

The footsteps draw closer, creaking loudly on the wooden stairs. My heart pounds with every step.

"You're late," she calls out, her tone dry, almost mocking. "I had to break myself out."

Emerging from the stairwell is a massive figure, a towering orc, his pale green skin gleaming faintly in the torchlight. His large tusks curve upward from his lower jaw, and his dark eyes fix lazily on my cellmate. A heavy tome hangs from one hand, open as though he'd been reading it mid-stride.

"I had nothing but faith in you," the orc replies, his voice dripping with sarcasm, deep and smooth as velvet.

"Sure," my cellmate mutters with irritation. "But I really would've loved the help. I had absolutely *none*. And a liability." She points with her thumb in my direction.

Ignore it. You're better than a response.

The orc shrugs one enormous shoulder, clearly unbothered, before his gaze slides to me. His eyes narrow slightly as he takes in the sight of my bow and my drawn arrow.

"A twilight elf," he says, voice carrying a sigh of vague exasperation. "That's new."

I lower my weapon entirely, letting the arrow vanish into starlight. My curiosity overrides my fear. "Are you from Dazzoran?"

Why is that your first question? This is why you have no friends.

The orc's brow furrows. His long braid swinging over one shoulder. "Yes. I'm from Dazzoran."

"He hasn't seen your friend either, don't bother." My cellmate is fiddling with one of her gloves, maybe adjusting the lockpick she slipped back inside.

"What's a twilight elf doing here?" the orc asks, "you're farther from home than I am."

"Who cares? Let's go, she isn't your problem," my cellmate says.

I laugh bitterly, the sound rough and hollow. "You can go, surely, it's fine. But to satisfy your curiosity, my brother tossed me from my bedroom balcony."

The words slip out before I can stop them, but I don't care. It's the truth, after all. I have nothing left to lose, right?

That causes my cellmate's mouth to fall open slightly, but only for a second, though her gaze avoids mine. "What? No, he didn't." When I don't respond, her eyes finally dart up to meet mine, searching my expression. Her voice tightens. "Why would he do that?"

"He was having a bad day," I reply flatly. I can't bring myself to voice the real reason. The way the tiny object I now clutch so tightly has shattered everything I held dear.

The orc lets out a weary sigh, rubbing a hand across his forehead. "Why are you looking for him, then?"

"I'm not."

I turn away, my mind mostly lingers on Syvis. She must be worried about me. She would never believe the traitor's brand Ilriel placed on me. But would she think I'm dead?

I wish she were here. I really, *really* need a guard.

The awful stranger breaks my thoughts again. "Why did he throw you from a balcony? What was your crime?" Her tone has shifted, harsher, as though demanding an answer she believes she deserves.

I press my lips into a thin line. *Why did he do it?* Because he believes the world orbits his ambitions. *What crime did I commit?* Trusting too easily.

She shrugs, unconcerned by my silence. "Well, how much is the reward?"

I blink. "Excuse me?"

"The bounty on your head," she clarifies with infuriating calm. "How much is the reward for bringing you home? I wasn't going to ask, but now I'm curious."

I fail to keep the tremor from my voice. "Are you a bounty hunter?"

"I could be. It must be pretty big if a *king* wants you dead."

King? The thought is so absurd it almost makes me laugh. Ilriel, is no longer a king. How hilarious.

I don't respond. Instead, I lift the Nightstrand, its bow form glowing faintly as I steady it, an arrow pointed directly at her head. She's standing close, close enough that even in my exhaustion, I wouldn't miss.

Her cold face doesn't falter. "You won't," she says, tilting her head as though unbothered by the arrow aimed at her skull.

"I will," I say through my teeth.

Her hand moves faster than my eye can follow. One moment I'm gripping the Nightstrand, and the next, it's gone. She holds it now, examining it with a mocking sort of curiosity.

"Don't try to shoot me," she says. "It won't work." Her fingers tighten on the golden hilt. "Anyway, how much is the reward?"

I stare at her, dumbfounded. *How did I not see her move?*

"I don't know," I say weakly, my voice barely above a whisper.

She grins. "Guess we'll find out, then."

"We?" the orc asks, still flipping through his book without much interest.

I look back at my cellmate. The tips of her ears stick out beyond her hair despite her efforts to keep them hidden.

"While I don't typically engage with royalty," she says, almost lazily. "I think I'd like to cash in. We deserve an easy payday."

"You must be out of your mind," I snap, though my words tremble with fear. I lunge for the Nightstrand, but her grip holds firm. Instead of wresting it from me, she pulls me closer with a sharp tug. I tell her, "I have a guard that can snap your neck with one of her hands."

"Where is she, then?"

"Enough," the orc commands, his deep voice cutting through the tension.

My weapon is released abruptly, and I stumble back, clutching it to my chest.

"Zemm," the orc finally introduces himself, tucking his book into his bag.

I press my lips together, grinding my teeth as I glance back at the now-empty cell. "I am finding another way home," I say with lingering anger. "Sorry to disappoint you."

I was never taught to survive beyond the palace walls, but I'll learn. I *have* to learn.

My cellmate, who has yet to introduce herself, laughs. Low and grating. "Where are you spending the night? Do you have a map? Are there more signs with your face on them?"

She doesn't give me a chance to answer before she continues. "This city is full of scum who'd sell you out."

"Like you?"

"Yes, like me," she answers with infuriating honesty.

Zemm exhales heavily. He closes his eyes briefly.

The last of my adrenaline fades, replaced by exhaustion that makes my legs feel like water. I can't fight, and I can't trust them, but I can do something else.

I can offer them more than whatever my bounty is. I'm a queen, I suppose. I can give them anything.

She's infuriating, but she's quick, strong, ruthless. I think I need someone like that. I don't have to talk to her, or be her friend, but I can *use* her. And I'm sure all she'll care about is earning enough coin to get out of this disgusting place.

I clutch the Nightstrand tightly, trying to steady my breathing. "My name is Faelyri," I say softly, mostly for Zemm's benefit. "My friends call me Lyri. My enemies mispronounce my name."

My gaze shifts to my cellmate, locking with hers. "Name?"

"Thorne."

She says it slowly, her expression shifting ever so slightly. Her sharp, captivating eyes narrow, almost as though she's waiting for something.

"Let's make a bargain," I say to her, "you will help me find my missing friend and deliver me to my home alive. Then, you will be rewarded with something of equal value."

"What can you offer me?"

"I know you won't believe me, but I am in a position to offer you whatever you desire. I promise."

I hope.

She and Zemm share a quick look. She says, "it has to outmatch your bounty."

Of course it does. I have no idea what that is, but it's okay; I can lie.

"You have my word. Anything my brother plans to offer you, I will always offer more."

She grins, nodding, "alright. You have a deal."

That was easy.

"Well, how do I know you won't betray me?" I ask.

"I always honor a bargain," she says, "at least I have that going for me."

"It's true," Zemm confirms.

I straighten my posture as much as I can, the way I've seen Ilriel do thousands of times. "As my guard, you may refer to me as 'Your Highness' or "My lady'".

Her laugh bellows louder than I have heard yet, "I will never do that."

My posture crumbles. When I look at her, my body tells me to run, like there is some instinct warning me of danger, the way animals evolve to be wary of their predators.

However, I hold out my hand for her to shake, which she takes and squeezes.

CHAPTER

EIGHT

"Can you move?" Thorne demands, her voice edged with impatience. "Up the stairs?"

"I can't walk quickly," I admit. "You'll have to be patient."

Every step, every moment standing here, has set my legs ablaze, the fire spreading through my calves and into my blistered feet. I'm dreading the climb.

Zemm exhales sharply, though he doesn't say a word. I try not to let guilt gnaw at me. I understand why we need to move; really, I do, but my body screams for rest.

"Right," Thorne says through her teeth.

She lingers at the door, opening it carefully to peer outside. We step through and ascend into the streets only when she gives the signal.

I keep my head down, shielding my gaze from the row of severed heads lining the gates. I don't want to see their empty, lifeless eyes staring at me.

I don't want to remember them.

As Thorne leads the way, I stumble into a slow, painful

84

rhythm, falling further behind with every step. My legs have turned to melted wax, and my feet, raw and bruised, throb against every uneven stone.

My eyes remain fixed on the back of Thorne's head as I limp forward, trying to focus on something other than the pain. Watching the strands of her hair blow in the wind.

"Hey!" My voice echoes slightly off the shadowed alley walls.

Neither Thorne nor Zemm stops, but Zemm does turn to look back at me, his brow raised.

"Where are you from?" I ask her.

I just need to focus on *anything* else.

I stagger forward in a desperate attempt to catch up, though my legs rebel. There's no strength left in them. They're little more than bruised jelly now.

"Why?" Thorne's voice cuts the air, and she finally halts.

My relief at any slight rest makes me nearly crumble to the ground.

"I already know where Zemm is from. And you're not human."

"Me?" Her pale, elegant hand rises to her chest as though she might deflect the accusation.

I nod. "You're Elven. What kind, I wouldn't know, because your ears are too short to be those of a high elf's," I persist, pointing to my own sharp-tipped ears.

"I'm not Elven," she replies, tone flat and unyielding.

I gesture again to my ears, and she reaches for her own. For a moment, her expression almost softens, but then she steps closer, seizing both of my ears between her chilled fingers.

A jolt shoots through me like lightning. I recoil, swatting her hands away. "Do *not* touch me! Ever."

"I'm not an elf," she repeats, colder this time, "elves are pretentious." Without further warning, she snatches my hood and yanks it forward, shrouding my face. "And keep your hood down."

Her command given, she strides onward, leaving me to stumble after. Perhaps she's no elf. Perhaps she's a demon risen from the depths of the underworld.

As we move, I steal glances from beneath my hood. The glow of the city's inn passes us by. "Where are we going?"

"A place to stay," Thorne says with a flick of her hand. "Try to keep up."

She veers sharply down a narrow alley, turning left when we reach a high stone wall to follow an even tighter passage between two leaning buildings. Zemm grunts as he squeezes through, his broad frame barely fitting. A twist right, then left, then right again.

Finally, we emerge onto a long, dismal road that stretches toward a burial ground. My chest tightens.

Perhaps they'll bury me alive.

Thorne leads us along the broken path, weathered stones groaning beneath our feet. At the ground's rear stands a gnarled old tree, its roots gripping a heavy, wooden door built into the earth.

Thorne grips the rusted handle, and with a mighty pull, the door shrieks open, dust billowing into the air. She coughs into her sleeve.

"A grave?" I ask, voice thin. "Are you burying me?"

"Should we?" She casts a glance into the darkness before her.

Zemm descends first, stepping without hesitation into the abyss. My breath falters. I peer over the edge and shiver; there's no light below, nothing but a black void. Memories stir of rushing wind and twisting branches clawing at bark. My gaze falls to my broken, blood-caked nails, and a chill seeps through my bones.

Thorne turns to me. "We don't have all day."

I bite my lip. "I just... what is *down* there?"

"Go find out."

Reluctantly, I grip the splintered ladder and begin my descent. The wood creaks beneath me, each groan echoing like a death knell.

Do not break, I beg the ladder silently. *Please, do not break.*

The door slams above me before my feet touch the ground, swallowing the world in suffocating darkness. For a heartbeat, I am blind. Though slowly, my eyes adjust thanks to my elven vision. Water glimmers faintly below.

A sewer.

Thorne lands behind me with a heavy thud.

Her voice cutting through the gloom, she nudges me into the muck. "Let's go."

Reluctantly, I press on, boots splashing through the stagnant water. I tread cautiously, but my companions do not. Their careless steps send filthy waves sloshing over my ankles, soaking my socks.

We take the first left, and my fingers instinctively twitch toward the walls, but I pull them back. Whatever slime coats these stones, I will not touch it.

As I step forward, something skitters beneath my boot. Rats scatter in the shadows, one of them brushing against my foot.

I want to scream. I should just scream right now.

But they are completely unvexed, and we take the third right.

I push forward, guided only by the chill in my spine and the low murmurs of my companions.

The door reveals itself easily enough. An old, rotting slab of wood half-swallowed by the wall. I step back, fixing Thorne with a glare. "You open it."

With an exasperated sigh, she unlatches the rusted mechanism. The door creaks open, and a narrow stairway descends into darkness.

But the faintest draft of damp air brushes against my face. At the bottom, another door awaits, older still, its wood blackened with rot and streaked with mold. This time, Thorne moves aside and gestures for me to enter.

A tavern. In the bowels of this wretched sewer.

I blink in disbelief before focusing on the smoky haze that clings to the low ceiling.

Dim lanterns swing on iron hooks, their flickering light casting strange, warped shadows. Patrons crowd the room, hunched over bowls of stew and tankards of frothy ale. The tang of stale beer mingles with an unmistakable rancid odor that coils in my throat.

"I might vomit," I blurt before I can stop myself, my face twisting in a grimace.

"Not as grand as your palace?"

"I don't need a palace," I snap. "I just need it to *not* be a sewer." My voice softens, uneasy. "Do they live here?"

"Some, yes," Thorne answers idly, her gaze scanning the room. "We live here."

"Of course you do."

That earns a dark scowl from her. She pivots to block my path, a glimmer of cruelty in her eyes. She leans in, her voice a whisper.

"At least *I* don't look like I haven't bathed in days. You're the one that actually looks like you live in a sewer."

I instinctually reach for my weapon, though she grabs my hand.

"Draw that weapon of yours, and they'll string you up like meat. The sewer will carry your rotting corpse away. How long would it take for an immortal being to decompose, I wonder?"

A hush falls as I realize others are watching. Suspicious

stares, some narrow and accusatory, others merely curious, land on me. Zemm now sits at the bar, his back turned.

I swallow hard. I open my mouth to speak, but she doesn't bother letting me get my words out.

Instead, she merely shoves me forward. "Don't trip on the broken stone. Damaging the asset would be inconvenient."

"Get your grimy, *sewer-soaked* hands off me," I hiss, shoving her away.

She leaves me standing there, and I hesitate before forcing myself toward the table where Zemm sits. The walk feels interminable.

Every eye bores into me with heavy judgment. My hood remains low, shielding my face, but the weight of their gazes cling to me like a wet cloth.

The barstool's wood groans as I sit beside Zemm, its splinters digging into my thighs. He's engrossed in a book, oblivious to my discomfort. Or indifferent, I can't tell.

Thorne, meanwhile, leans over the counter, addressing a barmaid who wipes a mug with a soiled rag.

"Where's Esra?" Thorne asks.

"Who knows?" she replies with a shrug.

I lean toward Zemm, my voice barely audible. "I'll be fine if we can't stay here."

His only response is a guttural groan, his tusked mouth barely moving. At least his disinterest lacks malice. I can't say the same for his friend.

I let my gaze wander, scanning the shadowed room. Somehow, no water flows into this place. It's as though the tavern is suspended above the muck and rot of the sewers. That's relieving, at least.

One patron still watches me: an elf seated at a far corner. I wave hesitantly, but she doesn't return the gesture. My hand drops, my chest hollowing as the silence stretches on.

You do not belong here.

The realization gnaws at me as my thoughts drift, as they so often do. I close my eyes for just a moment as if I might will myself elsewhere. Maybe when I open them, I'll wake on a ship bound for Frondvale, with Ilriel at my side. Perhaps this nightmare will fade into mist.

But when I open them, I see only my hands: bare, stripped of rings and dignity. Everything I had is gone. Stolen clothes cling to my frame, and my only possession hums faintly with its dreadful promise of its potential demise.

It whispers to me even now, in tones so soft it might be a lullaby.

My reverie shatters as I catch the tail end of the conversation. A man, tall and scarred, his lip bisected by a thin white line, leans casually against the stone wall, speaking to Thorne. His eyes flick briefly to me, a wolf's smile cutting across his face before he turns back.

"What d'you mean, leaving?" the man, Esra, I gather, asks.

Thorne takes a long swig from her mug, stabbing her fork into a shriveled potato. "We'll be gone by sunrise. Got a big job." She points the fork at Esra. "Don't wait up."

Big job. Shut up.

Esra's face clouds with something close to hurt. "I need spies. How can I convince you to stay? I need your talent. No one else can—"

"You can't. It's not personal."

Not a thief, a spy. A legendary sewer spy.

Esra's attention shifts to Zemm. "And you? What do you have to say?"

Zemm doesn't even look up from his book. "I hate this city."

Esra chuckles, or sighs, it's hard to tell. His gaze slides to me, sharp and assessing. "And you. Who are you?"

"I—"

"She's not a recruit," Thorne cuts in smoothly, silencing me with a look.

Esra studies me for a beat longer, his expression inscrutable. "You look worn down."

Worn down. Quite the understatement.

"You hungry?" he asks, voice softer now.

I hesitate. Am I? I have to be. Perhaps the hunger is why I keep feeling nauseous. Maybe something to eat would cure the hollow ache in my stomach. I glance at Thorne, whose attention is still on her meal, then at Zemm, who remains as unmoved as a statue.

Then, the scent hits me again. Sewage.

"No," I whisper, trying to keep my face neutral. Though the hunger may eventually outweigh the thought of eating in this place.

Esra tilts his head, the edges of his scar tugging slightly. "Your face, I've seen it. On a sign."

He steps closer, too close, filling a mug with ale and placing it in front of me. The smell alone, bitter and sour, makes my nose wrinkle.

I push it back slightly, wordlessly declining.

He doesn't seem to mind. Instead, he reaches beneath the counter. What he places before me sends ice through my veins. A crumpled *WANTED* poster, yellowed and torn at the edges.

My breath catches as I stare down at the image. The ink is faded, but the face is unmistakably mine, or rather, my brother's attempt at recreating me in the hands of some artist. They got the details too perfectly: the fine branching markings that sweep across my cheekbones and nose.

I don't want to ask, but the words crawl from my throat anyway. "Are these everywhere?"

Esra doesn't answer, doesn't even feign interest in my question. Instead, he simply says, "keep it."

I hesitate, my fingers trembling slightly as I reach for the parchment. It feels heavier than it should, weighted with unanswered questions and dread. I want to tear it apart, rip it to shreds until the face staring back at me ceases to exist. But something stops me, a gnawing instinct that tells me to hold onto it.

So slowly, I fold the paper and tuck it into my pocket.

How long did Ilriel search the bottom of the cliff for my body? Did he send out riders? Did he climb down himself, shouting my name into the wind?

How long did it take him to clean up his mess?

"What does it say?" Asks Thorne.

"I'm sorry?"

"The reward, at the bottom, what does it say?"

There was no gold amount, only an offering of land and a title, which is *not* good for me. How can I beat that? What would be greater?

I refuse to answer this ridiculous question. And lucky for me, she doesn't ask again.

I lean on my elbow, studying the chunk of potato at the end of Thorne's fork. What did Ilriel have for dinner? It isn't fair that he probably had a fantastic meal after what he did. Wine, freshly baked bread, vegetables of all kinds, meats, berries.

And I'm sitting in a sewer watching my...

I don't even know what they are to me, but they're eating sewer food.

Esra breaks the tension, "I haven't seen a twilight elf in a while."

My heart stutters, but I do all I can to steady my voice as to not appear too panicked, "you've really seen another twilight elf?"

Is it my brother? Is he here?

"She looked like you. Could have been a sister."

Thorne's fork makes a *clink* as it hits the plate.

I do not turn my gaze toward her. I keep it focused in front of me. The ringing tells me to keep prying, "when?"

His face scrunches into something like strained thought, as if to force the memories back.

He says, "two, no... three, years ago."

"A woman?"

He nods.

I grip the Nightstrand under my cloak to hush the song only I can hear.

"That's a long time ago," Thorne says, "probably dead by now."

I ignore her and ask Esra, "do you know where she went?"

"She told me she was heading toward the mountains."

"Do you remember her name? The ice peaks?" I ask, remembering back to the gossip in the halls of my home.

He shakes his head, "No, but she said she was on her way to see the dwarves."

I should find a map.

This is perfect. This is the lead I was searching for. It's tiny, just a sliver of *something*, but it's all I've got.

"You're interesting," he says, "you've got a look about you."

I fidget with the fabric of my cloak.

He continues, "you look like you're a survivor."

Thorne chimes in, "Survival's all she's done so far, and she's not very good at it."

My face turns hot, burning with shame and embarrassment. I am suddenly so aware of my vulnerability.

Dirty, broken, bloody.

Thorne slides her plate in front of me, barely touched and getting colder by the second.

I shift in my seat and push the plate away, the smell turning sour in my nose.

"Not hungry?"

I meet her gaze. Her mocking voice makes me want to rip my hair out.

"I don't want to owe you anything," I tell her.

I bow my head toward Esra. "Thank you for your hospitality and your information. I just have one more question about the elf."

"Hm?"

I almost don't want the answer, "was she running from something?"

His voice echoes faintly against the stone walls. "I don't ask."

"Get up," Thorne says, "time for bed. Long journey tomorrow."

To *where*? It better be a journey to the dwarves.

I follow her toward a narrow hallway at the back of the tavern, where the air grows colder, and the stone gets darker.

I almost look over my shoulder as we walk through the halls, but I don't.

She stops before a door, placing a hand on the old wood. "Here."

I step inside to find a tiny room where a cot sits in the corner, with a blanket folded atop it. Glowing weakly on the table beside it is a lantern, its flame flickering.

It's awful, but it's better than the floor, at least.

But there are people that live in rooms like this, all down these halls...

I scan the room again, a knot of unease tightening in my chest. I wasn't paying attention to the path we took to get here. How would I get out of here alone, if I need to? The twists and turns of the dark hallways blur in my mind like smoke.

My voice is quieter than I mean it to be when I confess, "I don't know the way back."

Her hand lingers on the door, her fingers flexing impatiently. She tilts her head toward the hallway. "First door to the left of yours. That's mine. We'll walk back together."

No. I *need* to know how to get back alone. I need to know where I am.

But, there is something more than that. Some other feeling that I haven't had the time to allow myself to even engage with. Or say out loud.

I shift on my feet, the weight of exhaustion pressing on my shoulders. "I'm scared," I admit, surprising even myself. The words sound small, fragile, as though they don't belong in this wretched place. "I've never... I've only ever slept in my own bed."

Thorne doesn't move, but her face grows taut with barely contained irritation. "Think of your bed."

There's no warmth, no understanding in her tone. Just sharp-edged disdain.

I glare at her. "Well, does the door lock at least?"

With an exaggerated sigh, she inspects the knob, her mouth twitching into a cruel smirk. "Nope."

Panic bubbles in my chest, and my voice rises, "what if someone comes in?"

Her hand tightens on the doorknob. "Do you think so low of these people?"

"If they are anything like you, then yes."

She sighs again. "I'm *right* next door."

"That's not good enough!" I snap.

I'm used to far more than a thin wall for protection. I'm used to guards stationed at my door, people with swords who would die before letting harm come to me. And even then... they still failed.

My throat tightens. I swallow my pride as I beg, "stand guard outside of my door. That's why you're here."

She scoffs, the sound sharp and derisive. "I'm not your guard dog."

"Please," I plead, my voice trembling as the words scrape against my pride.

I hate myself for asking. For needing someone. For showing weakness to someone who will surely use it against me.

"You have a weapon," her eyes travel to my hip.

I do, yes. Though I do not know how to use it, not really. Not enough.

"What did I do?" Finally asking. Finally needing to know where this disdain is stemming from.

"I don't like people like you. I don't like royalty, but you, in particular, are wealthy, useless, spoiled, rude, and *cowardly*."

I cannot control the flinch from the last word.

I say nothing as she pulls the door closed behind her, leaving me alone with the lantern's faint glow.

I sit on the edge of the cot, staring at my hands stained with grime.

I can't deal with this anymore.

But I allow myself to lay on the cot, more comfortable than I imagined it to be due to my exhaustion. I retrace the hallways in my mind, and without even realizing it, I doze off.

CHAPTER

NINE

My body betrayed me.

I didn't stir until a thunderous pounding rattled the old door, and the sound pierced my heavy sleep.

A groan escapes my throat as I clutch the thin, threadbare blanket against my chest. My limbs are dead weight. Bruised, bloodied, and aching in every joint. My head throbs with each shallow breath I take. My hair is a tangled mess, clinging to my face. I must look as broken as I feel.

"Faelyri?"

Zemm's voice is muffled through the cracks in the door.

A slow, dragging shuffle is all I can manage as I cross the short distance to the door. When I wrench it open, he stands there, his large frame blocking out the faint light spilling from the hallway.

He watches me with... pity? No. With a sympathy I don't expect, as I haven't received it in who knows how long.

It's almost worse than disdain.

"You overslept," he says, "the sun is almost at its peak."

Of course I did. I'm *useless* so of course I overslept.

Anger surges through me. Sharp, bitter, and directed entirely at myself. I don't have the time to oversleep.

I glance down at myself. Not a good look for a ruler. My clothes are stiff with grime and blood, my skin clammy, my body rank from days of running, hiding, and bleeding.

I am disgusting.

Zemm clears his throat, "we should go."

"Can I just..." I try to steady the voice that is raw with frustration and shame. "Can I just wash myself, please? Can you bring me something, *anything*, to clean myself with?"

He hesitates, his gaze flicking down the dark hallway behind him, as though he's weighing the risks of lingering here any longer.

"Please. I feel disgusting. I *am* disgusting," I admit.

His expression softens, and he nods once. Without a word, he turns and begins down the dim corridor, his heavy footsteps echoing in the stillness.

I close the door gently behind him, leaning my forehead against the rough wood. My breath shudders, and I press a trembling hand to my chest, where the ache is deepest.

You cannot afford to waste your time, I remind myself.

Thorne leads the way once again, cutting through the labyrinthine alleys of this cursed city like she owns every shadowed corner. I *let* her lead only because I must, for now; otherwise, I would be lost in this twisting maze.

Zemm asked me earlier if I slept well. How could I answer that? I slept so deeply I may as well have been dead in a dreamless void. But it wasn't *well*.

We are deep within yet another darkened alley, the buildings here leaning like rotted teeth. My grip on the weapon at my hip tightens.

I also need to know the way to the mountains. I know it lies to the West of this continent, but I need more direction than that. Not vagueness.

"Do you have a map?" I ask them.

Thorne glances back at me, her gaze sharp, as though my question alone is a crime.

"We do," Zemm answers instead, his tone flat.

"May I be its keeper?" I press, choosing my words carefully. *Play nice,* I remind myself. "I've never been to this continent. And, well..." My voice softens, feigning hesitation. "I would like to become more aware of my surroundings."

"No. You cannot have our map." Thorne answers.

"Well, are there actual shops here? Other than those tiny stalls in the square?"

"There are," Zemm says. "There's a district."

"Could we go there? And I can get my own map."

Zemm watches me curiously, but it's Thorne who replies, her voice dripping with malice. "You don't have any coin. Do you plan to steal?"

"I can barter."

"With what?" She sneers, eyes landing on my weapon. "That rod?"

My hand tightens around it. *Never.*

"Please," I say through clenched teeth. "Let me just look."

"You slept all day," she growls, her voice sharp. "We *let* you sleep all day, and now you want to waste what little time we have left?"

I stop in my tracks, anger igniting like kindling in my chest.

Enough.

I reach into my pocket and pull out the crumpled *WANTED*

poster, unfolding it with deliberate care. I hold it to my chest, facing them. Daring them.

Her eyes move to the parchment, then back to my face. For once, she hesitates. "Land and a title," she murmurs, the words slow.

"That's right," I reply, voice steady. "So why don't you kill me?"

For the briefest moment, I see it: her mask almost slips. Her eyes widen, just slightly, but she recovers quickly, her face settling back into cold indifference. It is both awful and, unfortunately, beautiful.

"We're not going to kill you," Zemm interjects after a gasp.

But Thorne's voice cuts through his like steel. "Our bargain requires you to be alive."

"Your bargain with me." I press, my tone sharper now. "What could two people living in a disgusting sewer ever want that is superior to this? If there is nothing else you would require, then what's stopping you from just killing me and delivering me to my brother?"

She says nothing.

"So what I am hearing, by your silence," I reply, deliberately calm, "is that you will *not* kill me."

Slowly, I fold the parchment again and slide it back into my pocket.

The air between us thickens, crackling with tension. This time, our gazes lock and hold. I see the anger simmering behind her eyes, feel it radiating from her.

But I do not flinch.

"Give me your map," the words come out slowly. A command.

For a long moment, there's only silence. Then, with a scoff, she says, "I don't have it." Her shrug is infuriatingly casual.

I turn to Zemm, locking eyes with him. "Give me the map."

His tusked mouth tightens, his voice rumbling low. "I need my map."

"*I* need your map," I bite back. "I need to know where Vum Dorahl is. That's where your friend said the woman I'm looking for headed, correct?"

"He said *three* years ago."

"It's my only lead!" It all erupts from me. I start to scream. Thorne rushes to me, clamping her hand on my mouth to muffle me.

It's warm, and she doesn't release me until my breathing settles. Then, she exchanges a quick glance with Zemm.

She digs through his pack, revealing the rolled parchment map, shoving it hard into my chest. "Take the fucking map."

As soon as her voice fades into silence, shouting from the heart of the city replaces it, directly to our right.

"That," she mutters grimly, "is our cue to vanish."

"What is it?" I demand.

"A slaughter," she replies, moving like a shadow, skirting the building's edge to peer into the square beyond.

A crowd has gathered as though summoned by some dark instinct, drawn to bear witness. And there, in their midst, I see her, the woman from the statue. The Baroness. Flanked by two grim-faced guards, she hauls a struggling man forward, thrusting him into the spotlight of the masses.

I have never seen an execution. Starview doesn't revel in public executions. Truthfully, we are a city that knows little of executions at all.

Her face is a furious shade of crimson, her features twisted, whether by rage or madness, I cannot tell. Her bulging eyes gleam like cruel jewels.

The man before her wails, his pleas for mercy carried away on the unfeeling wind.

And then the Baroness draws her blade, the steel singing as it leaves the scabbard.

Thorne tugs at my cloak, her grip firm, trying to drag me back into the shadows of the alley. Yet I cannot look away from her. Her eyes are sharp as glass.

How could anyone do this? What crime could demand such a grim spectacle? So public, so deliberately cruel and humiliating? Ilriel had warned me of such horrors, whispered grim tales fabricated and meant to frighten children into obedience. Meant to frighten me.

"Let's go. Now," Thorne growls, low and urgent.

I shove her off, breaking her grasp. My breath catches as the Baroness steps forward, her voice like a tolling bell.

"For the crime of treason."

The word burns. It coils inside me, hot and venomous, and I bite down hard on my lip to keep from shouting. My fists clench, trembling with anger I cannot release. The Baroness hesitates, drawing it out like some twisted game, her smile a cruel crescent.

And then her blade falls.

The man's head tumbles, rolling like discarded stone. The crowd goes silent. Not a cheer, not a murmur. Just stillness, heavy and suffocating.

I don't know when it happens, but my hood slips back, baring my hair. I am now as conspicuous as a star in an empty night sky.

And she sees me.

She laughs or rather, *shrieks*, a sound that grates like iron on stone. "*That's* where you went."

I lift my chin, "and who do you think you are?" I challenge, my words sharp and scornful. "I have never heard of you, and surely that means you are no one of consequence."

Her smile doesn't waver, but her gaze sharpens like a blade as she turns to Thorne. "Are you with the elf?"

To my horror, Thorne crosses her arms, "I'm collecting her bounty. How much are you offering?"

The breath rushes from my lungs as though I've been struck.

The Baroness's laugh-shriek echoes once more. "Nothing, but I will take her."

I am nothing to these people. No more than a sack of coin, faceless and disposable.

Thorne steps before me, throwing up her hands in mock exasperation. "Well, if that's the case, we're just passing through. Carry on!"

Carry on?

The Baroness raises a hand, a silent command. Her guards close in around us, steel gleaming in the dim light.

I'm frozen, paralyzed by myself.

"Get ready to run," Thorne mutters, fingers curling around the hilt of one of her daggers.

There's no time to snap back. The guards move in, swords raised, and Thorne acts first. Her fist connects with a jaw, the satisfying crunch met with a smirk.

I have no room to draw a bow, and I hated the sword. So instead, I call the Nightstrand, willing it to shape itself into a quarterstaff. The weapon shimmers, woven of starlight. With a sweep, it sings as it crashes into the skull of a charging guard.

It sings a song not of pain or death, but of life. Blood sprays from her nose, and she crumples to the ground.

"Sorry!" I shout instinctively.

An arrow whistles through the air. I shove Thorne aside, narrowly dodging it myself. But in the chaos, a brute grabs me from behind, his arms like iron bands. I swing the staff backward, aiming for his temple, but his grip halts the blow mid-arc.

Thorne curses and lunges toward me, her gloved palm slamming into the man's face. There's a hiss of metal. A hidden blade flicks from her wrist and into the brute's forehead with a sickening *thunk*.

The man drops, blood splattering hot and red across my cheek.

Before I can think, I'm shoved forward, stumbling into Thorne's side.

She seizes my hand, and we sprint through the narrow alleyways, shadows pressing close as the sounds of pursuit echo behind us. Their boots thunder against the cobblestones like the pounding of war drums. I swipe at the blood on my cheeks, futile, as it smears like an unwanted mark.

"Don't trip over yourself," she snaps, though the command feels more for herself than for me. She hides her fear well, but I can *feel* it. Sharp, like a blade beneath silk.

I won't trip. I *can't* be caught.

She drags me past the city gates where Zemm stands waiting, his arms crossed, his face a storm cloud.

Her grip tightens around my hand, and I wince.

"So, what in the name of the gods did you do?" Zemm demands.

Thorne shoves me toward him, my hand throbbing from the strain. "Never, *never*, do that again."

"You have no authority over me," I shoot back, my tone equally sharp. "In fact, *I'm* the one with authority over you. I am a princess."

"You are nothing." Her face floods with darkness, she grabs me by the chin, and my eyes widen. "Do you understand now," she growls, each word spoken with precision, "that you cannot linger just because you want to watch a poor man die? Is it fun for you to watch an execution? Do you sit in the front row, from your throne, while your guards kill those who are struggling? Do you do it yourself?"

I flinch as her hand releases my face and instead yanks my hood roughly over my head. "Hide your hair," she snarls.

I rip away from her, my chest heaving. I didn't want to *watch*. I wanted to *stop it*.

But an apology still tumbles from my lips, empty, perhaps, but spoken for the sake of keeping peace. She brushes past me, her shoulder colliding with mine in a deliberate, rough motion.

A wagon waits just beyond the outskirts of the city, the driver perched atop it, reins loose in his hands. A single horse paws at the earth impatiently, its hoof stirring up small clouds of dust. I scowl but follow, my steps heavy with reluctance.

"I *am* sorry," I repeat my apology.

The air stills, thick with tension, as if the world itself holds its breath. The horse snorts, digging its hoof into the ground, the only sound breaking the silence.

"Where ya headed?" the driver asks.

"West," Thorne replies.

"How far west?"

She runs her tongue over her teeth. "Vum Dorahl."

The wagon creaks as I climb inside, the win hollowed slightly by the dread curling in my gut. The ride will be long, the silence longer, and the tension stretching between us like one of my drawn bowstrings.

I settle into the splintered wood, resting my chin on the wagon's edge. The sunlight drips through the canopy of trees in dancing flecks, casting playful shadows on the ground below.

Zemm tries to make conversation as we rumble along, his

words an attempt to pierce the uneasy stillness. I humor him, offering half-answers and quiet murmurs, but my gaze stays low.

I don't speak to Thorne, and Thorne does not speak to me.

TEN

I sit on the cold, damp ground, hugging my knees to my chest. The wagon couldn't take us through the mountains' paths, so we've made camp for the night.

I've never camped before, unsurprisingly, but there's something soothing, even thrilling, about it. The stars ease the homesickness for a small, fleeting moment.

We've taken refuge in a cave, its opening framing the distant hills. My eyes wander across the horizon, hopelessly searching for a glimpse of home as though it might appear by sheer force of longing.

Really, I may be checking to see if it's even still there.

The Nightstrand hums in my mind. Its song has shifted. Back then, it was all-consuming pain, raw and unrelenting. The pain lingers now, though dulled, as if its grown weary of its own mourning. Or I've learned to bear it better.

I desperately hope it's the second one.

Across the cave, Thorne crouches over a careful arrangement of sticks, aligning them with precision. When she deems them ready, Zemm steps forward, his hand hovering over the kindling. His long hair glimmers faintly in the firelight as he draws a rune in the air. A spark ignites, and the fire leaps to life.

"My brother told me orcs can't use magic," I say to Zemm, over the fire's crackle.

He pauses, arching a brow at me. "Have you ever met an orc?"

I shake my head, heat creeping into my face.

"Has he?" he presses, his tone flat.

I shrug, lacking an answer. Thorne scoffs from her place by

the fire, and the weight of their judgment makes me sink further into myself.

Zemm settles beside me, cross-legged on the stone floor. He opens a battered journal, its pages yellowed and stubbornly clinging together. I lean in, curious, and he tilts it slightly so I can see.

His script flows in elegant curves, his language. I wish I had a journal of my own to write away the horrors of the past days.

Did the other girls make it to safety? Perhaps I should have followed them. Maybe I would be having an easier time.

Though, I suppose it could be worse. At least I didn't lose my head.

I let out a sigh.

"We don't have executions in Starview," I tell them. "I've never seen one before. That was the first, and I didn't enjoy it. I would never want it to be a regular occurrence."

"I believe you," says Zemm.

I wrap my cloak tightly around myself until only my head is visible. My gaze drifts to Thorne, who is furiously scribbling in her own book. Her expression shifts as she works, focused and intent. She smudges something with her thumb and immediately redraws it with her coal.

Her hair is tied back, revealing soft, delicate features that seem almost out of place with her sharp demeanor. It's infuriating, really, how someone so cruel can be so beautiful. Is that the source of her ruthlessness? Unchallenged beauty? She must have never needed to learn to be kind.

I crane my neck, trying to catch a glimpse of her work. The lines on the page hint at a landscape, but I can't quite see. My voice comes out without my control, "I didn't know you were an artist."

Her head snaps up, and our eyes meet. She slams the book

shut with a force that makes me flinch. "You should get a hobby."

I gape at her, stung by the insult, but she sighs and... softens?

"That wasn't meant to offend you. It's advice. When it's dark and cold and hard to go on, having a hobby helps."

Zemm grunts in agreement, lifting his journal for emphasis. I do have hobbies, I think. Music, for one. I could carve the Nightstrand into a lute, though I'd likely drive them both mad in the process.

"Well," I venture, emboldened by her momentary vulnerability, "what were you drawing?"

Thorne hesitates, her expression unreadable. And for a moment, I think she might show me. For some reason, I hope she does.

But then she tucks the book under her arm, "nothing."

I roll my eyes. Maybe she isn't as invincible as she pretends to be. It's strange to imagine that her endless, annoying, confidence actually has a limit.

But I think there *could* be something else there. Something she doesn't want anyone to see, or notice. Though it is possible I'm projecting.

Still, I say, "you saved me. Twice."

She doesn't respond.

"Thank—"

"Never thank me." She snaps quickly. "It's insulting."

"I was just trying to show—"

"I'm not here to serve you, so I don't want your thanks."

Never mind. I hate her.

The fire pops, sending a faint shower of sparks into the cave's gloom and I watch it as I try to will time to move faster. Fast enough so I can get through all of this as quickly as possible.

"Stop brooding," Zemm's voice cuts through my thoughts. "You'll drive yourself mad."

"I'm not brooding," I retort.

"You're always brooding." He flips a page in his journal with an air of finality.

"Well, I haven't gotten the chance to organize myself. All I can do is brood. Brooding is my new *hobby*."

I make eye contact with Thorne, and she almost smirks. I think. And then says: "So what did you do?"

Zemm finally peeks up from his journal. His eyes dart back and forth between us.

"What?" I ask.

"To be called a traitor. You never told us your crime."

"Why does my crime matter?"

"It's a big reward."

Zemm interjects, "I personally don't care about elf politics, for what it's worth."

I guess that's worth something. But now, I have two options here: honesty or lies.

I can admit that not only did I do nothing, but my brother is a usurper. I can admit that I was completely caught off guard and overly trusting in every aspect of my life, leading to this moment. And I can admit that I am very quickly taken advantage of.

Or, I could lie. I could tell them the story of Starview's first queen. The one about the bloodshed, and betrayal and the curse about the kingdom collapsing.

Which it, unfortunately, is.

That is the story I can tell. Honestly, it sounds more like Ilriel's story, which is very ironic because Filauria was always kind of my hero.

"I wanted to be queen so badly that I killed a man and stole a crown," I say.

I did kill a man, the man in the camp. And I didn't steal a *crown*, but close enough.

She grimaces. "Do you always twist yourself up in your lies?"

"No. I don't. I'm a perfect liar." I am not a perfect liar. "I know nothing about you, about either of you, and you believe you deserve to know everything about me?"

"Then tell me, at least," she says, "why are you searching for an elf in a dwarven mountain? *That* we deserve to know. If we're going there."

The ringing starts again, the soft song. I place my hand on the Nightstrand, hoping to soothe it.

Honestly, I have no idea what I'll do if I find her. *When* I find her. If my brother is searching for her, I need to be quick.

"She has something I need, and…" I sigh, "I think my brother will be searching for her. He needs her for something that I will not elaborate on. Is that answer sufficient enough for you?"

A traitor searching for a traitor is very ironic. However, I never considered what might come of this quest if she refused to help me at all. Why would she help me? She wanted this to happen. I need to be convincing. Perhaps I should cry.

"Not entirely."

"Do you have a problem with the dwarves the same way you have a problem with elves?" I snap back. "Is that why you're prying?"

"I like the dwarves," she says, "they aren't pretentious. And they have cool hammers."

Was that… a joke? I can't tell, but I let out a soft laugh. I don't know why. I quickly cover my mouth with my hand.

She doesn't look up at me and goes back to playing with the fire, and I go back to trying to decode her face.

The unique color of her eyes. Her thin nose. The way her

lips curve up at the side, even when she isn't smiling. It's otherworldly, like it was fabricated, and I believe her now when she says she isn't an elf. She's too beautiful to be an elf.

"Why are you staring at me?" She asks, "you think I'm pretty?"

I quickly say, "I believe you when you say that you aren't an elf," I want to rip the smirk off of her face, "you're too ugly."

Zemm speaks up as he writes in his book: "*The elf girl with the hair of stars snaps at the trickster in an embarrassed rage.*"

"Excuse me?" I ask him.

He peeks up.

"I don't care if you think I'm ugly. You *wanted to be queen?*" Thorne starts, "You're not a ruler. You're entitled enough to be one, but that's not all you need."

I flare my nostrils. I'm not entitled. I'm scared and home-sick and dealing with the reality that my country may have branded me a traitor. And I'm stuck with these people who don't care about *me*, just what I can do for them. And I need to worry about where my next meal will come from, scavenging for food. It's all quite a lot. I don't care if I appear self-centered to her. She's the self-centered one.

"Well, *you're* a queen, right?" I ask. "Queen of the sewer."

"And you're a princess of death and decay. A princess of a collapsing sky."

I need to physically stop my body from shaking. It takes everything to stay calm.

I don't care to respond to her and speak to Zemm again, "Are you writing about me?"

"Sure am."

Everything is awful.

"Good thing you'll never rule, though," Thorne continues to antagonize me, poking at the dying fire again. "That's your brother's job."

I should scream. I should scream until my voice box bursts.

Instead, I swallow the scream. Hard. So it isn't lodged in my throat. My hands tear at the fabric of my cloak.

She keeps going, "What are your plans after you get home? How will you lead?"

"Thorne," Zemm says, "come on."

I... don't know. I do not *want* to rule. I do not want the weight of Starview resting on my shoulders. I do not want to carry a dying relic bound to my very soul that may or may not kill me. I am not a queen. I am someone who loses track of her conversations and cries over squashed insects. I am just me.

She sneers, "Maybe you should get used to camping."

"Enough," Zemm demands. "We're done."

I keep myself from screaming, though I am unsure how. But I *do* raise my voice to a level that echoes through the cave. "How does it feel knowing that you'll probably be alone for the rest of your miserable life?" I say. "No one will remember you once you're gone. But they'll sing songs about *me*."

"Out of jest, not respect."

"Why?" I blurt out. "Why did you make this deal with me if you're just going to act like this this entire time?"

She seems like she's thinking of some kind of response. Maybe a snarky one. "My desire for what I will get from you is greater than my disdain."

Zemm creates another rune with his hand before lifting his arm. The fire turns into a wall, separating me from the monster across from the way. The wall stays for a few seconds, then slowly becomes smaller and smaller.

The fire finally dies. I stare at the ash left in its place. Thorne stands to her feet and stretches.

Her problem with me could be as simple as hating all royalty in general, like she claims. I can handle that, and I wouldn't blame her. However, this has to be more personal. It's me specifically, that she has a problem with. Perhaps it's because I fight back, and she isn't used to someone not bending to her will.

She calls over to me, "I don't care if you sleep, but you better be up in the morning."

"Don't let it get to you," Zemm urges me. "She has an issue with nobles."

How can it not?

"It won't." I pause before another insensitive question is blurted out before I can stop myself, "How long do orcs live?"

Why would I ask something like that? What is wrong with me?

"Not as long as you will." He closes his book, then changes the subject quickly. "Is there a library in your castle?"

Firstly, it's a palace, not a castle. Secondly, I guess it's his turn to ask weird questions. "Of course there is."

"With books on magic?"

I nod.

"I don't care about the title. I'll be taking those instead."

I don't even have the energy to argue. I hope once we reach the dwarven city, the queen can help me. A dwarven queen would have no interest in whatever my bounty is, and she would certainly know if Filauria was there.

Maybe she would even supply some kind of guard for me. Someone strong and brave.

ELEVEN

I have heard many tales of Vum Dorahl, the fabled Dwarven city deep within the earth. Said to be a labyrinth of endless caverns, brimming with veins of ore. Much like my own home, its entrance is a seamless part of the mountain itself, save for the intricate runes etched into the stone.

My gaze sweeps across the dormant volcano towering above us. It looms like a sentinel, still and silent for as long as anyone remembers. Or, so I've been told. Beneath its mighty peak lies the Dwarves' realm, the entrance hidden at its base. I once asked my brother why anyone in their right mind would build a city under a volcano.

He laughed and told me the Dwarves turned the volcano's fury into their ally: its molten heart fuels their forges and lights their halls.

To me, the benefits do not outweigh the risks.

I swallow the lump of unease lodged in my throat. The volcano won't erupt... will it? Surely not. It can't. I think? I glance at my companions, hoping to find some shared apprehension, but they seem unshaken. Or, more likely, foolishly confident.

They are so dumb.

The heat ripples the air around the enormous stone doors ahead, distorting everything around me like a mirage. Very few elves visit this place, as they struggle with navigation if they're not properly prepared for the dense air. I am not prepared.

Thorne rummages through her satchel, retrieving a pair of peculiar, clunky goggles, which she fastens over her head. She then tosses another pair my way.

"Spare set," she says simply. "You'll need them."

"Goggles?" I frown, inspecting the crude contraptions.

"The air here is dense," Zemm explains, pulling on his own pair.

I blink at them both. "You just have these?"

Thorne says, "We're *cultured*. And prepared for anything. Everything I own is in this bag."

I reluctantly pull the goggles over my head, trying to ignore the edges of them obstructing my vision.

"Do I look ridiculous?" I ask Zemm.

Thorne answers, "yes."

She gives a powerful strike to the doors, the sound echoing like a drumbeat. The ancient gates groan as they swing inward, releasing a gust of hot air. It wraps around us, thick and stifling, though not as unbearable as the stories claimed.

Step by step, we descend into the city's fiery embrace. The air grows heavier, the scent of sulfur clawing at my nostrils. Each breath feels like a battle, the pressure building with every step. The heat isn't just oppressive, it's alive, pressing against my skin and mind.

At last, we enter Vum Dorahl.

The city's architecture is a marvel of stone and fire, its walls adorned with gleaming orange hues from molten rivers that thread through its veins. Though not as towering as the cities of men or elves, there's a grandeur in its craftsmanship, a rugged elegance born of the earth itself.

In the city's heart stands no palace but instead a towering shrine, crowned with a statue of their goddess, Belvadon. It dominates the view from across a vast bridge, glowing faintly with reflected firelight. My eyes are drawn down, over the edge of the bridge, into the abyss below. A fathomless chasm that devours all light.

How funny would it be if there was a screaming princess down there about to be kidnapped?

"Don't look down," Thorne mutters. "That's not where we're going."

She's right. That's *definitely* not where we're going. I pull my hood lower, hoping to avoid the curious gazes of the dwarves we pass.

As we near the shrine, I whisper to them, "do you think the Queen is here?"

I pray my companions won't offend her or, worse, the goddess herself. Even thieves and spies must know better than to provoke divine wrath, right?

"She better be," Thorne snaps. "We don't have all day."

Yeah, no kidding.

Zemm strides forward and pushes open the shrine's grand doors, revealing a chamber of brass and gold. Towering pillars stretch to the ceiling, framing the massive stone effigy. Her gaze, carved in meticulous detail, pierces my soul. She's mesmerizing.

A heated argument pulls my attention away from the goddess. Before us, a dwarf girl with a glowing hammer squares off against an armored guard.

"She's a disgrace!" the guard barks. "Your sister endangers

not just herself but all who labor in the mines. Let her face the consequences!"

The hammer-wielding dwarf's hands blaze with light as she strikes at the guard, who meets her blow with his shield.

"Can dwarves wield magic?" I whisper to Zemm.

"Not in the way we do," he replies, his voice low. "But they have their secrets."

The room falls silent as a commanding voice cuts through the tension. "Enough!"

A dwarven woman with fiery red hair braided to her ankles steps forward, her crown gleaming in the shrine's light. Queen Satra. My heart skips. Perhaps my luck is turning at last.

The hammer-wielder dips her head low, her voice trembling. "Please, forgive me. My sister is trapped in the mines, and no one will help me bring her back."

The guard scoffs, his tone as sharp as a blade, "she's probably already dead."

That's rude.

"Excuse me," Thorne interjects, raising a hand as though addressing a gathering. "Not to intrude, Your Majesty, but... my companion here has a question." She gestures toward me with a flourish and then bows awkwardly.

Companion? I'm not her companion. Why is she suddenly so awkward? Is it the Queen?

"Really," she adds, her tone stiff, "I mean no disrespect."

My jaw clenches so hard that it's beginning to throb. So, she does respect *some* royalty. And she *can* be polite after all. She just *chooses* not to be. Always.

Queen Satra's lips curve into a small smile as she regards Thorne. "You are not the one showing disrespect here," she says, her tone warm but commanding. Her gaze lingers on her for a moment before she tilts her head. "There's something familiar about you. Have we met before?"

Thorne straightens, rubbing the back of her neck. What has she stolen from this place?

Her face grows tense as if pondering something before parting her lips to speak.

"No, Your Majesty," but it's Zemm who answers the question. "Though we've always hoped to find work that would bring us here."

I groan softly, pressing my fingers to my temple. The Queen's eyes move to me, one brow arching slightly.

"A twilight elf," she observes. "Is it not unbearably hot for you down here?"

The heat is stifling, and it *is* unbearable, but I mimic Thorne's bow nonetheless. "I can manage."

I yank Zemm down into a bow beside me, causing him to grunt. Straightening, I clear my throat. "Your Highness, we've come—"

Before I can finish, the hammer-wielder interrupts, her voice frantic. "There's no time for this! My sister—"

"Is dead," the guard interrupts coldly.

Thorne tilts her head, her curiosity clearly piqued. Her tone is soft as she asks, "where is your sister? What is your name?"

I frown at her, catching Zemm's resigned sigh out of the corner of my eye.

She hesitates, her voice heavy with desperation. "My name is Agnat. My sister, she's in the mines. They left her there, alone—"

"She ran off alone," the guard snaps. "The others left because they *had* to."

Thorne furrows her brow. "You're dwarves. Why are you afraid of the mines? Isn't that your job?"

The guard bristles, his voice rising. "We're not afraid of the mines! It's what lies deeper in the darkness, creatures that none of us dare face."

Thorne stifles a yawn, covering her mouth with her hand. "We'll go," she says lazily, her words muffled.

My stomach drops. "*We?*" I hiss. "You mean us? Into the dwarven mines? You want *me* to go into the mines?"

Agnat stares at her in disbelief. "You would? You can't go. You're a," her gaze narrows on Thorne's blades, "all you carry is a knife!"

She is correct.

"Three knives, actually," Thorne corrects, a smug grin spreading across her face.

I hate her. I truly, genuinely hate her and everything about her.

"This isn't a joke!" Agnat cries, her desperation bubbling over. "You don't understand. You don't know the way and your bodies are not made for that heat."

I agree.

Thorne shrugs, undeterred. "They're just mines. I'm feeling noble today. Besides, if your sister's half as lovely as you are, I can't let her die down there."

My face twists in revulsion. She is insufferable (though, yes, Agnat is very pretty).

Turning to Queen Satra, Thorne asks, "There's a reward for her safe return, I assume?"

I roll my eyes so hard it nearly hurts.

The Queen nods solemnly. "If you bring Lapis back unharmed, there will indeed be a reward."

Thorne claps her hands together. "Show me the entrance, then."

Crossing my arms, I glare at her. "Do you *ever* do anything just to be kind? We didn't agree to this." I jab a thumb in Zemm's direction for emphasis.

Zemm sighs. "I'm not invested enough to argue with her."

Thorne smirks, wagging a finger at me. "Wow, I can't

believe you're willing to leave an innocent girl to die. Shame on you. You brought me all the way here, only to deny me the honor of helping a kingdom in need? Or do you only care for your own?"

"Do not twist my words."

"Don't be so heartless."

My teeth grind together as she turns to the Queen. "Your Majesty, I apologize for my companion's callousness. She struggles to understand that the world doesn't revolve around her."

When I get her alone, I'm going to punch her in her striking jaw. I will ruin her perfect face. Maybe I'm being a little selfish, but not heartless. I'm allowed to be selfish, especially considering the circumstances. She did this on purpose. Now, I have this terrible urge to prove myself. I need to prove that I'm not a monster. If I don't do this, will the Queen even help me?

Now, I need to go into these mines.

※

We creep through the narrow, hand-hewn tunnels of the ancient mines. Unlike the glowing brilliance of the city above, the cavern is dim, the walls faintly illuminated by gleaming threads of ore. The veins shimmer. Does all raw ore glow like this? My curiosity overpowers my unease, and I stop to run my fingers across the rugged stone.

It's moonstone.

I trace the pale glow with my fingertips. This shouldn't be here. My people's island is the only place where moonstone exists. *Only. Place.* Its light was a gift from the goddesses themselves.

"What are you doing?" Thorne hisses.

"Why is there moonstone in a dwarven mine?" I murmur, half to myself. "It shouldn't be here."

"Who cares?"

I care. There's so much of it here. Does Ilriel know about this?

Thorne grabs my arm, pulling me forward and snapping me from my thoughts. The glowing veins fade as we move, leaving only the flickering light of torches mounted on the walls. Thorne takes one and holds it aloft, the golden glow barely keeping the encroaching shadows at bay.

But even still, I just can't take my mind off of it. I keep turning back.

The oppressive darkness is the only thing that refocuses my attention. My eyesight is useless here beneath these ridiculous goggles, forcing me to rely on the flickering torchlight. My hands instinctively grip the Nightstrand.

The silence is broken only by the crunch of loose stones beneath our boots. Occasionally, a dislodged pebble skitters into the abyss, its sound swallowed by the void. The air presses against me, thick and suffocating.

My heart is racing. This was not part of the plan. My body is shaking.

"You alright?" Thorne whispers to me, her tone so uncharacteristically gentle it catches me by surprise.

"No," I respond, confused, my voice trembling. "I hate you."

The farther we go, the darker it grows. The torch is also struggling now. I cling to Zemm, twisting the fabric of his robe until I fear it might tear.

The air is too heavy. The silence too suffocating. Swallowing me. My knees are weak. I need to get out of here. I need to turn back.

"Thorne..." I start to speak, but the words are caught in my throat. I have no idea if she even heard me. I open my mouth to try again.

And then; *something*.

A sound shattered the silence. A screech, bone-rattling and unnatural, reverberating through the stone. I scream, unable to hold it back.

"That sound was not normal," Zemm says, his calm demeanor fraying at the edges.

Which screech does he mean? The first one, or mine?

Before I could gather myself, Thorne bolts toward the

source of the noise. Why is she running *toward* it? We should be running *away*. Zemm follows without hesitation, leaving me alone in the suffocating black.

"Wait!" I call, but they vanish into the darkness.

I groan, near tears, before forcing myself to chase after them.

The tunnel opens into a wide cavern, and there, surrounded by writhing, nightmarish creatures, is the girl. Her hammer blazes with magic as she swings it with desperate strength, crushing the skull of one abomination. The sickening crunch echoes in my ears, and it twitches as the life leaves its body. I clap a hand over my mouth, suppressing the bile.

The creatures are monstrous. Grotesque amalgamations of humanoid and insect. Their charred, rotting torsos drag themselves forward on elongated arms, ending in razor-sharp claws. Parts of their body have almost been turned *into* the mountain itself. Their lower halves have a pointed, metasoma tail growing from the corrupted stone carapace of their back, complete with eight skittering legs whose tapping echoes through the volcano.

So gross.

She's panting, Lapis, exhausted but clearly determined to survive.

Thorne has vanished from my line of sight. I search for her in the darkness, but she's gone. Zemm is the one now holding the torch.

"Gorenaughts!" Lapis calls over. "Watch out!"

I have no idea what they are, but this better be the last time I ever encounter one. I loosen an arrow, the twang of my bowstring echoing in the cavern.

Thorne reappears from the shadows, her dagger driving into the base of another monster's skull, drawing their attention away from Lapis.

"You must be Lapis," she calls over the hissing of my nightmares. "Your rescue party has arrived!"

"Who in the hells are you?" Lapis shouts, slamming her hammer into another beast.

Thorne doesn't answer, dodging as one creature launches itself at her from the wall. Thorne is about to push her second dagger through the ugly thing's mouth, but my arrow intercepts it.

"Careful of the teeth!" Lapis calls. "One bite will kill you."

Thorne growls, sidestepping another strike. "Would've been nice to know *before* we walked into this cesspool."

The creatures swarm, their numbers overwhelming. Zemm, holding the torch aloft, begins tracing runes in the air with his free hand, the flame in the torch flickering unnaturally.

"Hurry up!" Thorne shouts, slashing through another gorenaught.

"These things are hideous," she says. "Why do they look like that?"

Lapis grits her teeth. "They were people, humans, elves, orcs, whoever got lost in the mines and... changed."

I cannot even imagine that kind of suffering. Starving, desperate souls, twisted by the darkness into these horrors.

I release another arrow, forcing myself to focus.

Maybe they ate other gorenaughts, fed off of each other, mutated further. I suppose I'll never know, but I'll always be curious. Questions to ask Ilriel.

I'm making a list.

Suddenly, from my side, a creature lunges at me. It's mouth wide, claws sharp. It's legs flutter as it jumps.

Oh, I'm going to die.

But then, like a shadow, Thorne appears. With a swift, practiced motion, she drives her blade into the beast, forcing it back.

Her knife slices cleanly through its gaping mouth, and dark, venomous blood sprays forth. Where the foul liquid touches her arm, her tunic hisses and smolders, holes burning through the fabric as if the blood were liquid fire. Then, she's gone again.

"Ready to run?" Zemm calls, his voice tight with concentration.

Lapis shook her head. "We can't outrun them. They're too fast!"

"There's no such thing," Zemm says. "Faelyri, cover me!"

Me?

I don't even know what I'm doing! But I keep shooting and step in front of him as he chants. The air crackles as Zemm finishes his spell, the runes glowing with firelight.

The cavern fills with a sudden, blinding light as Zemm unleashes his magic. Flame erupts, washing over the gorenaughts with a roar. The creatures screech in agony, their twisted forms writhing before crumbling to ash.

For a moment, the cavern is silent but for our labored breathing.

The tips of my fingers dig into my top as I clench my pounding heart. The palm of my hand presses back in protest against the beating.

One large exhale escapes from every one of us.

More hissing.

Then, we run.

As we flee through the twisting tunnels, my foot catches on a loose stone, and I stumble, sprawling to the ground. Before I can push myself up, Zemm hoists me over his shoulder with ease, his grip firm.

Though the indignity burns, I don't fight him. I'm too tired of running.

We race through the cavern, the heavy silence broken only

by the echoes of our hurried footsteps. At last, the entrance looms ahead, the faint glow of moonstone framing the way. Zemm sets me down gently on the cool stone floor. I steady myself, offering him a soft word of thanks.

Thorne leans against the cavern wall, wincing as she rolls up her sleeve to inspect her arm. The skin is blistered and peeling away in patches. An acid burn.

"Damn it..." she mutters under her breath.

Lapis exhales in relief, her blonde hair matted with dirt and sweat. "At least it's not a bite," she says, brushing ash from her face. "Their blood. It's acid."

I stare at her, my exhaustion giving way to exasperation. What is *wrong* with this place? What kind of cursed land is this? I have, so far, hated every moment in Farfell.

"You call yourself *cultured?*" I snap at Thorne, my voice dripping with mockery. "How could you not know about creatures like that?"

She glares at me, her tone sharp as steel. "I can't possibly know *everything,* can I?"

Lapis holds up Thorne's arm, motioning for me to take it. I grasp her arm, maybe a bit harder than necessary.

She winces again, but says nothing.

I loosen my grip, studying her face. Her eyes stay hard as she watches Lapis work. At times, her lips twitch, almost revealing teeth.

She lets out no breath, no sound. All she does is stand here and watch.

She's...

Bury it.

How bad is that pain? Would it be unbearable for me? Would I cry?

Surely, she wouldn't have risked so much just for a

reward... would she? Did she just want to save a girl's life? She saved me. Again.

She's no hero, of that, I'm certain. And yet, maybe she's not the complete demon I've always assumed.

No, I'm just seeing what I want to see.

Bury it.

She will never save me again, I won't allow it.

The pendant around Lapis's neck glows faintly, casting a soft light over the darkened entrance. Her hands hover above Thorne's wound, the same gentle light radiating from her fingers. The burn doesn't heal entirely, but the angry redness fades, and the acid's corrosive effects seem to halt.

"There," she says, her voice calm and steady. "Wrap it, and you should be fine."

I drop Thorne's arm as if her touch burns me like the acid.

Lapis turns her attention to Zemm, craning her neck up at the towering orc, double her size. "Nice tusks," she says with a grin.

Zemm groans, pinching the bridge of his nose in exasperation.

The stone around Lapis's neck continues to glow faintly, its light a soft echo of the power she wielded in the mines. We stand before the towering statue of Belvadon, her presence looming over us in silent judgment.

Queen Satra approaches Thorne, handing her a small pouch that clinks with the unmistakable sound of coin.

Was that meager reward truly worth the burns, the terror, and the brush with death? What would she have done if I'd succumbed to a heart attack in those dreadful mines? No land or title for her.

"You are free to go," the Queen says to her, her tone curt. "The rest is dwarf business."

Thorne tilts her head, that dangerous glint in her eye. "Meaning?" she presses.

Please stop.

"Lapis endangered the others and will face consequences for her actions," the Queen replies evenly. Her candor doesn't surprise me. She strikes me as a ruler who doesn't flinch from harsh truths.

Thorne, of course, cannot resist the lure of an argument. She crosses her arms and says, "Why? The team is fine, and so is she."

As much as I loathe admitting it, I agree with her.

"I agree," Agnat blurts out, her voice hasty and firm, almost as though she plucked the thought from my mind.

Lapis keeps her eyes trained on the floor, her shoulders hunched. Maybe her silence is from shame, but I also hope she's proud. Proud of her strength, her resilience. She put up an incredible fight against those horrors, and for who knows how long.

That courage shines through, even now when she sheepishly keeps her eyes down and interlocks her fingers together.

"Belvadon will most likely strip her of her power," Queen Satra says with a measured coldness, "which will render her useless to the miners."

Both Lapis and I flinch, her eyes squeezing shut as though the words themselves burn.

Useless?

"No one is useless," I voice aloud.

"With all due respect," Thorne begins, "I think that decision lies a bit higher up than you." She nods toward the shrine.

Lapis's snicker causes me to jolt.

"What do you know of our goddess?" the guard snarls.

Thorne shrugs nonchalantly. "Not much. But gods are all the same, aren't they? They hate being told what to do, and they *love* shaking things up. Something tells me Lapis will be fine."

I glance down at the Nightstrand at my hip. Again, I find myself agreeing with Thorne. I suppose even a fragile, unreliable sword can strike a target every now and then before it snaps.

"In fact," she says, "I am so confident that I would bet you on it."

Does she have a gambling addiction?

"I will make no bargains, bets, or deals with a devil. There are other consequences, even if the goddess spares her." The guard sneers.

I glance at Thorne, but she doesn't meet my gaze.

"Shut up," Agnat growls.

Queen Satra's gaze shifts to me, sharp and assessing. I shrink instinctively under her scrutiny.

"What do you think?" she asks, her voice softer but no less commanding.

I let out a nervous laugh, fumbling for words. "Why... would you want *my* opinion?"

Her expression softens, though the warmth in her eyes unsettles me. "If you were in my position, what would you do?"

My immediate thought is clear: I'd let Lapis off with a warning, a lesson learned rather than a punishment. But I hesitate, unsure if honesty is wise. Finally, I manage, "I... I'm not a queen."

The Queen's lips curl faintly at the edges, a ghost of a smile. "My mistake."

But if she wants my opinion, then I suppose I should give it, right?

"However," I begin, drawing in a steadying breath, "as much as it pains me, I have to side with my... companion." I shoot Thorne a brief glance. "Lapis may have acted recklessly, but she only endangered herself. Your miners left her to die. They abandoned her without hesitation. If Lapis is to face punishment, so too should those who so readily cast aside their comrade. Without unity, no society can stand."

Queen Satra raises a brow, her gaze piercing. "So you expect them to throw their lives away?"

"Of course not," I answer quickly. "But I expect them to try. Leaving a teammate behind to save themselves fosters division, not survival. It's unity that holds a people together. Not self-preservation at the cost of another."

Yeah, Ilriel.

The Queen regards me in silence, her expression inscrutable. Then, at last, she speaks. "I was not alive when a portion of the high elves fostered division and chose to seclude themselves on your tiny island."

Wow.

"Filauria made the right decision," I reply boldly, raising my hands for emphasis. "She didn't abandon the ancient high elves. She rejected their cruelty. And since you've brought her up, have you seen her? She and I have much to discuss."

"Who in the hells is that?" Lapis asks, breaking her silence.

I adjust my goggles, keeping my gaze on Queen Satra as silence stretches between us. She doesn't speak, doesn't even part her lips, and I force myself to stand tall with as perfect posture as I can muster, refusing to let her gaze unnerve me.

Thorne glances between the Queen and I. When neither of us breaks the silence, she redirects her attention to Lapis.

"Come with us," she says suddenly, her tone light but inviting. "You want to fight? All we do is fight. Travel with us."

Lapis's mouth opens, her bright blue eyes glittering with surprise. Before she can respond, Agnat's voice cuts through the air like a blade. "Absolutely not. Dwarves do not leave Vum Dorahl."

Twilight elves do not leave Starview.

Thorne chuckles, "I know plenty of dwarves on the surface."

Agnat's fear spills through her reply, "Yes, but they never come back."

I gather my courage, preparing to speak, but Thorne barrels ahead, as always. "Right. So stay here. Live a boring life, be a... priest... or something. Or come with us and do whatever you want." She shrugs and turns on her heel. "I'm getting a drink, and then I'm leaving. If you're coming, meet us at the entrance in two hours. You seem fun, so I hope you decide to join us."

My gaze shifts to the stone statue of Belvadon towering above us. What would she make of all this? If she cared, wouldn't she have struck Lapis down already? Her silence feels like permission, or perhaps indifference.

"Let's go," Thorne calls over her shoulder. "It's clear whoever you were looking for isn't here."

I ignore her, still staring at the goddess. The stone seems almost alive, as though she might shift at any moment.

Please help me.

"Hey, fallen star, let's go." Thorne's voice rises, almost a shout.

This time, my voice is steady, stronger. "Have you seen her?" I ask Queen Satra, finally peeling my eyes away from the statue.

Thorne sighs loudly, but the Queen smiles. "Filauria?" she

asks. "She comes and goes. I could not tell you where she lives, but she favors the south. She mentioned visiting a Seer in Sunstill."

The Nightstrand at my hip vibrates faintly.

"Sunstill?" Thorne interjects.

Queen Satra ignores her entirely, her focus still on me. "Why are you looking for her? Was she not cast off?"

So was I.

"Elf politics," I reply, my tone guarded.

The Queen tilts her head, her gaze sharp and probing. "Is it because of the news? Or the bounty on your head?"

An ache blooms in my stomach, sharp and twisting.

"A princess accused of treason and exiled. Attempted to murder the King for that weapon on your hip before fleeing," she continues with a sigh. "It seems your whole kingdom is unraveling."

Thorne's head snaps in my direction, her eyes wide with shock.

My pulse quickens. "How do you know that? Here in Vum Dorahl?" My voice trembles as I speak.

"Why would I not know? It's not hard to spot someone like you in Farfell. Be careful."

My heart sinks. Ilriel must have ensured this rumor reached every major city. His reach is larger than I hoped.

"Are you interested in her bounty?" Thorne asks the Queen, stepping closer to me.

I grab her burned arm, my fingers digging into the tender skin. She gasps through gritted teeth, lucky that's all I do.

The Queen shakes her head. "No. I have no interest in the bounty," she says evenly. "But you should know. It was your brother who sent word. From Frondvale."

I'm not surprised he's here. Ilriel wouldn't let his failure stop him; he always gets what he wants, no matter the cost. My fists clench tightly, nails biting into my palms.

"Ilriel is an idiot," I snap, my voice rising with anger. It spills over before I can contain it. I explode. "He's arrogant, delusional, jealous, and his guard is an insufferable brute who can't even pronounce names correctly!"

The words echo through the shrine, bouncing off the walls and the statue. Thorne places a hand on my shoulder, grounding me as I realize the gravity of what I've just done. I shouted at a queen.

Queen Satra doesn't react as I expect. She nods, perhaps in understanding, or perhaps she thinks *I'm* the delusional one. "I have never met him in person. Or his guard."

Lucky her.

I take a deep breath, "I'm sorry," my voice is as shaky as my bow, and I very much need to shut my mouth. But I ask another question. "Why is there moonstone in your mines?"

Thorne sighs again.

The Queen's eyes narrow slightly, a faint smile tugging at the corners of her lips. "Do you think Starview is the only land with moonstone?"

"Yes," I reply bluntly.

Her smile widens. "Did your King tell you that? Your people have mined Starview's mountain for centuries, but it's not unique. We simply do not trade with you anymore. The crown disagrees with the price."

I run a hand through my hair, as my shoulders slump. I have no more questions for her. Only for Ilriel.

Queen Satra's voice softens as she says, "Disingenuous leaders never last. Do not waste your time worrying about Ilriel. The Gods come for us all, even for the immortal elves."

She's right. If I don't deal with him, the Goddesses surely

will. "Moonstone is precious to Starview," I warn her. "I think... he's going to come looking for it."

Her nod is slow.

❦

We linger by the entrance, waiting for Lapis with no sign of her approach. I tap my foot against the ancient floor, eager to leave the heat of this city behind. Beside me, Zemm idly tosses rocks over the edge of the bridge, peering into the void below. We listen for the faintest sound of impact, but hear nothing.

As we finally gather our things and prepare to depart, a voice calls out from the distance.

"Wait! Don't leave me!"

Lapis emerges, sprinting across the bridge, her oversized pack bouncing with every step. The pale light of the cavern catches her ocean-blue eyes, which gleam with determination.

Thorne smirks as she approaches. "Ever seen the surface before?" she asks.

She shakes her head, a flicker of excitement crossing her face. "Lapis Gravelfist," she says, introducing herself with a formality that feels so out of place after all we've been through.

Her sharp gaze sweeps over each of us, sizing us up.

"I'm glad you're alive," I tell her. As much as the ordeal in the mines frayed my nerves, I *am* relieved she survived.

Lapis narrows her eyes, studying me closely. "You've got an accent. Where're you from?"

"What?" I stammer, caught off guard. "I don't have an accent."

She tilts her head toward the others. "She does, doesn't she?"

"A bit," Thorne replies.

I draw in a sharp breath. "Do I really have an accent?"

"It's subtle," Zemm says.

Crossing my arms, I tell them, "I'll just start speaking exclusively in Elven. Let's see how well you manage then."

Thorne smirks. "Thank the Gods." She gestures toward the heavy stone door, holding it open with a flourish. "Shall we?"

"To Sunstill?" I ask, needing confirmation that we're aligned.

"To Sunstill," she says, rolling her eyes.

I breathe a sigh. As I step toward the door, something halts me.

Perhaps it's the faint echoes of etiquette drilled into me since childhood, clawing their way to the surface.

My pride battles with that etiquette; in a rare surrender, I turn to Thorne. My gaze lingers on her burned arm.

"I'm glad you're alright," I say, my voice softening despite myself. My body stiffens, betraying my discomfort as I add, "And... I think it's admirable that you wanted to save a life."

"I didn't do it for you."

"I know. And I'm not thanking you."

Her expression doesn't soften. Instead, her gaze hardens, locking me in place. An unreadable intensity burns in her eyes.

Why won't she answer? Why won't she *stop staring?*
Stop staring.

I ball my fists, the tension finally snapping. "Are you not going to say anything?"

At last, she breaks her gaze, her hands fidgeting with the edge of her glove as her eyes drop. She clears her throat before speaking. "Sunstill is close to Sugarport," she says, her voice quieter than usual. "I hope your friend is there because your boat home is in Sugarport, and that would be very convenient."

She brushes past me as she exits the grand city, her

shoulder grazing mine in passing. The contact is brief but enough to make my chest tighten.

I linger for a moment, my gaze sweeping over Vum Dorahl one final time. The city glows with the light of molten rivers, its beauty carved into my memory. One day, I'll tell Syvis about this place, how breathtaking it is beneath the mountain's shadow.

Have my parents ever been here? Did they love it? I should have asked the Queen.

And then, I step through the door, leaving the heart of the dwarven realm behind.

CHAPTER

TWELVE

I lift my gaze as we tread forward, my eyes drawn to the skies. The burnt-orange expanse melts into a murky blue haze.

There's a town nearby, according to *my* map. With luck, we'll reach its gates before the sun sinks below the horizon. Until then, I'll let my eyes linger on the rust-stained heavens. It reminds me of home (the sky, not the rust).

I ache for that home, not for its palace halls, but for the solace found within them. To see the elder women again, to hear Syvis's laugh, to lay upon a bed that knows my shape. It's a longing for a comfort I can no longer claim.

Home is a dream now, a wish wrapped in shadows. Even if I dared to return now, would I even reach the gates in time to plead my innocence before someone loyal to my brother shoots me down?

Instead, I follow a ghost's fractured path through a foreign land. My hand tightens around my weapon, its presence a steady murmur urging me onward. This seer is my best chance at uncovering the truth. I don't expect to find Filauria there, but I will find the trail that leads to her. And I will follow it.

Ilriel's arrogance blinds him if he thinks he can get me. I don't fear him. While this burden, for lack of a better term, *sucks*, my desire to outwit my brother eclipses my distaste for any of this mess.

"We need a horse or two," Zemm mumbles with weariness from the walk. His deep voice pulls me out of my retrospection.

"You wouldn't fit on a horse," Thorne quips, a smirk playing on her lips. She points ahead. "Look there. That didn't take long. But it would have been faster if someone else had the map."

She sucks, ignore it.

In the distance, a dim light flickers. A village, at last. A broken wooden fence surrounds a small cluster of buildings, their silhouettes weary and sagging under the weight of time.

Why is everything in Farfell so plagued by decay? So far, every human city and town has been battered into the ground.

Why would the royal family allow this?

The dirt paths meander through the village, branching off from the main road like veins. But the town itself stretches in a narrow line, the buildings close-knit and uniform. A weathered sign creaks in the faint breeze: *Butterpond.*

"Cute!" Lapis steps toward the sign with an amused grin. "Ever been here?"

I shake my head.

Thorne's sharp gaze narrows. "No, but I'll bet there's an inn. Let's go."

The soil beneath our boots is damp with the lingering touch of evening dew. Lapis raises her lamp, its glow a beacon as we explore.

The village is eerily quiet; no footsteps, no voices, only faint lights glowing through shuttered windows.

Finally, a larger building with a hanging sign draws our attention. I point toward it. "There."

I trail behind Zemm as we enter, keeping myself shielded from view.

The tavern is small, almost cute. Dim light flickers from sparse lanterns placed upon rough wooden tables. Only a handful of patrons sit scattered about, their voices slurred and sluggish with drink.

Thorne strides to the counter, where an elven barkeep polishes a glass. Shoving her aside, my hand presses against the rough leather of her vest.

"Let me handle this," I mutter, before speaking to the elf in our tongue.

Thorne stumbles back, her eyes shooting daggers into me as she smacks my hand away.

He bows his head, "I'm sorry," he says, haltingly. "I don't speak much of our language."

I step back. "Oh... apologies. I—"

"Sorry about her," Thorne cuts in, placing her hand on my shoulder. I flinch, pulling away. "We need four rooms."

The barkeep shakes his head. "We haven't got that many available."

Why can't he speak Elven?

Thorne taps her long fingers on the counter. My eyes focus on them. There's a meticulous rhythm in the tapping. "How many then?"

"Three."

I pull my vision away from Thorne's hand. He has to be joking.

"Any with more than one bed?" Thorne's voice sharpens.

The elf shakes his head, unfazed.

The rhythmic tapping ceases. Thorne sighs. "That's fine. I'll take them." She scratches the back of her head, swiping the keys off the cracked and worn counter with the other.

I'm too lost in thought to notice her approach until she gently takes my hand. It was almost instinctual, as natural as her heart beating. It's brief but makes me shiver. There's a tingling sensation that spreads up my arm. She pulls me toward the others, who have claimed the largest table in the room.

"They've only got three rooms," Thorne announces, spinning the keys lazily around her finger before pointing one at me. A sly grin creeps across her face. "So, you don't get one."

I meet her gaze, unwavering. "Or we could share."

Her grin falters, just slightly. "You couldn't handle sharing a room with me," she shoots back, her voice low and sharp.

"Sounds like the excuse of someone afraid," I counter. "What's wrong? Don't trust yourself around me?"

Her fingers tighten around the last key, her knuckles whitening. With a quick flick of her wrist, she tosses it my way. I scramble to catch it before it clatters to the floor.

"Share with her," she says, nodding toward Lapis before stalking back to the counter.

I lean forward onto my elbows, letting the near-empty room swallow the tension. I'm glad she's gone, at least for a moment.

"I don't mind," Lapis offers, her voice calm.

"Neither do I," I smile at her. Thank you."

Thorne lingers at the counter, engaged in conversation with a pretty girl. Short hair, *dark* hair, human, and a crossbow at her side. Another traveler, maybe. Or perhaps she lives here.

Thorne's features soften as she laughs. It's uncanny, the way she smiles and effortlessly places a hand on the girl's knee. She meets my gaze once, quickly, and when she does, something rustles in my stomach. Nausea? She leans in to whisper something to the human girl, and the girl laughs.

Zemm, meanwhile, bombards Lapis with questions about her homeland, his quill scratching furiously in his notebook. I twist a strand of hair around my finger, trying to ignore the pair of men at a nearby table who are staring at us.

They can't recognize me. This town is too small, too remote. Still, unease coils in my stomach, and I pull my hood down further over my face.

"Hey!" one of them calls out, his voice as rough as gravel. My gut twists tighter.

"What?" Lapis replies, turning to them, her tone sharp enough to cut.

"Where's she from?" The human tears a piece of bread with his teeth. The lip-smacking could make me rip my hair out. His grin exposes teeth that are more yellowed and crooked than I thought possible.

Zemm, ever steady, answers, "Frondvale. Just passing through."

The man's companion, clearly inebriated, spills his cup of ale everywhere as he pathetically falls over himself. "No, no." He says to his friend. "The one on the sign was an *ugly* elf. Not that one."

My hand slams against the table, the sound echoing through the quiet tavern.

Ugly? How dare he.

Zemm puts his hand on my shoulder, urging me to let it go.

I make eye contact with Thorne, who watches from the counter behind her glass.

"Hold on, hold on," he reaches into his pocket, stumbling as he pulls out the yellowed parchment I so quickly realize is my lovely portrait.

My heart pounds. He begins to unfold it, only stopping when a blade glints against his throat.

"Did you call my friend ugly when you've got such fucked up teeth?" Thorne asks, holding her blade.

The second man, drunk and emboldened, stumbles toward her. Thorne stops him with a hand on his forehead, forcing him backward as if he's nothing more than a child. "There's a blade in this cuff. Sit back down."

He crumbles into his seat.

I glance to the barkeep who isn't interfering, but instead watching intently.

For a second, I really do think she's going to cut through this man's throat. However, with a swift movement, she yanks the parchment from his hand. It crinkles as she balls it in her fist before tossing it into the fire.

"We didn't mean it," he says, face pale, as Thorne walks off.

Zemm leans toward me, "You're not ugly."

"Oh, I *know*." As I sink into the hard wooden chair, I cross my arms.

My eyes meet the barkeep's. I mouth an "I'm sorry" to him. He nods, maybe in understanding.

Thorne returns to the table, seemingly unbothered by the chaos that unfolded moments ago. She plunks down four pints of ale, the frothy amber liquid sloshing slightly in each mug.

"Good news," she announces. "You can all have your own bed."

I grimace at the mug she places before me.

"What does that mean?" I ask, lifting the pint cautiously. I'm not much for ale, but I take a sip anyway. Sweet and fruity, with a subtle tang.

She doesn't answer. Instead, she shifts into a conversation with Zemm, as though the earlier insults and altercation were distant memories. How can they act like nothing happened? Those men were revolting. Their words still sting, even though I know they're nonsense.

My eyes wander to the pretty human girl, the one now gazing longingly at the back of Thorne's head. I rest my chin on my hands, sighing. How does someone so infuriatingly rude make flirting look so effortless?

Everyone is laughing, enjoying their conversation. The table shakes under their movements.

I'm staring into the depths of my mug when Lapis nudges me with her elbow. "You're awfully uptight, aren't you?"

The comment startles a reaction from Thorne, who spits her drink out mid-sip.

"I'm *not* uptight," I say, bristling. Ilriel is uptight—not me. "I am perfectly relaxed. Always."

Lapis takes another sip of her drink, utterly unfazed. "When was the last time someone held you?" she asks. "Maybe if you had a lover, you wouldn't be so tense."

Thorne's laugh bursts from her, rich and loud. My jaw drops at Lapis's bluntness, heat creeping up my face. What does she know about my love life—or lack thereof? Zemm hides his grin behind his hand. I glance around the table. These people are insufferable.

"Do you have a boyfriend back home?" Lapis presses, undeterred.

My face twists in distaste at the thought. "No," I answer quickly. "I'm not interested in a boyfriend."

"Really?" Thorne leans forward. "Why not?"

Who cares? Leave me alone.

"Because I don't want one!" My voice is sharper than I intend, and I immediately regret it.

"I want one," Lapis mutters into her cup, almost wistful.

"That's not much of an explanation," Zemm chimes in, taking a sip.

My face flushes with heat, cheeks burning. I wipe the sweat from the back of my neck and pull my hood even lower over my head, hoping to hide the growing redness.

"I don't owe you an explanation. The reason doesn't matter. I'm not uptight. I actually used to get scolded constantly due to my laxness."

"I just thought princesses always have boyfriends or plan to marry. Like for an alliance or something," Lapis presses.

I shake my head. "We don't do that. We don't…" I don't know why, but it feels embarrassing to get the words out, even if two-thirds of my companions know this about me. "We don't actually leave our island. Ever. I have never been to Farfell, or met a person that was not a twilight elf. We have no one to ally with."

However, that isn't stopping Ilriel from trying.

Thorne leans forward. "So it's up to you then, to find a partner? Maybe you just can't get one. Despite your looks and that *shining* personality."

The memory of Syvis hits me like a gust of wind. Does she count? She must… right?

"I do have someone, though. Someone who…" My voice falters.

Lapis leans forward, her curiosity piqued. "Who?"

"It's my guard," I say softly.

Thorne arches an eyebrow. "The one who could crush my neck with her hand?"

Why? *Why do you care?*

"Yes. She's kind. She cares about me. About my safety."

Thorne tilts her head. "Isn't that her job?"

I shake my head. "It's different. I miss her. She knows

everything about me and…" My voice trails off as the ache of that connection fills the void in my chest.

What if I never find that again? What if I'm always alone? What if I'm stuck here, surrounded by strangers who don't understand?

The thought sends a numbness through my body, as though someone has torn me open and left me to bleed. I wish they hadn't brought this up.

My breathing quickens, and I fold my arms tightly, trying to ground myself.

Just bury it away. Put on a face. Deal with the tragedy later. Deal with it later.

"It doesn't matter," I snap, my voice cracking. My glare lands on Thorne, but her expression is unreadable.

Her face is tinged with pink, most likely from her drink. She smiles, but its strained. Like it's a poor mask for whatever she's really feeling. "Isn't engaging in a relationship with your guard a little inappropriate?"

I slam my hands on the table. "You're one to talk about inappropriate."

The barkeep glances up.

Thorne grins behind her mug. "You're so easy."

This isn't me. I'm not this person. Slowly, I drag my hands from the table, clenching the fabric of my shorts in my fists. I can't let her get to me. The idea that I've given her any amusement churns my stomach.

"Enough, let's drop it." Zemm waves his hand.

But Thorne isn't finished. She leans back, her smirk sharpening. "So easy. And so rude. Always slamming things like a child throwing a tantrum. Stomping your feet and breaking anything in sight."

I'm rude? She thinks *I'm* the rude one?

"I was thrown from my bedroom balcony, branded a traitor, starved, and traversed across a foreign country. Forgive me if I've been a snippy with you, the person trying to collect my bounty."

Zemm sighs.

"Balcony?" Lapis mouths.

Thorne's eyes darken. "You are snippy. I bet that's why he tossed you off the cliff."

I press my lips together, holding back the words that could see us all cast out from this place.

Thorne raises her cup in a mockery of cheer. "At least you're alive," she says, her voice laced with venom.

That's it.

My fingers curl tightly around my full mug of ale. Before I can think better of it, I hurl it with all my strength. Thorne ducks, and the mug crashes into the bar behind her, shattering into shards. The amber liquid drips down in wide splatters, gleaming in the dim lantern light.

"Hey!" The barkeep yells, slamming a rag on the counter. "One more outburst and you're all sleeping outside."

"Sorry!" Lapis shouts back.

I'm not sorry. Not for throwing it. I'm only sorry it didn't smash directly into Thorne's smug face.

My chest heaves as the fire of my anger begins to dim. Across the table, Thorne's wide eyes are fixed on me. Her usually unshakable demeanor is cracked, if only slightly.

My next words are spoken through my teeth: "I am sorry for whatever cursed you to hate nobility. I truly am. But do not, ever, say something so awful again."

For a heartbeat, the only sound is the low murmur of the tavern around us. Then Thorne gives the faintest of nods and drops her gaze. Shame? Regret? Hardly.

"Can we please change the subject?" Zemm pleads with us, rubbing his temples.

Lapis shifts awkwardly in her seat, the wood creaking beneath her. She taps her fingers against her cup before taking a long sip, trying to drown the unease in her drink.

I lace my fingers together on the rough table, forcing myself to breathe deeply. Rage won't help now; I have more pressing things to do than argue with a demon.

My voice is steady when I speak again, directing my words toward Lapis. "You have moonstone in your mines, don't you?"

"Oh, yeah!" she replies, her face brightening. "Boatloads of it."

I click my tongue and lean toward her. "How much, would you say... if you have to estimate... gets exported out of Vum Dorahl?"

She tilts her head, tapping her chin in thought. "Hm... not all of it. It's expensive, y'know? We've got a big stockpile just sitting there, ready to go. That stuff is scary. Practically indestructible."

It really is. "Ready to go for what?"

She shrugs. "For selling, I guess."

"Do you actively sell it?" I ask quickly, anxiously. I need to pull back a bit, "Or are you just hoarding it?"

Her expression twists, hardens, and she sits up straight. "What are you implying?"

"Nothing about the Dwarves." I assure her quickly. "Who do you sell it to?"

She shrugs. "Don't know. Some high elf. It's always the same one. Some guy. But actually," she scratches her chin, her brow furrowed in thought, "lately a human has been wanting it as well."

I lean forward, too far forward and too quickly. I almost fall out of my seat. "What does he look like? The elf?"

Her brows press together as she tries to remember. "Uh... tall? White... uh..." She sighs.

"Markings?" I trace a shape over my forehead, mimicking the branching symbol of a tree. "Does he bear a tree sigil on his forehead? Is his hair long? Is he ugly? Mean?"

Lapis throws up her hands, squeezing her eyes shut. "I *don't know*! No long hair, though. And young. That's all I remember."

"Did he say where he's from?"

"Enough." Thorne snaps. "You're clearly stressing her out."

But I don't stop. "Is Haelhil buying up your moonstone? And the human, what about him?"

"I don't even know what Haelhil is," Lapis groans, exasperated. "Look, I just mine the stuff, all right?"

I lean back, a frustrated growl rumbling low in my throat. I should've asked the Queen. But I'd been too rattled, too overwhelmed to think clearly at the time. Next time, I won't let emotions cloud my judgment.

"How do you not know Haelhil?" I ask.

"No one cares about elf politics," Thorne interjects, her tone bitter. "No one cares about your endless, petty wars between ancient kingdoms. You live so long you lose all sense of humility."

"I don't want to lose my *home*," I snap back. "You *should* care. Ilriel plans to ally with the human king."

Thorne's eyes narrow.

I finish my thought, "He told me our moonstone is running low."

Thorne stares at the table, her eyes distant as if peering through it into some unspoken memory.

She clears her throat, "seems like a lot of trouble for some ore."

"It's not just ore, I think," I retort. "I remember once he claimed much of Farfell is unoccupied."

"It isn't." Zemm says. "Every inch of this place is claimed."

"I am quickly learning that." I say.

"Would Starview have the army for that?" Thorne questions.

"We have an army," I admit. Not a grand one, but an army nonetheless. "And Frondvale's forces, of course."

But Ilriel isn't the kind of leader who would arm the humans out of pure benevolence, so what is he asking of them in return?

"So," Lapis starts, "you think he wants to run the other races out? And take over?"

A month ago, the idea would have been unthinkable. Ilriel had always been ambitious, yes, even a touch selfish. But he was also kind, at least to me. He'd comforted me in my worst moments, held me while I cried. I used to think he could do no wrong, that any suspicion I felt was paranoia.

Perhaps I shouldn't have ignored the invisible crack in his face.

I don't want Starview to march to war. I don't want Syvis sent off to die in some distant land, pitted against whatever enemy my brother deems necessary. I'm already so worried about her.

And then there are the people here—the common folk of Farfell, going about their lives, oblivious to the storm brewing above them. They would be the ones caught in the fire, the ones who'd suffer most.

"Are your parents behind him in this?" Thorne presses, her tone biting. "What does the human king stand to gain from an alliance with a recluse?"

I clamp my mouth shut, swallowing the urge to snap back at the insult. "My parents... my parents are dead. I don't wish to talk about that particular subject any further."

"What about that weapon, the Queen mentioned it," Thorne presses.

"The weapon is what Ilriel wants," I admit, finally, "but he needs me to get it. You won't understand, but it is the most important object of our people. And I have it."

"How? Why?"

"I got unlucky," I answer.

I have no idea what happens to Starview if the Nightstrand goes missing. Queen Satra said my country is crumbling. She's probably right. Because we live for (and rule for) so long, a shift of power is massive. There's a ceremony and a speech and... I don't know. Other royal things.

Did I just... steal the weapon and run, according to my brother?

My hand drifts to my chest, resting there as if I can steady the chaos within. Across from me, for the first time, I catch something in Thorne's expression that resembles sympathy. But I doubt it's for me. No, she's thinking of the innocents, of the countless lives that would be upended if Ilriel's ambitions come to fruition.

Abruptly, Thorne rises from her chair, the wooden legs scraping against the floor. Without a word, she crosses the room to the barkeep.

"I'm not worried." Lapis declares, slamming her cup onto the table with confidence. "The dwarves are strong."

I force a smile, hoping she's right. Ilriel might not act until we're reunited. But he's searching for me, clearly desperate. He needs me. It must eat at him, keep him awake at night. I hope it haunts him.

Thorne sets a drink down in front of me with a pointed glare. "Try not to throw this one."

I can't even summon the energy to care.

I'm desperate for a break from the tense conversation. I need someone to say something. Anything. Someone who won't drag the room down like I do.

I just want *anything.*

Lapis comes to my rescue, because she's amazing. "So, uh, how do you all know each other?"

I laugh softly, more out of relief than humor. For a fleeting moment, I could weep. Thorne, surprisingly, answers first. She leans toward Zemm, her lips curling into a smirk. "We met in Frondvale, actually."

I'm taken aback. "Fronvale? I thought you were from Grimehold?"

"I *lived* in Grimehold. But I also lived in Frondvale, for a time. I'm *from* a place you've never heard of," Thorne corrects me. "None of you, probably."

"Where?" I suppose now is my chance to learn more about her.

"It doesn't matter. I was just a baby when I was sent to Frondvale."

Zemm cuts in, "I accidentally started a fire. Before I had proper control over my magic," he says with a grin. "She helped me steal some books from the palace to figure it out."

The tension among us has eased, replaced by something lighter, almost companionable.

Still, my fingers tap idly on the rough wood of the table. The sound is rhythmic until Lapis swats at my hand with an exasperated huff.

To keep my hands from fidgeting, I pull the crumpled wanted poster from my pocket. Its edges are worn and frayed from being handled too often, shoved hastily into corners of my cloak.

I lay it flat on the table, though it refuses to smooth entirely. The dark eyes staring back at me from the parchment pierce through my skin, as if they might tear me apart. I never imagined I could look so menacing.

A blade strikes the center of my drawn face.

The knife's hilt bears the crest of the royal human family. Thorne's hand grips it tightly. "I'm tired of looking at that damned thing," she mutters, leaving the blade embedded in the parchment as she leans back. Without a glance at me, she turns to Lapis. "We met our uptight elf friend in Grimehold. She was a damsel in distress, flailing about for a friend. So that's where we're headed before we cart her back home."

That's not the story, not even close. I'm not searching for *a friend*. I'm searching for a way to save my homeland, to stop its descent into ruin. And Thorne? She's not helping me out of any kindness. She's helping herself.

I yank the knife from the table and toss it back down, its point making a dull thud when it hits the table.

Lapis nods. "Never seen an elf city before. Looking forward to it."

She might want to temper those expectations. Just in case it's a shadow of its former glory.

Thorne turns her attention to Lapis. "What about you? What was your life like before all this?"

"You saw it. Mine ore, heal wounds, get scolded." She takes a sip.

"But that stone around your neck, it glows sometimes." I pry, "What is it?"

She holds the pale yellow stone up slightly, letting it catch the faint light. It's a smooth gem, tied securely with a leather cord.

"This?" she says. "It's why I can heal. Comes from Belvadon."

I tilt my head, "So... she can communicate with you through that stone?" My next question comes out quieter. "Does it sing to you?"

Lapis nods slowly. "Kind of? Not sing exactly, but if I do something too crazy, it'll glow. Mostly she leaves me alone, though. My sister keeps saying if I don't live a dull, morally sound life, I'll lose my power."

"You won't," Thorne says bluntly, her lips curling into a knowing smirk. "They love chaos."

I stiffen. My weapon hums in agreement, a faint echo of its presence brushing against my mind. She's right. They *do* love chaos. Why else would all of this be happening, if not for their insatiable hunger for disruption?

"Don't push it," I murmur, "I'm superstitious."

She rolls her eyes at me. "Uptight." Then she says, "you know, you're the first twilight elf I've ever met."

"I hope I am able to do my people justice."

Thorne opens her mouth, parting her lips to speak. However, as quickly as she does, she closes them.

"Want to say something?" I ask.

She shakes her head.

"Go on."

"No," she says, "I lost it. Never mind."

She reaches across the table, her fingers brushing over the battered parchment as she retrieves her knife. With practiced ease, she slips it back into the holster strapped to her thigh.

I glance down at the poster. A hole now glares from the center of my forehead. Slowly, deliberately, I fold the paper, creasing it carefully before slipping it back into my pocket. It doesn't matter how torn or pierced it becomes. The face staring back at me will remain the same.

I linger in the dim tavern long after the others have retreated to their rooms. My fingers trace idle shapes on the worn wooden table, the lines meaningless but soothing. My eyelids grow heavier with each passing moment, but still, I don't rise.

The barkeep moves about the counter, wiping it clean with slow, practiced strokes. His eyes drift toward me now and then.

He probably thinks I'm drunk.

I'm not.

"Can I ask you something?" I murmur, breaking the silence.

He raises a brow but humors me with a low, questioning hum.

"Why don't you speak Elven?" The words tumble out, and I immediately regret them. Was that offensive?

If it was, he doesn't show it. His tone is calm, almost indifferent, as he replies, "I never learned."

"How?" I ask. In Starview, we all learned Elven long before the common tongue of Farfell.

"The short answer?" He sighs, leaning against the counter. "Those of us who live in human territories, or who are half-elves, don't always have that connection. My parents left Haelhil long ago. I was born here."

Half-elf? Can that happen? Of course, it's possible. I can't keep being so naive. Then I smack my forehead lightly. Thorne's short ears.

There's so much I was shielded from back home, so much everyone deemed irrelevant for me to know. They never thought I'd leave the island. Never imagined I'd need to understand the broader world.

After all, Ilriel was meant to rule. Not me. I was only supposed to exist in the periphery, untouched by politics or responsibility. They told me I didn't need to worry about such things.

They were wrong.

"Why did your parents leave Haelhil?" I ask him.

"It's a dictatorship."

Yeah, that much I know. I'm glad they got out.

"And you?" he asks, turning the question back on me. "Why did you leave Starview?"

I hesitate, then admit, "I'm looking for someone. Another twilight elf."

Before he can respond, the creak of the stairs draws my attention. Thorne stands on the landing, silhouetted by the faint glow of a lantern.

"Still awake?" she asks, "I'm sure he wants to close."

The barkeep turns away, busying himself with the bottles on the shelf.

I slump further against the table. "Didn't you go off with some girl?" I try to keep my voice even, but the bitterness slips through.

She ignores the question, crossing the room to sit across from me. Her face is drawn, her eyes heavy. "Aren't you exhausted?"

I nod faintly but don't move. Sleep feels like a luxury I can't afford. My thoughts are too loud, too tangled.

I keep replaying conversations I haven't even had yet, imagining what I'll say to Ilriel when I finally face him. Because I will. It's inevitable. And with each passing day, my anger festers, growing sharper.

He kept me sheltered, kept me blind to the truth. He thought I couldn't handle the world as it is.

He was wrong. I'm adjusting just fine.

"Be glad I'm exhausted," I say at last. "I won't argue as much."

"Oh, lucky me," Thorne responds. Her expression remains stoic as she studies me. "How drunk are you?"

"I'm not," I say, my words slurred through exhaustion. "Everything is my fault."

She answers without hesitation. "Don't you think that's a heavy burden to put on yourself?"

My eyes drift closed, and I squeeze them tighter, willing the sting behind them to fade. "You wouldn't understand."

Her chair creaks as she stands. A moment later she's beside me, lifting my arm over her shoulder. She says nothing as she guides me toward the stairs.

Before we ascend, the barkeep speaks in Elven, his accent rough. "I hope you find your friend."

I blink as my throat tightens. "Thank you," I manage. "I will."

The stairs feel steeper than they should, my legs clumsy

and unsteady. Thorne bears most of my weight as we climb. I cling to her, the warmth of her presence oddly comforting.

I don't want her to let go.

At the top of the stairs, she pushes the door open.

"How long to Sunstill?" I mumble.

She sighs. "A day or two."

The sting in my eyes grows stronger, threatening to spill over. I want to cry, but I hold it back. Barely.

"I always wanted to be like my brother," I confess quietly. "Now there's nothing I want less."

She removes my arm from her shoulder but keeps a steadying hand on my waist as I lean against the doorframe.

Before I can step inside, she hesitates. "I'm sorry..." she says softly, "for what I said about your brother."

I don't even want to think about it. "Than—"

No. The words die.

The door closes behind me. I stagger toward the bed without bothering to remove my shoes. After collapsing onto the mattress, staring up at the ceiling.

What are the others dreaming of right now? Are their dreams light, comforting? I hope so.

I'm sure I'll oversleep tomorrow. It won't be fair to them, so I hope I can force myself awake. Ilriel always hated it when I overslept too.

Maybe that's why he tried to kill me.

Was there anything he actually loved, or even liked, about me? Did he really just think I was too paranoid and useless? Was my love nothing more than an inconvenience, something he endured because he had no choice?

Am I even worthy of love?

THIRTEEN

I peer over the weathered wooden sides of the creaking wagon, the salt-laden air stinging my senses. The skies above us churn with ominous shades of gray.

The journey is unbearably dull, the monotony stretching the hours into what feels like an eternity. Yet, it has only been a day and a half. Exhaustion gnaws at me, but its fear that has sapped my strength.

Thorne sits opposite me, her slender form leaning casually against the edge of the wagon. Her gaze is fixed on the passing scenery, her sharp eyes tracking the trees as they blur by. Loose strands of her hair spill from the tie meant to contain them, framing her pointed ears.

She has been unusually quiet. Is she also thinking of my brother? Is she worried? I doubt it. Her posture is far too relaxed, as if she has not a care in the world.

I touch my face absentmindedly, tracing the markings etched into my skin. The thought of my mother tightens a fist around my heart.

I wonder, if she were alive, if she would believe Ilriel. Or if she would stand with me. Would she come find me? I miss her more than words can bear. Her face haunts me, suffocating me. I can't even bear to look at my own, it's too similar.

And Syvis.

I toy with the idea of writing her a letter, of telling her I am alive, safe, and that I am coming home. But I can't.

"Lyri," Zemm's voice pulls me from my thoughts, "Are you alright?"

I swallow the lump in my throat and force a reply. "Just admiring the view."

He eyes me with suspicion but lets it go. "We're nearly there," he says, his voice a quiet reassurance.

I nod, but my mind drifts again to my city. To Ilriel. To the vile lies he spread. The people would never believe such venom. Yet, I dread to imagine the lengths he might go to silence them, to keep them from coming to my defense.

The wagon jolts to an abrupt halt, shaking me from my reverie. I glance up to find a large, weathered wooden sign: *Sunstill.*

"I need to find the seer," I announce, ready to disembark. "And then we're leaving."

"Don't go running off," Thorne commands, her voice sharp. "You have plenty of time to find your seer. The girl at the tavern mentioned a festival here, and I intend to stay for it."

Plenty of time? No. I really don't.

"A... festival?" I scoff, climbing down from the wagon. "I don't have time for that."

"Sure, you do," Thorne counters, a teasing edge to her voice.

Don't start a fight.
Don't start a fight.
Don't start a fight.

"Why are you trying to ruin my life?" I demand.

"Your life is already in ruins," she retorts, smirking. "Might as well enjoy what's left of it."

Zemm is the last to exit the wagon. He stretches his legs and says, "At this rate, I'll never see the starlight city."

Neither will I.

Despite its name, Sunstill is anything but sunny. Heavy clouds blot out the heavens, and thick fog rolls in from the nearby ocean, curling around the town's brick streets. It's eerie, fitting for a place that might house a seer.

They like eerie, right?

Yet, the town is alive with activity, its citizens bustling about in preparation for their festival. A sea of strangers that only heightens my anxiety. Each face could be the one to recognize me.

I cling to the back of Zemm's shirt as we weave through the throng of festival-goers.

"Why is this place called Sunstill?" Lapis demands. "There's no sun!"

"Probably to lure unsuspecting visitors," Zemm replies.

Half the people here are clearly travelers, much like us. "There are too many people," I whisper, my grip tightening. "Too many eyes."

"What does it matter?" Lapis asks, shoving her way forward.

"She's afraid someone will recognize her," Zemm explains.

I'm still clutching his shirt, biting my lip. Am I wrong to be worried? No. I'm not.

As we reach the shopping district, where temporary stalls stand alongside sturdy brick buildings, Lapis's eyes sparkle with wonder. "Let's buy something!" she exclaims.

"I can't—" I begin, but she cuts me off.

"Please," she says, her voice softening. "I want to get something for Agnat. For when I see her again."

Her words hit me like a blow. She's homesick. Oh...

Lapis, Zemm, even Thorne, they all must long for their homes, for a sliver of normalcy amidst this chaos. I've been so consumed by my own burdens to see theirs. I just assumed that because they chose to come on this journey, they wouldn't bother to miss their past.

Maybe they want a place where people are laughing and enjoying themselves rather than us crammed in a tiny wagon, or cave, with no idea where our next bed will be.

They made it here, so they deserve that tiny bit of relaxation.

"Lapis..." I murmur. "I'm sorry."

She tilts her head, confused. "For what?"

"You must really miss her," I say, my voice barely audible over the clamor of the crowd.

"Well," she grins, "she didn't try to kill me."

I smile at her. She's got a great point. Agnat didn't appear to be the murderous type.

"Yeah, I'll go shop with you. What kind of gift are you thinking?" The corners of my mouth begin to twitch upward, almost forming a smile.

I'll blend in with the crowd. No one will notice me.

She scratches her chin. "I... don't know. She likes jewelry and stuff. Gemstones."

I start to speak quickly, "A bracelet. She could wear it in the mines. A ring would be too distracting. Hard to grip a hammer with something digging into your fingers." I think a bit before shaking my head. I end up raising my voice in excitement, "No. Maybe a hair clip, actually!" Something with blue gemstones would be good, to match the eye color they both share. She can use it to keep her hair back.

"Jewelry isn't supposed to be practical," Lapis says.

I'm grinning now. The largest grin I've probably had in... who knows how long. "Right. But isn't she down there most days? At least she can feel pretty while she works." My attention turns to Zemm, and I'm still grinning, "Doesn't that make sense?"

"I guess..." His eyebrow is cocked.

Maybe I can get Syvis something, as well. I can bring her a memento.

'Sorry for worrying you.' I'll say, handing her a necklace, or ring, or brooch, or... I don't know. I just know that she'll love whatever I bring home to her.

However, Lapis's wish isn't granted. The soft fabric of Zemm's shirt slips out of my fingers as I'm whisked away into the nearest dark alley. My back slams against the stone wall of the building. Thorne keeps her back to me, leaning against the wall as if to shield me from the main road.

Lapis rounds the corner, her presence hidden from my view but her voice cutting through the air. "What are you doing? Give her back." She says, irritated.

"Soldiers. Go away," comes the curt reply from Thorne. The single word sets fire to the unease in my chest, a flicker that quickly grows. It roots me to the spot. They can't be here for me. Surely, they're here for the festival.

But Lapis, fierce as ever, doesn't yield. From my spot behind Thorne, I peek out, catching the fury carved into Lapis's face, her lips pressed into a line. "I just wanted to shop—"

Zemm, ever loyal to his awful friend, shoves Lapis back into the busy street without a word. I am convinced they can communicate telepathically.

"Stay behind me," Thorne commands, her voice a low growl.

"They can't be here for me."

She doesn't even glance back. My instincts scream to flee, so I check behind me. There *is* a way to run. But as I try to move, the quick twist of her hand catches my cloak, pulling me closer to her side.

"What did I just say?" she murmurs, her tone sharper than a dagger.

The clinking of armor grows louder, cutting through the hum of the street. Once, that sound filled me with comfort. A reminder of my old friend.

Now, it only sends a spike of dread through my heart.

The metallic clang halts abruptly. Thorne, calm as stone, doesn't flinch. She leans casually against the wall, one hand lifted to examine her nails.

I ache to peek around her.

Waiting for someone?" A guard's voice cuts through the alley.

"No," Thorne replies, her voice cool and distant.

Another voice joins his, deeper and laced with false author-ity. "Strange to find someone lurking in an alley when the streets are so lively."

"Not one for crowds," Thorne says.

The two men exude an arrogance that sends my stomach churning. My grip tightens on the back of Thorne's vest. I don't know why, but I need to resist the urge to wrap my arms around her entirely. I'm yearning for the comfort I felt when she brought me up the stairs in the tavern. I want that version of her right now.

"Are you with someone?" the second man presses. "I see a shadow behind you. Seems suspect for someone cloaked in black to hide in the alleys."

"Seems suspect for a priest to walk with a royal soldier," she counters, her tone biting.

A priest? My breath catches. If the church is involved, what business could they have with me?

The sharp scrape of a blade being unsheathed shatters my thoughts. My breath quickens as panic claws at my throat.

Thorne laughs, cold and mocking. "You're joking."

"You match the description of someone King Claude seeks," the priest says. His voice is thick with triumph. "Someone with an elf spotted in Grimehold."

"Do I?"

"You do," the priest replies, his grin audible. "The Gods have blessed me today."

"Doubtful," Thorne quips, her tone dry as bone.

"They have," the priest insists, clapping his hands together like a child gifted a toy. "I'm going to be rich."

"An encounter with me is no blessing," Thorne replies. She steps aside, revealing me to the men. "Just ask her."

My heart pounds, and before I can think, my bow materializes in my hands. How did it get there? I don't know.

All I know is that Thorne is lifting my arms, and they are full of tension as I aim.

The men step deeper into the shadowed alley, far from the noise of the street. The string releases.

The guard's body crumples with a crash, his armor ringing faintly beneath the song that now fills my head.

"Good job," Thorne says, her smirk wicked. "You're turning into a real killer."

Am I?

My stomach clenches as nausea rises, and I collapse to my knees, clutching at my middle. The bitter stench of blood is overpowering, and I dry heave.

I can't keep doing this.

A heavy thud echoes in the narrow alley. The priest is down. His lifeless body sprawls across the blood-slick stones, and the air thickens with the sharp tang of death.

I gag as the stench grows unbearable, bile rising in my throat. *Not here*, I beg silently. *Don't vomit here.*

"Get up," Thorne commands, "We need to get away from these bodies."

"I can't," I manage to rasp between dry heaves. My legs feel like lead, my body frozen in place.

She doesn't wait for me to recover. Her hand clamps around my arm, pulling me up with cruel strength.

We don't head toward the main road; instead, she drags me into the shadows of the back alleys, away from prying eyes.

How many others know who I am?

Everyone seems ready to claw at the chance for riches, no matter the cost. I'm not safe—anywhere, with anyone. All I wanted was to buy a simple gift for my friend.

"You killed a priest," I mumble, pulling my cloak tighter around my face to block out the stench.

"I'm not particularly religious."

"*I am.*"

"Good thing you killed the guard, then."

When we've put enough distance between ourselves and the bodies, she releases my arm. I sink against a wall, hiding my face in my hands as the world spins around me.

Zemm and Lapis appear from the gloom, rounding the corner to join us.

"Are you alright?" Zemm asks, concern in his voice.

"Yeah," Thorne answers quickly, not giving me the chance to respond. She glances at me with her sharp eyes. "We should get you a mask."

A mask? That... might actually help. Something to hide my face, to shield me from the stares.

"Here," Lapis interjects, pulling a small scarf from her bag, "just use this for now."

I nod in thanks as I wrap it around the lower part of my face, making sure to give myself room to breathe.

We weave our way back toward the market, searching for a real mask and any trinkets that catch our eye. The lively hum of the marketplace feels unreal after the stillness of the alley.

Laughter draws my gaze to the left, where a group of children are gathered, their carefree giggles a balm to my frayed nerves. They remind me of home, of the children spilling out of the schoolhouse in my own city.

What are they laughing about? Are they sharing fun stories? Is some teacher telling them horror stories about the fey?

And then I murmur, half to myself, "I wish I could change my face, like a faerie."

Thorne stops dead in her tracks, turning to look at me. "A faerie?"

I nod. "Yes. Those terrifying creatures that eat children and wear their faces. Could a faerie change the face of another person?"

"Why are you asking me?" She snaps.

"Because you seem to know everything," I reply with a shrug. "Or at least, you like to pretend you do."

She grinds her teeth, irritation flashing in her eyes. "They probably couldn't. No."

"I could find one and ask," I suggest.

"You don't want to make a bargain with the fey," she says firmly.

"I used to have nightmares about them when I was a kid," I admit, "but I believe I could outsmart one."

"You can't," Thorne says with finality.

"But I read a book—"

"And how have all your books served you so far?" she snaps.

Zemm pulls his attention from elsewhere and looks between us. "What's going on now?"

"She wants to find a *faerie*," Thorne explains with exasperation, "the kind that *eats children*."

Zemm's eyes narrow in confusion, then shift to me. "Why? Do you eat children?"

"No! Because they can change their faces," I say, hopeful. "And I want one to change mine."

Thorne lets out a frustrated sigh. "I told her that's not how it works. If she ever made a bargain with the fey, it would only lead to death or servitude."

"But they can't tell lies!" I protest.

"No, they can't," Thorne agrees. "But they can twist their words into something more dangerous than a lie. Just leave it alone."

I pause, my voice softening just slightly. "Are you worried about me?"

Her eyes meet mine for a brief moment. "I'm worried about myself."

"You are an awful person. Selfish and awful."

"Yes, I am."

In my rented room at the Sunstill inn, I'm pacing in my slip, unable to sleep. I'm afraid that if I sleep, I'll have nightmares of guards and blood and invasions.

Worse than that, I'm worried my nightmares will be full of being chased. I'll have one of those terrible dreams where I'm trying my best to run, but my legs aren't moving. Behind me, something is creeping up. It can move, but I'm frozen in place. It'll catch me.

What happens when it catches me?

I always wake right before it does... but one day I might not wake up at all. One day it *could* catch me.

My arms are pulled tightly into me as I pace. If I don't have anyone to hold me, at least I can hold myself.

There's a creak outside my door, and then a soft knock. My arms drop, one now holds my weapon and the other is reaching for the knob. I take my time opening the door.

It's Thorne. Of course it is.

"Can I help you?" I ask, not very politely.

She walks past me, not waiting for me to invite her in, and closes the door behind her. "You wouldn't speak to me for the second half of the day and are *clearly* upset, so I came to check in. Is this about the fey?"

"No." Too exposed in this nightgown, I wrap my arms around myself to cover me. "I don't care about the fey. It was a stupid idea. I'm angry because you don't care about my safety."

"The mask will be fine. We have a deal, and I'm going to make sure you get home alive."

"That doesn't mean you *care*. You'll bring me home alive, but what if I lose a limb? What if I go blind?"

She shrugs.

"Deaf," I keep going, "or my tongue gets cut out?"

"Well, I hope so."

I think back to her accusation about tantrums and keep myself looking as calm as possible.

"You are capable of doing good," I surprise myself by saying. "I know it. I have seen it. Sometimes I think I'm just seeing what I want to see, but I don't know." I keep going, She can be comforting and even sometimes admirable.

"I know what people must see when they look at you. A person living in a sewer, stealing and spying to survive. They think you are bad, so you want to be worse to get ahead of it."

She takes a step closer, and instinctively, I take a half step back.

I say, "I suppose I am your exact opposite. I was given everything, and it made me useless. Turned me to rust. People used to bow when they saw me, now they punch me in my face. I didn't even notice those men staring at us. Too oblivious."

"Stop talking," she demands.

The harshness throws me off guard a bit. My face is hot in the aftermath of my vulnerability, as we linger in the silence.

I'm not sure if she's even aware that she's doing it, but she runs a finger over the markings on my face.

I swat her hand away and break the silence, "you came to check in. Are you satisfied?"

Still nothing.

"Is that a yes?" I demand. "Answer me."

"How do you want me to answer?"

"Honestly."

There's nothing I want her to say. There's something I expect her to say. The difference is important.

"Honestly? I think you're lucky that it was me that found you."

I frown at her. "*Lucky?*"

"If anyone else found you, you wouldn't be standing in this inn trying to analyze me." She flares her nostrils.

"No. I would be standing in this inn trying to analyze someone else. I think you're delusional."

"Delusional? Am I the delusional one? Am I the one that wanted to be a queen? Do you think you'll be a good leader?"

I'm taken back by her question. I keep my gaze to the side. "What?"

She repeats her question, but a bit slower this time, "Do you think you'll be a good leader?"

When the barrier falls, do you think you can lead an army to fend off Haelhil?

There's a tingling in my chest now, I place my hand over it. My breath shortens. I try to fill my lungs, but it's impossible. I start to chuckle nervously. I move my hand to my mouth to keep the laughter in. It doesn't work, and now I'm laughing behind my palm.

She crosses her arms, shifting her weight from one leg to the other, and cocks her head. I'm still laughing.

I take one deep breath. I reach for the door, but don't open it. "What time are we leaving?" I ask.

"What the hells was that?" she demands.

I don't know. Her ridiculous question made me nervous, so I didn't want to answer. And now, I'm getting angry. She's just standing there, being annoying.

Her voice becomes too playful for my liking. "Are you going mad?"

"No. My brother is the one going mad."

"Does he also break out into maniacal laughter?"

Perhaps. Maybe that's become a trait of his, just like it's become a trait of mine apparently.

"If you're satisfied, you should leave," I say.

"Maybe I'm not." She won't take her eyes off me. "I have another question. Why are you always staring at me?"

"I'm watching you to make sure you don't kill me when I'm not looking." I lie.

She has no reason to know why I stare, that's no one's business but mine. Besides, I stare for no other reason than jealousy. Because I'm jealous of her features, and her eyes, and even her hair. And I wish I looked like her. I wish I could be beautiful enough that I didn't need to care about anyone else's opinion.

I wish I could be beautiful enough to be unkind.

As she takes a step forward and I take another back, my back presses against the wooden door.

"You're lying," she says.

"Is that an accusation or a desire?" I press my palm against her stomach to push her back, but she doesn't move. "You are so arrogant. And incredibly disrespectful."

Her eyes darken. "Am I? You said you had everything I didn't. Should I shower you with praise for that?" She takes my face in her hands, getting so close that our noses almost touch, and she whispers, "should I kneel?"

Her eyes are clouded with an intense, unreadable emotion. I expect her to laugh at me again, or insult me while I just stand here. My face is blushing hot. My heart is exploding. Her hands are in my hair.

"Well?" She asks again.

I'm immobilized. I don't know what to do. What do I do?

"Stop staring at me unless you're going to kiss me." She drops my face and steps back.

I scurry to the side, away from the door, and away from her.

"Get out of my room. I won't tell you again."

When she leaves, I slam the door behind her. I lean against it, needing to catch my breath. What the hells was that?

FOURTEEN

I don't want to see her.

Just the thought of going downstairs twists my insides. I'm dreading it. Dreading the way she'll look at me and the way she'll speak, like she knows exactly what I'm thinking. Last night, I felt something, something I despise. It was more than anger. It was a tangled snarl of emotions, as if someone bottled my heart and shook it.

It's like handing her a weapon, letting her have that power over me.

What is wrong with me? She's a monster.

I cocoon myself in the sanctuary of the blanket, pretending I'm anywhere but here. I won't join their stupid revelry. No, I'll remain here, in this bed that feels more like a fortress.

"Lyri!" Lapis's voice booms behind my door, followed by the insistent thud of her fist. "Come on. We're going!"

"I'm not feeling well," I lie, "go on without me!"

The pounding halts, thankfully. But then, her voice returns, laced with suspicion. "What the hells do you mean? Are you sick?"

I fake a loud, dramatic, cough, hoping it's convincing enough. "Yes! I've come down with something. Please leave."

The doorknob rattles, but it doesn't budge. I made sure to lock it after last night.

"Lyri!" She shouts, exasperated. "I'll knock the door down and then you'll have to pay for it."

Me? Why would I have to pay for it?

"Leave me alone!" I shout back, the words escaping before I can stop them. Perhaps I should just tell her the truth. Lapis is my friend... I think. I can trust her. Probably. "I do not want to go downstairs! I don't want to see Thorne. She's making me crazy."

There's a pause, and then another voice speaks.

"You really should come down," Thorne says smoothly. "You'll miss out on all the fun."

My face flushes with heat, and I bury myself deeper within the blanket.

The doorknob rattles again. This time, there's a soft click, and I feel the air shift as the door swings open. My heart drops.

"Why do you have a key?" I demand, my voice muffled by the layers of blanket I refuse to uncover.

"I don't," Thorne says casually, her boots thudding heavily against the floor as she approaches. "You're sick?"

"Mhmm." I fake another cough.

"Let me feel your head," she orders.

"No!"

"Are you actually sick, *your highness*, or is it true that you don't want to see me?" She lowers her voice. "Did I excite you last night? Did you not want me to leave, and now you're angry at me?"

My cheeks burn, and I whip the blanket tighter around me. "Shut up! I *am* sick. I don't want to see you, just like I didn't want to see you last night."

"Then, if you're really sick, I want to help." The blanket is bunched in her fingers as she gives it another pull. But she doesn't press hard, and I'm still able to keep myself buried. She lets out an exasperated sigh.

Something lands on the table with a thunk.

"Fine," she says. "Drink this. It'll help."

I reveal only my eyes. I narrow them on her, and then to the mug she placed on the table. "What is it?"

"Slugroot. I had some in my bag."

"That sounds horrendous." I scrunch my nose in protest. I'm not drinking anything by that name.

"It's just a name," she says, rolling her eyes. "It's tea. It'll help with whatever it is you have. Fever, chills, lies."

I sit up just enough to peer suspiciously into the cup. It smells earthy, like damp leaves after a rainstorm or bark stripped fresh from a tree. Thorne slips off one of her gloves, and before I can stop her, her hand brushes my hair back, tucking it gently behind my ear. Her fingers are warm, her touch featherlight as she presses her palm to my forehead.

"I've been standing too close to you," she says, her hand still resting on my skin. "Wouldn't want to catch whatever plague you've conjured."

I don't respond, my gaze fixed on the far wall. Her hand lingers too long, her presence too overwhelming. I also don't want to meet her eyes. They frighten me. When she finally pulls away, she scoffs.

"If you feel better, come join us," she says, her voice sharp again. "They'll miss you." She leaves without waiting for a reply, the door slamming behind her.

I touch my cheek, her warmth still haunting my skin. Monster.

I finally bring the mug to my nose. I don't know if I should drink it... because I'm not actually sick. But the warmth of the mug in my hands is strangely comforting.

It's hot, but not as terrible as I'd feared. Bitter, yes, but manageable, with a hint of something almost sweet at the edges. Before I realize it, I've finished the drink, save for the small leaves that rest at the bottom of the cup.

I groan and let myself fall backward onto the bed, staring up at the wooden beams of the ceiling. I've already made such a scene... but I can't just stay here. I came all this way. I've faced worse things than this. Am I really going to cower in fear of a single person?

No. I'm not. But still, I'll have to be cautious. Going alone would be foolish. So I *should* hurry to catch up with them...

Instead, I find myself sitting on the edge of the bed, legs swinging back and forth. My thoughts wander as the muffled sounds of the tavern below reach me. Laughter, the clatter of mugs, the hum of voices sharing stories over breakfast.

My friends might be down there, gathered at a table. Are they talking about me? Do they even notice my absence? Do they miss me?

A pang of homesickness hits me like a sharp blade. If I were home, Syvis wouldn't have let me stew like this. She'd have marched into my room, pulled the blankets from my bed, and dragged me down the hall by the ear if she had to. She wouldn't let me hide away. Not from anyone, not even myself.

But here, left to my own devices, I make the wrong decisions. Always.

Frustration wells up, and before I can stop myself, I grab the pillow and hug it tightly to my chest. It does nothing to soothe the ache, so I slam it back down onto the bed.

Enough. Enough wallowing, enough hiding, enough of this self-pity that's taken root in my heart.

I swing my legs to the floor and stand, planting my feet

firmly. My hands ball into fists at my sides, and I take a deep breath. I force myself to move, step by step, toward the door.

❧

The heart of the town isn't hard to find. The festival pulled me in like a tide, carried along by wide-eyed tourists swept up in its colorful current. When I finally reached the bustling square, though, I don't look for my companions. Instead, I linger in the shadows of a towering stone building, tucked safely away from the watchful eyes of soldiers and the vibrant crowd.

Dancers twirl, their laughter ringing out like bells. Beautiful women in beautiful gowns spin with men whose faces melt into the background. I glance down at my own plain attire and sigh.

I am severely underdressed. Embarrassing.

A towering tree blooms at the square's center, its branches heavy with blossoms, and at its roots stands a small shrine where people kneel one by one to offer their respects. Others browse stalls glittering with jewelry and trinkets.

I wonder if that's where Lapis is.

That's where I should be as well. But without coin, like Thorne will never allow me to forget, I have no place at the market. She handles our expenses: meals, lodgings, everything. That's another thing that gets under my skin. It's like she doesn't trust me to handle it myself.

A sigh, heavy and rasping, breaks through my thoughts. I turn to see an old woman lowering herself to the ground beside me, the shadows draping over her like a second cloak. Her hood conceals most of her face, but her tan, wrinkled hands peek out as they fumble with a small package.

She looks up, and pale, clouded eyes meet mine. Her face is

strangely ageless but her smooth skin clashes with her gnarled hands.

"You're too pretty to hide in the shade," she says, her voice smoother than I expect.

"I always stand in the corner at parties," I reply.

The woman unwraps the bundle in her hands, revealing a small loaf of bread.

"I'd go to the shrine, but I scare the children. So, I also sit in the shade." She nods toward the tree.

I hesitate before sinking to the grass beside her, pulling down my mask at last. Without a word, she tears the bread in half and hands a piece to me. I take it instinctively. I can no longer tell friend from foe, but something in me trusts her.

"Are you blind? Is it your eyes that frighten them?"

"My eyes don't work well, but I'm not blind," she says evenly.

I bite into the bread, the rough swallow catching in my throat. "Gods..." I nearly choke. "You're a seer!" The Night-strand coils within me, its song rising in a warning hum.

The old woman smiles, a knowing gleam in her cloudy gaze. "I suppose I am."

I can't believe my luck. I found her. Though, I suppose she found me, not the other way around.

The only other seer I'd known was in Starview, and Ilriel despises her. He won't let her near the palace after her vague but haunting predictions.

What did she tell him? Something about... being blind, I think? Yes. She'd told him he'd go blind one day, and I'd never seen him so afraid.

"They like me when they need me." She chuckles a bit. "Otherwise, I'm the witch who eats children."

"Do you eat children?" I furrow my brow.

"I prefer fish."

I laugh at her joke, but not loudly. Passersby glanced at us with unease: a pair of hooded figures lost in the shadow of a festival.

"So, you're not a fey then?" I ask.

"I am very much human, sorry to disappoint you."

"Do you live here, in Sunstill? I've been looking for you."

"All my life." She ignores my second statement. She keeps staring at the shrine, or in the direction of it.

I stand, brushing dirt from my knees, and extend a hand. "I'll take you to the shrine."

She hesitates but finally takes my hand. Her grip is firm as I pull her to her feet. The crowd thickens as we near the tree. In fact, it almost seems as though some intentionally block our path. So in response, I shove my way through to clear one myself.

At the shrine, she kneels, murmuring some human prayer.

While she prays, my gaze wanders, and I spot Thorne in the distance. Her head tilts in confusion as she catches sight of me. I quickly return my eyes to the seer, who is now standing and ready to leave.

Together, we weave back through the crowd to the safety of the shade.

"Thank you," she says. "Normally, I wait until nightfall, when everyone is gone."

"That's a shame," I reply, settling back into the grass.

I swallow the rising nerves in my throat. Building the courage to ask her my questions.

Her downturned eyes meet mine, and without waiting, she says, "I don't see your home. I've already looked."

My fingers dig into the cool grass, nearly tearing it from the ground. I wasn't even going to ask that.

"What? How is that possible?"

She doesn't flinch. "A cunning trickster shall weave deceit, stealing what is yours by sleight and guile. Shadows shall creep where sunlight reigns, casting a cloak over a city of golden brilliance. And deep beneath the earth, where no eye dares wander, starlight shall slumber, hidden from the world above."

Her voice carries a chill that seeps into my chest, tightening around my lungs.

"Can you clarify?" I ask, even as dread tells me it's hopeless. "I have no idea what you're saying. That wasn't even my question..."

"I know," she says evenly. Her pale, clouded gaze fixes on me. "But I've just told you the answer to your question."

My hand instinctively goes to my weapon, gripping its hilt. Not in threat but to steady the trembling that matches the rapid beat of my heart.

"No, I'm looking for someone," I say quietly.

"Yes," she replies, her tone calm. "I know."

This is why Ilriel hates seers. Their answers are riddles, their clarity an illusion.

"Well, which part was the answer?" My voice rises despite my effort to contain it. "Where is she?"

Pressing her hands to the ground, she struggles a bit while standing to her feet.

Breathe through your frustration. Don't snap.

Once she's on her feet, she turns down to me and says, "Your relationships are not a competition, you know."

That's hardly a clarification.

My head reels with confusion, and my mouth opens, but no words come. Of course, she would leave me with that. A fragment of wisdom that feels like more riddles.

She walks away, disappearing behind a building, leaving only shadows and questions in her wake. I sit there, the grass cool against my palms, staring after her. I don't know what she means, but maybe Zemm will. He's smarter than I am.

My gaze drifts back to the square, where my companions are lost in the revelry.

Thorne, with her arm draped around a woman, wears her look of easy confidence as she addresses her. Lapis leans into a conversation with a human man, her laughter bright even from a distance. Zemm is chatting with an elf man, his usual reserved demeanor softened by a rare smile.

I want to be there. I'm *yearning* to be there.

But something keeps me rooted here, knees pressed into

the earth. Thorne certainly doesn't want me there. She'd probably revel in the sight of me sitting here alone, miserable and on the verge of a breakdown.

I clench my fists. I don't care.

At least, that's what I tell myself.

It doesn't matter. I need to figure this out. I need to focus.

Shadows shall creep where the sunlight reigns.

Sunstill may have sun in its name, but there is certainly no sun here. Dark shadows from the sky already cast a cloak over the city.

Ugh. I don't know enough about this cursed land to figure this out.

So, I pull out the map tucked away in my bag. Desperate for answers, and scan the faded lines. My eyes catch on Frondvale, where the crest of the human royal family marks the territory.

A blazing sun. Or some sun-adjacent symbol, for their deity whose name escapes me.

That has to be it.

Will Thorne go to Frondvale? Will the rest of them? They have to.

When I glance back up, Thorne is watching me, her gaze sharp and unreadable. Anger? Disgust? I can't tell. Last night's mockery still stings, and I have never been more confident now that she despises me.

A cunning trickster shall weave deceit, stealing what is yours by sleight and guile.

She's going to betray me. Has she already? Is she biding her time? I cannot let my guard down.

It isn't until droplets of water hit the map, smudging the ink, that I notice how hard my eyes are stinging. I've never cried so much in my life and now I feel like it's all I do. I rub them fiercely. Crying is weakness. Weakness is unforgivable.

Enough. Stop crying. Pathetic, sad, annoying.

I roll up the map and shove it into my bag. When I glance back, Thorne's eyes are still on me. The weight of her stare is too much. I need to leave.

What would Ilriel think of me right now?

The tavern is packed. Somehow, we've managed to claim a small table, though we're crammed together. Poor Zemm is having the worst of it.

"Did you find your seer?" Thorne asks, taking a lazy sip of her drink. Her smirk is cutting. "I saw you with that old woman. Unless you've developed a thing for hanging out with grandmothers."

Actually, I do have a thing for that. That's funny.

"I did. No thanks to you." I won't tell her that she found me, and not the other way around.

"And?" She raises a brow.

"She was... cryptic," I admit.

"Not shocking," she replies, dismissive as always.

"Thorne, stop being rude! Lapis steps in, her voice sharp. "Lyri, what did she say?"

Lapis, my saving grace. I could hug her.

"She said something about sunlight," I begin, repeating the words to the group: "Shadows shall creep where sunlight reigns, casting a cloak over a city of golden brilliance. And deep beneath the earth, where no eye dares wander, starlight shall slumber, hidden from the world above.

"I think she might mean Frondvale," I finish.

I will not say the beginning. Not to anyone.

Will Zemm also betray me? How loyal is he to his friend?

"Oh?" Says Zemm, "why there?"

"The human crest," I explain. "It's a sun."

Thorne interjects, her tone biting. "What if it's not about Frondvale at all? What if she's talking about two completely different things, and neither of them lead to your friend? Did you ask *specifically* about your missing elf?"

I shake my head, "no, but—" I grit my teeth. "She told me it was the answer to my question."

"But you didn't even get to ask your question, did you?" Thorne presses, her smirk widening. "So, how do you know?"

"I just—" My words falter under her scrutiny.

"I'm starting to think this is the biggest waste of my time."

"Then leave!" The words burst out before I can stop them. "No one's forcing you to stay."

Leave before you betray me.

Zemm cuts in, his voice calm but firm. "We promised to help you find your friend. That was the bargain." He tosses Thorne a glance.

I straighten in my seat, meeting Thorne's challenging gaze. "You will take me to Frondvale."

Lapis raises her mug in a cheer. "To Frondvale!" She takes a long sip before adding, "What's the name of this elf, anyway? I just realized I've got no idea."

"Filauria," I say quietly, the name a lifeline and a weight. "She won't be hard to miss."

Lapis grins. "That's such an elf-y name."

CHAPTER

FIFTEEN

The skies hang heavy over the seaside town of Sugarport, their gloomy cast painting the world in hues of slate and ash. The town itself is a patchwork of small, fragmented islands stitched together by sagging wooden docks, each plank warped by years of salt spray and relentless tides. Scattered houses cling to the edges of the islands, their weathered walls leaning against the persistent wind. At the heart of it all stands the tallest island, crowned by a solitary lighthouse.

It's quite a grim sight.

Fishing nets sprawl like webs across the docks, their fibers stiff with brine. Arching metal lanterns sway gently, their flickering lights casting pale reflections on the water below. The wood beneath our feet creaks with every step, though its protests are nearly swallowed by the ceaseless roar of waves crashing against the pilings. The air is thick with salt, so sharp it sits on my tongue.

Zemm nudges me a bit. "Alright?" he asks.

"Of course," I say.

My gaze drifts to the ship docked ahead, the one that could take me home if I wanted. But instead, we're heading Northeast, toward Frondvale.

Thorne had done nothing but argue over it, but dismissed me without offering any alternative or a decent enough reason *not* to go. Because she's annoying.

We approach the end of the longest dock, where a man stands supervising the loading of a large ship. His rough features turn toward us. "Yeah?" he asks gruffly.

Thorne steps forward, revealing her coin purse. She dangles it before him, the sound of clinking metal cutting through the air. "How much for a ride to Candlewood?"

The man's eyes sweep over us. "Candlewood?" He scoffs. "Nothing."

Thorne yanks the pouch back, her grip tightening. "Nothing? That's lucky for us, I suppose."

"Not really," the man says. "I'm not going to Candlewood."

Thorne laughs. My eyes dart behind him, searching for another ship, but most had already set sail.

I step forward, desperation edging my voice. "What can I give you to take us to Candlewood?"

The man doesn't waver. "Nothing. I'm not going that far for fun."

"It isn't for fun. We'll pay you." My fist clenches. "I really, really need—"

"I'm too busy," he interrupts, his tone flat. "Take a horse."

Take a horse? Is that a joke?

"Do you know how long that would take?" I ask.

"No idea, but it's not my business."

"I can do anything for you." I offer, my voice slipping into a plea.

His resolve remains unshaken. "No. Have a nice day." With that, he turns and walks away.

I want to scream, but the crashing waves would drown the sound before it left my throat.

For once, Thorne stays silent, though her expression is a smirk of vindication.

"Well," she says finally, her voice laced with mockery. "Guess Frondvale isn't the right place after all. You were wrong."

"No, I wasn't," I snap, anger boiling over. "Queen Satra told me my brother is in Frondvale. The guard said the human king is looking for me. Sunlight? Are you kidding? I'm not wrong. We need to go."

"You want to walk right into his grasp?" Thorne counters.

"Maybe he has her," I said, my voice trembling. "Maybe I need to free her."

"I think Lyri, is right," Lapis interjects. "We need to figure out another way."

Thorne smirks wider, addressing me, "why don't you just relax for once?"

"Relax?" The word come out as a snarl. "I can't! Why do you constantly have to argue with me?" My anger flares hotter, directed squarely at Thorne. My hands shake, and I press one to my chest, trying to steady myself. "This is your fault."

An exaggerated laugh escapes her. "Ha! My fault? That's hilarious."

"This is no one's fault," Zemm says.

"It is! It's her fault. She's led by greed and hatred."

Thorne shrugs with a pasted smile on her face. "It's not my fault the ship won't go to Candlewood. You're so superstitious, don't you think that's your goddesses telling you you're wrong?"

Her jokes aren't funny. They never have been. Without

thinking, I snatch a dagger from her hip and press its cold edge against her neck.

Lapis and Zemm freeze, their faces pale with panic, but Thorne, Thorne keeps smirking. She doesn't flinch, doesn't cower. Instead, she stares back at me with infuriating calm, as though daring me.

"I let you do that," Thorne breathes, her voice like a coiled snake.

"No, you didn't." I reply, the tension in my hands betraying my calm tone.

Before I can react, she moves fast, drawing her other dagger and pressing it to my neck. Her thumb applies more pressure than mine, and though my hands tremble, I don't back down. The cold steel against my skin sends a shiver down my spine, but I meet her gaze unflinchingly.

"Enough!" Zemm shouts.

Thorne's lips curve, parting slightly as she whispers, "Do you even know how to use a knife, Faelyri?" My name drips from her tongue, barely audible but sharp as the blade she wields.

And I just realized this is the first time she's ever used my name.

"You told me I was turning into a killer."

"Not like me." She leans closer, the blade pressing deeper into my skin. Our noses nearly touch, and her breath brushes against my cheek. I won't let it distract me. "Don't get me excited. Drop the knife."

"You first." My voice trembles, failing to sound as threatening as I want it to be.

She doesn't move, her smirk unwavering. In response, I press my blade just a bit further. I could do it. End this now. It would be justified. I can cut her life down before she has a chance to enact whatever plan she has to betray me. Just a little farther...

"Stab me," she says, her tone daring. "Do it."

Her eyes lock me in place, their intensity rooting me to the spot. She mouths something—*come on,* maybe? I can't tell. I can't think.

Then she exhales deeply, closing her eyes for the briefest moment. Her blade drops, clattering against the wooden dock with a sound that echoes in my ears. She raises her hands, surrendering. My hands are still trembling as I pull the dagger from her throat and offer it back, blade pointed outward. She takes it, her hand brushing against mine.

"That's not how you pass off a knife," she says.

I jerk my hand away and yank my hood over my head, my body still trembling. I take a final look at her, at her neck. There is no cut, only a harsh burn.

As I finally turn and storm off, the rotting wood beneath me cracks. My foot plunges through, and a sharp cry escapes me.

Behind me, Thorne's laughter rings out. My face burns with embarrassment as I pull my foot free and continue my dramatic exit.

I walk down the docks, away from the group, away from her. I don't know where I'm going, maybe to find a place to sleep, maybe to follow that irritating man's advice and find a horse.

Or I could go home. That's always been an option. Go home and find Syvis.

My choices seem to boil down to two: find a ship to take me home, where I might be killed immediately, or go to Frond-vale in search of Filauria, where I might also be killed immediately.

And if I run into Ilriel? What will I say? What will I do?

I already know what I *want* to do. Use the last bit of life in this weapon to snuff out his.

There is a third option, of course. There has always been a secret third option: toss the Nightstrand into the ocean and live as a hermit in the woods.

The weapon hums angrily on my side.

I stop on a patch of solid ground away from the docks and glance around at the bleak town with it's oppressive air. Very few people roam, wearing expressions of irritation. I need someone, anyone. Someone who doesn't look like they'd immediately turn me away.

"Lyri!" Lapis calls. I turn to see her jogging toward me, her blonde hair catching in the wind.

The fabric of my hood threatens to fly out of my fingers as the gusts threaten to expose me. "I'm leaving," I tell her. "Thank you for being kind to me. I'll never forget you."

She sighs deeply, her face exasperated but gentle. "Stop being dramatic. We're going to Frondvale."

I cross my arms, skeptical. "We? You're the only one here."

She shoots me a half-smile. "You excited Thorne too much. She needs a cold bath."

Gross. I twist my face in disgust. "You can come with me. Just you. And Zemm, actually."

She shakes her head. "We can't leave Thorne behind."

"Why not?" My voice sharpens. "She doesn't need either of us. She's mean and arrogant and collects shiny new women to fill the void in her soul."

Lapis raises a brow. "Want to hear my theory on why she acts like that?"

"She's a lonely pervert," I don't care for the real answer. I don't care about Thorne's tragic backstory.

Her expression softens, her eyes warm and kind. "No," she says gently. "I think she just wants to give people a fighting chance, but I also think she's guarded. Afraid of something. Maybe herself."

The words hit me harder than they should. My chest aches, and I hate it. Lapis really is too kind for this hard world.

She steps closer and wraps her arms around me. For a moment, I freeze. It's the first real hug I've had in... gods, how long? I've forgotten how warm they are, how safe they make you feel. All I've wanted is comfort, and now that it's here, it threatens to break me.

"You know," she murmurs, "Zemm really wants to see your light-up floors."

I push away gently, unable to meet her gaze. If I look up, I'll cry, and I've already cried too much lately.

"Just let me be by myself for a little while," I say softly. "Let me... meditate or something."

She nods, understanding.

CHAPTER

SIXTEEN

The map trembles in my hands, its edges curling under the relentless gusts. Sugarport lies at the southernmost edge of Farfell, while Frondvale is far, *far*, north.

A direct path would lead me straight into the shadow of Mirrormire: the deepest, darkest, most dangerous forest on the continent.

I can't go through there. No, I'll have to go around. It would add a day, but if I hurry, push myself, I can make up that time. I *will* make up that time.

I clutch the parchment tightly as the wind lashes at me, tugging at my cloak. The storm is rising, its fury growing stronger with each passing moment. My cloak flutters like a desperate bird. At my hip, the rope tethering the Nightstrand in place barely holds. Its faint hum vibrates a melancholy song, begging for a safety that has been denied to us both.

With a sigh, I roll the map and tuck it into my sack. My eyes scour the desolate landscape for shelter. Through the swirling rain, I spot a stable. A small, rickety structure with sagging beams.

Good enough.

I force the wooden door open against the wind's resistance. The smell inside is thick and rank. Wet straw, old leather, and the musk of horses. It's vile, but it's better than the open fury of the storm.

Making my way to the back, I sink onto a pile of coarse hay, its prickling digging into my skin. Thunder shakes the walls, and the shutters on a lone window slam like a drumbeat. Rain splashes through the gaps, icy droplets stinging my skin.

Still, it's far better than the fall from the cliff, the wagon I'd been imprisoned in, or the cold cell of Grimehold.

I wrap my cloak tightly around me, drawing my knees to my chest as I lean against the wall. What would Syvis think of me sleeping in a stable? Her heart would give out. I'll keep this bit to myself when I see her again.

I'd like to get something for Agnat. For when I see her again.

A pang cuts through my stomach. "Everything is awful," I mutter under my breath. The Nightstrand hums again in quiet agreement.

The worst part of it all? I miss Ilriel.

Perhaps I should have made more friends. I would have had others to spend my time with and I wouldn't be so stuck on him. We did everything together. I want to go back to that time. I want to go back to the lunch before he told me about that trip to Frondvale. I want to go back to when he was the one using this stupid, dying thing that has me trapped. I miss my life, and I miss Syvis, and I miss my bed.

But I truly miss Ilriel more. Or at least the memory of him.

Perhaps, when I find him again, I can reason with him. I have no desire to fight. I will if I have to, but I really don't want to.

A creak of the opening door pulls me out of my self-pity.

Peeking out from under my hood, my stomach drops. The last person I ever want to see. The one person who seems destined to shadow and torment me.

She steps inside, her wet boots scuffing against the worn wooden floor. Lowering herself to sit, she folds her arms over her knees, eyes fixed on the door she entered through.

She doesn't speak, so I break the silence. "How did you know where to find me?"

Her head turns, and loose strands of hair fall across her face. "You're predictable," she says, voice low but edged with that familiar sharpness. "I knew you wouldn't have the nerve to knock on a door and ask for shelter. And you'd never head back to Sunstill in this weather. You're too—" She pauses, her lips pressing into a thin line.

Whatever insult she's holding back dies, and she turns her gaze forward again.

"Where are you staying?" I ask.

She closes her eyes, leaning her head back against the wall without answering. After a moment, she rises, crossing to the violently slamming window. With a swift motion, she pulls it shut.

"You'll catch your death letting yourself get soaked like that," she says without looking at me.

"It doesn't matter," I reply flatly.

"It does," she counters, her tone sharp. "I used up the last of my Slugroot while you played your game of pretend."

She retakes her place beside me, pulling her arms around her shivering body.

"What are you doing?" I ask.

And, nothing.

"Why are you here?" I grind my teeth when I get no response from her. "Go inside," I order.

Her teeth chatter.

We lapse into an uneasy stillness. Wonderful. "Answer me."

"I have to get you there alive. So I have to make sure you *stay* alive. Don't mistake it for a personal concern over your wellbeing."

"It feels more like you delight in tormenting me at night."

Like she needs to get me alone to strike.

Thorne leans back against the barn wall, eyes closed. She shifts, probably trying to get comfortable in the freezing cold.

I sigh. "So, what? You're just going to let yourself freeze to death out here to make sure I stay alive?"

"Don't read into it."

The weight of the air presses down on me, the kind of weight that's impossible to ignore. I need to shatter it before it smothers me. I just need to change the subject.

I have questions for her, but I don't want to know anything about her, personally. Not her past, her habits, her dreams. Nothing. That knowledge feels dangerous. I don't want it.

I do not care why she has that knife with the crest of the royal human family on it. Or why, when no one is around, she almost melts into someone else. Or how she got caught up living in a sewer. I do not want to know where she is from.

But I *do* want to know her plan. And I need to know something else.

"Why have you been fighting me on Frondvale?"

"Because it sucks."

Does it?

"Are you a fugitive?" I demand.

"Are you worried about me?"

"I'm worried about myself," I repeat her own words from Sunstill back to her.

Her expression stays perfectly blank. Her mask never falters as she gives her vague answers, "maybe."

Her gaze falls to my face, her eyes tracing the bridge of my nose. I glance at her neck and the faint burn across her skin where I pressed the blade's edge to her neck.

"What happened to your neck?"

"You tried to slice it open. Terribly."

"Would it not have cut?"

"The blade was hot." She turns her head away, her lips curling upward into a smile. "I can never decide if I hate you or not."

"You can't decide?"

"Don't you feel the same?"

"No. My hatred for you has never wavered."

She tilts her head. "Do you know what your face looks like when you're panicked? Have you seen yourself?"

"I don't often prioritize finding a mirror when I panic, no."

She chuckles, "it's funny."

"So you think it's funny when I panic?"

She reaches for a strand of my hair, her fingers brushing against it as she watches the colors shift in the dim light. I bat her hand away, but before I know it, my own hand reaches out, grasping *her* face.

Her chin rests in my palm as my eyes scour her features. The bold lines of her brow, the delicate sweep of her lashes, the sharp elegance of her nose.

"You want to kiss me?" she whispers, her breath a ghost against my skin.

"No." Heat flushes my face as I pull myself away. This is part of it. To make me vulnerable. To trust her.

"Panicking," she murmurs, a sly grin tugging at her lips. "I want—"

The barn door creaks open, cutting her off. Two figures tumble in, soaked and shivering. Lapis and Zemm, dripping water all over the hay.

Thorne lets out a sigh.

"What are you doing?" I ask, my voice sharp.

"We decided we should all sleep in the barn," Lapis says with a grin. "Good for bonding."

"You'll freeze," Thorne snaps.

"So will you," Lapis shoots back without missing a beat.

Zemm shrugs. "We thought it was better than leaving you two alone to kill each other."

I exhale loudly, avoiding Thorne's eyes. I won't ask what she was about to say. I'm not sure I even want to know.

But here, now, there's a warmth growing in my chest as I watch Lapis and Zemm attempt to get comfortable on the hay. Sitting in this horrid stable. I'm not alone. I have friends. Two of them, right here.

&

As we walk, I fidget with the edge of my sleeve, my stomach twisting itself into knots. My earlier outburst gnaws at me and my cheeks flush with embarrassment.

We tread across the slick, waterlogged docks, the warped boards groaning beneath our steps. Ahead, the town entrance looms, framed by the soft glow of lanterns swinging in the damp breeze.

"I knew you'd get over it," Lapis says, her voice carrying a smug confidence. She turns to Zemm. "Didn't I tell you?"

"You did," Zemm replies, his tone flat but amused.

Wait, what?

"Have you been talking about me?" I ask, narrowing my eyes at Zemm.

His gaze stays fixed ahead. "Of course. It's all in my book."

I blink. "Your book? What does it say? What have you been saying about me?"

Before he can answer, Lapis points ahead with exaggerated cheer. "Oh, look! We're here!" She makes a beeline for the wagon waiting by the town's edge.

I grab Zemm's sleeve and tug, lowering my voice. "Is it bad?"

He doesn't answer, but the faint twitch at the corner of his mouth scares me.

Near the wagon, two women are huddled together, gossiping. Their whispers carry just far enough for me to catch fragments of their conversation.

"A twilight elf! Imagine! They say she tried to kill the King of the twilight elves."

I stiffen. What an absurd lie. My fists clench, but I force myself to keep walking.

Ignore it.

The other woman gasps, her voice sharp with scandal. "Where is she now? Surely locked up."

"They never caught her," the first woman whispers. "King Claude sent orders across the kingdom. She's left a trail of bodies in every city she's visited, along with her servants. They say she's trying to wipe out Farfell itself. It happened right in Sunstill!"

The second woman's gasp is so loud it turns heads. I pull my hood lower, grateful for the mask hiding the lower half of my face. My heart thunders in my chest, but I fight to stay composed.

Is *that* the story they're spinning about me? That I'm some ruthless killer? A monster pulling strings from the shadows?

Ridiculous. I roll my eyes under the hood. I was a hostage and yet somehow I've become the villain.

My anger bubbles over, and before I know it, I'm striding toward them, ready to interject.

"Hey—"

A hand clamps down on my shoulder. Thorne steps in front of me, her face a mask of cold authority. "Ignore it. Keep your head down."

I exhale sharply, my heartbeat slowing. She's right. I bite back the words on my tongue and let her guide me away.

"Did you *hear* them, though?" I mutter as we pass the women.

"You're famous," Thorne says, her voice dry.

If only they were talking about the truth. About how I've survived the impossible, dragged through this cursed underworld of a land, and persevered, coming out stronger for it. But no. How many believe those lies?

What happens if I become a queen with a reputation so tarnished no one dares speak to me, let alone trust me?

"Lyri, you okay?" Lapis nudges me.

I nod stiffly, though my thoughts are spiraling. I want to tell her I'm fine, that I'm just tired, but the words stick in my throat.

I might pass out.

We reach the wagon, and Zemm extends a hand to help me climb in. It's small and cramped, not enough seats for everyone, so I settle on the floor. A week ago, I would've been furious about that, but now? I don't care.

I focus on keeping my emotions locked away, like Thorne does. Like Ilriel does. Queens don't cry. Queens don't falter.

I've let myself be blinded by love, ignoring the cracks beneath my feet until the ground gave way. Never again. If I'm to be a ruler, I can't let my emotions cloud my judgment, not even when faced with blatant lies about me. That's really no way for a ruler to behave.

But how does a ruler behave? I know how Ilriel behaves, but what about me?

But... I think my friends believe in me. And I think that could be enough.

You do not have to understand it. You just have to do it.

Syvis's words are haunting, mostly because she's right. I have to do it, even if doing things is hard. My first job as queen is to make sure my country doesn't collapse, that's easy. My second job, confronting Ilriel, will be much harder.

CHAPTER

SEVENTEEN

The wagon jolts to a stop, and my head thuds against the side. I groan, rubbing my temple as I blink away the haze of sleep. My vision is blurry at first, but it doesn't take long to realize we haven't even reached a town.

"Wha—?"

"Main roads are too risky," Thorne interrupts. "This is as far as the wagon goes."

"Great." I slide out onto the dirt path, still half-asleep. "Won't that take too long?"

"Actually, it's shorter," Zemm replies as he hops down beside me. "We can cut through the forest."

"Exactly," Thorne says with irritating smugness. "This is a shortcut."

As the wagon clatters away, leaving us behind, we turn and head toward the dense line of trees. I tilt my head back, gazing up at the canopy as we walk. The woods grow thicker with each step, the air turning cooler and more shadowed. Soon, the underbrush becomes so dense it's nearly impossible to move without brushing against branches and vines.

This is *not* a good shortcut.

I glance at Zemm, who's far better with direction than the rest of us combined. He should be leading, he's the smart one. Instead, I'm stuck swatting at branches while Thorne hacks through them with a knife. The others follow her path. I refuse. Her method is undoubtedly more efficient, but I will not admit it.

After an eternity of battling the forest, the trees finally start to thin out. My relief is short-lived. A rustling catches my attention from the shadows to my right.

"Do you hear that?" I whisper.

"It's probably just an animal," Thorne says, much louder than she should. "Leave it alone."

I strain to listen, and when I glance at Zemm, he meets my eyes. His voice is hushed. "The movements are too deliberate to be an animal."

I nod. Someone is out there, watching us. Before I can say as much, an arrow whizzes past Zemm's head, embedding itself in a tree trunk.

"Told you." My smirk comes automatically, but it really isn't the time for that.

Thorne scowls, her other dagger already in hand, as if her blades could block arrows. Two figures step out from the shadows: human bandits. One of them grips the bow that releases the arrow. I can't wait to see who's faster.

I keep my focus on the figures ahead as Thorne steps in front of me, both blades gleaming. "You didn't have to shoot," she snaps at them.

A third figure emerges from the trees, and my heart drops. A twilight elf. Her unmistakable ghostly white hair glows faintly under the pillars of sunlight filtering through the canopy.

Farren.

Oh, lovely.

She found me. She followed the trail I left behind by being reckless.

I grab onto Thorne's shoulder and pull her down a bit. She keeps her eyes locked on Farren as I whisper in her ear. "I know her."

Farren's cold gaze locks onto mine, her lips curling into a smile that doesn't reach her eyes. "Princess Faelyri," she says, her voice smooth and mocking. For once, she pronounces my name correctly. "I have come to bring you home."

Home? That's doubtful. More likely, she's here to deliver my head in a sack. Farren would never be leading a search party for me, Syvis would.

"You're lying." I square my shoulders, puffing out my chest in an attempt to look braver than I feel.

Farren's expression doesn't change. If she's angry, she hides it well.

"I have a portion of the reward right here, which I was told to offer your... *companions*," Farren says coolly, motioning to one of the humans. They hand her something wrapped in deep green velvet. She unfolds it slowly, taking her time.

It's my crown.

Thin golden branches adorned with moonstones glint in the light. Its shape is unmistakable, perfectly molded for my head.

Bring me my sister's head, and you can have her crown. How twisted.

Farren holds it up for all to see. "Land and a title!" she calls out, her voice ringing with twisted glee.

"Shit," Thorne mutters under her breath, though there's an infuriating smile playing on her lips. It is heart-shattering.

My shattered heart feels like it's shriveling into nothing. Time slows. The world is distant. Warped.

This is the betrayal.

"Well, there you go," I say, my voice not as harsh as I intend as I turn to Thorne. "You can finally move out of your sewer." The word drips with venom, and I hope it stings.

"The crown for the girl," Farren begins, her voice dripping with mockery. "You'll want for nothing for the rest of your short lives."

Thorne sheathes both of her daggers, and my stomach tightens. "Really? The crown?" she asks, her tone sharp.

"Yes," Farren replies smoothly.

Thorne tilts her head. "And my land? Does the crown come with the title attached, or is that something I'll have to invent myself?"

"You'll have it all," Farren says, gesturing grandly. "After I get the girl. So hand her over."

My legs feel like they're made of water.

"Nope," Thorne snaps, her tone resolute. She nods toward the crown in Farren's hand. "Not until you're far away from that. No offense, but I don't trust you."

"You can't sell her!" Lapis cuts in, her voice panicked. "Are you insane?"

Thorne ignores her, as if her voice doesn't even register.

Over the static building in my ears, I force out a question. "Where's Ilriel?"

"You'll see him soon," Farren says with her usual infuriating calmness.

I've been tired of her for years, and now, I've reached my limit.

I unclip the Nightstrand from its holster. My hands work almost of their own accord, shaping the bow. I draw it back, aiming the glowing arrow directly at her. "That's not an answer."

Thorne's voice cuts through the tension, low and tight. "Drop your weapon, you idiot."

But I'm past caring. Farren's plan is sloppy, reckless, and stupid. She should've sent someone else, *anyone* else, and maybe it would have worked.

I am very gullible, after all.

But she came herself, cocky. I really hate her. I steady my aim, the arrow pulsing with its own energy, its thoughts mingling with mine.

"You're going to shoot me?" Farren asks, her voice dripping with condescension.

"You tried to shoot me," I snap, my grip tightening as my heartbeat roars in my ears.

She laughs, a sound that grates on my nerves. "Faelyri," she spits, mangling my name. "Put the bow away. You were always terrible with it. You can't even hit a stationary target. You were far better suited to your other... mindless hobbies."

Thorne, however, steps closer, her smile gone. "You shouldn't talk to her like that," she warns, her voice sharp as steel. "In fact, you shouldn't even look at her."

What? My eyes dart to Thorne before snapping back to Farren. Thorne continues, "I've changed my mind. I won't be handing her over and we'll be on our way. But I'll take the crown."

Farren scoffs, her lip curling. "And what are you supposed to be? Her guard dog?"

"I'm no one's guard."

"Drop the bow," Farren orders, "I won't ask again."

In response, I loosen the arrow. It streaks through the air, whistling as it embeds itself into the eye of the human standing beside her, the one who had handed her my crown. He drops with a dull thud.

Another arrow forms in my hand. Its energy crackles as I notch it. "You've always been the worst—" I begin, but my words are cut short by the rustling behind us.

More humans emerge from the thicket, accompanied by a massive wolf. My stomach sinks. Of course, she wouldn't come alone. But the wolf? I don't want to shoot an animal.

The beast lunges at me, teeth bared and snarling. I release the arrow, but it misses.

Before it can reach me, Lapis's hammer crashes into its muzzle with a sickening crack. The wolf howls and collapses, its body twisting as it scrambles to its feet.

"Don't touch my friend, you stupid, ugly animal," Lapis growls, her voice as fierce as the blow she landed.

"Incredible," Thorne mutters under her breath.

Shut up. Nothing about this is incredible.

I let out another arrow, taking down the woman to Farren's left.

The wolf rises again, its jaw hanging at an unnatural angle. It whimpers. To my left, Zemm is locked in combat with one of the bandits. A shimmering barrier flares between them, dropping briefly as he casts fire toward his opponent. She dodges until a flame catches her arm, and she screams, gripping her blade tighter.

Then she retaliates, slashing across Zemm's chest. He staggers, blood spilling from the wound, but his fingers spark with energy. A bolt of lightning leaps from a rune near his hand, striking her dead. The smell of charred flesh fills the air.

Lapis, meanwhile, brings her hammer down on another bandit's shield. The sound reverberates like a gong as the metal fractures. When the wolf leaps at her again, she swings backward, shattering its jaw entirely. It collapses, lifeless.

I raise my bow, ready to take aim at another man, but the Nightstrand's bow vanishes from my grip. The celestial energy that had pulsed in my hands just moments ago is gone, leaving only the lifeless hilt. I try to summon it again, but nothing happens. Panic wells up in my chest.

How could it just vanish? I smack the Nightstrand against my hand in desperation.

Lapis swings her hammer with a ferocious cry, slamming it into the skull of the bandit she's fighting, and he crumples. She stumbles back, panting, then sprints toward Zemm, who's still grappling with his injuries.

I'm frozen, staring at the lifeless weapon in my hand, my mind racing. I pour every ounce of willpower into it, channeling everything I have left.

"Now's not the time to die," I whisper through gritted teeth. "Please work. Just for a little while longer. I've almost found her, I promise."

Maybe this is punishment for turning my weapon against my own people. Maybe the Goddesses saw it as an insult.

But I've let my guard down for too long.

I have never felt such intense physical pain as when the knife plunges into my arm. The scream that rips from my throat is like nothing I've ever heard before. Raw, blood-curdling. I stumble back, the blade still lodged in my flesh. My arm hangs uselessly at my side, but I refuse to let go of the Nightstrand. Even dead, even silent, I won't abandon it. Not while Farren is still here. Not ever.

I grab the knife's hilt. At first, there's no pain, just a strange, hollow numbness. But as I rip it free, the agony comes roaring to life, shooting down my arm like fire. My breath hitches as my skin tears, the shock leaving me reeling.

The man who stabbed me doesn't last long. Thorne's dagger slashes across his throat in a messy arc, spraying blood as she snarls. Her gloves are soaked crimson, her teeth bared in a feral expression. Even after he's dead, she doesn't stop. She plunges her dagger into his face. Once, twice, three times, before throwing him aside like trash.

I've never witnessed anything so terrifyingly unhinged.

Farren is the only one left, and I know I can't fight her like this. My arm is useless, and the Nightstrand is silent. I can't even lift it. But Farren doesn't come for me. Instead, she charges at someone more worth her time: Thorne. Her blade comes down toward Thorne's crossed daggers. Thorne is quick, and skilled, but she's incredibly outmatched. Farren keeps her on the defense, forcing her back with every calculated strike.

There's a reason my brother chose Farren as his guard. Thorne is going to die.

I whisper in Elven, begging the Nightstrand to return its power. The pain in my arm is a constant, searing reminder of my failure, but I smack it against my palm again and again. Nothing.

The weapon is dead.

Thorne, against all odds, manages to knock Farren's long blade out of her hand. It clatters to the ground, and for a heartbeat, Farren's composed mask slips. She reaches for it, but Thorne kicks it aside. Farren, ever prepared, draws a dagger and lunges. Thorne blocks, but she's running out of space, her movements slowing under the relentless assault.

I can't let everyone die here.

My body shakes as I fight the pain, forcing my arm to lift. My grip on the Nightstrand falters. "Wake up," I plead. "Please. Just this once."

For a moment, there's only silence. Then, the faint, familiar hum. The low, resonant song of the Nightstrand returns, and the bow reforms in my hand. The celestial energy steadies me as I notch an arrow. My aim is shaky, my body barely holding together, but I don't care.

I let the arrow fly. I hope I don't miss.

It strikes Farren's hand as she raises it for another strike, pinning her to a tree. She cries out, clutching the wound as the arrow dissolves into starlight.

"Tell my brother I'll see him when I get home."

Farren doesn't waste a second. She bolts, vanishing into the woods like a shadow to escape the blade Thorne is going to thrust into her. The Nightstrand fades from my hands again, and this time, I let it. I drop to my knees, clutching my arm as the blood continues to flow.

The world shakes, my breathing ragged. Thorne appears beside me, sweat glistening on her brow. She kneels, her face tight with concern. "Are you alright?"

"Do I *look* alright?" I snap.

My body is cold, my throat is tight, and my brother's betrayal stings like the fresh wound on my arm.

He's a coward. Sending his guard after me across Farfell, to clean up his own mess, insulting and hurting my friends. What kind of ruler sends his lackeys to hide in the shadows and ambush his own sister in the woods? A terrible one. A wretched one. A coward.

Thorne ignores my tone and presses her hand over my wound, trying to stem the bleeding. Her touch is steady, sure.

"Zemm is worse," I mutter, glancing toward him. "Go help him."

She doesn't move. Instead, she wraps her arm around me, holding me upright. "It's not that deep," she says. Her voice is... soothing? "You'll be fine. I've had worse."

I want to believe her, but I've never been stabbed before, unlike her. So I won't put much weight in her words.

The pain burns, but I hold on. I have to.

"It hurts," I admit, eyes locked on her blood-covered hand.

Thorne eases me down until I'm sitting against the rough bark of a tree. She glances toward Lapis, who is crouched over Zemm, doing her best to tend to his wounds. "Are you almost done?" she calls.

"Yeah!" Lapis shouts back.

She's still holding pressure on my wound, her bloodied

hand steady despite the slickness. I place my good hand over hers, willing the bleeding to stop.

"Faelyri, I promise you, you will be okay," she continues, "what did you do for fun at home?"

"What?"

"All day, on your island, what did you do for fun?"

"Nothing. I did nothing."

"That's not true."

I groan. She's going to make fun of me. Use it in some way to hurt me. "Music. I like music. My weapon sings to me."

She lowers her voice, "sing to me."

I can't. I wouldn't be able to. I'm no good and my mouth is too dry. My body is too full of too many different things. I can't sing to her.

"I can't believe I'm going to die here," I mutter, my voice thin and tired.

She smirks, her confidence infuriating. "I told you, you're going to be fine. But you really shouldn't have pulled the knife out."

"I'm going to die here," I insist, "and I've never even had a girlfriend. Or kissed anyone. I'm going to die lonely and sad."

"Yeah, that's pretty embarrassing," she says.

I groan, the humiliation almost worse than the pain. Great. Dying *and* embarrassed.

She closes her eyes and leans forward until her forehead rests lightly against mine. Her breath is warm, calming, despite the storm raging in my chest. I think she's trying, really trying, to reassure me in her own awkward way.

"I thought she was going to kill you all," I whisper. The words escape before I can stop them, unbidden and strange.

"Don't underestimate me," she breathes.

"It's impossible to underestimate you."

Her head tilts, her nose brushing against mine. My lips almost part, almost.

"You were worried about me?" She asks.

No. That would be impossible.

"You would be no use to me dead," I answer.

She lifts her head, looking away from me. Any compassion in her expression has faded.

I move her hand away from my arm just as Lapis finally joins us. She kneels beside me and begins working on my wound. The bleeding slows, though the ache remains. When she finishes, I stand, light-headed but determined. I need to check on Zemm.

I kneel next to him, where he's lying on the ground. "Are you okay?" I ask, my voice low.

"Yeah," he grunts. "Just hurts to get up."

Thorne sinks to the ground as well, sitting amidst the carnage. "Why don't you believe I always have a plan?" she asks.

"Because you don't tell anyone your plans," Zemm replies.

Lapis walks over, holding something bundled in her shirt. When she lets go, a cascade of gold coins and coin purses spills onto the ground. My crown is among the haul, its familiar branches gleaming. "I checked the bodies," she says, proud.

"Awesome. You're the best," Thorne says, grabbing the crown and inspecting it with a smile. That smile.

Stop smiling.

Before anyone else can respond, I cut in. "I'm sorry, but I think we need to go."

Thorne clears her throat, then places the crown on her own head. She doesn't say a word as she adjusts it, tilting it slightly to the side. She wears it like it belongs to her, and in some frustrating way, it suits her. Regal. Confident. Infuriating. Beautiful.

"That's mine," I snap.

"After what I've gone through, dealing with you?" She retorts. "Half now, half later."

She finally removes it and shoves it into her bag without bothering to wrap it in its velvet covering. The clink of metal makes me flinch.

"We need to go," I repeat, my voice cracking. Every second we linger feels like a risk. The bodies around us, the open forest. It's all too exposed. And if Farren comes back with reinforcements...

"No," Lapis protests. "Zemm can't walk. You can't move someone this injured."

Zemm struggles to sit up, groaning as he rubs his chest. "I can walk," he says through gritted teeth. "Just not fast. I'm an orc. My body can take this."

"We're going to get you a better shirt, buddy," Thorne tells him. "No more cloth."

As Lapis begins to argue again, I help Zemm to his feet. His arm drapes over my shoulders, the weight pressing into my injured arm. I flinch but try to hold steady. Still, I droop a bit.

"I've got it," Thorne says, standing and taking my place. She shifts Zemm's heavy weight onto herself with ease, standing tall.

"We're close to an inn," I persist. "If we push through, we can make it."

"We need to stop!" Lapis snaps. "If we push too hard, we'll die. You can barely move your arm."

"My arm is fine," I lie, the pain shooting through me even as I say it.

"No, Lyri's right," Zemm says, his voice strained. "I'll be fine. Let's just get there."

Lapis exhales sharply, clearly exasperated. "Do you even know how long it'll take?"

"What if I go ahead?" I suggest. "I can run to the inn, get a horse, and come back. It'd only take a few hours."

"No," Zemm says firmly. "If I need to stop, I'll tell you."

Lapis places her hands on her hips, glaring. "And what if he dies?"

"He won't," Thorne says with a shrug. "He's too stubborn to die."

EIGHTEEN

The closest inn isn't in a town, just a lonely building tucked away in the middle of nowhere. We were lucky that it wasn't far, as Zemm struggled with the walk. I promised him we'd find a horse as soon as we could, but for now, I had to keep us moving forward.

The faint, fading hum of the Nightstrand spurred me on.

As we reach the inn's entrance, my gaze drifts north to the path that winds through the darkening forest. "I don't want to stay here," I say, my voice barely above a whisper. "I'm sorry."

"You'd rather camp?" Thorne scoffs.

I shake my head, "I'd rather keep walking. I need to get to Frondvale."

She sighs, rubbing the bridge of her nose "I understand the urgency—"

"And I appreciate that, so I would like to keep going."

As the two of us stand here, teetering on the edge of an argument, Lapis has already led Zemm inside. He stumbles slightly as he crosses the threshold.

"He can't walk." Thorne motions to the door, shoulders sagging.

"I have to go," I insist. "My brother knows where I am, and my weapon is dying. I can't stay here. I don't have the time. You can catch up once you find a horse."

I rub my stinging eyes, fighting to suppress a yawn. My lips press tightly together as I hold it in, my cheeks puffing out.

"One night won't change anything," Thorne says firmly. "You're injured, exhausted, and not thinking straight. And it's getting dark."

"One night can change everything. I've spent my whole life in the dark. I'm used to it."

Thorne's hand moves to the doorknob, her resolve cracking just slightly. The wood creaks as she opens it, her head dipping low. "Please," she says quietly, "just go inside. Or I will make you go inside."

I hesitate but enter the dimly lit inn over the cracked and weathered floorboards, with patches of greenery sprouting through the gaps.

At the back of the room, Lapis and Zemm are already seated at a worn table. Zemm's breathing labored. My own arm burns, but it must be only a fraction of his pain.

Perhaps I shouldn't have pushed so hard.

I slide into the seat next to him, crossing my arms over the table. My eyes dart between him and the rough wood grain beneath my hands. "I'm sorry for rushing you," I murmur.

He holds his chest, managing a faint smile. "It's alright. I get it."

My leg bounces under the table. The scent of fresh bread drifts through the room, making my stomach growl. I run my fingers through my tangled hair, wincing as they catch on knots. I'd been neglecting myself for too long.

"Lapis," I say, leaning toward her, "can I use your hairbrush again?"

"No," she snaps. "You keep losing it! How do you lose something when you don't even have anywhere to put it?"

I groan, slumping back in my seat.

When Thorne joins us, she isn't carrying mugs of ale. Instead, she holds a handful of room keys and a single drink for herself. She hands a key to Zemm. "Go upstairs," she instructs.

He doesn't hesitate, though he flinches when he stands too quickly. His breathing quickens as he takes the key with a trembling hand.

"Do you need help?" Thorne asks, her voice soft.

He shakes his head. His legs drag, but he manages to climb the stairs.

Thorne takes the seat next to me and slides another key to Lapis. "You should go too, if you're tired."

"I'm exhausted," she admits. "But I won't be able to sleep."

Fair enough.

I toy with the ends of my hair, leg still shaking. "I should go upstairs," I mumble.

Thorne's head is buried in her hand. Unsure if she heard me, I repeat myself louder: "I want to go upstairs. Can I have the key to my room?"

The loud chime of the inn's door cuts through the quiet murmur of the room. My head snaps toward it instinctively. A guard steps inside. The room falls silent, the air thick with unease. The crest on his armor catches the flickering light of the hearth. A member of the royal human army.

Before I can react, Thorne grabs my hood and yanks it down over my face, shoving me forward into the table. My chin nearly slams against the rough wood as she pins me there.

"Stop!" I hiss under my breath.

"Shut up," she snaps, her voice low and urgent. She pulls my head against her chest, her grip firm.

I do as I'm told, hiding myself within the folds of my cloak. My head so pressed against her chest that her heart pounds beneath my ear. It's racing, faster than I thought possible, bursting out of her, and the rhythm sends my own heart into overdrive.

"I'm looking for someone," the guard announces, "I have word she may have come this way."

My instincts betray me, and I start to turn my head toward him, but Thorne's arms tighten around me, holding me in place.

"Who're you lookin' for?" the barkeep asks, his voice gravelly. He's a small, wiry man with a hunched posture, but there's steel in his tone.

"A twilight elf. Her name is Faelyri."

He butchers my name. Great.

Thorne's heart pounds harder, and so does mine. Her breath is shallow and quick. This is precisely why I didn't want to stay here. We should've kept moving, even if it meant pushing through exhaustion. Farren must have tipped them off. This inn was the only logical place for me to stop, and now it's a trap.

Did the barkeep notice me when I came in? He hadn't paid me much attention, but now I can't be sure.

"Haven't seen one," the barkeep says casually. Is he lying, or did he truly not notice me?

The clink of armor grows louder as the guard steps further into the room. "I'll check anyway."

"I've got no one in the rooms," he lies. "The ones down 'ere are tired, get out."

"You can't order me to leave."

"Sure I can. The crown's done nothing for me, or my family. What do I care about you?"

Thorne lets out a short breath, maybe a chuckle.

The unmistakable sound of a sword being unsheathed rings. "I'm checking the place," the guard says coldly.

The barkeep doesn't argue further. The heavy thud of the guard's boots grows louder as he approaches, each step rattling my nerves. Thorne's arms tighten around me, the pressure bordering on painful. I pull my cloak tighter, wishing I could see what was happening.

The footsteps stop. He's here.

"Seen a twilight elf?" The guard asks, voice directed at our table.

We can't handle another fight. Not now.

"Nope," Lapis answers casually. "Where the hells is a dwarf gonna find a twilight elf?"

The guard doesn't laugh. "What about you?" he asks Thorne.

Thorne takes a long sip of her drink, the movement pressing against me as I stay hidden. She sets the mug down slowly. "Didn't he tell you to leave?"

"I don't take orders from a barkeep," the guard sneers.

Thorne tilts her head, her tone turning icy. "Right. Who do you take orders from, then? Which member of the royal family?"

What is she doing? Is she stalling?

"The King."

Thorne laughs. "Sure." She holds the fabric on the back of my head. I keep my eyes open, even if there's nothing but darkness as I'm pressed up against her.

"I know you, old man." She says. "Miserable, mean, always subpar with a sword."

She knows him?

The guard slams a fist against the table, making the mug jump. "Shut your mouth."

"Still trying to make captain of the guard, huh?" Thorne goads. "Always failing. So now you're here, harassing a kind old man in his inn?"

He lunges for her, but Thorne shoves me aside just as her knife flashes. The blade pins the guard's hand to the table, embedding deep into the wood. I hit the ground hard, dazed but scrambling to my feet.

With Lapis's help, I steady myself, just as Thorne twists the knife deeper. The royal crest on the blade gleams in the dim light, deliberately displayed.

"I don't want to kill you, because you're old and sad and your life is pointless," Thorne growls. "But now I'm worried that you'll come back with your friends and cause more issues for that kind man behind the counter."

The guard cries out, his face twisted in pain. "Why do you have that knife, thief?" he spits.

Thorne leans closer, her voice low and venomous. "Mind your business."

Her gaze darts to Lapis, and with a nod, Lapis swings her hammer into the guard's head. The blow echoes through the room. He collapses, lifeless, his blood pooling across the table.

Thorne rips the knife free, splattering crimson, and wipes it clean with a cloth before sliding it back into its sheath.

"Sorry!" I blurt out to the barkeep.

The old man barely reacts. After a moment, he grabs a mop bucket and mutters, "take him out back. I'll bury him."

Thorne kicks the table, the legs scraping loudly across the floor. "Fuck you," she snarls.

I can't stop staring at her. There's something raw and electric in her anger, in the way her shoulders tense and her breaths come sharp and shallow. She looks at him in the way I look at Farren.

"Are you alright?" I ask softly.

All she does is grunt.

"Who was that guy?" Lapis whispers.

Thorne doesn't answer. Instead, she slams a key onto the table, probably mine, before grabbing the guard's arms. Despite the weight of his armor, she drags the body across the floor with ease. With one hand.

The barkeep gestures toward the back door, and without another word, Thorne disappears through it.

Lapis turns to me, her face pale. "What... was that?"

I shrug, rolling the cool, chipped metal key between my fingers. My gaze drifts back to the door Thorne exited through, narrowing.

As I'm changing, there's a sharp sound of knuckles rapping on my door. Quickly, I slip my sleeping gown over my head, the fabric brushing against my arms as I softly step toward the door. One hand grips the doorknob, the other my weapon.

"Hello?" I call out, my voice quiet but steady.

There's no response, only silence. I try again, louder this time. "Hello?"

"Yeah, sorry." Comes Thorne's voice at last.

I open the door just a crack, sighing, peeking out to confirm it's really her. Her vest and gloves are gone, as are her boots. She's dressed simply in her black tunic and pants, weaponless. I step aside, setting my own weapon down as she slips in and closes the door behind her.

"You shouldn't keep coming into my room so late," I try to scold. But, actually, I think I'm almost grateful not to be alone.

"I came to check in," she says. Her eyes dart to the walls.

"My arm is okay."

"That's not what I meant," she replies, dropping onto the edge of my rented bed. Though it was almost a stumble back.

I wrinkle my nose at her. "You don't have to check on me."

I fidget with the ends of my hair, my gaze darting to the door and back to her. The words stumble out of my mouth. "Are you here for me? Or do you want to talk about downstairs? Do you just... need someone to talk to?"

She exhales heavily, the sound more resigned than frustrated. "No," she says sharply.

When I don't respond, she lays back on the bed, legs hanging off of the side, feet pressed to the floor.

"Then why are you here?" I ask. I want to press her about the guard, about everything that happened, but I'm afraid she'll leave if I do. And I don't want her to leave.

Why do I want her to stay? Am I that desperate for company?

I twist my hair tighter around my fingers, bracing myself for some flippant remark meant to amuse herself at my expense. Instead, she turns her head to look at me, her hair falling into her face. Her green eyes lock onto mine.

What is this expression? I don't know. Soft? Warm?

"Tell me about your guard," she says.

"Syvis?" I half-laugh, caught off guard. "Why do you care about Syvis?"

She shifts on the bed, the frame creaking as she rolls onto her side, propping her head on her hand. "Because you never talk to anyone. Anyone but the three of us."

"So?"

"So, do you think it was just proximity that drew you to her? Why her, specifically?" Her words are slurred.

"Are you drunk?"

She doesn't answer.

"I—" I stop myself.

I'm not going to admit how impossible it's always been for me to make friends or how Thorne herself is the only person who hasn't treated me like glass. And how much I think I like that, even when she's insufferable. Even if I have to constantly be watching my back.

I can never decide if I hate you or not. Don't you feel the same?

"What does she look like?" she asks suddenly.

I bite back a laugh. "Are you being serious?"

Her gaze sharpens, and I can't tell if she's teasing or

genuinely curious. My grip on my hair loosens slightly. "I don't know how to explain it."

"Does her hair shine like yours?" she presses.

"No."

"Does anyone's? Or are you the only fallen star in your kingdom?"

I shake my head, sighing. "Why are you asking me this? I'm not unique among the elves, no."

I'm actually very unremarkable, believe it or not. Nothing like some of the other elves. Like my mother. Nothing like Thorne.

I used to think my mother was the most beautiful person in the world. I was wrong.

"Because I'm curious."

My legs, too tired to keep me upright, finally give in. I sink to the floor, leaning my back against the bed. Thorne shifts again, lying on her stomach, her face now just above mine.

"You can't be too close with her," she says, her voice lower now, almost a growl. There's something new in her eyes, something raw and unspoken. Hunger, maybe. But the ale is strong on her breath. "Not with what you said when you were bleeding out. Dying in my arms in the woods."

My face burns at the memory, my gaze fixed straight ahead. "If you're drunk, you should leave."

She leans over me, her weight shifting onto her forearm as she closes the space between us. "Do you ever want to try?"

I pull my knees up, resting my chin on them as I curl into myself.

Her brows furrow as she searches my face. "Do you know what I'm asking you?"

"Of course I do." I don't know which question I'm answering, to be honest.

Her hand finds my chin, tilting my face toward hers. Her eyes bore into mine. "...Do you think I'm a monster?"

The words catch me off guard. I don't know how to respond. Two weeks ago, I might have said yes, called her a demon wrapped in beauty. But now, in this moment? After she insisted we rescue Lapis. After she saved me, too many times, from sudden death. After she comforted me while I was bleeding out. Now I'm not so sure. I'm still leaning toward yes, but not enough.

But perhaps Lapis was right. Perhaps she's just afraid of herself. Guarded like I am.

Her hand stays on my chin, her gaze steady and piercing. This isn't going to happen. Not here in this tiny inn where the walls are so thin that our neighbors may hear the conversation. I don't remove her hand from me, but I admit, "I don't know what to say."

"Tell me I'm not a monster," her voice trembles just enough to make my chest tighten. "Lie to me."

I exhale slowly.

"Just lie if you have to. You can lie. So lie to me."

"I—" If I tell her she isn't, she will think I'm lying. But if I don't say anything, she'll think I believe she is. Is this what she wants from me? Is she going to kiss me? Now? Drunk? Drunk would be the only way she'd do it. But she isn't drunk when she flirts with everyone else. Does she need to be drunk to flirt with me? That's cruel. She's cruel to me because she doesn't like me. She doesn't care. She just wants to embarrass me.

"Yes, I do."

The answer doesn't seem to satisfy her. She doesn't pull away, though. Instead, her hand moves to the back of my head, her fingers tangling gently in my hair. Her eyes follow the way it shifts and glimmers with each movement as if the sight has mesmerized her.

"I don't want to be," she whispers, "but I know I am. I'm wicked. I don't know if I can ever change. If I'm capable."

"Everyone is capable of change."

"You're naive," she rests her forehead on mine. "You have a very narrow view of the world. It's…"

It's what? Childish, is what I assume she was going to say to me.

I need to change the subject. Now. I need to pull away from her, but I can't. "How did you know that guard?"

"I had a job in Frondvale."

Oh… really? She never offers anything real. This is rare. My breathing slows, matching hers.

"My job, specifically, was…" Her voice trails off, and instead of finishing, she presses her cheek against mine. The warmth of her skin sends a strange shiver through me, and suddenly, I'm floating outside of my body.

I hate this. I hate the way she makes me feel weak, the way it feels like she has some invisible string tied to me, holding me here. I don't want anyone to have this kind of power over me.

"My job was very hard," she whispers, her breath brushing against my ear.

"In what way?" I ask, my voice barely audible.

She opens her mouth as if to answer, but the words don't come. I can see it in her eyes. She wants to tell me. Not me, just someone. Her face inches back so I can see her fully. Then, she gestures to her throat, her mouth still open, the words stuck there.

"That burn?" I ask.

She shakes her head.

"Did the royal family do something to you? Something you're too afraid to say?"

Again, she shakes her head, her expression unreadable. "They suck, trust me," she sighs. "But it wasn't them."

"Can you write it?" I press.

Her head moves side to side for the last time.

Her hand slides from my hair, trailing down to my back. Her fingers grip into the fabric of my dress and she's leaning in. Her touch sends a jolt through me, and I scramble away from the bed, suddenly unable to bear the closeness.

"You don't have to leave," I say quickly. "But I will. I know you're drunk. You can keep the bed."

She rises slowly, nearly staggering as she gets to her feet. "I'll leave."

She doesn't say anything else as she walks to the door. Her movements are slow, deliberate. The door creaks softly, and with a final glance back, she steps out, closing it behind her.

I stay frozen where I am, my chest heaving as I try to calm my racing heart. Sleep feels impossible now. The room feels too still, too empty, her absence more suffocating than her presence had been.

But that's part of her plan, I think.

CHAPTER

NINETEEN

I couldn't sleep at all last night. Every moment of our interactions replayed endlessly in my mind, each one worse than the last. At some point, I began to wonder if I'd gone entirely delusional, my thoughts fabricating scenarios that never even happened.

I shove it all down, locking it away where I can't feel the sting of it. I don't have the time, or the energy, to untangle the humiliation gnawing at me. Most of it comes from the fact that she was drunk, I'm sure.

I do not have the time to let myself feel anything for *anyone*, lest I forget the dangers of attaching myself to a person who is only my companion for monetary gain.

It goes beyond that. When I like someone, when I get attached to someone, they die. And then I have to go through that again and again and again. I'm too selfish to ever want to go through that again.

And yet, as we walk along the open dirt road, I can't help but watch her. The way she smiles at Lapis and Zemm. The way her gaze darts toward me when she thinks I don't notice.

Trickster.

I pull the map from my sack, unrolling it carefully to check our route. I have no sense of how far we've walked since leaving the inn. Not far enough, that's certain. And we won't be staying at another one anytime soon. It's too dangerous now.

I glance over my shoulder, a quick, paranoid sweep of the road behind us, then return my attention to the map.

A heavy sigh comes from beside me. Zemm is doing his best to keep pace, but there is strain in every step.

"How much longer do you think it'll take to reach Frond-vale?" I ask, raising the map for him to see.

Through labored breaths, he answers, "If I wasn't wounded, two days. Now? Three, maybe four. Maybe longer."

"It's alright," Thorne calls back over her shoulder. "We'll get there."

My arm aches. A sharp, persistent sting. I rub it absent-mindedly as if it would help. Lapis asks if I'm alright. I nod, brushing off her concern. It better not scar.

A forest looms ahead suddenly, a dark, tangled wall of trees rising from the earth like ancient sentinels. The edge of Mirrormire. Shadows cling to the gnarled branches, with air heavier and colder than any normal wood. I stop in my tracks, staring at the foreboding woods.

"When did we get here?" I murmur, panic creeping into my voice. "I can't go into Mirrormire."

Thorne stops beside me, arching a brow. "Why not?"

"I won't be welcome there," I reply, my voice tight.

Lapis stumbles over an exposed root, catching herself with an awkward flourish. "Why not?"

"Elf politics," I mutter.

Thorne, ever irreverent, waves a dismissive hand. "Oh, I'm sure you'll all get over it."

We truly will not. Mirrormire isn't just another wood, it's the domain of the swamp elves. We do *not* get along. We were separated by centuries of strife and bitterness too vast for her small mind to comprehend.

When Filauria led her exodus, she had been both brilliant *and* paranoid. Only her most loyal supporters were granted safe passage to Starview, while others, those who had hoped merely to escape the cruel grasp of Tae'ril, were left behind. Some found refuge in Farfell's caves or the snowy peaks. Others wandered the seas, the swamps. The deep forests.

I can't blame them for resenting us. We thrived in Starview's haven while they fought for scraps in harsh, unforgiving lands. But the resentment has grown like a festering wound, and I can't forget how unwelcome I'd be here. For normal travelers, this forest is dangerous. For me? It's a death sentence.

"We need to go around." I hold my ground.

Thorne crosses her arms, her expression hard. "We don't have time for that. Or have you forgotten how you insisted we hurry?"

I press my lips together, frustrated. This is exactly why I rushed them. So we wouldn't have to deal with this.

"Let's take a vote!" I throw my hands up, turning to the others.

Take my side.

"I'm not taking the long way," Lapis says without hesitation. "Not after you pushed us to get to Frondvale as fast as possible. You're being a hypocrite."

"I'm not being a hypocrite," I argue, though it sounds weak even to me.

I turn to Zemm, trying my best to appeal to him with the most pitiful expression I can muster. He taps his chest in response, shaking his head.

Right. Of course.

And Thorne? She shrugs as though the forest were no more dangerous than the market square. "I've never been in there, but I'm sure it'll be fine."

Fine? She's insane. I can't believe I almost kissed her. Twice. I've been away from home for so long that my standards must have fallen into the sewer she crawled out of. "Do you have any idea what this forest is?"

Her eyes squint as she angles her head up. "Well sure, I heard exaggerated tales about a changing forest."

I cry out, my voice rising. "This forest is alive. It changes. The stories aren't exaggerations. The trees whisper. They—"

Thorne doesn't wait to hear the rest, stepping boldly into the shadows, Lapis close behind, and Zemm following with a resigned sigh. My heart thuds painfully as I linger on the threshold. Then, with a deep breath, I step forward.

When my boot hits the mossy ground, a hushed sound passes me. With the light from above immediately choked by the dense canopy, shadows stretch and swirl like living things, and the ground breathes beneath my feet.

A hushed voice, speaking in Elven. I shiver. Is it a warning? A threat?

"Thorne, please." My voice edged with desperation. "This is a mistake."

She doesn't even glance back. "This is the fastest way."

"Then I'll go the long way," I snap. "Alone. I'll meet you on the other side."

"You'll do no such thing." She shoves me forward, too far forward, and I stumble deeper into the forest.

I whirl back toward the entrance, my pulse racing. But it's gone. The trees have closed in. "The entrance is gone!" I cry, my voice shaking.

"It's still there," Lapis said without concern, her gaze calm.

No. It isn't. I'm certain.

Ilriel had told me once how to escape Mirrormire. But I can't remember. Why can't I ever remember anything? Why am I so spacey? I clench my fists and push forward, each step sinking into the soft ground. My boots squelch. The whispers grow louder, words I can't quite make out.

I need to remember. If I don't we are going to be trapped here.

The roots of the enormous trees twist up from the ground, rising to my waist, and even higher on Lapis. The woods stretch endlessly in every direction, dark and suffocating.

"We just have to walk straight ahead," Zemm says. "If we walk straight, we can find the exit." How can someone be so intelligent, and yet so ignorant?

"It's dark in here..." Lapis breathes.

The deep green of the moss and leaves drink in what little light filters through the canopy. The shadows stretch longer, darker, and the air colder with every step.

Whispering? What did Ilriel say? Fire?

Should I burn this forest down?

A whispering pulls me from my racing mind, and I turn sharply. Nothing. My paranoia.

"Keep up," Thorne calls over her shoulder.

She's right. I can't keep getting distracted. My eyes dart between the trees, searching for the source of the noise. My fingers tighten around my weapon as it begins to vibrate faintly, its energy stirring. "Did you hear that?" I ask.

"No," Thorne replies.

Of course not. The only silver lining is that it can't be Farren. The thought of her scurrying back to Ilriel to report her failure makes me smile, if only briefly. But more whispering wipes the smirk from my face.

This time, I'm certain I didn't imagine it. I turn again, my weapon raised, scanning the darkened forest for movement. The twisted branches stretch like skeletal fingers. No sign of life.

Nothing.

I sigh heavily, letting my shoulders drop. *Paranoid.*

When I turn back, my heart stops. They're gone. The shadows have swallowed them whole.

"Hey!" I shout. "Thorne!"

I knew this would happen. Why does no one ever listen to me? Ignored in Starview, ignored here.

Are we all separated, or is it just me?

I lift the Nightstrand high, its faint hum of energy now silent, and wave it like a truce flag. Calling out in Elven, I try to summon any semblance of diplomacy or negotiation. Still, there's no answer.

The elves can't leave me here to die. They wouldn't, right?

So I walk. In which direction, I'm not sure anymore. The forest shifts, the paths bend, and I have no magical ability to dispel the illusions woven into them. How will I know if I've already been here? How will I know if I'm just walking in circles?

With no other choice, I do something I've never done before, I transform the Nightstrand into a knife. Its blade glints faintly in the otherworldly light. I mutter a quiet apology to the nearest tree, its ancient bark gnarled and twisting like veins, and carve an X into its surface. It's the largest tree I can find, its roots knotted around one another in a tangled embrace.

I'll keep track this way.

Knife in hand, I continue my hike. Every third or fourth tree bears my mark, and I keep my eyes forward, though I can't help but call out every now and then. Nothing answers me. Not my friends, not the forest, not the whispering voices that taunt me from its shadows. The silence gnaws at my resolve. The thought of the elves leaving me here to starve, to wander until my sanity frays and my mind slips... it's unbearable.

Just keep walking straight, right?

A breeze stirs my hair, and with it comes a memory, faint and elusive. Ilriel's voice, speaking of flame and the wind. The details slip through my grasp, but it's something.

I pause to mark my twentieth (I think) tree, stepping back to examine the X carved into the bark. My heart plummets. The roots at its base are familiar, twisting in the same knotted pattern.

This is the same tree.

My mark is gone. Their stupid forest rejected my attempt to outsmart it.

Adrenaline surges through me, cold and sharp. I've been walking for at least an hour, haven't I? I know I have.

As I stand frozen, one of the roots moves, slithering toward my leg like a snake. I stomp down, grinding it beneath my boot with all my strength. I swear I hear a faint cry, high and sharp, as the root recoils.

"Are you joking?" I shout in Elven, my voice cracking. "At least give me a chance!"

I stab the knife into the center of the X I carved. The forest falls silent again, save for the soft rustling of leaves as the wind picks up.

Wait, I remember.

I pull the knife free, holding it vertically. "Can you become a torch? Is that something you can do?"

It responds. The blade shifts, and a flame bursts to life at its tip, flickering. I hold it out, watching as the embers are carried by the breeze. They drift left.

Turning as needed, I let the flame guide me, though I don't know where it's leading. I just follow the flame, wherever it takes me.

Just follow the flame.

Then, in the distance, I see it: a faint light breaking through the trees. The exit. My heart leaps.

I figured it out. I'm a genius. Brilliant. Beautiful. Smart. Wonderful.

But my celebration is cut short. The flame sputters, flickers, and dies. The singing stops, and the light ahead vanishes.

The Nightstrand falls silent in my hand, its glow extinguished.

"Seriously? I don't have time for this," I mutter, shaking it in frustration. "Not in here. Don't die in *here*."

A voice answers me, smooth and laced with malice. It speaks in Elven. "So, you return."

My head jerks toward the sound. My grip tightens on the now-lifeless weapon. I *really* don't have time for *this*.

"Drop your weapon, Filauria."

Filauria? This forest must attract the mad and delusional. Farfell is where the mad come to die. Ilriel will fit right in.

I grit my teeth. "Let my friends and I out of your spell, and I will lower my weapon," I say, my tone firm despite the trembling in my hands.

"Friends? You have no friends," the voice taunts.

Harsh.

The voice shifts, now behind me. I whirl around, trying to find its source.

"The others are not in our spell," it continues. "They are free to leave these woods unharmed."

"Meet with me, face to face," I demand.

"No. You are not worthy."

"What then? You are going to let Starview's queen die here in your swamp?"

"You are no queen."

My hands shake as I strap the Nightstrand back to my hip. As if it matters now. I raise my hands in surrender, my voice bitter as I say, "Fine. Let us talk."

I've never attended one of my brother's negotiations, let alone led one. I have no idea how these things are supposed to go, but I'll try. I have to. If I can gain even the smallest measure of control here, I might just get out of this wretched forest alive.

The wind stirs the leaves, whispering in the silence around me. Then, from behind one of the massive, ancient trees, a swamp elf steps into view. His skin is a deep green, darker than Zemm's, with mossy horns of bark curling above his long ears. He leans on a staff, the wood gnarled and knotted with intricate patterns.

"I am not Filauria," I say, my voice steady despite my racing heart. "Faelyri Miavyre. Queen of Starview." I keep my hands raised, trying to project an air of calm authority.

"Liar." He spits at the ground in disgust. Fantastic. "Ilriel Miavyre is the king."

So he's heard of me. His information is outdated, though. That could work in my favor. Perhaps the rumors about me haven't reached these woods.

"Faelyri Miavyre is the traitor," he adds coldly.

Never mind.

He tilts his head, the maroon strands of his long hair falling over his shoulder as he listens to something unseen. His narrow, piercing eyes never leave me. The rustling of leaves grows louder. At last, he speaks again. "I was wrong," he says.

Obviously.

"Venali," he introduces himself. "Why are you in my woods?"

Why am I in his woods? Because no one ever listens to me. Of course, I can't say that. I have to be careful. "I would like to propose an alliance."

He growls, his teeth glinting faintly as his lips curl back. "Lying again. The trees tell me you are passing through, on your way to Frondvale. You lie like her."

Then why. Did. You. Ask?

"It is not a lie... entirely." Sure, I'm passing through, but an alliance would be nice. "Why do you think I am Filauria?" I ask, genuinely curious. I've never even seen her.

"You have her face," he replies, gesturing to his own markings.

I lower my hands slowly, but the motion makes him raise his staff. I touch my face, frowning. He must be mistaken. I'm tired of strangers telling me about myself. My jaw tightens, but I force myself to stay calm.

Keep it together. Keep it under control. Don't throw a tantrum.

"We are not related," I say firmly. "My mother's name was Narunn. My markings are from her. She is no longer with me."

"Who was her mother?" Venali responds swiftly.

I hesitate. I... don't know. I've only ever known my immediate family.

Venali tilts his head again, his attention drifting as he listens to the trees. I wish I knew what they were telling him.

"Does she come here often?" I ask, breaking the silence. "Do you know where she is now?"

"No," he replies curtly. "I have not seen her in ages. Perhaps she left Farfell," he continues, "though I doubt she was brave enough to return to Haelhil." His gaze sharpens. "You claim to be the Queen?"

I raise one hand, holding the Nightstrand out with the other. The weapon remains lifeless, silent. Can he sense that?

"You have her face, and the weapon, but the trees do not lie. Even if you are not her, you are a descendant. You sit on your isolated, dying throne of stars."

I flinch at his words. *I'm not a descendant.* My parents would have told me. Ilriel would have told me. Of all the secrets they kept, that wouldn't have been one of them.

"Listen," I say, my tone sharpening. "I am sorry for coming into your woods. I did not want to be here. My friends were the ones who chose this path. As you can see, I was on my way out."

"None of you ever take responsibility for your actions. You say your *friends* brought you here? Do you have no free will? " Venali sneers. "You are a terrible leader and worse at diplomacy."

We're not even having a discussion! I want to scream at him.

"You said I do not have friends, but I do," I argue. "And they will come back for me."

"They have no idea you are missing," he says, his voice like a dagger. "By the time they notice, they will be out of these woods, unable to return for you."

Well, that's just cruel.

"Well, Venali," I say, forcing my voice to remain steady, "what can I do to get out peacefully? I am alone, obviously not a threat, and I do not wish to fight."

He waves his staff, drawing a rune with the glow radiating from it, and the forest shifts around us. The towering trees and mossy roots give way to a strange village. The houses are built into the trees, their walls dripping with moss and fungus, the air thick with the sour scent of decay and vegetation.

I'm surrounded now by swamp elves emerging from the shadows, their eyes fixed on me, unblinking. They watch whispering in hushed tones, their voices like wind moving through reeds.

How long have they been here? Were they always watching, silent as fish behind murky glass? Or is this just another of Venali's illusions, designed to unsettle me?

His staff thuds softly against the ground with each step he takes. He leans on it, using it for balance, and I don't bother asking why.

But, how old is he?

"Starview's Queen and descendant of Filauria," Venali announces with a sharp edge to his voice. The whispers cease instantly. "She would like to ally."

Ignore it.

"What kind of alliance?" one of the elves asks.

That's an excellent question. Unfortunately, I do not have an excellent answer. I didn't think I'd get this far. My mind scrambles, searching for something that might sound convincing.

"You know my country is crumbling," I begin, my voice somehow steady despite the pounding in my chest. "My brother, Ilriel, claims he has a right to my throne. He has built a palace of greed and cruelty, forged an alliance with the human king, and now he seeks power, any power. He will come to

Mirrormire." I pause, drawing a breath. "If there is anything I can offer Mirrormire, let it be this warning. As a peace offering."

"Why would he come here?" another elf asks.

"Are you serious?" I scoff. "Your magic is extraordinary. He needs it. Once Starview falls, what else will he have left to conquer?"

If I don't get out of here, Starview *will* fall.

From within the stirring crowd, another voice rings out: "And why should we trust you, scion of a traitor? Your ancestor left us to die."

"I–" My voice falters when another joins the clatter.

"We were hunted, driven into this swamp, while you lounged in your gilded palaces."

"Well–" I try again.

A third voice, sharper than them all, a woman: "You shine while we have turned to rot."

Finally desperate to get a word in, *anything*, I turn to her, "that is not a very nice thing to say about yourself."

Her face twists into a snarl. Oops.

"Are you here to finish the job?" she snaps, voice brimming with venom. "Here to drive us out, just as Filauria cast us from your pathetic mountain?"

"I am *clearly* not a threat to you," I repeat myself from earlier.

"Then it will be easy to kill you," she retorts, eyes flashing with malice. "Let us end this now; an eye for an eye."

A murmur of agreement ripples through the crowd while my pulse pounds in my ears. I just have to force myself to stay calm. I can stay calm. Stay calm.

Ignoring her, I turn to Venali. "Were you there?" I ask.

He nods.

"I only know fragments of the story," I admit. "Pieces told

to me by my family. I know they were skewed. Will you tell me? Why you're here, in this swamp, while I sit in a..." I toss a glance to the woman, "gilded palace?"

Another elf steps forward, "your people attacked us when we landed on your island. They slaughtered us. Drove us onto this continent."

"Well," I say, fumbling for the words "I know... she was paranoid."

"And that gives her the right?" Another snaps.

"She was escaping a tyrant!" I protest.

"So were we!" someone cries out. "We were driven from the forests near Haelhil, but your ancestor deemed us beneath her!"

That can't be true. Can it? Paranoia drives people to madness. I would know.

The speaker gestures toward Venali, voice trembling. "He protected us. And now look at him. His leg is no longer flesh, but root."

Venali doesn't move to confirm, but the cane now makes a lot of sense.

The elf speaking aims an arrow toward me, and Venali doesn't stop him. "Keohwen is correct, we need to kill the girl."

"Slow down," I say, "I just want to understand. How did you even reach Starview, to be driven away?"

"We commandeered a ship. Your ancestor slaughtered us. Even the children."

"Herself? Or her allies?" I press.

The archer hesitates. His aim wavers.

"Do you even know?" I continue. "Were you there?"

The arrow slackens on the string, but it doesn't fall.

The woman, Keohwen, answers in his place. "She is one of them. She never punished them for their crimes, which makes her complicit."

"Did she know?" I can't keep myself from snapping. "Do *you* know if they were punished?"

Silence.

"I'm not excusing the slaughter, I promise" I say, "but you do not know if she sought retribution."

Venali finally speaks, his voice low. "She claimed she did."

"And what do your trees say?" I ask him.

His expression hardens. "They tell me she was not lying. It was one of her rare truths."

Keohwen growls, "the trees could be wrong!"

"Yes," Venali concedes. "They could be. But they have not been. At least not in all my years of listening."

She huffs, turning to the others. "Enough! Let us kill the girl and move on."

"Can I just leave?" I ask. I don't care how desperate or pathetic I sound.

Venali's voice softens, "my people requested this meeting. I wanted to give them the chance to speak."

"They've spoken," I reply, gesturing to the agitated crowd. "Let me go, and you will never see me again."

"As your apprentice," Keohwen starts, "I have made the decision that the girl must die."

She surges forward, blade flashing. I reach for the Night-strand, but it lies dormant in my grasp, silent.

Breathe. Breathe. I beg myself. My chest stings.

The blade arcs toward me.

She's fast, too fast, but Venali's staff strikes out, intercepting her blade before it can reach me.

"We have the right to kill her," Keohwen insists, her eyes blazing. "She is a trespasser. Our laws are clear."

"Yes," Venali agrees. "We have the right."

"So why do we not?" she demands.

Venali turns his gaze to me. "I was never a friend to Filauria. I lived in the forests near Haelhil, far from her. But when tyranny found us even there, I journeyed to her, hoping to plead for my people. She refused me an audience, saw me as a trickster, a threat."

He pauses. "Desperate, I took what I could. I fought her allies, stole a ship. I thought we could find safety in her lands, but we were met with bloodshed. We fled here, to this land now known as Farfell. When even these forests offered no safety, we came to this swamp. Protecting it with the same magic you sought to escape.

You call us elves of the swamp, but we were not always such. As you were not always what you call twilight. And as Keohwen mentioned to you: now I am this, roots and vines and scars. And you shine ostentatiously."

"Well," I try, forcing a weak smile, "being able to talk to trees is pretty cool."

"It is not a new ability," he replies flatly.

Right. That makes sense I suppose.

"Why would Filauria come here, then?" I ask. "Even to speak with you?"

"She was desperate, as you are now," Venali says.

"You are right. I am desperate. Please, let me go. I am so sorry this happened to you, I am, but I need to leave. My brother is a tyrant, and your trees must know he needs to be stopped."

Keohwen grinds her teeth, her jaw tightening. "And how do you propose to stop him?"

"I don't know. Kill him, I guess," I blurt out before my mind can catch up with my mouth.

Why did I say that? That's not what I want to do. That's not who I want to be.

Venali turns away, his gaze drifting beyond the village and into the shadowed woods. The other elves remain silent. Do they still think I'm lying? Maybe they believe their magic can stall Ilriel. It won't.

"My brother can navigate your forest. He knows how to dismantle resistance."

If they kill me here, they'll learn the truth the hard way.

But, if they kill me here, maybe that would be the best thing for Starview. The Nightstrand would be lost, hidden from Ilriel and the high elves. But how many people would die as they search for it?

"And if you are a liar?" Venali asks.

"Assassinate me and end my rule. Free me from my burden."

The air falls still. No rustling. No whispered voices. The forest remains silent.

Finally, Venali speaks. "I will lead you out," he says, "so I may keep an eye on you."

Fair enough.

"You will just let her leave?" Keohwen demands.

Venali's cane digs into the ground and he takes his first step forward, passing me.

We walk in silence.

The exit is close now. I can feel it. My friends are waiting just beyond. My hip vibrates faintly, finally. It's weak, but it's there.

When we emerge, the panic leaves the faces of my allies. Lapis rubs her forehead, letting out a sigh. She wraps her arms around me, squeezing me so tightly that my shoulder hurts. "We couldn't get in."

I step back, shaking my head as a way to reassure her I'm okay.

I turn to Venali and bow deeply to him, still speaking in Elven, "Thank you. And I truly am so sorry. I wish I could make it right."

"Many years ago," he sighs, "we fled from a miserable and wretched villain. The trees tell me one day he will finally fall. I do not want another to rise in his stead."

Thorne takes a step forward, voice sharp, "are you the reason for our wasted time?"

Venali turns to her, responding in Elven with a snide remark I really shouldn't repeat.

"He can't understand you," I lie quickly to Thorne.

"Great," she mutters

Venali's steady gaze meets mine. He nods once. "You are more civil than Filauria," he says. "She is a nuisance, though I do hope you find her."

Before I can respond, he's gone, vanishing into the shadows of the forest like a ghost.

Thorne grabs my arm the moment he leaves, her grip firm and demanding. "What the hells happened in there?"

"Elf politics," I reply, brushing her off. I'm too tired to explain more, and she wouldn't care to hear it anyway.

Zemm pulls me into another sudden hug, almost knocking me off balance.

Lapis is muttering more apologies, her words tumbling over each other in a rush. "We should have listened to you," she says, repeating it like a mantra.

 In my lightest tone, I ask, "were you going to leave me in there?"

"No! We couldn't get back in," she insists, her face pale with guilt.

"Every time we tried," Zemm chimes in, his voice quieter than usual, "the forest just spat us back out. Even if we walked forward, it always led to the exit."

I nod slowly.

"I tried to dispel their magic," he adds, frustration creeping into his tone. "I couldn't. I'm sorry."

"It's fine," I say, offering a faint smile. "Really. I got out, and that's what matters."

Thorne doesn't say a word. No apology, no explanation. But I don't expect one from her. It's not her style.

Instead, she glances toward the horizon, her expression unreadable. For a moment, the four of us stand in silence, the weight of what's just happened hanging between us. Then, with a deep breath, I adjust my pack and start walking.

"Let's get to Frondvale," I say, not looking back. "We, unfortunately, have a long way to go."

CHAPTER
TWENTY

They still feel guilty, even now as the fire crackles in our camp, flickering its shadows onto our faces. Lapis fidgets, sometimes glancing in my direction, while Zemm's eyes lock on the flame, his book open in his lap.

Did he write about this?

They don't need to feel guilty. I'm fine, everything is fine. In fact, I'm glad they didn't listen to me, just once. It worked out in my favor. I have a new, odd lead.

I'm looking for a woman who wears my face.

And according to my map, we're almost there. Just one final hill, I think.

This continent is nothing but hills. There have been hills everywhere we go. Walking up hills, walking down hills, walking beside them. The land was only flat in the south. Though I haven't been near Dazzoran, or the wasteland in the southwest, so I don't know what the terrain is like there. So I'm just going to imagine everything else is hills as well.

Leaning back against the trunk of a broad tree, the fire's warmth washes over me. The flames pop and hiss in a soothing rhythm. My gaze lingers on the dancing embers. Maybe I'll throw Ilriel into a fire one day.

"You look shaken." Thorne's voice takes me out of my trance. She's sitting close to me, her ever-present sketchbook resting on her lap.

"What?"

"You look shaken. You're not speaking."

"I never speak."

"You never shut up."

Ugh.

I haven't been speaking, no. I'm not angry. I've been thinking. Planning. Scheming? Attempting to dissect the rest of the riddle. The bit about the starlight hidden from the world. Then, I'll deal with the trickster bit.

"I'm not shaken," I tell her, "I'm thinking."

"About your home?"

"No," I reply quickly, shaking my head. My thoughts aren't on Starview. Not now. "Why can't you speak Elven?" I ask, deflecting.

Her pencil pauses, and her eyes dart toward me briefly. "Why would I speak Elven?"

"It seems no one can," I say, frustration creeping into my tone. "No one here. It must be a dying language."

"So?"

"I've never met a half-elf, you know." I say to her, eying her ears.

"Neither have I."

I sit up straighter, leaning forward to grab her ear.

She yelps, swatting my hand away. "Don't touch my ears," she snaps, her hair falling loose from its tie and framing her perfect face.

"You're not a half-elf?"

"No."

"Why do you lie? About everything?"

"I never lie."

"You do nothing but lie."

My gaze drops to her sketchbook. She's drawing *me*. But also, not? It certainly does not look like my *WANTED* poster. The face on the page is familiar, but it is not mine, it looks like my mother. The resemblance is unmistakable, like staring at her portrait come to life.

Why is she drawing my mother? Why is it watching me? What is my mother thinking about me right now as she stares up from the page? Has she been watching me from this book the entire time? Watching me cry?

Watching me kill?

"Who is that supposed to be?" I ask, frowning.

Thorne glances at the page, her brow furrowing. "It's you," she says dryly. "Or did you forget what you look like?"

"Why are you drawing that?"

"I'm drawing everyone," she says, flipping through the book to show me. The sketches are all unfinished, some rough outlines, others more shaded.

"That's not me," I say, shaking my head. "You're an awful illustrator and should quit."

She bares her teeth.

"Show me!" Lapis calls from across the fire.

Thorne holds the book out to her. Zemm peers over, nodding as he glances between the sketch and I.

"That's not me," I insist.

"It's like, perfect," Lapis says.

"No. It's all wrong. All of it. The entire thing."

"Fine," Thorne says. Without hesitation, she rips the page out, crumples it in her hand, and tosses it into the fire. My mother's face is consumed by flames in seconds freed from her prison inside the book.

"Can I see mine?" Lapis asks eagerly. Thorne moves to sit beside her, flipping through the book.

Zemm takes her place next to me, nudging my shoulder gently.

"Can I tell you something?" I ask him, my voice quiet.

"Of course."

"I know I said I didn't want to talk about it, but I miss my mother."

His expression softens. "Is that why you avoid looking at your reflection? In water, or glass, or mirrors?"

I nod slowly. The poster doesn't bother me the same way. It's distorted enough that it doesn't feel like her.

Zemm's large hand rubs my back. "If it helps, I miss mine too."

I glance at him. "Is she...?"

"No," he shakes his head. "But I am."

I tilt my head, confused.

"Orcs with magic aren't rare," he explains, "but we're sought after. My mother made me hide it. She was afraid they'd take me from her."

"Would they have?" I ask without thinking.

"Most likely. I'd have been chained, used as a weapon." His voice darkens. "But I couldn't ignore it. I practiced in secret. When they discovered me, I faked my death. Burned my home with a body they'd mistake for mine. Even my mother believed it."

I stare at him, horrified. "You can't ever go back?"

He shakes his head. "Never. I fled to Frondvale. That's where I met Thorne. I set that fire and she was just a stranger that had my back. The guards treated me far worse than her, and I think she hated that. She helped me. Found me work, gave me the space to learn my magic."

"She *helped* you?"

He nods, a small smile tugging at his lips. "She's my best friend."

Thorne's eyes meet mine from across the fire. How long has she been watching us?

"I'm sorry I didn't ask sooner," I say softly. "I should've asked. I shouldn't be so focused on myself."

"I didn't offer it. I'm sure you have many secrets that you keep."

He pats my back once more before returning to his bedroll. "Let's pray to your Goddesses," he says lightly. "Just in case they're finally abandoning you, with that magic fading in your weapon."

"What?" I ask, alarmed. "You think they'd abandon me? Can they even do that?" My fingers dig into my knees.

Thorne stretches her leg out in front of her. "That's why I'm not religious."

Zemm settles in. "That's not the reason."

My thoughts churn as I stare into the fire, as if it can provide the answers I need.

"I wonder if your Goddesses are also fallen stars," Thorne remarks.

Fallen star.

And deep beneath the earth, where no eye dares wander, starlight shall slumber, hidden from the world above.

A woman with my face. With my hair. Beneath the earth. In a cemetery? Buried, dead? No. Not yet. I know she isn't dead. Something is telling me she isn't dead.

Where sunlight reigns.

It must be under the castle. That is the only explanation. Somewhere. A dungeon. Ilriel has her locked away. All he needs is me.

I glance at Thorne. Whatever job she was assigned to, her connection with the royal family will prove useful. I'll need her knowledge if I'm going to break into the palace. If I'm going to find her. She'll know every entrance, the layout of the dungeons, and where my brother might be hiding.

I'll need her for this. I'll betray her before she has the chance to betray me.

CHAPTER
TWENTY-ONE

The city of Frondvale sprawls before me, magnificent and alive. Even under my hood, I can't help but peek, taking in the bustling streets and gleaming spires. Everything here breathes with a vibrancy Starview just can't replicate. The scent of fresh bread and blooming flowers fills the air, and the hum of life surrounds me. I love it. Every chaotic, beautiful inch of it.

Thorne, on the other hand, appears to be walking into her own personal hell. Her scowl is deep, her jaw tight, twisted into a snarl, as we cross the massive stone bridge leading past the front gate. When we pass a pair of guards, she lowers her gaze and mutters, "Keep your head down."

"I am."

It's unfortunate that I'm not here under better circumstances. Beyond the crowds and lively streets, the castle looms in the distance, its high towers reaching toward the sky like spears of white stone.

"Where are we staying?" Zemm asks.

"I don't know," Thorne admits flatly. "Ideally, we wouldn't be here."

Too bad. I don't have a choice. I *need* to be here.

"You still got friends in the city?" Zemm presses.

"I don't know." Her eyes dart around the streets, and she quickens her pace. "I might know where to go."

"Please don't say another sewer," I groan.

"Too bad."

I hate that the sewer spies are here, too. Is there some kind of secret underground network of sewer-dwelling criminals spanning every major city? Do they have meetings? Messenger rats? I deserve answers.

The crowd thickens as people urgently rush toward the center, their expressions tense.

"We should take another way," Zemm suggests.

"No," I blurt out. "I..."

I need to know what's happening.

Before I can be stopped, I slip into the throng, following the flow of people. The streets are so bright, so clean. Sunlight bounces off polished stone, and flower boxes overflow with vibrant blossoms. It's a world away from the oppressive decay of Grimehold.

I slow, distracted by the beauty of the city, and my companions catch up to me.

"There's a crowd," Lapis says, pointing ahead. We're nearing the city's heart, where a large group has gathered in front of the castle gates. My stomach twists.

Please don't let this be another execution.

"Shit," Thorne mutters under her breath. She veers left into a shadowed alley, motioning for the others to follow. They go, but I linger, caught by the strange stillness of the crowd.

My gaze locks on the gleaming star positioned dead center

of the city. The one that shines so brightly, beyond and above the rays of the sun. Brilliant.

"Faelyri!" Thorne shouts. "I'm not doing this again!"

The sight, the perfect star, holds me captive.

On the steps of the castle stand four figures: King Claude of Frondvale, Queen Edithe, *Ilriel,* and a twilight elf guard.

My brother, valiant and statuesque, shining, commands the scene. His posture is perfect, his face carved in stone. Beside him stands not Farren but someone far more familiar.

"Syvis," I whisper, my voice barely audible. "That's my guard. That's my friend. That's Syvis."

Thorne's green eyes are locked on the scene before us. She says nothing.

Ilriel steps forward, his voice booming over the hushed crowd. "I love my country, and I love my sister. But I cannot forgive her heinous crime. She attempted to murder me for the throne. A throne she had no right to claim." His voice cracks dramatically. "And she is still out there."

"*What?*" The word bursts from me, sharp and raw, before I can stop it. Thorne's arms are around me in an instant, pulling me to the ground. Her leather-clad hand clamps over my mouth, muffling my protests.

I thrash against her, trying to claw my way free. Around us, the crowd stirs faintly, but the attention remains on Ilriel. The collective murmurs and gasps swallow my outburst.

"Stop," Thorne hisses in my ear. "You need to stop."

My nails dig into her arms and will no doubt leave scratches under her sleeves.

"Breathe. This isn't helping." She orders. "And you're hurting me."

I exhale shakily, taking in deep, steady breaths. Five of them. Slowly, painfully, my heart begins to calm. Only then do I notice Ilriel is still speaking.

"I have made contact with the other prominent cities of Farfell: Grimehold, Deadbell, and Hollow Haven. I have been following the trail she left behind. She has something of mine, and it is imperative that I get it back."

Thorne loosens her hold, helping me to my feet. My legs shake, my thoughts muddled. I glance back toward the castle steps. Ilriel clutches his chest dramatically, his expression etched with false sorrow.

"There was no one I loved more than my sister," he says, his voice heavy with false emotion. "But as the King of Starview, it is my duty to ensure justice is enacted."

What a joke.

The fury in my chest reignites, but I force it down. I can't afford to lose control again—not here, not now. My gaze darts to Syvis. Her jaw is set, her eyes cold as she watches the spectacle unfold.

Thorne scoffs, rolling up her sleeves to assess the cuts I left on her arms. Her face hardens, but she freezes as her gaze drifts toward the royal family standing on the castle steps. Her focus lands on the royal children. Three sons and a daughter.

The sons are typical, their arrogance practically glowing as brightly as their ceremonial armor. But the daughter...

She has Thorne's face, almost. The shape of her features, the cut of her jaw. It's there. But her eyes are vacant, hollow, like a puppet whose strings are pulled by unseen hands. Like someone has taken her from her body and left something lifeless in its place.

My head snaps to Thorne, studying her profile. Her ears, her expression, her beauty, everything about her.

"Oh my Gods," I breathe, realization finally dawning. "You're a fey creature."

She ignores me completely, her eyes locked on the girl.

The fey can glamour themselves into whatever you most desire to see.

Is this what I desire? Someone like her? Is this how she sucked me in?

"You're a faerie. Or a pixie. Or..."

"Stop talking, now." She snaps.

Meanwhile, Ilriel continues, his voice carrying over the crowd: "With the help of the royal army, I will investigate every inch of this continent until she is found."

I should scream. I *could* scream. Right now, I could unleash every ounce of my fury and ruin Ilriel's carefully crafted speech. But that would only prove his point. That I'm unhinged. That I'm dangerous. Maybe I *am* unhinged.

My eyes move again to Syvis, searching for some sign, some reassurance. She meets my gaze briefly, her wide eyes betraying a flicker of emotion. But she's good, and her face fades into its stoic mask. With quiet precision, she excuses herself from the others and steps away.

Ilriel drones on, because he never shuts up: "In exchange for their help, I plan to offer my services to King Claude. Much of Farfell has been taken from the humans. Together, we will reclaim it."

Oh, so he's completely insane.

My hand tightens around the Nightstrand as it shrieks in my grip. I lift it, feeling its weight shift as it takes shape. Why is it screaming? Is it my madness? Or, perhaps, it's because she's here. In the city.

"What are you doing?" Thorne hisses, her voice sharp with panic. "Put that away."

"No," I whisper, my voice steady despite the chaos in my chest. My arrow is nocked, the string taut. Ilriel is far, but not far enough. I can hit him. I *will* hit him.

I thought I could reason with him, but I can't. He's insane.

Thorne lunges, grabbing my arms and yanking me back. The arrow slips from my grip and vanishes before I can release it. "We need to leave," she snaps, dragging me away through a nearby alley.

"Let me go!" I growl, struggling against her. "That's an order!"

"Ha!" She pulls harder.

I swing the Nightstrand at her arm, the impact making her gasp, but she doesn't relent. Her grip only tightens.

"Why did you stop me?" I demand. "You *heard* him."

"I know how insufferable you are. You'll regret it for the rest of your life if you don't at least try to reason with him."

"I don't want to reason with him."

"And what happens when your cover is blown?" she snaps, hauling me farther down the alley.

"I don't care."

"Shut up."

We reach the end of the alley, where it opens into a small, secluded space behind a cluster of poorly placed buildings. Thorne shoves me behind a stack of crates, the rough wood scratching my back. I glare at her as I crouch, but before I can say anything, a commanding voice calls out:

"Halt!"

Thorne steps into the clearing, hands raised. "Yeah, I know."

"I have seen your picture, thief. Where is the Queen?" The voice is familiar. Too familiar. I inch forward, peeking from behind the crates.

It's Syvis, her sword drawn, the faint glow of her enchanted armor reflecting the sunlight. Her stance is rigid, her expression severe.

"I don't know any queens," Thorne replies with an exaggerated shrug and mockery. "Did I look pretty in my picture? I really hope so."

I step out from my hiding place, my voice trembling as I call her name. "Syvis..." My breath catches. "I've never been happier to see anyone in my life."

Thorne lowers her hands as Syvis sheaths her sword. The guard's face softens, a faint blush rising to her cheeks. "I am very happy to see you, as well," she says quickly. "I am so sorry. I should have done something."

I throw myself into her arms, and she holds me tightly. For the first time in weeks, I feel safe. I linger there. I need to.

Behind me, Thorne lets out a loud, pointed sigh, her foot tapping impatiently against the stone.

Syvis kneels before me as she releases me. "I am sorry I let you down."

"You didn't," I assure her. "I promise. I missed you so much."

Her beautiful face lights up. She must have gone through as much as I have, especially traveling with Ilriel. He wouldn't have trusted her. He kept her around to keep an eye on her. I hope he wasn't too cruel.

"Syvis," I begin hesitantly, "was he being honest? About an invasion across the continent?"

Her smile fades, and her eyes drop to the ground. Not the reaction I wanted. "I do not know," she says softly.

"How?" Thorne interjects.

She narrows her eyes on her and then says, "That speech was the first I heard of it. I promise."

"What happened after I was..." I just can't say the rest.

"That next morning, after we discussed your journey to Farfell and your position as Queen and keeper of the Night-strand," Syvis begins, her voice steady but heavy, "I grew concerned when there was no response at your door. I entered unannounced. I apologize for that."

I wave my hand dismissively, urging her to get to the point. "Not important."

"Your room was uncharacteristically pristine."

I roll my eyes.

"But you were gone. I searched the palace, but Ilriel intercepted me. He claimed there was an issue with the Nightstrand, that you needed to remain in Starview longer for safety reasons. He refused to let me see you and instead hurried me down the mountain and onto a boat bound for Farfell. I traveled across the sea with only a small team of guards." Her voice catches briefly. "I did not learn of your supposed crime until he arrived here. The accusation came directly from him. I never believed it."

"Did you put up a fight?" Thorne asks, her arms crossed and foot tapping impatiently.

I stay silent, letting Syvis answer the question, though I know her answer. Her dark eyes meet mine as she speaks. "No. I did not. I am worth more to the Queen alive."

Thorne lets out a derisive breath, gesturing toward me. "Well, your fallen star and I don't have the luxury of wasting time, as she keeps reminding me. Nice to meet you, though." She salutes Syvis mockingly, her hand lazy and insincere.

Syvis's face twists with disdain. Her gaze travels over Thorne, her expression one of pure disgust. "Your Highness, is she holding you captive? Do you know she is a wanted criminal?"

The tension cracks between them, sharp and dangerous. I don't have time for this right now.

"We made a bargain," I say, the words tumbling out. And then it hits me like a physical blow as soon as the word leaves my lips.

Oh. I made a bargain with a faerie. With the fey.

My hand flies to my mouth, and the blood drains from my face. Thorne is watching me, her eyes gleaming with an awful, wicked amusement.

Syvis narrows her gaze at Thorne. "I do not care to travel with her, and neither should you."

Without waiting for my response, Syvis pulls a heavy coin purse from her belt and tosses it into Thorne's hand. "Enjoy," Syvis spits.

Thorne grips the bag tightly, her knuckles white as the coins scrape together inside. She tucks it into her pocket. "I appreciate it," she says with a smirk, "but, unfortunately for your friend, I was promised far more than gold. So, I have to finish the job."

Syvis responds, "no. You are leaving. Protecting her is my responsibility."

"I'm not here to protect her."

"Stop," I command.

Thorne turns to me, her expression sharp and predatory. "Do you think you can leave without me? Do you *want* to leave without me? Let's set aside your little revelation about bargains for a moment and think logically. You're leaving with someone who has no idea what your plan is, someone who won't protect you from her comrades, her army. What happens when you return to Starview after finding your long-lost friend? When they call you a traitor, do you think she'll stand by you?"

"I... uh..."

"And you think you'll survive on your own?" she presses, her voice low and biting. "With your bow dying at the worst moments? With arrows that won't pierce the armor they wear?" She gestures toward Syvis, her point punctuated by her disdainful tone.

Thorne steps closer, too close, her voice dropping to a dangerous whisper. She grabs my chin, holding my face in place. "Are you going to break the bargain you made with me? With *me*. Did you really think you could outwit me?"

If she ever made a bargain with the fey, it would only lead to death or servitude.

The sound echoes through the alley like a whip crack when Syvis's palm connects with Thorne's face in a resounding slap.

Thorne stumbles back, cheek flaming red. She touches the mark gingerly, flinching at the sting. Her eyes blaze with fury as she lifts her fist, lunging toward Syvis. But Syvis doesn't flinch. Doesn't even blink.

Thorne hesitates at the last second, her knuckles brushing past Syvis's face and slamming into the wall instead. The impact not only reverberates through the stone but actually damages it, and her other hand grips the hilt of her sheathed dagger. When she removes her hand, the stone is cracked.

Syvis straightens. "You should never speak to royalty that way. Apologize."

"She's not my ruler."

I wish I was the one who smacked her.

I can't help but stare at the red mark blooming on Thorne's cheek. It mars her sharp beauty, but is this even her real face? What is her real face?

They are horrors, haggard nightmares that twist your will to their own ends.

"What happens if I leave?" I ask her quietly. "If I go with Syvis now? What happens then?"

Thorne's smile is a dagger's edge. "Is it worth finding out?"

I drop my gaze, my mind racing to formulate a new plan. "Syvis will come with us."

It isn't much of a plan, but right now it's the best one I have. I can do better, and I will.

Syvis stiffens. "Your Highness, I cannot leave now. Not yet. I know you have tasks to complete in this city, and I can guide you after. But for now, I know where you can find Filauria."

My head snaps in her direction, "where?"

"Your brother has her in a cell, in the castle."

So, I was right. I'm grateful to be right. Not grateful that's she's in a cell, of course, but grateful for the fact that she's somewhere I can easily get to. Where she can't run off to the next location. I will find her, release her from her prison, and she'll owe me. She'll come to Starview with me.

Syvis hesitates. "Your Highness... I do not think I can sneak you in."

I turn to Thorne, my voice steady. "Thorne can get me in."

Thorne meets my glare with her own. But in her eyes, I think I can see the faintest flicker of interest. Or challenge.

The river's murmur echoes faintly through the sewer's tunnels as Thorne peers over the algae-covered steel fence above the rushing waters below. The stairs to our left wind downward to the inevitable: a sewer gate waiting at the bottom. My nose wrinkles at the thought of it. Another sewer. Of course. What is it with her and sewers?

I wonder if the rest of them are already there, eating sewer fish and drinking sewer ale.

"I'm sorry she hit you," I say, my voice flat. I'm not sorry, but I figure peace is better for now.

Thorne grips the fence tighter. "You're not the one who hit me. Your *girlfriend* did."

I arch an eyebrow. "She's not my girlfriend. She's my guard. And my friend."

"Fine. *Guard-friend.* Whatever."

I sigh, clicking my tongue. "You're going to have to get along with her. She's coming with us."

Silence.

The gate's lock proves no match for her, and with a click, she yanks it open. The rusty hinges squeal. With that, we crawl through the opening, and I immediately do my best to avoid the filthy water flowing beneath us. Thorne, however, stomps through it like it's a paved road.

"We're close," she says over her shoulder. "Try not to insult anyone."

"That job you mentioned before," I begin cautiously, "the Princess—"

She stops so abruptly I nearly crash into her. Her hand grips my shoulder as she turns, her green eyes sharp. "Do *not* bring up what I told you. Not around anyone. Do you understand?"

"I have too many questions for you."

"What I told you was a drunken mistake," she hisses. "That regret haunts me. Your only concern regarding me should be my reward."

The sound of her boots splashing through the water echoes as she stomps off. I follow her deeper into the dark, the stench growing stronger with every step. I clamp a hand over my nose.

After what feels like an eternity navigating the labyrinthine pipes, we reach a door. Sturdy, better kept than the one in Grimehold. Of course, it leads to another tavern, because why wouldn't it? This one is larger, fitting for a city like Frondvale.

Zemm waves us over from a table in the corner. We approach, and Lapis wastes no time. "What happened?" she demands.

"She found her *guard-friend*," Thorne mutters, pulling out a chair with a screech of wood against stone.

"You did?" Lapis's eyes widen.

Zemm slides Thorne a drink, and I watch it longingly. Everyone has one, except me. I grab Thorne's cup before she can take a sip, and without thinking, I down it the way I've seen them do countless times. The burn is sharp, but I don't care. I slam the mug on the table and immediately reach for Zemm's, gulping it before anyone can stop me.

Their voices fade into the background, distant and muffled now. My mind races as I trace the grooves in the wooden table. What did Ilriel promise the humans? Territory? Elven magic? Power?

I sink a bit farther into my seat.

Grimehold. Deadbell. Hollow Haven.

Deadbell is near the Hailstone Peaks, home to the snow elves. Grimehold lies close to Mirrormire, too near Venali's people. And Hollow Haven... I don't even know who resides in the Hollow Wastes, but are they human?

And of course, all three flank Dazzoran and Vum Dorahl.

Where is Thorne from? Where do the fey hide? Are they scattered across the land, or do they have their own kingdoms, their own magic-filled strongholds?

"Lyri." Lapis snaps her fingers in front of my face.

I look up, dazed. They're all watching me now. "Filauria is in the castle."

"Yeah, we know." Lapis says, "Weren't you listening? She just said that."

Did she? My hand pulls at the ends of my hair beneath the table.

Lapis leans closer. "I'll go with you into the castle."

My head throbs as I lean forward on my elbow, gripping my forehead. In Starview's palace, the kitchen is always bustling. People constantly coming and going. One person sneaking in would be easier than two. Filauria might not even talk to me if I bring anyone else. Every story paints her as paranoid.

I'm nudged again, my head snapping up. Lapis is speaking, but her words blur. I nod anyway, and the table erupts in laughter. What did I just agree to? Whatever. They can laugh. Maybe they need it. I know I do.

"I'd like another drink," I mutter, standing too quickly. My head spins, and Thorne's hand shoots out, forcing me back into my seat.

"*Sit. Down.*" She pulls my hood lower over my face, her hand firm. I hate when she does that.

Zemm gestures around the room. "They won't sell you out, but there might be shadows lurking."

Thorne slides another drink across the worn wooden table, the mug scraping slightly against its coarse surface. When did she get a new one? I can't pay attention to anything...

"Here. Don't do that again."

Do what? Stand?

I lift the cup, its cool rim pressing against my lips, and drink deeply. The bitterness lingers on my tongue as I set it back down. "Can you tell me which way to go from the kitchen?" I ask.

Is that my voice?

"Tomorrow. You won't remember if I tell you now."

"Will you sketch it for me?"

Her own mug meets the table with a thunk. "Tomorrow."

I reach out, gripping her hand where it cradles her drink. My vision sways, and the room spins softly around her face. Her gorgeous, horrible face. Her face that was fabricated just for me. "Are you all right?" I ask, my words slurring.

Her eyes dart around the table before meeting mine, her expression guarded. Her mouth opens briefly, but she hesitates. "Why wouldn't I be?"

My hand slips from hers, falling to the edge of the table. Though I don't want it to. Why don't I want it to?

Her fingers tap against the mug, a steady rhythm I can't help but watch to keep myself grounded.

"Lyri, can I have a crown?" Lapis asks suddenly, breaking the quiet tension.

"What?"

"When you go home and you're a Queen, can you get me a crown? Not one that means anything. Just a crown."

"They all mean something," Thorne says, taking a sip from her mug. My eyes trail her movement, trying to hold onto some semblance of focus.

I tear my gaze away. "Sure, whatever. I can get you a crown. You've earned it."

"What's your home like?" Lapis presses.

My home. The word pulls at something deep within me. What is my home like? Do I remember? The first thought that comes is *beautiful*. Beautiful, pristine, unbroken. I spread my hands wide, attempting a grand gesture.

"Mountains," I say. "Lots of them. The castle is made of stars."

Okay, I might be a little drunk.

The words keep spilling out. "The palace floor lights up like the sky, and the moon fills the throne room with her light. Especially when she's full. The city is carved into the mountains, in tiers, layered with starlight. And there's no sun at all.

"There's a reason for that, the lack of sun. A barrier protects Starview, keeps it cloaked in starlight. The barrier must never fall."

As if in response, the Nightstrand hums faintly. Has it already fallen?

Lapis leans forward, "Why?"

Because I don't want to lose my home.

I slam the empty mug down, my voice rising despite myself. "It doesn't matter, because it's already in ruins! And I bet Tae'ril is already there!"

"Who?" Zemm asks.

"The day I got this." I hold up the Nightstrand, its singing soft in response to my agitation. "That was the day my life fell apart. I used to think Ilriel deserved this. He doesn't. No one does."

"You should go to bed," Thorne says, her hand firm on my thigh. Her leather gloves are rough, but her fingers are soft.

But I can't stop. The words pour out, one after another. "I'm related to the only twilight elf ever accused of being a traitor. The trees told the swamp elves that." My voice cracks.

I'm fumbling over every single one of my words. I probably sound insane.

"Trees...?" Lapis whispers to the others.

"She was a traitor," I say, my head now cradled in my hands. "Just like me."

"You're not a traitor," Zemm says gently.

"Exactly!" My voice wavers, rising again. What am I even saying?

"So that's why you don't drink a lot," Lapis states.

I let my head fall against the table, groaning into the wood. My outburst, while embarrassing, is also freeing.

Thorne hauls me up, draping my arm over her shoulders. Her strength is steady, her presence grounding.

"Time for bed."

I cling to her, resting my head against her shoulder as she walks. She looks like a painting, one too perfect to be real.

"Why didn't the guard recognize you at the inn?" I whisper, my words slurring. "The Princess's face..."

"He didn't see the face you see."

When we reach the room, I collapse onto the bed without

removing my boots, curling into myself. My head pounds, worse than the Nightstrand's relentless song.

Do you think I'm a monster?

"Do you think I'm useless?" I ask her.

"What?"

I groan.

"Why do you care what I think?" she asks, her tone sharp.

"Because I think you can see me," I whisper.

Lie to me

"Yes, I do," she says.

"Thorne..." My voice falters, the words spilling out unbidden. "I'm going to be trapped on my island forever. Ruling a kingdom forever. This isn't a gift, it's a prison."

The bed creaks and dips as she sits beside me.

"Show me your face," I demand. "You have her face. I have so many questions."

"She has *my* face," she corrects with venom in her voice.

So, they *can* change other faces.

My eyes are closed so tightly as I cling to the pillow. My face pressed deep into it. "I'm going to be alone forever."

"I have so many questions for you..." I repeat.

The bed shifts as she stands, and the quiet click of the door shutting is the last sound I hear before sleep claims me.

Is this what a hangover feels like? A sharp, relentless pain stabbing through my skull, splitting it apart with every pulse? Does this happen to everyone who drinks? Why would anyone willingly do this to themselves?

I'm curled up in my bed, still fully clothed from the night before, when the door creaks open. I don't need to look. I already know who it is.

"How's your head?" she asks.

I respond by tugging the thin blanket over myself.

"That good?"

I mumble from under the blanket, "Everything hurts."

"Well that's awful, because we have to go."

I don't move. The blanket is my sanctuary, and I'm not ready to leave it. But Thorne sighs and yanks it away without hesitation, leaving me exposed to the cold, merciless room.

"How do you deal with this?" I ask. How can anyone function with a headache like this? Nausea builds in my stomach and throat.

"I don't," she says with a shrug. "This doesn't happen to me because I'm a professional."

I roll onto my back, pressing a hand to my forehead. "I think I'm dying."

She pushes my hand aside, replacing it with her own. Her touch is cool. "You're not. Haven't you ever had a drink at home?"

Not ale. Never ale. Wine, sometimes, with dinner, but never enough to feel like this. This was the first time I'd even finished a glass of anything stronger. I shake my head slightly, and the motion sends a fresh wave of pain crashing through me.

She steps back, giving me space. I swing my legs over the side of the bed. When I stretch, my joints pop and crack in protest.

"Can I ask you a question?" I venture, my voice still hoarse.

"No," she replies flatly, not missing a beat.

I ignore her. "What do you want? When I find her, when I bring her back to my home, what is it you want from me?"

Her expression doesn't shift. "I want you to uphold your end of the bargain."

"You told me never to make a bargain with the fey."

"And you shouldn't," she says, a slight smirk tugging at her lips.

"But I made one with you!"

She shrugs.

"I didn't know," I argue, my voice rising. "It has to be void if I didn't know."

"That's not how it works," she replies, still smirking.

"Really?" I breathe out. "Fine. Will you at least answer my questions? Who are you? Where are you from? Why does the Princess look like an empty puppet wearing your face? You say it's your face, but is it? And why do you have that knife?"

"None of that is your business."

I falter, almost admitting the fear that's gnawed at the edges of my thoughts for so long. "What if I can't reward you?" My voice is quieter now, almost a whisper. "What if my home is already destroyed? What if I return and there's nothing left. No way to fulfill my promise to you?"

She smiles then, but it's not the kind of smile that brings comfort. It's wicked, calculated, and yet still so achingly beautiful that it twists something deep inside me.

Stop smiling. It's easier when you don't smile.

"I planned for that," she says simply.

Something is wrong. I feel it in my chest. A sharp, aching pain like something vital has been torn out of me. My heart feels like it's been ripped from its place, leaving me bleeding and hollow.

CHAPTER

TWENTY-TWO

"I used to do this all the time," Thorne tells us. "It's easy."

The castle looms above us, an enormous structure of unyielding stone. It's both beautiful and imposing. Its towering spires almost out of place against the fortress's stark, square design. This is a place built to withstand a siege, to house warriors rather than nobles. The artistry in the architecture is undeniable, but it lacks the lightness of my own home.

My own palace is far more elegant and more welcoming. This one feels heavy with the weight of defense and strategy.

How many people live here, I wonder? It must take a lot of upkeep.

"You... used to do this all the time?" Lapis asks, and I slip out of my trance.

Thorne nods, her face calm, nonchalant. "There are constant deliveries, people coming and going, cooks, servants. The kitchen is the best entry point. The servant's entrance is always active."

I already knew that. "I *know*."

Thorne sighs, glancing back at Zemm. "Wait here, or as close as you can without being seen. Just in case."

He nods in agreement.

She crouches low, her body melding into the shadows of the wall, and begins to move with ease. I follow, doing my best to stay hidden among the trees, though I know I'm far less stealthy. There are only a few guards patrolling, but Thorne doesn't take any chances. Her movements are fluid and precise.

"There's a door in the back," she whispers to me. "We just have to pass through anywhere a guard *could* be. The rest is nothing."

A wooden door creaks open ahead of us, and several workers spill out, carrying heavy sacks of flour and other crates. Thorne watches them with the calm patience of someone who already knows what will happen next. Her eyes travel upward to the windows before settling back on the door.

As more workers arrive, shouting to each other and dragging a cart loaded with crates, Thorne leans close. "Do not say a word. Keep your mask up, your head down, and grab one of those crates. Do you understand me?"

Her eyes lock onto mine. I nod, my throat dry.

"There will be an opening for you to slip out of the kitchen. Do not miss it," she says.

And then she stands. Not crouching. Not hiding. Standing tall and walking into the open like she belongs here.

My breath catches, but I force myself to move. I grab the smallest crate I can find, apples, I think, but even it is impossibly heavy. Thorne, of course, chooses a larger one because she's frustratingly annoying.

But we're not hiding. Why aren't we hiding?

We follow the workers into the kitchen, slipping seamlessly into the bustling chaos. Most of the staff are too preoccupied to notice us, but one woman stands near the center of the room, her sharp eyes scanning each worker.

When her gaze lands on Thorne, her expression softens. "Your Highness," she says, her tone a mix of surprise and reverence.

I nearly drop the crate. *Highness?*

Thorne stands there, smiling. Just Thorne. And her smile is easy, as though this is all perfectly natural. "I wanted to help," she says smoothly, raising her voice higher than usual.

Her boot nudges my leg, a subtle kick that snaps me into motion. I set the crate down and slip away into the shadows.

Her laugh, light and infuriatingly confident, echoes behind me as she exits the kitchen, closing the door behind her.

In the golden-lit hallway, my chest tight with frustration, I snap: "What was that? She thought you were the Princess? In *that awful* outfit?"

"I wasn't wearing this outfit," she replies, unbothered.

We reach the first intersection, and Thorne pauses. Her eyes fix on the empty hall stretching out to our right, her expression suddenly distant.

"Did you forget where we're going?" I ask, stepping to her side and waving a hand in front of her face.

Her gaze remains locked on the hall. "No," she says quietly. "I didn't forget."

"Then what are you doing?"

Heavy footsteps echo from somewhere beyond. Thorne doesn't move.

"What are you doing?" I repeat, more urgently this time.

Still no answer.

With a huff, I shove her into the left hallway, snapping her out of whatever trance had claimed her.

At the end of the corridor, we find a door leading to a

narrow, spiraling staircase. The air grows colder as I push it open, the faint scent of damp stone wafting up from below.

"Do faeries have good eyesight?" I ask as I peer down into the darkness.

"Yes," Thorne says, taking the lead. "Close the door behind you."

I obey, and the darkness deepens. My hand instinctively finds the wall, fingers tracing its cold, uneven surface. A breeze seeps through the cracks of the walls and over my fingers.

I take my next step, and then the next.

My other hand rests on the hilt of my weapon as we descend in silence.

Neither of us speak. It's almost as if the dungeons are guarding the silence.

The faint glimmer of iron bars comes into view, and my stomach churns. Before we reach the bottom, I grab Thorne's arm.

"Listen to me," I say firmly. "If we get caught, take the Nightstrand and hide. He won't kill me unless he has it."

She scoffs in response, which I take as agreement.

We step into the dungeon, the dim light casting long shadows over rows of cages. To my right, a skeleton hangs limp in a cell, its hollow eyes staring out from eternity.

How long has that been here? And how many more of them are there?

To my left, there's a low groan. A human man, gaunt and pale, starving to death in his cage and reaching weakly for the bars. For us.

Thorne ignores it, but I can't. She needs to take my hand and lead me forward.

"Do they get fed?" I ask, my voice trembling with horror.

"I don't know."

Why would anyone do that to someone? Leave them to

waste away? It's uncivilized. Unbearable. I need to get out of here.

Filauria's cage is at the far end, set apart from the other prisoners, isolated in the cold shadows. My heart pounds as I half-hide behind Thorne, who strides forward with a calm that I can't muster. I let out a breath as I see her.

She's here. Her head is bowed, her hair cascading over her left shoulder like a waterfall spun from starlight. It shimmers, just like mine.

Thorne nods toward her, urging me forward. I shake my head, panic rising in my chest. What am I supposed to say? How do I introduce myself to someone like her? What's my name again? I've forgotten my own name.

"Filauria, I presume," Thorne says, her voice firm and steady where mine falters. "We're here to break you out."

Filauria lifts her head slightly, her eyes locking onto Thorne's. Thorne nudges me with her shoulder, and I step into the dim light.

Filauria's gaze shifts to me, and she leans forward.

"Ah." She's speaking. She's speaking to me. "You must be the sister. Faelyri, correct?"

She knows my name. I try to speak, but the words stumble over themselves. Her face is thin, her cheeks hollow. "They haven't fed you..." The words trail off awkwardly.

Why was that the first thing I said?

"Once every few days."

He wants to keep her weak. Deliberate cruelty meant to keep her powerless. Unable to defend herself.

I bow deeply, dragging Thorne into the motion with me. I should have bowed first, before speaking. I'm doing this all wrong. I've forgotten my grace.

"Why are you bowing to an exiled traitor?" Filauria asks me.

"Great question. You have no idea how long I've been stuck searching for you," Thorne says, but I cut her off with a sharp stomp on her foot.

Filauria's laugh is a low, rasping sound, almost like a sigh. "Come here, little elf," she beckons, and I step closer to the iron bars.

Her eyes study me, tracing every feature. I do the same, unable to stop. Venali was right.

"Did you ever... have a child?" I ask.

"I did," she says, her voice softening. "A little girl. They took her from me when they exiled me."

"I'm... so sorry."

"Don't be," she replies, her lips curving into a faint smile. "You are proof that she lived a long life."

My palm slaps against my forehead. Why would *no one* ever tell me that?

Thorne throws a glance between Filauria and I, "are we glossing over that?"

"Yes," I answer, removing my hand from my forehead, "that really isn't my concern right now." Handle it later.

Filauria's gaze lingers on me, warm despite the pain etched into her features. "How old are you?"

"Eighteen," I answer.

"A baby..." she murmurs, her eyes drifting to the Nightstrand at my side. They narrow slightly. Can she hear it as well? "My sisters have a terrible sense of humor."

I furrow my brow. "What?"

"You are just a baby." Her gazed fixed on the Nightstrand. "Why would they give you such a burden?"

I can't help but flare my nostrils. "I'm not a child."

"I do not mean to offend you," she says gently. "You have come this far, so I know you are capable. But would you not rather enjoy your youth?"

I pull the Nightstrand free from my belt and let it rest in my hands. "It's dying," I say, cutting straight to the point.

Filauria sighs, a sound heavy with weariness. "Another reason they should not have given this to you. Did they think using my descendant would make it easier to find me?"

I press on, "How do I fix it?"

Thorne groans, rubbing her temples. "We don't have time for this. Can we go? We can do this later."

Filauria's expression hardens. "I will not be returning to

Starview, baby elf." There is pain beneath her voice, raw. "I am so sorry."

I breathe outward. It slips from my chest like a fragile thread. I try to hold it in, but the ache in my throat rises. "You have to come with me. I came all this way."

She shakes her head gently. "Your brother told me about you. Thank you for thinking I am a hero, but I am not. I cannot go back. I cannot face my sisters." She shifts where she sits, crossing her legs as though settling in for a long conversation. "Do you even know my story?"

I hesitate, my mind scrambling. "The... split? Um..."

"Keerla and Velle, your lovely goddesses, are my sisters," she says with a bitter smile. "I was once one of your deities. I gave up that life for this mortal one." She groans, glancing around the cell. "And look how that turned out for me."

"That's all very nice, but can we go?" Thorne interjects, tapping her foot impatiently.

Filauria ignores her. "I once met someone with power unlike anything I had ever seen. He could travel between this world and the spirit vale. He made himself a god." Her voice grows wistful. "It was... impressive. He was not a god, though. So he decided to pursue one. I thought his courtship was charming at the time."

"Fascinating." Thorne says.

"Shh!" I wave my hand at her.

"He convinced me to leave my sisters behind, to relinquish my power. I did it willingly. I came here to be with him. That weapon of yours, it was my parting gift from them. 'Use it to keep yourself safe down there,' they told me. I had no idea that tiny little thing would hold my power. All of it."

Thorne scoffs. "Why would you ever give up that power?"

"I fell in love." Filauria spit a curse in Elven, sharp as shattered glass, before turning her keen gaze on me. "Never give up anything for a man, baby elf."

Thorne's laugh rings out like a crack of thunder. "Don't worry, she doesn't have that problem."

Heat flares in my cheeks, burning my face.

"Please keep going," I beg her.

"He did not love me in return, unfortunately. I was the youngest, and easiest to manipulate. When he discovered the power he sought lay in that little weapon, he demanded it. But it was the only connection I had to my sisters. I couldn't give it up."

"So, you left?" I ask.

"I left. But I did not leave alone. There were elves, many of them, who had grown tired of his rule. Some came with me, while others fled to Farfell. The altar on your island stood long before your home. I built the city around it, enclosing it in a protective spell. I wanted to be closer to my sisters."

Her voice wavers, but she presses on. "They begged me to return, but I could not. I had a child, she was only ten. They expected me to abandon her, but how could I? After our argument, my weapon stopped working for me. My sisters thought they could control me by taking it away, as if I were a child throwing a tantrum. They often told me I was childish. To them, I was throwing tantrums. To me, I was expressing myself."

Thorne glances at me, but I do not turn my head to face her.

"They gave it to someone else, a man who planned to ally himself with the one who betrayed me." Her eyes harden. "So I stabbed him in the heart. I do not regret that decision."

Her gaze finds mine again, unflinching. "And there I was: a traitor. You know the rest. I suppose you are living it."

I blink, and my vision blurs when I open my eyes. The

stinging in my nose rising. "So... sending me to you, with this, is their way of making amends?"

"Perhaps," she said, her tone unreadable. "After the incident, they decided only my descendants could wield the weapon. Once my daughter was old enough, of course. This was always going to fall to you. I imagine they finally tired of your brother's arrogance."

"Why give it to Ilriel at all?"

"I have already said. You are a baby."

I wipe my eyes hastily, startled by the wetness on my cheeks. When did I start crying? "My mother used to tell me your story," I began, my voice trembling. "Your last words... when you said you were coming back when it crumbles—"

"I remember what I said."

"I'm sorry," I grip one of the iron bars. The cold metal bites into my palms. "I came all this way. You have to come with me." I hold the Nightstrand toward her. "Take this. Fix it."

"That does not belong to me."

"I'm not leaving without you."

"I will not be coming with you," she replied, her tone resolute. "I want to move on with my life. I suggest you do the same."

"I can't if everyone dies!" I cried, my voice echoing in the stone chamber.

"You are not responsible for their lives. They are. They can choose to stay or leave."

"I lost everything. I can't lose my home!"

"Your home may already be lost."

Frustration boils over. I rattle the bars violently before stepping back, gripping the Nightstrand in both hands. I tried to twist it, snap it, do something, anything.

It doesn't snap in half, unfortunately.

"This was it," I admit to her. "This was what I thought I

needed to do. I am so useless. I am so purposeless. *This* was my purpose. I was so certain. I finally had *something*."

"You can find a new purpose. I suppose your brother still needs to be dealt with. That is a purpose."

"With *what* weapon?"

"Do you not know how to wield a real bow?"

No. I don't. But that doesn't matter.

I keep going: "With *what* army? With what city behind me? We're family!"

"Is that what you believe?" her eyes drop, "you look too much like my daughter. In truth, I do not know if I can bare to look at you."

I let out a loud, frustrated breath. I can't do this. It's too much. She won't come with me? Fine.

"Open her cage," I finally order Thorne.

"What? No," Thorne replies, crossing her arms. "She said she's not coming. Let her rot."

"Please," I said through clenched teeth. "Just open her cage."

I don't want to argue with her. Not now. I just want to go home and never see either of them again. I want to waste away in my crumbling palace. Waste away in the filth of it.

Thorne sighs before begrudgingly working on the lock. The door creaks open with a sharp clang that echoes through the room.

Filauria struggles to her feet, pressing heavily into the seat for support. She bows low to me, the gesture so unexpected it makes my heart ache. "Thank you for believing in me, baby elf, when no one else did. I am sorry that I let you down."

"*Really?*" Thorne snaps, her voice sharp with fury. "*You're sorry that you let her down? Is that it?*"

Her jaw clenches before she speaks again. My hand twitches to reach for it, to get her to stop, but I just can't.

"Do you know..." Thorne starts, "do you know what a nightmare this has been?"

"I do not care about the deceitful fey or your discomforts," Filauria answers.

"Fine, because personally? I don't give a fuck about yours either. But look at her," she holds her hand out to me. "Don't you think she looks pathetic?"

What?

"Almost murdered, kidnapped, beaten, starved, held for ransom," Thorne continues, her voice rising. "Do you think she deserved that? Do you know how far she's walked, how many times she's retraced your trail, circling this continent with barely a lead? The only thing guiding her was hope, a sliver of hope that she could fix whatever this is." She snatches the Nightstrand from my hand. "This isn't her responsibility. It's yours. She's making herself sick worrying about a kingdom she's barely had the chance to enjoy because she's a friendless recluse."

Is she insulting me or defending me? I might get sick right now.

"She doesn't deserve the crushing guilt of this mess," Thorne growls, pointing the Nightstrand at Filauria. "You should be ashamed for putting this annoying girl through this. I've never met someone more determined to persevere, even when everyone, including me, worked against her. Do you know how insufferable that made her?"

My chest tightens as tears blur my vision again. I step forward, gently taking the Nightstrand from Thorne's hand and strapping it back to my belt as it begins to sing faintly.

Filauria doesn't respond. None of us speak. The silence stretches, thick and suffocating.

After a moment, I break it. "How can I call your sisters? How can I fix this?"

"You cannot speak our language," Filauria replies after a pause, her voice flat.

"I'll learn," I said stubbornly. "What's it called?"

"There is no word for it in Elven or in the common tongue."

Thorne finishes her rant: "That is entirely unhelpful. This is why I hate the gods. You all want to be worshipped, revered, but you act like children. You create chaos and then leave those you deem beneath you to sweep away the wreckage. You want us to believe you're greater than us? To trust in your *divinity*? Then prove it. *Be* better.

"I could force you to come with us, you wouldn't even realize if you were glamoured. But, frankly, I have no personal stake in whether you do or don't. I'm getting paid either way. I just think you're a real asshole and I hate when my time is wasted."

Filauria opens her mouth to speak, but the hope in my chest crumbles to dust as she turns away after a moment of pause, retreating into the shadows of the dungeon. My heart drops into my stomach as I watch her vanish.

Wherever she's gone, I hope she finds peace. I hope she can rest.

Unfortunately, there will be no peace for me.

CHAPTER
TWENTY-THREE

"Now what?" Thorne finally asks, her voice breaking the tense silence.

Good question.

I keep my voice barely above a whisper. I just have to ask. "Did you mean it?"

"Mean what?" she replies, not looking at me.

"All of it, I guess."

She rubs the back of her neck, letting loose strands of hair fall across her face, veiling her expression. "Yes. You're insufferable and annoying."

"You can't lie," I sigh.

That's fine. It doesn't matter. Not really. "Take me home, please. I'll fix my problem myself."

Take me back to Starview, to my crumbling kingdom. I'll be its last queen, reigning over a land of ruins and ghosts.

My graveyard awaits me.

She groans. "She said you need to speak her language."

I begin walking through the damp, foul-smelling jail. "I'll learn it. I only need the basics. That should be easy enough."

"Uh, no." Her footsteps are heavy and reluctant as she follows. "I know you're disappointed, but you've done all you can. It's time to move on and go home *without* doing this. All empires fall."

Perhaps all empires fall, but not mine. I refuse to let it. I dragged myself across this accursed continent. I won't let some capricious deity dictate my fate. There must be books in Starview's library, ancient tomes with fragments of her forgotten language. I'll find them. I'll learn. And Zemm can help. He's smart.

"What about our bargain?" I ask.

"I helped find her. I didn't say she needed to go with you."

A faint sound drifts from the stairs ahead. A shift of weight, perhaps. Perhaps it's her, making her escape. If so, good for her.

"Stop," Thorne whispers sharply behind me.

I don't. I can't stop. My feet carry me forward, head down, until the steady rhythm of footsteps makes me freeze.

The boots in front of me are too clean, too finely made for this filthy dungeon. They're sharp, elegant, and painfully familiar: Elven craftsmanship, like those worn in the court of my home. My gaze travels upward, slowly, reluctantly.

Ilriel smiles down at me. A perfect smile on a perfect face carved from arrogance and control. Perfect posture. Perfect person. He looks every inch the ruler I am not.

"I came to check on my prisoner," he says. "Did you meet her?"

The hair on the back of my neck rises. My body burns from the inside out. "Yes," I reply, my voice steady despite the heat surging through me. "I released her."

We're alone now. Thorne is gone, probably hiding in the shadows. Good. I don't want her to be part of this. I'm already humiliated.

Ilriel nods, his smile unwavering. "That's a nuisance."

Could I crack his jaw right now? Lapis's hammer could. I should have brought her with me.

I clench my shaking fist.

"Excuse me, Ilriel," I say, keeping my tone even, calm. He doesn't deserve courtesy, but I give it to him anyway. Let him see that I am better. "I'd like to go home now. I have work to do."

"Work?" He laughs, a cruel, hollow sound. "Do you even know what that is?"

The heat boiling in my chest explodes. Before I can stop myself, my fist flies forward, slamming into his jaw with a satisfying crack. Ilriel stumbles, hitting the dungeon floor hard. Pain shoots through my hand, but I bite it down. I won't give him the satisfaction of seeing me flinch.

"Have you lost your mind?" he shouts, cradling his jaw.

I have. Completely.

As he rises, he keeps his hand on his face. Does it hurt? I hope it does. I hope I loosened a tooth.

"How dare you strike me!" he shouts.

"How dare *you* throw me from a cliff!" I snap back, my own voice rising to an uncontrollable shout. "How dare you keep me locked away from the world! How dare you lie to me, Ilriel! And how *dare* you send Farren, of all people, after me!"

"I'll excuse this outburst." He snarls. "I'll attribute this to your cracking mental state."

How generous of him.

He extends his hand toward me, commanding, imperious. "You can come with me now, as you are. Or I can put you in shackles."

Rage flares again, hot and insistent. My throbbing fist trembles at my side. One more punch, and I'll break my fingers.

His sword flashes, the blade cold and steady beneath my

chin. "There are guards everywhere," he warns. "You won't get far if you run."

"You can't kill me," I say through gritted teeth, reaching for my weapon only to realize it's gone. Thorne took the Nightstrand.

For once, she listened to me. Maybe that was a very bad plan.

"No," Ilriel says, a dark smile curling his lips. "I can't kill you. But I can make you wish I had."

The blade presses closer as I swallow hard. My breath slows. I force myself to calm the storm raging inside me.

"I'll come with you," I say at last. "But don't touch me."

For a moment, he doesn't move. Then he steps back, lowering his blade.

❧

Ilriel swirls the wine in his glass. His gaze is on me, his smile as sharp as a dagger. "Isn't it funny? We came to Frondvale together after all."

I don't respond, keeping my lips pressed tightly together.

"How did you survive the fall?" he asks, his tone as casual as if he were inquiring about the weather.

Stay calm. Stay cool.

"I had a graceful landing," I reply evenly.

He takes a bite of his meal, nodding as he chews. When he finishes, he points his fork at me. "The Nightstrand, right?" He doesn't wait for me to answer. "Eat. You look like you haven't had a proper meal in weeks, maybe longer."

The spread before me is lavish, the kind of feast I haven't seen in ages. Rich meats, vibrant fruits, steaming breads. Everything smells divine. To him, this is nothing special. Just another day, another *light* lunch. A mockery.

This journey has broken me, stripped me of everything I thought I was, and rebuilt me wrong, with jagged edges that don't quite fit. And here he sits, unchanged, untouched, as if the world beyond his gilded walls doesn't exist. Life moved on as normal for him while I've seen things I never even knew existed.

I used to think of the world as fragments of stories. Ones that have been weaved together for my amusement. I could be told every day that there are stories and worlds outside of my windowpane, but they never existed until I was thrown through it. I yearned to see the base of our mountain, thinking it was some grand adventure. But that was only our doorstep.

There are sewers where people make their homes, there are awful creatures lurking in mines born from torment and madness, and there are cities rotting under the rule of tyrants (though I guess he's met plenty of tyrants).

There are orcs with magic, gentle souls, and a love for storytelling. There are dwarves with hearts of gold whose laughter shines brighter than the steel of their hammers.

There are insufferable, beautiful, wicked trickster faeries with the strength to carry an armored man with one hand.

Being a ruler isn't about sitting at a well-set table or drinking wine from a goblet so expensive its cost could feed a family for a year or more. It's about the people. Their lives, their stories, their struggles.

Ilriel doesn't care about being a good ruler. Not about me, or our country, or the families he's so willing to crush beneath his boot.

I won't eat his fucking food.

"How did you find Filauria?" I ask, bluntly.

His lips curl into a small, smug smile. "Magical friends. And I'll find her again. Your hero will be locked away in another prison, marked a traitor just as you are."

Don't have an outburst here, you're unarmed.

"I suppose so," I say coolly. "But if I were in her place, I'd have done the same. And now, I get the chance to."

He laughs, low and dismissive. "I don't want to fight with you, Lyri. I don't have the time. I have a country to lead. Finish your final meal, please."

Final meal? He really is delusional. "If you don't have the time for me, then why am I here?"

"Because I love you," he says simply, as if those words hold any weight. "And because I'd like your final moments to be civilized. I never wanted you to be rolling in the mud."

I scoff. "You, quite literally, threw me into the mud."

"To be fair," he replies, utterly unfazed, "I thought you'd die on impact."

His face betrays no emotion. He's a statue. Cold, unyielding, empty.

"Even if you kill me," I say, my voice steady, "you won't get what you want. Deep down, I think you already know that. So tell me, what's your grand plan for this 'new power' of yours?"

"You *want* me to tell you?" His grin sharpens.

I nod, keeping my breathing even. I need to know. He won't kill me. Not yet.

"Well," he begins, leaning back in his chair. "As you know, we've run out of moonstone. I'm sending the miners farther afield, just as I said at the party. Vum Dorahl has plenty of it. I'll raid their mines."

I laugh, unable to help myself. It's not funny. None of this is. But his ignorance is almost laughable. "Do you know what a gorenaught is?"

His fork stills on his plate, his eyes narrowing with curiosity. "A what?"

Not caring to elaborate, I press on. "What else do you plan to do?"

He shrugs, taking another bite. "I'm tired of living on a tiny island. I want a castle like this one. I deserve it." His gaze sweeps the grand room, filled with ornate tapestries and towering ceilings. "I'll conquer the continent with the humans. We'll split it down the middle."

"Don't they already control most of it?" I ask, my heart pounding.

"Forty percent," he answers, as if that's not enough. "We're going to split our forces. The human princes have already set off. Lovell to Hollow Haven, Cyrill to Grimehold, Quent to Deadbell."

"And then?

"Spread, conquer, destroy if necessary," he says, as casually as one might discuss a game.

"The other races?" My mind flashes to Vum Dorahl, to Dazzoran, Agnat, Zemm's mother. To all the lives that don't deserve to be caught in his ambitions.

"Everyone," he says with finality.

"And you? Where will you go?"

"Haelhil," he declares, his eyes gleaming. "I will take Haelhil."

Oh... oh no... he really is insane. "Tae'ril will kill you on sight."

"Not after I've built my army," he replies with chilling confidence.

Maybe I should let the high elves kill him. It would save me the trouble.

"How did you know you would be chosen, after our mother?"

"I knew the goddesses wished to clean up their own mess. That our family alone can wield the weapon."

Of course, he knows everything.

"Ilriel," I have one final question for him. One question that has haunted me, but I have never been able to allow creep into my consciousness.

"Hm?"

"Did you kill our parents?"

"I did, yes."

I'm going to kill him. Not in this moment, but the moment I have my weapon back. I will put an arrow directly into his eye and kill him. I will rip the crown from his head and strangle him with it, somehow.

There's nothing left to ask. I have my answers. His madness is clearer than ever, I just needed to know his plan so I can know how to stop it.

"Can I ask you a question now, Lyri?" His tone is smooth, almost kind, but I know better.

I hold my breath, bracing myself.

"Do you know how to fix it?"

I meet his gaze, unwavering. "No. Do you?"

His grin spreads wider, cruel and knowing. "Of course you don't."

A wave of heat engulfs me, and I clench the tablecloth beneath my fingers, wringing it. With a sharp yank, I drag it forward, forcing Ilriel's chair to scrape back. Chaos follows. Plates, cups, and a half-full wine bottle crash to the floor. The shatter of glass jars me from my haze, my gaze snapping to the crimson-stained marble where his dinner lies in ruin.

The cloth dangles precariously, half-off the table now, but I don't give the silence time to settle. I clap my hands sharply, the sound echoing in the room, mocking him. "Bravo, Ilriel. You've won. You have everything you want."

His eyes move to the scattered silverware and shattered glass, his lips curling in disdain. Good. Let him stew in it.

"Not everything," he says finally, his tone colder than the marble beneath us. "Give me the weapon."

A smile tugs at my lips, sharp and humorless. I sing the words to him: "I don't have it."

His fork clatters to the table. "I'm sorry?"

"I lost it," I lie, stepping back and sweeping my cloak aside to reveal empty hands. "Pickpocketed in the city. My mind was elsewhere." I wave a hand.

His fist slams against the table, rattling the remaining dishes. "You can't be trusted with anything."

No. I really can't be. He rises so abruptly his chair topples backward, the crash startling. Before I can react, his hand is in my hair, yanking me forward with enough force to make me stumble.

I let out a cry as he drags me by a chunk of my hair, almost tripping as he stomps to the door.

"Stop!"

"No," he snaps, his grip tightening.

My vision blurs with tears, but I force myself to keep moving. He hauls me down the gleaming golden hall, his boots pounding a rhythm of fury. My scalp aches, but I bite back the pain. Shackles would almost be kinder. Almost.

Maybe he's bringing me to the gallows. Maybe my head will be severed in front of the whole city, just like that man in Grimehold. He won't do it himself. He's a coward.

"Ilriel, release me. That's an order from your queen."

He doesn't even flinch. My eyes dart down his side, catching the glint of steel at his hip. A knife. My fingers twitch.

In one motion, I grab the blade and slice through the strands he holds captive.

My hair falls free, and I shove him forward, retreating a few steps. The knife trembles in my hand as I meet his shocked gaze.

"I told you to let me go."

For a fleeting moment, I think I've won. But I should have just stabbed him.

His fury ignites. He tosses the severed hair aside, his hand snapping out to seize my neck. The knife slips from my grasp, clattering uselessly to the floor. He shoves me forward, and I hit the marble hard. Pain explodes in my head, the impact leaving me dazed and spinning. My limbs feel foreign as I stagger.

The walls ripple until we enter the throne room. Here, the world steadies. Guards line the gilded walls, their armor catching the light. Farren stands among them, bowing low before Ilriel like the sycophant she is. And there's Thorne, arms raised in submission, a guard at her side ensuring she doesn't flee.

The room is vast, its golden pillars towering like giants. Sunlight streams through a massive stained-glass window, its sunburst design casting fractured rainbows across the throne. One throne. I wrinkle my nose at it.

Ilriel narrows his eyes at Thorne. What does he see? Does he see the same face I do?

"Your Highness, we found her sneaking through the castle," Farren announces, her voice sickly sweet. "She doesn't have the object. We checked."

She *doesn't*? What did she do with it?

"If she doesn't have the Nightstrand," Ilriel says, his voice low and dangerous, "why is she here?"

I should have kept it. If I had, I wouldn't be standing here now. This could've ended in the dungeons, with Ilriel rotting alongside the starving humans he pretends not to see. Instead, I'm here while he tightens his grasp on everything.

Thorne's expression is a mask of icy composure. "I'm completing my end of a bargain. That's why I'm here."

Ilriel doesn't even acknowledge her, waving the statement

off like a gnat. He orders the guards to search the city for the tiny object he's so obsessed with, already discarding this conversation as beneath him.

At first glance, Thorne seems as calm and collected as a statue. But her fingers twitch, her gaze darts restlessly around the room. I can see it. The nervous energy coiled tight beneath her skin.

She better have a plan. She always has a plan.

"Can I lower my arms now?" Thorne asks, breaking the silence with an out-of-place, casual tone. "You've got my weapons, and my shoulders are killing me."

Ilriel nods curtly, and she lets her arms drop, rolling her shoulders with an exaggerated sigh. Then she gestures at me, her voice sharper. "And maybe let her go? She looks miserable, and we both know she's not going anywhere."

I'm shoved forward when Ilriel releases his fierce grip on me. I stumble directly into Thorne, who catches me, her arms wrapping firmly around my waist.

"What happened to your hair?" she asks, her voice low. "It looks awful."

I groan. I run my fingers through the uneven, short chunk. Sorry, mother.

"There were others, Your Highness," Farren, the ever-obedient snitch, pipes up. "We couldn't locate them, but the guards are still searching. Syvis is with them."

"Of course she is," Ilriel mutters with a weary sigh. "She's insufferable."

"Agreed," Thorne chimes in, glancing toward the door as though expecting something, or someone.

Her hand tightens on my waist as she leans closer, her breath brushing my ear. "I really hope you got what you needed from him because you're out of time."

I did, actually.

"Where is it?" I whisper.

"Shut up," she snaps, her grip on my waist tightening even further. I'm not sure if she realizes, but her fingers are practically digging into me now.

"Take my sister to a cell," Ilriel commands his guards, his voice cold. "Kill her *friend*."

Before anyone can move, one of the guards bursts into flames, their scream ripping through the air. The acrid stench of burning flesh follows, making me gag.

"Oh thank the fucking heavens," Thorne breathes.

Ilriel draws his blade, like a true hero.

It's me he charges at, but his strike never lands. Thorne intercepts him with a knife, one I hadn't even seen her draw, pressing it to his throat. "You shouldn't hit your sister, shame on you."

"Where in the hells were you hiding that?" I ask, muffled by my hand as I cover my nose against the smell.

She doesn't answer. Instead, she drives her knee into Ilriel's gut, sending him stumbling back. "I'm not one of your simpering little guards, *Your Highness*," she spits. "I fight dirty. I live in a sewer."

"Disgusting," Ilriel spits back. He's right. It's disgusting.

Thorne snatches a dagger from the incinerated guard's remains and deflects Ilriel's next attack. The clash of blades rings through the air, sharp and grating.

"Move," Ilriel growls, his teeth bared.

"No. The only reason you're still breathing is because I don't want her angry with me," Thorne says, her knife pressing closer to his throat. "Because she's *really* annoying when she's angry."

I stand there, useless, my eyes darting around the room. Syvis, Zemm, and Lapis are all locked in battle, outnumbered and outmatched by the human and twilight elf guards.

Zemm's spells crowd the air, freezing one guard before incinerating them. Only for another to slam a hammer into his face, breaking his nose. Somehow, he retaliates, bloodied but unrelenting.

Syvis wields her massive sword, holding her own until a crushing blow to her arm shatters her focus *and* her bones.

The sickening crack makes me cringe.

Lapis swings her hammer down with a crunch, shattering the skull of the guard she kicked to the ground. She's breathing hard, her hands raw and bleeding, but she's still standing. Still fighting. Hopefully unbroken.

I don't have time to wonder. A guard barrels toward me, swift and determined, and I'm still unarmed. She's almost on me when a starlight arrow whistles through the air and buries itself in her head.

"Baby elf!" Filauria's voice rings out. The Nightstrand glows faintly in her hand. "Do you always just stand around during battles?"

I shake my head violently, trying to deny it.

"Yes. She does," Thorne answers for me.

Filauria rolls her eyes and lets her bow fade into light before tossing the Nightstrand toward me.

She shouldn't have thrown it.

My fingers barely graze the weapon, and it slips through my grasp. Thorne snatches it midair, a grin spreading across her face.

"See? I told you I—" The words choke off abruptly. Her body stiffens, and her grin falters.

Ilriel's blade is buried in her side.

My heart is a wild, frenzied drumbeat in my chest. My limbs tremble uncontrollably. I can't move, can't even think. Thorne's eyes widen, blood spilling from her lips as she coughs onto my cloak. Ilriel tears the Nightstrand from her grasp, triumphant. He finally has what he's been chasing.

A golden paperweight.

Thorne's grip on my shoulder tightens as she leans against me, refusing to collapse. I wrap my arms around her, holding her upright, though my own legs are shaking beneath her weight. Ilriel's hand still clutches the knife in her side. If I pull her away, will it kill her? If I leave it there, will she bleed out?

I can't breathe. My lungs burn as if the thorny vines of panic around my heart have tightened.

And then Thorne laughs.

A broken, wet, chilling sound.

"If I die, will my curse be over? Will it lift?" Her bloody lips twist into something like a grin. "Can I finally leave this place behind?"

Curse? Does she mean being stuck with me? Is she joking? *Now?*

I clutch her tighter, my knuckles pale, tears blurring my vision. My body trembles with rage. I can't let this end here. I need to fight. To do something. Anything.

She's bleeding out. I don't have a weapon, but I need to do something. Just, *anything*. So I take Thorne's hand. Not in the same way as when she drags me along through a dark alley. Or when she covered my wound, and I held her. Or when she plays with my hair and I swat her away in embarrassment.

No, I take her hand in anger. In a fit of blind rage. I take her hand with the intent to kill.

I interlock our fingers before I slide mine down to her wrist. There's a blade in her wrist cuff, I remember. There's a button, a small spring.

I hold my breath. I don't hesitate. I thrust her hand forward, toward my brother's face. I press the button.

I'm aiming for his eye.

Ilriel jerks back, but not fast enough. The blade slashes through his left eye, and he howls in pain, blood pouring from the ruined socket.

He stumbles, clutching his face. The Nightstrand slips from his fingers, clattering to the stone floor.

I drop Thorne's hand and scramble for the weapon. My fingers tremble as I grasp it, the vibrations of its power rippling through me. Around me, the sounds of battle rage on: metal striking metal, the screams of the dying, the choking stench of blood and scorched flesh.

But all of it fades into nothing.

He lowers his hand from his face, revealing the bloody ruin of his eye socket. His remaining eye burns with a hatred so pure, it's almost alive.

"You stabbed me," he growls, his voice a rasp of pain and disbelief. "In my face. In my *eye*."

My eyes are locked on him. Everything around him is in black and white, but he's shining like the night sky. A beacon, or a target.

I steady the bow, the weapon vibrating in my hand, aimed at his chest.

"Don't shoot me," he whispers. His voice cracks, trembling with a fragile plea. Tears streak his face, mixing with the blood. "Please, Lyri. Don't. I'm sorry." His words spill over, choked and desperate, the way he cried the day he threw me from our home. I wonder if it hurts.

I hate him. I hate him for crying. For making me see this. For making me hesitate.

I should be the one crying.

"Please shoot him," Thorne rasps, her voice coarse.

"You're not a killer," Ilriel says through his sobs. "You have a good heart."

Is it real? His tears? His sorrow? It feels forced. Cheap.

He's wrong, though. I am a killer, but I'm not a murderer. There's a difference.

But it's too late. His words have already wormed their way into my head. My hand is trembling too much to hold steady. It's over.

"Faelyri," Ilriel sobs, his voice cracking like brittle glass. "Please don't shoot me. Just talk to me. I've always been there for you. I've done everything for you. I protected you."

A crack of lightning erupts to my left. Zemm's spell. The familiar, deafening clang of Lapis's hammer follows, echoing in my ears and fading into groans.

The battlefield is quieter now, the chaos dimmed to nothing more than the low whimpers of my injured friends.

I try to steady my bow, the arrow pulled taut. Ilriel's crying fills the space between us. Thorne clings to consciousness, barely able to stay upright.

My brother looks pitiful. Hunched over, groveling, a pale shadow of the noble figure immortalized in the grand portraits of our home. There's something satisfying about this, seeing him stripped of his power and pride. This is the release I've crawled through the dark to find, the moment I've dreamed of.

But will it even matter? Will it bring me peace?

"Lyri, I know you love me," Ilriel says, his voice trembling. "And I love you."

But he doesn't. Not really. If he did, he wouldn't be here,

wouldn't be trying to twist my emotions, wouldn't be manipulating me like this. It's true that I love him, though.

And that would almost be funny, if it wasn't so heartbreakingly tragic.

"Lyri," he continues, his breathing uneven, "if you kill me now, while I'm trying to make peace, they might take it all from you."

I laugh bitterly. "Who cares? Even now, you can't see that I'm not like you? I don't care about power the way you do. Grow up."

Behind me, Thorne coughs. The wet sound of it sends a chill through me. I don't turn to look. I'll get her out of here when this is over.

"Fine." Ilriel's voice grows sharper, though his words are broken, his strength fading. "Go back to your tiny, dark island, Faelyri. Hide. But when I recover, I'll hunt you down. You'll never have a moment's rest. I'll conquer this place. I'll destroy you. I won't just kill you. I'll break you."

Bold words for a man who just lost an eye. I draw my arrow back further, ready to release, but Thorne collapses into me, dragging us both down.

I push her off me in a panic. She's pulled the blade out of her side. The blood pours freely now, staining her hands, mine, the floor beneath us. Why would she do that? She told me not to do that!

I press my hands to her wound, trying to staunch the bleeding. My cloak is off in an instant, wrapped tightly around her waist in a makeshift bandage.

"Lapis!" I scream, my throat raw. "Lapis!"

My head throbs from the collision with the ground, but I can't focus on it. My hands are slick with Thorne's blood, trembling as I try to keep her alive.

"Lapis!" I call again, desperate.

She's breathing, but her face is losing color. She opens her bloody mouth. One of her eyes is closed, but the other meets mine. "You're such an idiot." She spits up blood.

We should have just left. I wasted way too much time.

Finally, Lapis is here, shoving me aside with one battered arm. "We need to move her. Back to the guild."

"You're not supposed to move someone who's—" I start to protest.

"You want to stay *here*?" she snaps. No. I don't want to stay here.

I glance back toward where Ilriel had been, but he's gone. Farren's gone. All of Ilriel's guards lie dead on the floor, their blood mingling with the others.

Syvis is writhing in agony, cradling her broken arm. Zemm's face is a mess of blood, his nose broken, but he's still standing.

This is my fault. I let him get in my head. I let his crying weaken me. I let him escape.

Just yesterday, this room might have been filled with laughter, music, the cheers of a merry court. Dancers spinning, jesters performing.

And now we're here, and my friends are dying.

TWENTY-FOUR

Thorne is sprawled upon the narrow cot, her skin as pale as the moon's glow. Her chest rises and falls with agonizing slowness, and the copper tang of blood fills the air. Beside me, Lapis hovers over her.

"I need to remove her shirt," Lapis says, her hand already reaching toward the leather ties of her vest.

A weak cough escapes Thorne's lips as her trembling hands move to the ties, but I brush them aside. "I'll just do it," I say.

My fingers, unsteady as they are, work at the laces. I move slowly, fearful of causing her further harm.

"Could you *hurry*?" Lapis snaps.

"I'm trying," I mutter, throat tight. But I can't hurry. This isn't just a nameless soldier. I know I'm taking too long. I can't make it worse.

And... this isn't how I'd ever imagined undressing someone for the first time. Not that I'd been thinking about that. At all. And not her. Just someone. Not her.

My face burns even as Thorne's gasp of pain drags me from my spiraling.

Beneath the vest, her black tunic clings to her skin, sodden with blood, the crimson stain spreading from where the blade had pierced her.

The blood-soaked leather is rough beneath my fingers. I trace its edges with my thumb. Whatever this is, wherever it's from, it saved her life.

When my gaze finally meets Thorne's, her lips curled into a faint, bloody smirk, despite her agony. "What are you staring at?" she rasped.

Ugh.

The smell of iron hangs thick, mingling with sweat. My heart pounds as I linger here, at times leaning forward to watch as Lapis pulls a thread through Thorne's skin. The color hasn't returned to her face yet, her eyes flutter closed against the pain. I wish I knew what she was thinking.

I should check on the others. But I can't help them.

"Syvis has a broken arm," I begin, only for Lapis to cut me off.

"And Zemm's got a broken nose. I can't even stand without wincing, and you *definitely* have a concussion. I *know,*" she snaps.

Okay. She knows.

I sit back, fidgeting with my clothing and uneven hair. My leg bounces uncontrollably until Lapis slams her bloodied hand against it. "*Stop!*"

I clasp my hands over my knees to still them, watching helplessly as she works. With each movement of Lapis's, each time the needle pierces the skin, Thorne gasps through clenched teeth.

"Don't be so dramatic," Lapis mutters as she finally tightens the last of the wrappings. "It'll numb soon enough. You can move, but I wouldn't. It'll hurt."

With a final sigh, Lapis wipes her hands clean and turns

toward the door. "On to the next one," she says before the heavy wooden door slams behind her.

Once we're alone, Thorne shifts with a groan. "Get me a clean shirt."

I obey, rifling through her belongings until I find something, likely her last one. She snatches it from me without a word and begins peeling the blood-soaked fabric from her body.

I should look away, but I can't. I'm staring at her for too long. At her body. She's thinner than I am, taller. And muscular, but that's not surprising. She's so strong; of course she's muscular. Why wouldn't she be?

Am I still staring?

"Do you mind turning around?" She snaps.

"I was looking at the blood," I say, but oblige.

My hair tightly winds around my index finger as my gaze follows the grooves in the wooden door.

She scoffs. From now behind me, she says, "if you knew you couldn't handle it, you should've let someone else take care of it. I got stabbed, you know."

I know. Everyone is dying, and my brother is gone.

"Would you have cared if I died?" she asks.

"I would care if *anyone* died!"

"You can turn around now."

Slowly, hesitantly, I turn.

She runs her hands over her chest briefly before combing her fingers through her blood-matted hair.

"I went into that awful place for *you*," she says, picking up her torn and bloodied shirt. The sound of fabric tearing under her hands follows.

"I'm sorry," I murmur. "I know this was my fault." Apologizing is all I can muster.

"Yes."

Ouch.

I glance at my twisting fingers as my mind scrambles for something, anything, to ease the tension. But there was nothing I could say to undo what had happened.

"How did they catch you?" I finally ask her.

She sits back on the bed with a heavy expression, "I went to the Princess's room, and I stayed too long," she admitted. "Laid in that bed. In *her* bed. That's how they caught me."

My mouth twists into a snarl. "They caught you with her? Don't you really think it was the time to—"

"I have a sentimental attachment to the room. I don't care about her."

Hard to imagine she can have a sentimental attachment to anything. Though, of course, she would. "Who swapped the two of you? Did you do it yourself?"

"As a baby?"

"Well, I don't know! I don't know how it works. Why would someone do that?"

"Why would someone infiltrate the royal family with a hold on over half of the continent?"

Right. "But, why her? Why not an advisor... or..."

"Because no one cares about a princess."

I clutch my chest.

"That wasn't an insult."

She raises a hand to her throat, the lingering burn now faint but still on her skin as a reminder.

"Iron burns the fey," I said softly. "You're a changeling. The princess was taken, and you were put in her place. How long?"

Silence.

"And there's something binding you, a curse," I continue. "You can't speak of it, can you?"

Thorne's mouth opens, and for a moment, it seems she might try. The silence stretches before a whisper finally breaks free. "I can twist my words within reason. But I don't like to risk it."

I exhale. "Was that truly her? Standing there when Ilriel made his speech? Does she even know?"

"I don't know what she knows," Thorne admits. "If she has my memories, her own, or if she's nothing at all."

"Is this face you wear fabricated? Intentionally fabricated for this unique position you were placed in?"

She shakes her head. "I was just blessed with this one."

Yeah, no kidding.

"And hers?"

"Glamoured, maybe. Who knows what's under there. Or, maybe she was also blessed."

A sharp groan pulls her back to the present, her hand clutching at her side.

"You had an entire life. Living like royalty," I snap. "Like a princess. You made me feel like I had everything, and you had nothing."

"I was not a princess. I was absolutely powerless my entire life. I was a shadow living in the cracks of—" She tries to continue, but whatever magic binds her renders her words inaudible.

Her hand goes to the royal blade strapped to her thigh, unsheathing it with deliberate grace. The silver edge gleams as she turns it over in her hands.

She tries again, "sent away from home, from everything familiar, just for—"

She sheathes the blade.

"Where are you from?"

"Thistleglade."

"I didn't think someone like you could be from a place so whimsical."

"That's because it isn't."

"Have you been back? Since you were sent away?"

"Once," she says. "And never again."

"And who cursed you?"

No reply.

"How did you get out? Why aren't you still there?"

More silence.

"Why are you entertaining me right now? With what little you can say?" I finally ask.

An answer, at last, "as much as I regretted any moment of drunken vulnerability. I also felt relief."

I'm finally getting it. I'm getting everything. Every answer to every mystery she is shrouded in. The pieces of her life are forming a picture. But I need to know more. I need to know the things she can't tell me. I have to find a way to free her from this curse.

Because I have to know.

"To answer a question I'm sure you have," she starts, "I have never glamoured any of you. I promise you that."

"But no one recognizes you other than that woman in the kitchen..."

"I said I have never glamoured any of *you*."

"Does Zemm know?"

"He knows I'm a faerie, yes."

"And he let me make that deal with you?"

She smirks, sharper this time, "it's a big payday."

And then, a flush of anger as I say, "you can make anyone do anything. You could have *forced* Filauria to come with me."

"She showed up, didn't she?"

Oh... I guess so.

"Would you like me to?" she continues. "Do you want me to force her to swear to do anything you need, no matter the cost?"

It's tempting. But I can't be that person. "No."

But then she straightens, stepping closer. Her eyes lock onto mine, and her next words come out in a quiet rush. "I have to confess something to you. I think it's eating me alive. Rotting me from the inside."

I freeze, my heart thundering in my chest. Her intensity pins me in place as I study her face, waiting.

"I think about you," she says, her voice trembling slightly. "All the time. At night, when I'm alone. That's why I come to your room."

I swallow against the lump forming in my throat.

"There's something about you," she continues, stepping so close our breaths mingle. "You fight back. I like that. Maybe I'm just a freak." Her hands find my waist, holding me firmly.

And I like that she doesn't treat me like glass.

But I let out my breath. "What are you doing?"

Her lips curled into a faint, pained smile. "I hate it," she says, "I hate that I think about you. Someone so sad that your sadness comes out in outbursts of anger. I hate that I *want* you."

"You don't believe that," I say, "The stuff you said—"

She interrupts me, "But you're a fallen star, and that's why you act the way you do. Because you fell from the sky, and crashed into the darkness. And now you're wandering down here, trying to return to your sky. I hate that you're beautiful, too beautiful."

I don't know what's happening. I'm afraid, but also not. My eyes linger on her soft lips. In return, she's eyeing me. I need to make a choice now.

She grabs my face, hand tightly holding my jaw. My lips are parted. My breathing is heavy. Her lips brush against mine. I close my eyes.

Her mouth is soft, but her kiss isn't. It isn't gentle or safe. It's full of built-up frustration. She drops her hand from my jaw. She's kissing me as if she needs to hurry. Like she's trying to prove something or is running out of time. Her hands are in my hair, gripping tightly to me as if to keep me here in this spot forever.

I've never done this before. I don't know what I'm doing, or if I'm even doing a good job. But she presses farther into me. And I like it. I like it too much, My body is on fire. I can't like it this much. Not with her. Not with someone so beautiful and dangerous and terrible for me.

A cunning trickster shall weave deceit, stealing what is yours by sleight and guile.

When she lets out a soft moan in my mouth, that's when I push her away from me.

"Is this a joke? Are you playing a prank on me?" I ask.

"What? N-no, of course not. I—"

"Never do that again. I won't be something for you to use and throw away. Like all of those women in the taverns."

Her expression darkens, voice cold. "Who cares about them?"

"Exactly."

"You kissed me back. You *wanted* to kiss me."

Yes, I did. I wanted to kiss her so badly that my body aches and my heart cracks. And cracks. And cracks as I stare at her face. I want to keep kissing her.

But I just can't. I cannot do this. Not with her. Not with someone who had tricked me into a bargain whose price I don't yet know. Not with someone who could so easily manipulate me if I let her in. Servitude or death? No.

I cannot like her. If I like her, it'll be easier for her to gain power over me.

"So you're jealous?" she asks.

"You got it out of your system," I answer, "so I assume you're satisfied."

"*You* wanted to kiss me."

"Don't you know when people are lying? Haven't you learned to tell?"

Her teeth grind in her mouth. "Not everyone."

Without waiting for her response, I turn and leave, my steps echoing in the corridor. The door creaks shut behind me, but something stops me when I turn the corner.

I can't believe my first kiss was in a sewer.

Filauria stands against the wall, her posture casual but still so regal, almost sucking the air from my lungs. She tilts her head as I stare, and then she begins to approach.

She's here? Why wouldn't she have just left?

When she stops in front of me, I bowed instinctively.

"Your brother is gone, baby elf," she says. "Most likely retreated to plan his next move. It does not matter. We have more important things to worry about."

"You're... coming with me? Why?"

"Your friend," she pauses. "Hunted me down in the castle and begged. She was very pathetic."

"I was also inspired by your courage," she continues. "It has been many long years since any elf has shown me kindness."

A heat rises to my face, unbidden, and I fight the urge to shy away. Courage? Perhaps I am. More courageous than my brother. "You shouldn't have been treated so cruelly," I say.

"The same could be said of you."

No. It doesn't compare. She has centuries over me.

"Was I truly your hero?" she asks.

"Yes." Embarrassment doesn't matter anymore. "I admired

the way you carved your own path, forged your own destiny. I wanted to follow that example, but I never managed to. It's actually kind of funny," I finish, "I never thought I could do much of anything at all."

"You did so much. Be proud of yourself."

I let out a breath. I had clung to that tale told to me in childhood, blissfully ignorant of how far it strayed from the truth. Though, perhaps, I had always known on some level. Or I had been drawn to her by some ancient, weird, ancestral bond.

Her laugh is melodic. "You look like my child, you know."

"Actually, I look like my mother. Her name..."

What was I saying? These walls are so gray. Everything here is gray.

"I'm sorry," I shake my head, "Her name was Narunn."

Filauria's face tenses, her brow furrowing. Like to grasp the threads of a forgotten memory. "You say *was?*"

Is it cold in here? The emptiness of the corridor presses in around us, a chilling breeze raising the hairs on my arms. "She... was... yes," I manage. I try to continue, but my voice falters, my jaw clenching against a welling tide of grief.

"She is dead?"

Ilriel...

Can I say it? Can I even get the words out? "I..."

Breathe. Breath and it will all be okay. Five breaths. It's okay. It will all be okay.

The weight of her hand on my shoulder steadies me. Grounds me here in this moment with her. "My parents were..."

"They would be very proud of you."

"I know," I whisper. "So, we need to reach Starview. Immediately. Or as soon as we can. So they can continue to be proud."

She nods.

I can't talk about my parents anymore. I refuse. I can't tell anyone about what Ilriel did, not yet. "And then I need to find my brother. Or..." What did he say? Uh... the princes. "Hollow Haven, Grimehold, Deadbell."

I don't want to go back to Grimehold. Even the name makes me shudder. "I need to go there. Stop them, right? I need to make sure Agnat is okay."

My mouth won't stop. My voice breaks, as does the seal holding my tears in. "For Lapis. Vum Dorahl is her home. And Zemm, his mother in Dazzoran. And are there people in the wastelands? And Venali..."

"Breathe," she says softly, reaching out with steady hands. "One thing at a time. Right now, our only concern is that weapon. But wait... You've met Venali?"

Right. Yeah. Right. I take one long, deep breath, expanding my chest. "He thought I was you."

"Senile old man."

He's not. But...

"Filauria," I breathe, "did you command swamp elf children to be killed?"

Her gaze does not waver. "I saw to the punishment of every soul who harmed the swamp elves," she replies. "I sought out Venali in Mirrormire to offer restitution, to assure him that I played no hand in the deaths of his kin. And to beg forgiveness for my silence when he came to me, for failing him when he needed me most. I wished only to set things right."

All I can muster is a nod.

"One thing at a time," she repeats.

She *is* right that I need to focus on one thing at a time. Right now, the Nightstrand is my focus. That was my original plan when I got this responsibility, and I'm finally seeing it through.

I'll let Ilriel rest while he can. He will never get in my head again. His good fortune has been used up, if he had any to begin with.

"When should we leave?" I ask her.

"Once your friends are able to travel again."

❧

The path to Candlewood was grueling, but the voyage across the open sea was worse.

When the relentless churn of the waves didn't render me seasick, I found myself in silence. What will happen when I get home? Perhaps I won't even make it through the gates. A stray arrow might shoot me down, loosed by a would-be bounty hunter seeking what was promised for my head.

But... perhaps they don't believe it.

And my parents, immortalized in the painted portraits that hang within the halls of our home. They are waiting for me. They're going to be so happy to see me. My mother would be furious over the jagged cut of my hair. She was obsessed with Elven tradition.

What will I say to them first? *Did you know orcs can wield magic?*

They would delight in that. They would love my friends. They would be glad to see Syvis and I reunited, even if they have never been introduced. They would find solace in knowing I am guarded well.

Ilriel will come back though. *I'll torment you.* What more can he even do? I'd say I'm pretty tormented. I could invent a new stage of grief.

I tear my gaze from the shimmering horizon, the stinging salt air pulling me from my thoughts. There, above the waves, I can see it now: the grey mountain crowned in mist, where my city rests. Starview is close.

With my companion's injuries, the climb will be strenuous. I need to push them a bit more, they can rest at the top. They'll be in awe when they see it. The walk will be worth it.

There's never been a more beautiful city than Starview.

CHAPTER

TWENTY-FIVE

The ivy-covered gates of my home stand before us. Only silence lies beyond. Once we pass through, the wind stops, and the air becomes still.

"This is it?" Lapis asks, "It's a mess…"

The lanterns that once brought me comfort through the starry streets have been shattered, their glass scattering along the road. Gardens have been stomped out; the life of the well-loved flower patches cut short. Along with the broken glass, there are weapons littering the ground. Some are broken, but at least there are no corpses to accompany them. Many of the once beautiful buildings have begun to fall apart…

Everything looks as though it's been looted.

At least it's all still shrouded in the night sky, still beautifully covered in stars. The barrier is still holding strong.

Thorne lets out a short breath behind me. This is nothing like I envisioned when I brought my friends to my home. There was supposed to be joy, a celebration in our honor, or something.

There's no joy here now, only horror.

"It was not like this when I left, Your Highness." Syvis assures me. "He must have done this afterwards. He stayed behind…"

"Where is everyone…? This is creepy," Lapis mumbles.

"They're sleeping." I say. "It's the middle of the night."

"How do you know?" Zemm asks, "Isn't it always night here?"

"I can tell."

I tread softly through the silent remains of the once-glorious city. Faint glimmers of light flicker in some of the windows, defying the oppressive quiet.

However, there are no soldiers.

"Your Highness," Syvis calls, "Please be careful."

My steps carry me onward along the peaceful, eerily serene path toward the castle. The others follow at a wary distance, their whispers muffled by the wind. As I move, the breeze carries the delicate fragrance of moonflowers to me, a sweet, intoxicating aroma so vivid it seems almost tangible. I pause briefly, letting myself be enveloped by its haunting familiarity.

My gaze shifts to the left, to the small garden near the softly murmuring stream.

Then, the castle comes into view, its spires rising like sentinels of memory. My balcony juts over the cliff's edge, a faint silhouette against the night sky. I should have listened to Syvis about leaning over the edge.

Steeling myself, I press forward, each step heavier than the last.

The massive double doors loom ahead. It takes every ounce of strength in me to push them open, their groaning protest echoing in the stillness. Gasps of awe ripple through the group behind me as we cross the threshold, but I barely notice. My goal lies beyond the throne room, to the altar.

The ancient floor beneath us glows, just like they wanted.

The only sounds that accompany us are the soft clinks of Syvis's armor and the steady cadence of our boots against stone.

As we pass the portraits of my family, I crane my neck upward to meet their solemn gazes. I linger for but a moment. Their faces, regal and eternal.

Are they proud?

"Your Highness," Syvis urges.

Yeah, I know.

Weariness claws at my resolve as I reach the throne room doors. With a surge of determination, I throw my weight against them. Thorne moves to assist, but I brush her off. I need to do this.

The doors creak open, and behind me comes a shriek. The voice is distant, meaningless. My attention is fixed on the thrones.

Noise fades. The world itself seems muted, save for the haunting melody emanating from the weapon strapped to my side. It sings a song of anguish, each note a shard of pain piercing through me.

Moonlight spills through the high windows, its pale beams shimmering on the still waters of the pool in the center of the room. I do not lift my eyes to the heavens. Instead, I focus on the reflection in the water.

A hand seizes my arm. "Faelyri..." Thorne whispers my name, her grip firm but trembling. Her voice carries an edge of desperation. "Fallen star," she shakes me lightly.

Slowly, I raise my head.

My parents sit upon the thrones, their forms regal, waiting to welcome me home.

But their eyes... Their lifeless eyes stare into nothingness. Their faces are bloated and pale, their bodies waterlogged, the ocean's cruel mark. My mother's face is twisted. That's it, that's my face.

He dug them up. He desecrated their graves and placed them here, twisted effigies of the lives they once led.

Filauria's voice cracks as she murmurs, her words trembling. "That is my child..."

I step forward, the weight of grief threatening to crush me. The shallow pool is no obstacle; I wade through it, moonlight shattering around me as my cloak drags through the water. My footing falters, and I stumble, scraping my knees against the cold stone.

Still, I rise, trembling and unsteady. My hands shake as I reach for my mother's cold, lifeless hand. Kneeling before her, I press her hand to my face, the chill seeping into my skin.

Silent tears give way to violent sobs, and then to a scream: raw, guttural, and agonized. My nails tear into the delicate fabric of her gown as I cling to her, desperate for the impossible.

I pull myself to my feet, using her still form for support. Her head lolls as I wrap my arms around her, shaking her, begging her to wake.

She won't wake, of course. She never will.

Her body slumps lifelessly to the side, her right arm dangling over the carved armrest of the throne. When she does not stir at my touch, despair drives me back down the short flight of steps, collapsing onto the cold floor.

I turn to my father, grasping at a fading hope, and reach for his hand. I shake it with trembling desperation, pulling as if to summon him back from the abyss. His body shifts, but only to lurch forward, hanging limply in final resignation.

Even now, his hair glimmers faintly, a halo that mocks the lifelessness that has claimed him.

Suddenly, rough, damp arms encircle me, the leather of

gloves pressing firmly into my skin. They do not pull me away, but hold me steadfast, grounding me in this unbearable moment. Thorne and I both sink to the floor as she embraces me, as if she means to fuse her strength with mine.

"Release me," I command, though my voice carries no actual authority. I don't want her to let go.

"No."

Syvis looms above us now, her voice strained. "We… we should bury them."

"No!" My voice breaks. "No, I don't want to!" I clutch the fragments of what I have left. I can't let them take my parents from me again.

"They cannot remain here, Your Highness," Syvis insists. "We must return them to their graves. They deserve to rest."

She falters briefly but then calls to the others, she kneels and begins to lift my father with reverence. "Help me carry them to the burial site," she commands.

In desperation, I struggle to rise, to stop her, but Thorne's hands are strong as she holds me down. I twist against her, my body writhing. My fist connects with her face, a wild and clumsy strike fueled by grief, but she absorbs the blow without faltering, her grip steady.

My gaze darts to Zemm, who gently cradles my mother's fragile form, lifting her from the throne. My hand shoots out, grasping hers one final time. The weight of her touch anchors me, but it slips away as Zemm pulls her from my reach. Her ring, delicate and ornate, slides from her finger and into my trembling grasp.

"Please," I plead, my voice breaking. "Please, don't take her from me. I need her."

Zemm pauses for the briefest moment, sorrow etched into his features. "Lyri, I'm sorry," he murmurs. With great care, he supports her head, though the gesture feels hollow in the face of death. He follows Syvis, their forms retreating into the shadows, carrying with them the last remnants of my heart.

Never feel this again.

A single shallow grave had been prepared long ago, a haven where my parents once lay together in peace. Now, their bodies are lowered gently into its embrace, Syvis and Zemm performing the task with solemn care. I clench my fists at my sides, resisting the primal urge to throw myself into the grave.

How could he have done this? What filled his twisted heart as he orchestrated this desecration, satisfaction? Regret? How long had they been sitting there, reduced to grotesque ornaments of his malice?

I will find him. And when I do, his body will be left to rot in disgrace.

Syvis clears her throat, breaking the oppressive silence. "They were noble and loving parents," she says, her voice steady but filled with reverence. "They gave life to a brave and brilliant young woman. It has been an honor to serve their name." She bows deeply to the grave before turning to me. "Your Highness, would you like to speak?"

I say nothing, so Filauria steps forward in my stead, her tone soft and measured. "No mother should need to bury her daughter. The lands beyond this mountain are serene and untouched by sorrow. Please find peace there."

"May Belvadon's light guide them," Lapis intones solemnly, her hands clasped in prayer.

"I... I'm sorry, Lyri," Zemm says haltingly, his usual composure faltering. "I don't have the words. None seem right."

Thorne steps forward, as though summoning the courage to speak, but after a deep inhale, she falters. Taking a step back, she lowers her gaze.

I toy with the ring that now adorns my finger, the last vestige of my mother. Zemm uses his magic to cover their bodies with earth. The soil moves swiftly under his command, far quicker than any tool could manage.

Syvis comes to my side and places a firm hand on my shoulder, and I let my head rest against it, closing my eyes as the finality of the moment washes over me.

"Faelyri," she murmurs gently, leaning her head against mine, "are you certain you do not wish to say a few words?"

"I spoke my words to them long ago," I reply, my voice

quiet. But then, after a deep breath, I add, "Still... I'm sorry. Sorry for all the times I overslept. For never taking things seriously when you wanted me to. But you should know... I'm taking this seriously. I've kept my promise, I found her. And now..." My voice wavers, and I steel myself. "Now I'm going to find him. I'll throw Ilriel from the highest balcony if I have to. Did you know he did that to me? It doesn't matter, I suppose."

I glance skyward, the weight of the grave too much for my gaze to linger upon. "I don't know if I was ever the daughter you hoped for. I know I didn't have a lot going for me, but I really hope you're proud of me now."

The wind stirs the tree above, its branches creaking.

There is no reason to remain any longer. I turn away from the grave, away from my parents, and begin my march toward the altar.

Filauria alone follows me.

CHAPTER
TWENTY-SIX

Filauria grips the Nightstrand tightly, its glow pulsating with an eerie, rhythmic light. The artifact hums its haunting melody.

"It's loud," I murmur, gripping the side of my head.

We stand before Starview's ancient altar, its stone weathered by time, but still magnificent. Older than the city itself, its grand steps stretch upward, each carved with runes that hum with dormant power. This was a place of union and eternity, where my parents had been bonded many lifetimes ago. I remember coming here as a child, drawn to it.

Filauria begins to speak, but the words that leave her lips are unfamiliar. Neither the Elven tongue nor the common language of Farfell, it is something older, something primordial. Her voice is steady and commanding, carrying authority.

Suddenly, light erupts around us. Blinding, overwhelming. I shield my eyes against its brilliance, and when I lower my hand, the world has changed. A dense fog envelops the altar, the starlight extinguished, leaving behind an unnerving emptiness. The altar itself is drained of color, its vibrancy replaced with the pallor of death.

I glance down at my hands. They are nearly transparent, a ghostly sheen overlaying my skin like a fine film. I raise one hand, peering through my palm, disoriented by its semi-ethereal state.

Did I die? Did she kill me?

Filauria continues her incantation, the strange language pouring from her lips as if drawn from another realm. From the fog, two luminous wisps drift forward, their forms radiating a pale, otherworldly glow. They circle me with an unnerving curiosity, scanning me as though assessing my very soul.

Filauria addresses them in their cryptic tongue. One of the wisps transforms before my eyes, shifting into a radiant spirit, her form shimmering like living flame. Her features are intricate, her body detailed and human-like, yet entirely composed of light. She extends a hand toward me, the particles of her skin disassembling into specks of brilliance before reassembling seamlessly.

The second wisp lingers behind me, smaller and less assured. Her movements are tentative, her curiosity tempered by caution.

The first spirit speaks, her voice a melodic echo. Though I cannot understand her words, Filauria responds, and a flicker of frustration crosses the spirit's luminous face.

Then, abruptly, she addresses me in Elven. "Why is a mortal here? Have you come to visit your parents, child?"

My eyes widen, "what? My parents are here?"

The spirit turns back to Filauria as they exchange sharp words in their ancient dialect. Filauria steps between us, her expression unyielding as she slams the Nightstrand into the spirit's outstretched hand.

"Keerla," she says, her voice edged with exhaustion, "I am weary of this. Fix the mess you caused. This girl has endured enough."

The spirit, Keerla, returns the Nightstrand to her sister, her luminous face unreadable. "Do not lay this at my feet. I am not to blame for your precious weapon's decline. You are the one who abandoned your home."

Even goddesses hate their siblings. Good to know they aren't too far above us.

The second spirit, who must be Velle, steps forward, her

movements hesitant. She takes the Nightstrand from Filauria's hand and examines it closely.

"Can you speak our language?" Velle asks me in Elven, her voice softer than her sister's.

I shake my head.

She places the Nightstrand into my palm. "How, then, can you wield this?"

"It sings to me," I admit. "There's a song that guides me."

Her glowing hand closes over mine, warm despite its ethereal nature. "Do you know how to restore it?"

Again, I shake my head.

Velle glances back at her bickering sisters, a flicker of exasperation crossing her radiant face. She hesitates, as though on the verge of saying something more, but remains silent.

I follow her gaze to the others. "Do they always fight?"

She nods. "Terribly." Her hand tightens around mine. "I am sorry about your family. This was not meant to happen to you. Not yet."

"Yet?"

She nods again. "This was foreseen, but the timing was not ours to choose. The Nightstrand should not have waned so soon."

Destiny, it seems, has a cruel sense of timing. Yet, if they required a descendant of hers, I guess it had to be me. Ilriel is too far gone.

The thought of my brother ignites a fire within me, and I find myself speaking before I can stop. "I don't know what to do about Ilriel," I confess. "Do you know where I can find him?"

"He is in Farfell," Velle replies, her voice carrying the weight of certainty. "He will not return here. If you wish to draw him out, sever his ties to the great cities. Leave him with nowhere to run."

"How?"

She mimics the motion of a blade slicing across her throat, her glowing face unyielding. "Kill his allies."

His allies. The human princes? A knot tightens in my chest at the mere thought of facing them. "I don't know if I can do that," I admit, my voice barely above a whisper.

"It was merely a suggestion."

I should use this to my advantage, being in the presence of a deity, a being with knowledge far surpassing anything I could ever hope to grasp.

This might be my only chance to gain an answer to every question I'll ever have.

"How old are you?" I ask her.

Really? That's what comes to mind?

Velle's radiant visage flickers gently, like the calm embers of a fire. "I am the eldest, though I cannot say when I was born. Keerla came after, and then Filauria." Her tone shifts slightly, almost playful. "Does my form unsettle you?"

"No," I reply honestly. "I think you're beautiful."

I hope that when I die, I take a form much like hers. Being a spirit wouldn't be so bad if I was made of light.

Time here feels strange, slippery, as if it has no anchor. How long have I been here?

"How do I fix it?" I ask at last, my voice laced with desperation.

Velle's luminous eyes bore into mine. "Oh! You agonized over this for so long, and the answer is so simple. It simply requires an exchange of life. Easy."

"What does that mean?"

Before she can respond, Keerla does, her voice louder and more casual than I expect. "It needs a sacrifice at the altar."

I whip my head toward Filauria, panic surging through me. "You didn't tell me I would need to sacrifice someone!"

Filauria's eyes widen slightly, then narrow as they settle on Keerla. "I did not know," she admits. "Why is this necessary?"

"Why would it not be necessary?" Velle interjects. "Its power comes from life."

Keerla snaps, "if you are so attached to your selfish obsession with the mortal realm, sacrifice another. Keep your power and your filthy city. Or choose the more reasonable option and come home."

My legs weaken beneath me. My voice shakes as I point the Nightstrand at Keerla. "Take a soul from here. Use someone who's already dead."

Velle recoils, her light dimming in dismay. "That is vile. Would you condemn a soul to be bound here with us?"

"I don't know," I admit, my voice trembling. "Maybe. I don't want to. But I've come this far."

Keerla tilts her head. "Any soul?" she muses. "Your mother's, perhaps?"

My mother? No. Never her.

Keerla's tone turns icy. "The weapon fades, the home she built will crumble, and with nothing left, our sister will have no choice but to return to us."

Myself, Ilriel, my friends. All pawns in their cosmic game. They shattered my family to mend their own. Why did I have to go through that?

"Foreseen," I repeat Velle's words, "but you mean orchestrated."

"That is correct," Keerla answers.

Filauria, unbowed and resolute, steps forward, her light burning brighter. "You cannot control me, Keerla," she says, her voice like steel. Then she turns to me, her gaze softening. "Granddaughter, I will be your sacrifice. I am tired. Two thousand years is a long time to walk this mortal realm."

"*What?*" I ask.

"I will give myself to your cause," Filauria declares, her voice unwavering. "I am tired of my sisters trying to govern every fragment of my existence, treating me as if I were still a child. They destroyed your life in their schemes, and I cannot abide it any longer. End me with the Nightstrand, hunt down your brother, and avenge your parents. Avenge my daughter."

"Filauria, this is madness," Velle snaps.

Her expression remains calm, serene even, as she responds, "I am volunteering." She turns to me, "thank you for listening to my story."

My grip on the Nightstrand tightens, my clammy fingers trembling as the artifact's dim glow flickers faintly. When it begins to hum, louder than ever, I can't hold on any longer. I drop it, the hilt clattering to the ground.

"There you go," I say, my voice hollow. "I... I don't care anymore. I'm sorry."

I think I'm going mad.

"I am so sorry, but I just don't care," I continue, turning to Filauria. "I'm not going to kill you."

"But I am—"

I raise my hands to cut her off. "I won't do it. Everything I've been through, every harrowing step of this cursed journey, led me to my home, and that was the worst moment of my life. I can be a killer, but I am not a murderer. And you... do not deserve to die."

I shift my gaze to her sisters, steel edging my tone. "But my brother does. If it's him you want, I can do that instead."

Keerla begins to change. Her once-pure glow deepens, shifting to an angry red that burns like molten fire. "Oh? I do not want your brother," she spits.

"Why?" I demand, my voice rising with defiance. "He's a descendant, isn't he? Doesn't he share your bloodline? Isn't that enough?"

Keerla's rage intensifies, her heat forcing beads of sweat to form on my brow. Her voice rumbles like a storm. "Because your brother is worthless."

The words spill from my mouth before I can think. "Tae'ril?"

Velle gasps, her glowing hand covering her mouth. She murmurs something in their ancient tongue, her light flickering faintly.

Filauria interjects, "do not bargain for me."

Keerla's red hue begins to fade, shifting back toward white, though it doesn't fully return. "You believe you can bring him to me?"

I actually wish Thorne were here. She is very good at making bargains. What would she do? How would she word this?

"Yes." Am I mad? Probably. "I'll bring him to you. *After* I deal with Ilriel, I'll hunt him down and deliver his soul. Just give me time."

Keerla's gaze pierces through me, her light shifting to an icy calm, as if savoring my desperation. "You have been watched," she says coldly, her voice carrying an edge of cruel amusement. "We have seen you and your companions. And because of that, we know how slim your chances truly are."

Her words sting, but I force myself to stand taller. "Then let Filauria come with me," I counter. "Let her help. Give her the chance to find closure. You believe she betrayed you by choosing that man? How sweet would it be for her to deliver his soul to you herself?"

Keerla glances at Filauria, the two exchanging a silent, weighty look.

"How much time do you need?" Keerla finally asks.

"As long as you can give us," Filauria answers before I can.

Keerla's focus shifts back to me. Her voice is colder now,

calculating. "Time flows swiftly, mortal. And the so-called immortality of your kind is an illusion, a vanity of the flesh. But I will grant you this: you have until the final breath of one of your companions to bring me the elf monster. And in the interim, as my gift to you, you may continue to wield the object your people revere."

"I'm not betting the lives of my friends," I retort sharply.

"It is only a window of time," Keerla counters, her tone devoid of sympathy.

"And if I fail?"

"If you fail, as punishment for wasting my time, I shall also claim the soul of your fallen companion."

"That sure sounds like I'm betting their lives."

"That is all I offer," Keerla replies, finality in her tone. "Make a decision."

My friends are strong. They have all come so far with me and survived so much. They would survive this. I have plenty of time. We're all going to live so long.

"I accept your deal."

The blinding light once again engulfs me. The world shifts, the air grows familiar, and when the light fades, I find myself standing beneath Starview's night sky. The altar looms silently behind me.

"Welcome back," Thorne's voice cuts through the silence, steady and calm.

I turn toward her slowly, every movement weighted with exhaustion. She stands on the stairs, arms crossed, her expression unreadable. I can't bring myself to meet her eyes for long and quickly cast my gaze to the ground.

"How long was I gone?" I ask, my voice low and subdued.

"Hours," Filauria is the one who answers from behind me. "We were gone for hours."

"Where are the others?" I ask Thorne.

She lowers her arms and ascends a few steps toward me. "Syvis went door to door, checking on as many people as possible. They're alive but rightfully terrified. There isn't one person here who believes you're capable of what he accused you of. They panicked when they discovered he dug up your parents, and some of them even took what they could and left. That's why this place was a mess. At least he wasn't the one that destroyed it…" She lets out a sigh. "He took anyone he deemed important enough. His counsel and any guard that was willing to follow him. There *are* some left, though, don't worry."

Oh, at least they're safe. That's good news.

Her eyes have concern in them, maybe. Or I'm just seeing what I want to see. They are so beautiful.

I hold my chest, taking a step away from her. My words are soft, as if they were a whisper drowned out by a hurricane. "Please step back."

"They're all awake now," she continues, looking up at the sky. "Though it's the middle of the night. How can you even tell?"

"They are? What is everyone doing? I have to go to them." I take a step down the stairs, but she holds me in place.

Her touch makes everything so much worse.

"Cleaning up the city," she replies, her voice softening. "Zemm and Lapis are helping. You should go to bed."

Are Zemm's wounds going to kill him first? His walk is getting better. He's healing. How long do Orcs live? Lapis won't die. She's far too strong.

Oh, what did I do?

"I can't. I have to go. I have to find my brother." And then I have to find Tae'ril immediately.

"You just buried your parents. Again. I think you deserve to rest."

I can't rest. I don't have the time to rest. "Don't touch me."

Filauria steps in, pulling me away from Thorne. Facing me she says, "I will check on them for you, but your friend is correct. You should go to bed."

Friend? Thorne is not my friend. Thorne has no part in this. I have to check on Zemm, and Lapis, and Syvis. My actual friends whose lives I may have gambled away in selfishness.

CHAPTER

TWENTY-SEVEN

A single sheet of parchment rests on the ivy-clad stone podium before me. The delicate paper trembles in the soft breeze. I reach for it, fingers brushing against its fragile surface, only to let it fall back, fluttering to its quiet perch.

No one has spoken.

A sweet, floral scent rides the wind, curling around me, carrying echoes of home. For a heartbeat, my mind is flooded with memories: soft laughter, warm sunlight. But as swiftly as the scent fades, so do the memories, leaving behind an aching longing I know will never be satisfied.

I've seen my brother stand here countless times, always steady, always unshaken. I stood behind him then, a quiet shadow. The endless sea of stars before us never seemed so vast, so threatening. He was my shield against the enormity of it all.

Now, there's no one to shield me.

My heart pounds in my chest, a wild and erratic drumbeat. My palms are slick, and my hands tremble.

I have to speak. I have to do this.

What did Ilriel say when he stood at this podium? I can't remember.

I clear my throat. "Sorry about the mess!" The words tumble out before I can stop them. *Really?* That's all I've got?

But the silence demands more, so I press on. "We are going to clean it. I promise. I know many of you have already started, thank you for that, but I will help too." My voice falters for a moment. "I am not like Ilriel."

The crowd remains silent, their expressions unreadable in the dim light.

Finally, a voice rises from the front. "We know, Your Highness. We have all been waiting for your return."

My weapon hums softly at my side, as though urging me forward. I take a breath and continue, though my words come slowly. "But I am also not like him in another way, I do not have grand, inspiring speeches prepared. I am sorry for that as well. But... I need to do something that might seem strange. Once we have rebuilt, I will be leaving for a time."

The crowd stirs, their murmurs like the rustle of leaves. Questions ripple through the assembly.

"What about Haelhil?" someone calls.

"They will not come here," I say, though even I can't tell if I'm lying. "Look around you. Our city is safe from the high elves. But Ilriel, he *will* return, and he will bring an army. So I must find him first. I will name a retainer to rule in my place while I am gone."

The murmurs grow louder, disbelief mingling with concern. "How is that possible?" someone demands. "Our rulers don't leave. It's never been done."

"Sometimes," I reply, meeting their eyes, "we must adapt faster than we would like."

"And who will rule while you're gone?"

The first name that comes to mind spills from my lips. "Filauria."

The crowd reacts with a mix of surprise and skepticism. I don't turn to see Filauria's face, but I can feel her incredulity burning at my back.

"I know you are probably confused. Much like I am not a villain, neither is she. Please just trust me," I continue, plowing forward. "And Syvis will train new soldiers. We will need them. If you have ever wanted to learn the sword, now is your chance."

We haven't talked about that, but she'll get over it.

Someone else speaks, their tone wary. "Your Highness, there's still so much to rebuild. What do we do?"

"One piece of stone at a time," I say simply. My gaze drops to the parchment before me. It's blank. I never wrote a word. "Thank you for listening."

A voice rises again. "Why are you thanking us?"

"Because you did not have to stay. Many left when they could. But you are still here, waiting for me. For that, I am grateful."

I crumple the empty sheet and set it back on the podium, stepping aside to bow deeply, an act my brother has never done. He was too good to bow. But these people deserve it.

The crowd erupts into cheers, but the sound rings hollow. There's nothing to celebrate.

Turning, I finally meet Filauria's gaze. Her expression is a storm of disbelief and indignation. "Me?"

"I trust no one else," I admit softly. "It has to be you. Please."

She lowers her voice, "we are supposed to find Tae'ril—"

"And we will. I'll come back for you. This is just for now."

"Why would they want *me*? They do not trust me. A traitor."

"Make them trust you. Retell your story. I'm a traitor, too. You'll be fine."

And Syvis's head shakes, vehement and sharp. "Who will protect you on your journey? I need to go with you."

"Who else could train a new army?" I force a smile I don't feel, "I've made it this far. I'll be okay."

I have to protect myself.

CHAPTER
TWENTY-EIGHT

The moonlight filters through the lattice windows, painting the room in silvery shadows. I sit at a small, ornate table, my fingers wrapped around the stem of a silver wineglass. The other hand cradles the cool, heavy pitcher of crimson wine I'd acquired for myself. The set is beautiful: silver accents curling around the base of the cup like ivy.

But it's also unused, essentially a relic.

Syvis never drinks on the job. Other than her, only my brother and the servants have ever stepped into this room, obviously.

I should be furious with the servants. Furious that they left my parents slumped on those thrones, humiliated. But I just can't be. They were paralyzed by fear of my brother's return.

I barely notice the tears until the dampness soaks through the tablecloth beneath my hand. Grief wells up, sharp and unrelenting.

My grip tightens on the fabric, now translucent and

clinging to the wood beneath. The knock comes, low at first, then louder until the very walls seem to rattle.

I ignore it until it's impossible.

Reluctantly, I rise. When I yank open the door, I'm ready to snap. But it's Thorne, standing there, disheveled in her sleepwear. Her hair tumbles loose over her shoulders, and a blanket is tucked under her arm.

I sag slightly, "What do you want?"

"Want me to stay with you tonight?" she asks.

I blink. "...*What?*"

She holds up the blanket like a peace offering. "I'll sleep on the floor, but you shouldn't be alone. Not here."

"Do you think this is funny?" I demand.

Her gaze scans the room behind me, and she steps inside. She pauses near the table, delicately setting her blanket on one of the chairs.

"How did you know this was my bedroom?"

"I didn't."

I shouldn't let her stay. This room isn't for her.

But the ache of solitude wins.

Her fingers curl around the silver pitcher, lifting it to her nose. "Drinking alone?" she asks, frowning. "You never drink."

"I haven't poured a glass yet, or are you blind?" I motion toward the untouched goblet.

She hesitates, then fills it with a steady hand and passes it to me. Her tone is lighter as she pours one for herself. "I don't even like wine."

"Then why are you drinking it?"

She sips, wrinkling her nose. "Because you shouldn't drink alone." With that, she pulls out a chair and sits as though she belongs here. For once, I don't argue. She's right.

I join her, sinking into the chair opposite hers and lean on my elbow. I take a cautious sip; the bitterness prickles my tongue, better than ale but still foreign. She mirrors me, resting her head on one hand.

"I haven't *really* been in a palace in so long," she says. "Feels strange. I thought it'd remind me too much of home, but it doesn't."

"Well, that's because it's not your home," I reply.

Her eyes glimmer. "Does it feel like home to you?"

My gaze drifts across the room. To the carved canopy over my bed, the faded paintings on the walls, the fireplace reduced to embers, the cool marble beneath my feet. Finally, my eyes settle on the closed balcony door.

This room feels empty. It feels like betrayal.

"No," I admit quietly. "I suppose it doesn't."

I could have let the Nightstrand crumble instead of rebuilding this place on a foundation of chaos. I could have run off with my friends instead of gambling lives like currency. Doing to them what was done to me.

Am I turning into my brother?

Thorne is already pouring herself a second glass. For someone who hates wine, she has no issue drinking it.

"Can I go out there?" she asks, pointing toward the balcony. Her question pulls me from my trance. I hesitate, my chest tightening, but I nod.

I haven't opened that door yet.

She strides to the balcony door, wine glass in hand, and unlatches it. A cool breeze sweeps into the room, carrying with it the scent of night air and something faintly floral. "It's nice out here," she calls.

I believe her. Despite my fear, I finish my glass and follow but stop at the threshold, lingering in the doorway.

She leans over the edge of the stone railing, her hands gripping it tightly. "I won't throw you off, I promise," she teases, glancing back with a smirk.

She steps up onto the ledge, the wind tugging at her hair, her balance perfect and infuriatingly effortless.

She lifts another foot from the ground and my heart leaps into my throat.

"*Get down!*" I shriek at her, my scratchy voice echoing through the air.

Thorne turns her head, eyes wide, before she steps down from the balcony railing.

"It's a long way down," I say, my voice strained. I swallow and add: "You don't want to fall."

My stomach churns, twisting itself into impossible knots. Why am I so frightened? I used to spend hours out here. I'd dangle my legs over the edge, letting them swing through the bars like I had no care in the world. I leaned so far over the railing that my feet lifted off the ground.

I *slept* out here, under the stars.

"I had one of these," she mutters, almost to herself. "Well, *she* has one of these. It's how I'd sneak out." Her voice drops lower. "Gods... that's a long fall."

Despite every instinct screaming at me to stay inside, I step closer, gripping the railing tightly. My fingers curl around the coldness like it's the only thing keeping me tethered to the ground. My breath is shallow, quick. I need to steady it. I need to breathe.

Why can't I breathe?

"Are you alright?" She asks.

I'm struggling, trying to deepen my breath. The mountains in the distance are serene, the calm wind brushes against my face. But this is too much. Why can't I feel my body? I touch my arm, but it isn't my touch. It's someone else's. Or is it mine? I just don't know.

Is it my arm?

"I feel..." I start. My mind flashes to my parents, their lifeless forms, the betrayal. "I feel everything. And nothing. Is that possible? I don't know if I'll ever be alright."

I think this pain is eternal. A bottomless pit I will never climb out of. I'll never forgive my brother for what he's done. One day, I'll drag him here myself and throw him from this very balcony.

My hands clench the railing as I force myself not to look down. "I never wanted anyone to see my home like this. It was... it was so beautiful."

Thorne places a hand on my waist, her touch grounding me. "It still is," she says gently. "Let's go inside. We won't come back out here."

She guides me back into the room, each step feeling like a battle. My breathing steadies the moment I cross the threshold, the heavy door shutting out the night and all its shadows. I pull away from her as soon as I can, retreating to the edge of my bed. The silk sheets ripple beneath me as I sit.

"Why are you really here?" I ask, my voice sharp and cold.

"I came to check in."

"No. You didn't. Don't lie to me."

"I can't lie," she sighs, "But..."

Here we go.

"I hate to be that guy," she starts, " but I also came to discuss our bargain."

Of course. I roll my eyes and lean back slightly. "Oh?"

Her gaze doesn't waver as she repeats my own words back to me, "'You will help me search for my missing friend and deliver me to my home alive. Then, you will be rewarded with something of equal value.'"

I let out a bitter laugh, the sound cutting through the quiet. "And that's all you care about. You came in here pretending to care about me, but it's just the bargain."

"I can care about multiple things," she says simply.

"But you can care more about one over the other."

"Of course, but you'll never truly know which," she smirks. Infuriating.

"I see it now," I say, my tone biting. "You stay silent so often, always, because you can't lie. And it's not worth your time to weave false truths. So tell me, what about our bargain brings you here now? Why now, of all times? Without even giving me a moment to breathe."

Her voice is calm. "You have yet to fulfill your end. I returned you home alive. We found your friend."

I grit my teeth. "As you can see," I snap, "your title and land are not my priority. You already have my crown. Keep it."

"That wasn't the bargain."

My brow furrows. "What? Yes, it was. Land and a title."

She steps closer, looming over me like a shadow. "No. It was something of equal value to your life."

"*What?*"

Her eyes meet mine, unflinching. "The trade was for your life."

My heart pounds, anger flaring hot and wild in my chest. "So you want to control me? Own me? Kill me? Which one?"

"I haven't decided, but certainly not kill."

"You *can't* do that," I hiss, my voice trembling. "I will not offer you my life."

"You made a deal."

I clench my fists, "I'm useless to you. As you always remind me, I'm a queen of a broken land."

"You are. For now."

"You're stealing my free will," I say, my voice breaking. "That's not okay."

"Unfortunate for you," she replies coolly.

My life? Absolutely not. Are the fey immortal? Am I going to be controlled until something kills me? My brain traces through the countless books I've read and stories I've heard about the fey. Maybe I can offer something else.

I can try.

"Wait," I say, my mind still racing. "What would you die for?"

It almost seems as though the question catches her off guard. Her face shifts to intrigue before collecting herself and saying nothing,

I push forward, grasping at the only thread of hope I can see. "The curse on you. What if I help you break it? Is that enough? Is your freedom enough?"

She steps closer, her presence suffocating. "I don't need to talk about that," she says. "This is more valuable to me."

"Why?" I demand. "So you can rule a kingdom from the shadows? Control an army? What if I refuse? What if I force you away?"

"If you are not by my side," she says evenly, "you will die. Until, of course, I consider your debt repaid."

Death or servitude.

Too bad she isn't my friend. Keerla could take her and be rid of this nightmare for me.

"I deserve to know why."

She tilts her head, "because I don't care about my curse in the sense of ending it. I care about ending the lives of those who cursed me. And I think you would be useful." Before I can interrupt, she says: "To answer what I assume is an unspoken question: killing them will not necessarily mean my curse will fade. But it will mean that they can no longer control me."

Unless someone else takes over, I bet.

She steps closer as I sit frozen on the edge of my bed. "I don't need your army," she continues, her voice softer now but no less dangerous. She leans over me, so close that I instinctively fall back, propping myself up on my elbows. Her hands come up to cup my face.

"But *you*," she says, her eyes locked onto mine, "are an oddly useful person with an oddly useful gift for surviving dire situations. I should be dead. Zemm should be dead. That fall from that balcony? *You* should be dead. But here we all are. Perhaps it's the luck of the goddesses you pray to."

Yeah, well, that luck ran out.

"I'm not going to find your enemies," I snap, gripping her wrists tightly and forcing her hands away from my face. "I have my own to deal with. And I won't be wasting my time to travel to some odd fey realm."

"I can wait, and so can the realm," she replies smoothly. "The more time you take, the longer you're stuck with me."

"You said you wouldn't glamour me."

"I said I *never have* glamoured you. This isn't a glamour, it's a bargain. Listen to me," she says, "the desperation, the drive to save your land, the visceral hatred you feel for your brother. The desire to pay him back. The mourning of your parents. Everything inside of you that has been drowning you. How deeply do you feel that?"

I lower my eyes to her lips.

When I don't speak, she does, "that raw pain that eats away at you. That makes you fight your own emotions. Makes it hard for you to trust anyone, even yourself. Makes your first instinct to flee from something you consider dangerous. I feel a similar pain."

My eyes move back to meet hers.

"I need you. You are a magic that I have never encountered," she finishes.

"You will promise me two things," I demand, "the first is that you will *never* glamour me. The second is that you will never kill me."

"Faelyri," she breathes, "I promise that I will never glamour you, and I will never kill you."

With that, I shove her away, planting my foot against her stomach and pushing her back with enough force to make her stumble. "Leave my room. I don't want you sleeping on my floor."

She regains her balance effortlessly, brushing her hands over her clothes, "fine. Suit yourself," she says, her voice light. She steps toward the door. "Have a nice, lonely night. Alone with your melancholy."

The blanket she carried in lies abandoned, draped haphazardly over the chair as she moves to the door with the grace of someone who always commands attention, whether deserved or not.

The groan from the door's hinges prompts me to bolt upright, heart pounding.

I don't want to be alone. I can't be alone.

Bare feet sliding across the chilling marble, I rush to the door, propelled by something forbidden. My palm pushes against the wood.

She's terrible. Cruel. Manipulative. She uses me, twists me like a marionette. And yet, she's here. Always here. When the world forgets me, when my friends bury themselves in distractions, she feels the pull of my darkest hours and answers it.

Like some part of her is tethered to the chaos inside me.

The faint whistle of wind is this room's only sound. The silver pitcher and glasses still sit on the table, glinting faintly in the moonlight.

Her eyes narrow on me, her silhouette framed in silver moonlight, but there's a faint hint of a smirk on her soft lips.

What am I doing?

She is maddeningly beautiful; every movement steeped in an infuriating elegance that pulls me in even as it enrages me.

She's *awful.* Mean, selfish, wicked, fearless, compassionate, and unshakably confident in a way that I can never be.

I hate her.

I want her gone. Gone from this place, from my life, from the suffocating corners of my mind.

Does she really think I'm magic?

"No," I say.

"No?"

"No. I don't want to be alone here, with my melancholy."

And before I can rethink or regret, my hand slides to the back of her head, fingers tangling in her hair, and I close the space between us with the press of my lips against hers.

She doesn't falter, not for an instant. Her arms snake around my waist, pulling me closer.

CHAPTER

TWENTY-NINE

I overslept.

The warmth of the blankets tempts me to stay cocooned, but I know better than that. There's too much to be done. I should check on the people again, or start packing for the journey back to Farfell, or join the efforts to clean up the wreckage. *Something.*

A deep sigh from behind me fills the air.

Thorne. Asleep on her back, one arm flung over her head. The blanket barely conceals her, leaving her shoulder and collarbone bathed in the dim light seeping through the windows.

Oh... what did I do?

Why did I do that?

Was this... was she... what I wanted?

No. She wasn't. No this is not good.

Before I can second-guess myself, I shove her shoulder. Hard. At the forceful shove she stirs with a startled gasp, her eyes blinking into wakefulness.

"Get out of my room," I demand.

Her gaze sharpens as she props herself up on one elbow, her voice drowsy. "Good morning to you, too."

"I'm serious," my jaw tenses. "Get out."

Instead of leaving, she leans closer. "You didn't want to be alone, remember?"

"This will never happen again." My heartbeat roars in my ears. "It can't. It won't. You... you must have done something. Some sort of fey glamour trickery—"

Her expression darkens instantly. "Do not ever accuse me of something so awful."

Okay... too far. Even for me. But what if someone sees her here?

"You can't be here. What if someone comes in? A servant? And sees you here and thinks..."

She laughs. "And thinks what? That you have no self-control? That a wretched faerie thief has stolen your precious innocence?"

I've never done that before... why did I do that with her? Why did I not hate it? Why did I actually enjoy it? What's wrong with me?

I hate her.

"I mean it. No one can ever know about this," I say.

"Fine," she says, rising from the bed. "This stays between us. Don't make it weird."

"I won't make it weird! I never make things weird!" I snap, retreating under the covers as she moves to dress.

"You *always* make everything weird."

"This isn't funny!" My voice cracks, heat rising in my face from its humiliation. "This is serious. I know this meant nothing to you, but it was my—"

"I know."

"And..." what am I doing? "I don't even know if..."

"You're making it weird."

Why am I embarrassed? Why am I worried about whether or not I did a good job... or... I don't know, something? Why does that matter?

Now this is another thing I have to deal with. Another thing that will haunt my consciousness. And I'm stuck with her for who knows how long. Stuck looking at her, being around her, hearing her laugh, talking to her.

I want to reach for her right now. She can be so comforting. But none of it changes the fact that she is also very awful and that was a very bad idea.

If she really cared about me, she would have let me out of my end of the bargain. She wouldn't try to have a claim on my life.

"It wasn't meaningless to me," her eyes drop.. "But you won't believe me. Even though you know I can't lie to you."

I clench my jaw, forcing my expression into something colder than the storm brewing in my chest. Perhaps I can appear unfeeling.

"I understand now," she continues, "why your trust issues run so deep."

"*You tricked me*! And then... How could I ever trust you?"

Her face hardens, her mouth curving into that awful smirk. "I suppose you can't, then. So don't, if that's what you want."

With that, she finally storms from my room. The forceful slam of the door rattles the fragile canopy hanging above me.

Bury this, deal with it later. There are more important things to do.

The world won't stop for my tangled emotions.

With a groan, I force myself upright and throw on the clothes I've been wearing for weeks. They reek of sweat, blood, and something more indefinable, grief, maybe, but I don't care. These are the clothes that have carried me through everything.

As I tug them into place, a thought stops me. This was

instinct, pulling these worn garments over my shoulders. I had forgotten entirely about the closet full of silken gowns and ornate finery waiting just a few steps away. Dresses befitting a queen, untainted by the life I've lived these past weeks. Something that doesn't smell like depression.

I glance toward the closet, then shake my head. No. This is fine. I don't want to wrap myself in elegance while my friends wear the same clothes they've endured in. It would feel... wrong? Like a betrayal or detachment from them. The only thing of worth on me will be my mother's ring.

When I pull open the heavy wooden door, Syvis is there, standing like a sentinel as always.

Oh no...

Her gaze sharpens as it sweeps over me. "Your Highness, why did she just step out of your room? So early in the morning?"

Oh no...

"She needed to give me a message."

"What message?"

Yes, what message? Think quick. Hurry.

"I'm sorry, Syvis," I mutter, "it was a personal message from Zemm. Something's going on with him. Don't bring it up though, or he'll be embarassed."

"Ah, of course. Well, breakfast is ready. You should come. And..." Her brow quirks upward as her lips press into a line. "You should change."

Breakfast? Do I even have time for breakfast? Should I eat? I suppose so. Yeah, I'll go eat.

Thorne will be at breakfast, won't she? Oh no.

"I'm not changing," I say, brushing past her expression. "Thank you. Will you walk with me?"

Syvis lets out a quiet sigh, but she bows with her usual grace. "Of course."

The ladies in the palace practically buzz with excitement now that I've returned. They swarm around me, adjusting my newly cut hair, fussing with my clothes, eager to make everything perfect.

I swat them away and send them off to Lapis, who is much more enthusiastic about the attention.

They've seated me at the head of the table in the great hall. A placeholder crown gleams on the table in front of me. Surrounding it is an extravagant spread of food. Far more than we could possibly eat. It's a waste, really. Though my friends are ecstatic. They haven't seen a meal like this in ages, if ever.

Syvis sits at my right, Filauria at my left, with the rest of my companions almost filling the chairs down the length of the table. The seat directly across from me, my real seat, remains empty.

"This is amazing," Lapis says, already reaching for her second helping.

Thorne studies me out of the corner of her eye. Her expression sharpens from behind her glass. I must look either miserable or entirely blank.

Do not look at me. I should scream at her. Why is she looking? *She's* making it weird.

I don't think we did everything. There's probably so much more we didn't do. But we did enough things to make me want to run and hide.

Don't make it weird.

Did she want to do anything else? Did she just get it out of her system and will never want to do that again?

No. You don't want to ever do that again. Focus on your task.

My focus drifts instead to the portraits on the walls. They

flank us, one side bearing my father and Ilriel, the other my mother and me. There are portraits of us everywhere in this palace. We were all so vain.

My gaze locks on Ilriel's portrait. He looks heroic, even noble, in a way that twists something deep inside me. My friends are laughing now, eating and drinking with a joy they've so long been denied. They deserve this moment, after all I've dragged them through. They deserve the world.

My eyes drop to the silver knife beside my empty plate. It gleams in the light, sharp and elegant, more suited for slicing meat than spreading butter. My fingers trace the engraved accents on the handle before wrapping around it. I lift it, weighing its balance, and turn it in my hand.

"Lyri?" Zemm calls from farther down the table. His voice cuts through the chatter, which falters into silence. "Are you alright?"

I glance up, the knife still in my hand, my grip tightening around it. My pulse pounds in my ears as I turn my attention back to the portrait of Ilriel. Without thinking, I hurl the knife. Thorne ducks instinctively as the blade flies true, embedding itself squarely in Ilriel's painted eye. In his right eye.

"Can someone please remove that?" I say, my tone as calm as if I'd asked for more bread.

The servants stationed against the walls exchange uneasy glances before one steps forward. "Where should we put it, Your Highness?"

"In the fire pit," I reply. "There's another portrait of him in the hall. And one of my family, you know the one. Cut him out of it. I want every image of him gone from this place. I want him burned."

The servant bows low before scurrying off to fulfill my orders. The table remains still, tension thick in the air. I shouldn't have done that. But I couldn't stand his eyes watching me, mocking me, gutting me.

"Well, guess that's a no," Lapis mumbles through a mouthful of food, breaking the silence.

I don't want the talking to stop. I want them to keep enjoying themselves. "I'm sorry for that," I apologize to my friends.

"It's alright," Zemm says casually, chewing as if nothing happened. "It was an ugly picture."

"*He* is ugly," Syvis mutters, her nose wrinkling in distaste.

He's not ugly. She doesn't need to lie.

"I thought he was handsome..." Lapis murmurs under her breath.

The conversation lulls for a moment before Zemm speaks again, "what's our plan?"

The question coils in my chest. Before I can respond, Lapis interjects with a grin. "I'm not leaving until I get my crown. I was promised one."

Right, of course. She has earned it, after all. I have old tiaras and circlets, ones that I never wear. A large collection of things. It would be wasteful to have a new one made for her. An irresponsible way to spend coin that can be used for more practical things. I can just give away the ones collecting dust.

I glance up at her, "would Agnat like one as well?"

Her eyes light up. "Yes!"

I nod. They can have them. The servants can take my dresses. Zemm can claim whatever he wants from the library. I'll strip this palace of everything unnecessary if it brings them joy.

I already know what Thorne wants. What Thorne *has*. I can't even think of it. I can't think of her.

I need her to stop staring at me.

"Zemm has asked an important question," Syvis says to me, "what is our plan?"

"I actually have one," I say. "Believe it or not." I take a breath. "Velle told me Ilriel is in Farfell—"

"Wait, *Velle*?" Syvis interrupts, her brow furrowing.

"I'll explain later," I say, brushing past her question. "Anyway, Ilriel is in Farfell. That's all I care about. I'm going to hunt him down. That's the plan."

"Sure," Zemm says, raising an eyebrow. "But what's the *actual* plan?"

"Hollow Haven, Grimehold, Deadbell," I say, listing the cities. "He'll either be hiding with allies in one of them, or we'll draw him out by taking them out."

"Take them *out*?" Thorne asks, her fork tapping against her plate.

"Yes. I'm going to kill the human princes."

Lapis grins. "I'm going to be a folk hero. The dwarves will sing about me."

Do I have a war council? Or a council at all? Wasn't it supposed to be twilight elves?

"Are you all helping me?" I ask the table.

Zemm shrugs. "I'm not going back to the sewer, but I'll go to Grimehold. Temporarily."

"Of course we're helping," Lapis says, her mouth full again. "We're family."

Thorne scoffs.

Family. The word feels foreign, strange. I always thought family was tied to blood, immutable and binding. But maybe not. These people have shaped me, stood beside me. I think of them as my family more than I ever thought of Ilriel as such.

I still have family.

And one day, I'll have their portraits hung in these halls. Though, not Thorne's. Never her.

I'm slouched in the throne where my mother's corpse sat just hours ago. The soft cushions seem determined to swallow me whole, as though the throne itself knows I don't belong here. A pit has been growing in my stomach ever since I lowered myself into this seat, and it only deepens with every passing moment.

I've never sat here before, not even as a child. I never wanted to. I thought that maybe it would feel like a warm embrace, like my mother's arms wrapping around me.

It doesn't.

The temporary crown dangles from the armrest, neglected. I can't bring myself to wear it. Not yet.

To my right, my father's throne stands empty. My gaze drifts toward it, unbidden, and now I can't unsee the ghostly image of him seated there, stern and silent.

Which throne did Filauria use when she ruled? Which will she use now? Was there only one then? How much has this place changed since she last saw it?

The sound of footsteps pulls me from my thoughts. Thorne approaches, stopping at the base of the short steps leading to the throne. She doesn't ascend, but she tilts her head, her gaze sharp.

"Fallen star," she says, her voice carrying that infuriating mix of familiarity and mockery.

Gods, I hate that nickname. My scowl deepens as I lean on my fist, my elbow braced against the arm of the throne.

Why is she here *now*?

"Want me to kneel?" Thorne smirks, and it's somehow worse.

When I don't answer, she takes the liberty of climbing the steps. She stops partway, one boot resting on the center step while the other plants itself firmly between my feet. Her hand reaches for the crown, still dangling from the throne's arm. I flinch as she picks it up and places it on my head.

"I like this throne," she murmurs, her smirk returning. "I thought I could kill you for it, but I suppose now I don't have to."

"You don't have the brain power to rule a country," I shoot back.

Thorne leans on the armrest. She adjusts the crown slightly, her fingers brushing my hair, and crosses her arms. "Fae," when she speaks again, her voice is quieter, "are you frightened?"

I shake my head, though a little caught off guard by the nickname. Frightened would have been the right word the last time I was in this palace. But now? Now, there isn't a word for what I feel. It's something deeper, heavier, impossible to articulate.

My hand grips the opposite armrest, the one she isn't leaning on, and my gaze falls to the pool beneath the throne. The water ripples gently, its surface catching the light of the hall. It's always been captivating. If I look hard enough, I can see faint reflections of the past.

I see myself as a child, splashing the water with small, eager hands, the ripples spreading out in chaotic patterns. My brother was there, older and steady, his laughter mingling with mine as he joined in. Our parents were gone on one of their trips, but he stayed with me, kept me distracted.

But he knew. But... he kept me happy, if only for a fleeting moment before the weight of the world descended.

That short memory with my brother is a good one. I can keep it, but I won't let it weaken me.

I'll follow the light of the stars, those same stars that have guided me through every sleepless night, until I find him. Until this is finished.

ACKNOWLEDGMENTS

I can't believe I wrote a book. That's pretty wild.

I won't bore you with my life story, but it's been a pretty bad time. I don't say that to feel sorry for myself, or get sympathy. I really mean that, and I like being honest, starting from when I was Violet Jr crawling around on all fours.

I'd like to spend this page thanking my friends. They are the most important people in my life. I think a lot of queer people can really relate to the importance of chosen family.

Firstly, I want to give space to the people who contributed to the making of this novel: Paulina, one of my oldest friends (and basically sister). Thank you for drawing not only the wonderful art seen throughout this book, but also the cover. You're incredibly talented, and I hope you see that every single day.

Justin, thank you for being the reason why I was able to completely turn my life around. Thank you to my friends (and fellow authors) G.L. Tomas for all of your help and guidance during this incredibly scary process.

I would also like to thank my cat. She can't read this, but I would throw myself into a volcano for her.

I have a lot of friends that I want to mention by name, but that would be an extra ten pages. I have a deep connection with everyone in my life and I feel as though they all deserve to be recognized.

Shayne, you are so incredibly kind and selfless. And Sam,

your ability to persevere through hardship inspires me. Anna, Katie, Cariann, Rin, Matthew... the list really does go on forever and I could write an essay about you all. I love you all so much. And to the others I didn't name: I love you just as much, I promise.

And thanks to everyone who read my book and connected with Faelyri's story. And thanks to the ones who read it that didn't connect at all, that's still important. I know that I have a long way to go, and this is just the beginning.